THE HAND YOU HOLD

OBSIDIAN

M E Karbowski

Cover designed by Cover Designer

This book is a work of fiction. Names, characters, places, and incidents either are products of the author's imagination or are used fictitiously. Any resemblance to actual persons, living or dead, events, or locales is entirely coincidental.

M E Karbowski

Printed in the United States of America

First Printing: March 2018

ISBN-9781980407317

CONTENTS

PROLOGUE

A t nearly 3 AM in the maternity ward of Saginaw General Hospital, for one family at least, things were not going well.

Her water broke some five hours earlier, and that had made it nearly *two months* too early. She had endured the painful delivery and now she and her husband awaited the news from the doctor. She lay in the bed, covered with a thin, yellow hospital blanket sipping water from a plastic cup with a bendable straw. The water tasted like the room smelled: uncomfortably sweet and sterile with almost a sickening aftertaste. *Probably has some electrolytes and some other stuff*, she thought absently. She was mentally and physically exhausted, but there was no way she could sleep. She had to know, not that there was anything she could *really* do.

It was a warm night for the end of April, the rain falling from the sky was more of a mist, not so much falling on things and people, but coating them in a fine layer of water. The moisture seemed to bring the smells of the earth, the budding trees and the growing grass, into focus. There was a smell of newness, of growth. Spring had come to Saginaw, Michigan. There was no wind, and it was eerily still. Very few cars were on the road and no one, it seemed, was moving about. The snow was gone now. Even the towering, dirty black piles where the snowplows had pushed it for months were now just small humps of debris--blackened paper cups, discarded McDonald's bags and colored Styrofoam containers bearing the arched "M" logo; papers that had lost nearly all of the identifying ink, all smashed and worn, lying ready for the street sweepers, if they came at all.

The small television mounted near the ceiling was off, as there was no sense having it on with no programming available after 2 AM. All the better since the news coverage mainly was on the so-called "Eastertide Offensive" being waged by the North Vietnamese forces on their neighbors to the south. That conflict was a world away, something unimportant to them since he had been discharged from the Navy some four years earlier. And they had more pressing matters to occupy their minds. There was a small transistor radio beside the bed, but that too was off as that just seemed to be more of a distraction. Only the loud *tick--tick--tick--tick--tick* of the clock on the wall filled the silence and punctuated the passing of time. Reminding them that no matter how much they wanted time to speed up or reverse itself it was in constant motion, moving toward an uncertain future.

Finally, the heavy wooden door pushed in and light spilled in from the hallway. A shadowed figure stood silhouetted for a moment before he stepped fully in and allowed the door to close. The doctor had arrived.

"He survived the birth," the doctor began in a warm tone.

Oh thank you God, she thought. This was her third child, the previous two were girls. This would be their final child, they had decided, and both were elated that it was a boy.

"The next 48 hours will be critical, however," he continued, still smiling. He was a short man, only 5' 4", balding, thick black-rimmed spectacles obscuring hazel eyes and bushy eyebrows. A stethoscope hung around his neck. He had changed out of his scrubs and was wearing brown polyester slacks, and a tan button down shirt under his opened white lab coat. He was pleasant and capable.

"His lung has collapsed," the doctor continued in a somber, but somehow supportive tone as he stopped at the foot of the bed and read from the chart. "We have him in an incubator, where--if he survives the next few hours--he will remain for as long as necessary. Which could be several weeks." He looked at the couple and met both of their gazes before continuing. "His weight is severely low--only 2 lbs. 9 oz. We are doing everything we can for him. You're welcome to stay here for that duration if you like...I'll let you know when the situation changes. In the meantime I'll give you something that will help you sleep."

She looked at her husband who was squeezing her hand, tears in both of their eyes. Her heart was racing, its pounding was thundering in her ears. She had a hard time hearing the doctor's words. The antiseptic smell that wafted in from the hallway with the doctor filled her nostrils and made her sick to her stomach.

"That would be helpful," she said, referring to the sleep aid. "But first, I need to make a phone call."

She'd been raised in a Christian household. Her grandfather was a preacher, from a line of preachers. Her father was raised on the Word, as he called it, and tried to instill those beliefs in her as well. She believed, yes, but did not really practice much. Did not have much faith. But she knew who did.

The hour was late and she was sure he would be asleep. She picked up the heavy handset of the yellow rotary dial phone that was next to the hospital bed and slowly dialed the number she knew by heart.

It rang five times before a quiet, small voice answered, "Hello?"

"Dad?" she began, tears streaming down her face and thick in her voice, changing the timbre and tone of it. She took deep breaths, fighting back the tears.

Her husband held her hand tightly for support. He would have made the call, but he knew it was something she thought she should do. "They're not sure the baby is going to make it," she continued without awaiting his reply. "His lung has collapsed and he's in an incubator," she managed to say before the sadness, fear, and anxiety broke her voice. "Can you please pray for him...for us?" She managed to squeak out after a sobbing pause.

"Yes, honey. I sure will...How are you holding up?" He asked with much sincerity.

"Not sure yet, Dad," she replied honestly.

"I understand. Just know that if God has a plan and a purpose for him, he *will* make it," he reassured her. "Try and get some sleep...Call me tomorrow and let me know how things are. As for me, I have some phone calls of my own to make."

"Thanks Dad. I love you," she squeaked.

"Love you too, honey," he said before he depressed the plunger on the phone and hung it up. He waited three seconds and released it. Once he heard the dial tone he began the tedious process of scratching out the numbers to his pastor.

In the time before answering machines the phone would just ring and ring until someone answered it or the person calling gave up and disconnected. The phone rang 16 times before a tired but concerned voice answered, "Hello...this is Pastor Gary?" he said, using his first name.

"Pastor, we need to wake up the Prayer Chain," he began, and then explained to him the dire situation.

That's how it began with the two of them calling two people. Then those four calling four more, and so on until nearly the entire congregation was up at 3 AM praying for a tiny baby boy that had been pushed into this world too soon.

*				*				*

The brass door knob to her room rattled. The wooden door began to shake violently. "Young lady open this door, right now!" Her stepfather yelled. He had been drinking. He was always drinking. Him and her mother were also putting medicine into their arms with a needle. Mom was probably sleeping now, like always. She had not heard her mother yelling for a couple of minutes now. It always happened a few minutes after her mom fell asleep on the couch, after putting medicine in her arm and after drinking. That's when he came for her.

She was crying softly, tears streaming down her face. She was under the bed. Not under the covers, not in the closet. Most kids at school thought that monsters lived in those places: under the bed, and the closet, in the basement, in the dark places. That's where most kids thought the monsters waited. But she knew better. Since she had been six. Real monsters were out in the world, they looked like ordinary people. They offered you candy, and toys, ice cream and everything good.

They were not gifts, these things. They came with a price. Something had to be given back for these treats. These monsters were relentless. The dark places were not where the monsters lived, rather they were the places that you went to hide from them. But no matter the place she chose, the dark wasn't dark enough, the space wasn't deep enough to truly hide her. The monster always came and found her.

CHAPTER ONE

There was a knock at the door. More of a pounding, really. There was an urgency to it that implied distress. Or anger. The sound echoed throughout the house. It came from the side door, not the front which intimated that it was someone he knew, as people he didn't know tended to go to the front door, which he never used. In fact it was basically blocked with an armchair that was adjacent to the 8 foot pool table of the great room. He happened to be in the bathroom, which was located on the same side of the house as the side door so he could clearly hear the pounding. Whoever it was had opened the storm door and was pounding directly on the steel entry door. Loudly. Persistently.

"Son of a bitch," he said as he rolled his eyes and looked towards the ceiling. "Every time I'm in the damn bathroom," he said to himself, exasperated. "Just a minute!" He yelled as loud as he could, hoping the person at the door could hear him through the wall.

Apparently they had, as the pounding then stopped. Daniel Gibson finished his business, flushed the toilet and washed his hands. Daniel checked himself in the mirror and, seeing that he was still presentable, having just gotten out of the shower, shaved and dressed some fifteen minutes prior, opened the door to the bathroom and proceeded through the master bedroom--past the unmade bed, pillows and blanket askew, dirty clothes piled into a plastic bin in the corner next to the dresser--skirted the great room which he had cleaned the previous day, dusted the wood furniture and electronics and even vacuumed with the "fresh linen" scented powder, and continued through the kitchen--also clean and ready for company--and finally made it to the side door.

He could see the man standing there on the side porch, as there was no curtain and the half lite of the steel door was clear glass. The man saw him walking through the kitchen, and as their eyes met he stuck up both fists and gave Daniel a double-middle-finger in way of saying "Hello."

Daniel laughed and returned the greeting. A few steps more and he opened the door and gestured for his friend to come in.

"About time," his friend said as he pushed his way past Daniel into the kitchen. "What were you doin', jerking off?" He said with a laugh.

"Not hardly," Daniel replied quickly, leaving the door open. "I was taking a deuce, if you must know."

"That explains the smell," his friend shot back, as he opened the fridge and helped himself to a bottle of Michelob Ultra. "Still drinking this 'diet' beer?" he asked as he twisted the top off and took a swig, flipping the cap into the sink that was set in an island across from the refrigerator. Daniel ignored his friend's lack of etiquette. He was used to it. In fact, it was expected.

"Ah, you're just jealous that you can't afford it," Daniel replied.

"I have much better things to spend my hard-gotten gains on," he said as he continued to walk into the living room and plopped himself on the overstuffed leather couch.

The man's name was Paul Glendening. He was tall, about 6 foot three and weighed in usually around 200 pounds. He was one of the very fortunate and few individuals with a high metabolism that provided him a strong, muscular body that he didn't have to do a thing to earn. He had black hair with a receding hairline. He kept it longer in the back, hoping the extra length there would somehow compensate for the lack of it on top. Even though Paul smiled, he hardly ever showed his teeth when doing so. When he did smile with his teeth it seemed more like a grimace, and Daniel would tease that he was "scaring the children" with it. His lips were thin and sat on a face that was angular and also thin, but still held strength. Paul's eyes were a unique shade of steel blue and at times they seemed to look into a person's soul. To look into them for too long was unsettling, at least that was Daniel's experience.

It was early September in Petoskey, Michigan. Labor Day weekend to be exact. It was Saturday and the sun was out and it was hot. Eighty-one degrees, which was record-breaking high but very welcome that time of year. The last weekend of Summer for kids and most vacationers, or "Fudgies" as the northern locals referred to them, as a summertime visit to Northern Michigan wasn't complete until you had your fill of some of the thirty different varieties of locally handmade fudge. It could be found as far "south" as Gaylord and Traverse City, and seemingly in every small village and town right up over the Mackinaw Bridge into St. Ignace and beyond. Daniel hadn't eaten a piece of fudge in over twelve years. Even when he was a Fudgie before moving "Up North" he didn't eat the super-sugary treat much. He preferred chocolate, or chocolate-coated whatever.

There was a slight breeze and Daniel had all of the windows open in every room of the fifteen hundred square foot house. He had a small window air conditioner in the bedroom, but that was usually reserved for night sleeping or for times when it was unusually hot and he laid there with his cats and watched television. Which was what he would probably be doing that day since it was so hot, but he had other plans. Good plans. The sound of someone mowing their lawn purred through the windows, bringing with it the smell of the fresh cut grass and even the scent of sunshine.

His house sat on an acre of flat land that used to be a farmer's field. In this parceled up space there were twenty lots, but only six were currently developed. The grass around his place was field grass--hard and uninviting. He planned on getting a "lawn" someday, but that day had not arrived yet. There were no trees in any of the yards, though some five hundred yards from the private gravel road state land began and all there were were trees. Now they were lush green, their leaves flowing gently with the wind current, rustling when the day was quiet. Someone was grilling, the smell of searing meat floating through the window now along with the sound of an angry Blue Jay. Daniel's stomach growled as the smell triggered his appetite, something he didn't have much of lately.

As usual, Paul was wearing long, silky basketball-style shorts and a matching tank-top which allowed his muscular arms to be on display. His basketball shoes were all white and very clean and bright, looking new, though Daniel knew they were not. Today he wore the colors of the Detroit Tigers. He had the matching top and bottoms of all of his favorite sport teams, all of which were from Michigan. One day in April, the Detroit Red Wings, Tigers, and Pistons had played televised games. Paul insisted on watching them all and he had changed his clothes to match and support the appropriate team being aired. If his team won he celebrated, if they lost he cursed, pouted and immediately removed their outfit.

The two had been friends for many years and even worked together from time to time at different jobs. They enjoyed working together as they both had a strong work ethic and were very capable and competent in what they did. They didn't get together very often lately, for various reasons. Life, mainly, Daniel mused. But today was a special day. Sort of.

Actually, Daniel Gibson was having a really shitty day. Shitty *year* for that matter. But he hoped that today would be a good day. A singular bright spot in his darkening existence.

Daniel was 6 foot tall himself, with red hair cut short, buzzed around the ears and at the back, military style. He had an easy smile and was seemingly always laughing, on the outside at any rate. His eyes were hazel and could convey intelligence, kindness, and at rare times, a want for violence. His face was oval, his nose thin, and his hairline was starting to recede, though not nearly at the pace his friend's was. At his heaviest as he was 205 pounds, though currently he had been working out regularly, changed his eating habits, and along with the stress, he was down to 170. Looking and feeling better than he had in over ten years. Physically that was. Emotionally, that was something totally different. And the reason for Paul's visit.

They never called him Paul. And "they" meant everyone who knew him, except for his parents and his sister. Everyone else: his friends, coworkers, acquaintances, and even enemies knew him as "Nevver." In fact, that is how he introduced himself, and all of his ever-present sports jerseys bore that name across the back. That and the number 69, both because of the sexual connotation and it just happened to be the year Paul reluctantly allowed himself to be removed from his mother's womb. When asked why he spelled his nickname with two Vs Paul would reply, "The first V is for violence...The second V is for victory, and I never lose!" That may have been Paul's narcissistic and egotistic reasoning for it, but Daniel also noted that he was a very negative person, pointing out at seemingly every opportunity that something or another would "never" happen. So it was a fitting nickname, one that would be with him forever, and probably etched on his tombstone as well.

"So where's Nimrod at?" Nevver asked.

He was sarcastically referring to the third part of their group who was yet to arrive. His name was David Reed, and like Paul no one hardly ever called him by his given name. The nickname that was forced upon David and which had stuck since they were in high school was "Church." He had gotten it from Nevver, who at the time could not stand him. It was meant as slander and a way for Nevver to be above and belittle David, who was a devout and unapologetic Christian. Though he talked openly about his faith if someone inquired, Church did not push it on people or act as if he was better than others. He felt that he should live as an example, though he'd be the first to admit he really wasn't Christian role-model material and struggled with life just as anyone else had.

It was a mystery how the three of them ever really became such good friends. Daniel supposed that it was because they had all worked at the Little Caesars pizza restaurant during high school, and while Nevver was just one of the douche bag workers you had to deal with, it was Church who had not only endured the almost constant ridiculing and antagonizing, but had turned it around and somehow befriended Nevver. Their senior year in high school the three seemed to be inseparable, and really for several years after that as well. Until Daniel got married and moved "Up North." That was nearly eight years ago.

They heard a car crunching down the gravel driveway. Nevver quickly looked at Daniel and smiled as he jumped off the couch.

"The asshole has arrived!" he shouted excitedly as he quickly made his way to the storm door, throwing it open and stepping out onto the side porch. The sun hit his body and for a split second Nevver stood still, smiled and tried to absorb the rays. "Hey douche bag, I thought you'd never get here!" Nevver yelled. "You're late as usual! That means *you* gotta provide the girls!" He continued as he gave their newly arrived friend the double-fingered salute.

"Nice to see you too, Nevver," Church said as he made his way to the porch, a wide smile across his face. The two men shook hands. Nevver held the door and motioned with a grand gesture for his friend to enter. Just as he was passed, however, Nevver kicked him in the ass, not hard but enough to remind his friend who the Alpha Dog still was.

"You're such an asshole, Nevver," Church said shaking his head, ignoring the assault with calmness and dignity.

Daniel was in the kitchen and held a beer for his friend. He actually had one in each hand, because by now he knew Nevver was ready for a second. Both men thanked him, and Church stepped in and gave his best friend a long, welcoming hug.

Church was a little shorter than Daniel, standing five foot ten inches tall. He wore a baseball cap as usual. Because of the season this time it was navy blue with the white stylistic "D" of the Detroit Tigers. He always wore a hat, unless he was at church or a wedding or funeral. Mostly to hide his balding scalp. Daniel had told his friend that he should just shave his head, but Church refused. He liked the cap. He wore jean shorts and a quality copy of the button-up uniform shirt of the Tigers. His smile was warm and bright. Daniel always felt better when Church was around, he guessed it was because of his smile and genuine friendship they shared. His eyes were a pale blue, about three shades from being white. Nevver had called him an albino more times than Daniel could recall, because of his light eyes and his skin was also very pale, though he was not albino.

"Do I need to leave you two alone for about 30 minutes?" Nevver said sarcastically as he slow punched Church in the right shoulder. And though it was acted out in playful slow-motion, at the last instant Nevver put power behind it and gave it nearly as much force as a normal punch would have been, rocking his friend back a step.

"OW!" Church exclaimed. "Do you have to do that every time? You're such a dick."

"Never said I wasn't," was all he said as he walked back into the living room and claimed his preferred spot on the couch.

Daniel just shook his head and smiled. "It's good to see you, Church. It's been too long."

"So how you holding up?" Church asked with all sincerity. He was referring to Daniel's recent divorce. His wife of nearly 6 years, Stacy, had seemingly went through a midlife crisis early. She was barely 31. She had told him she just didn't want to be married anymore. All told they been together for over 10 years if you included the years they dated and the short period when they had broken up.

"I'm doing okay," Daniel lied.

Good, tell him that. You don't want to get into it right now, and he really doesn't want to hear it, Daniel's mind told him.

Church looked into his eyes and he could see the sadness and he knew that something wasn't right. His friend definitely wasn't okay.

"Come on, let's go in the other room and sit down," Daniel said quickly before Church could press the subject. So they did.

Nevver was seated on the left-hand side of the couch, Daniel took his usual spot on the right. Church sat on the matching leather loveseat to the side of the wooden coffee table perpendicular to the couch. The stereo was playing classic rock from a compilation CD. The volume was moderate, the music could still be heard and enjoyed while the conversation could be held at normal voice levels. On the coffee table Daniel had a bowl of pretzels, all bowl of potato chips, and a smaller bowl filled with peanut M&Ms. Nevver was already hungrily helping himself to the treats.

"So, you never saw this comin'?" Nevver blurted. Daniel gave him a pained look, and Church shot him a dirty one. But, it was how he was, and they would expect nothing less.

Well, here we go anyway, his mind chirped.

"No... I knew *something* was wrong," Daniel said as he began to remember small details.

Well, at the time he told himself they were small details. Thinking back now he realized they were actually much larger signs. Ones that he should not have ignored. "For weeks before she left me 'the note' she quit wearing her wedding ring...And she became cold and distant, didn't want to talk about much of anything... Seem pissed all the time, you know? I thought it was her work. She was stressed out and hated her job."

"Ahh, but she was always kinda bitchy," Nevver quipped. He got the same looks as he had before. "What? You guys know it's true," he said in his own defense, then taking a drink from his beer still looking at them.

Church ignored him and asked, "You didn't say anything to her? You didn't confront her about this behavior?"

"Nope...I asked Steve, my friend at work, what he thought. He said that she would get over it, whatever it was, that I should just give her some time and that she would come around...He was wrong."

"So then you just came home one night and there was this letter on the couch?" Nevver asked.

Daniel remembered distinctively coming home that night. It was a cold night at the very beginning of March. There was still snow on the ground and more in the forecast. He'd come home like he usually did after closing up the restaurant. It was well after 11 pm. Stacy was already in bed, which wasn't that abnormal. After he had taken his shoes and coat off he noticed the piece of paper lying on the otherwise empty coffee table. He sat on the couch and opened it up, hopeful it was something good. Hoping that she was finally going tell him what was wrong, so he could help her with whatever it was.

As he read, it seemed like the couch had slanted and tilted. He had to grab onto the side of it as though he might slide off. It seemed as a black hole, a singularity, had opened up in his living room and was pulling everything towards it--his dreams, his goals, his life, *their life*--into it. Into oblivion. He thought he could feel his heart tearing out of his chest and being drawn into the chasm as well.

Daniel wasn't one for crying. It took him longer than most people, it seemed, for distress and grief and mourning to register and manifests itself in the form of crying tears. When his grandfather had died from cancer it had taken him six weeks for the reality, the grief, to set in before he cried. This time however the tears were immediate.

He felt the weight in his chest, his head felt immediately thick and heavier. His ears seemed to plug with the sound of his own beating heart. Tears flowed from his eyes as his mind struggled to comprehend what he was reading. He had come home in a good mood, hoping that they would enjoy some late night dinner, or might even have sex--wouldn't that be a novel thing? He was not prepared for *this*. At all.

It was like he was riding a bike fast, downhill, feeling the wind in his face, smiling at the thrill. Then suddenly a parked car. No time to stop, no time to swerve. No time to think, to evaluate, to decide. WHAM! Going from twenty to zero in a split second. The unexpected, sudden impact. The jolting of every bone and fiber in your body. The feeling of nauseating weightlessness, uncertainty. The horrifying anticipation of the fall, the hard secondary impact on cold pavement. The mind trying to make sense out of the senseless. *Was this real?*

In her handwriting, on a yellow legal-sized single sheet of paper with blue ink, Stacy wrote how she wasn't happy. She didn't want to be married anymore. She felt that he had settled for her and he really wanted somebody different. Somebody better. Deserved somebody better. She didn't know what she wanted, but what their life had become wasn't it. She said he was a good man. She said she was sorry. She made it clear that no matter what he would say, she could not be convinced otherwise. It was over. And there was nothing he could do about it.

He had wept and sobbed as he slowly walked into their bedroom, and standing at the side of their bed he could tell she wasn't asleep.

"You don't want to work on it?" He asked, his voice thick with sadness and pain. He clutched the note in a trembling hand.

"No," was all she replied. Cold. Hard. Emotionless.

"What about counseling?" He pleaded.

"I asked you for that a while ago...*You* refused," she spat. Anger now.

Oh shit. It was true. He couldn't recall exactly when she had asked, but she had said, "Maybe we need to go to counseling."

He remembered automatically getting defensive and replying with anger, "Maybe *you* need counseling!" The subject wasn't brought up again. That was the end of that. Or so he had thought.

He grabbed his pillow and the extra blanket and, still sobbing, went to the other end of the house and laid down on the single bed in the spare room.

He was angry at himself, replaying several specific interactions over and over again in his mind. *Why didn't I say something to her sooner?* He could tell something was wrong, and when he had asked her what it was she would reply "Nothing." Which he knew was a lie, but he didn't want to pressure her. He knew she was under a lot of stress at work. So was he. So he let it go, figuring she would talk to him about it when she was ready to. But it had festered and had grown out of his control.

No matter how much he wanted to he couldn't go back. He couldn't fix what was broken. He couldn't undo whatever it was in her mind that he had done-- whatever singular or multiple things that had made her come to that conclusion--he could not change it. And it broke his heart with crushing feelings of frustration, sadness, and anger. This wasn't supposed to happen. They both believed in God and the sanctity of marriage. Divorce wasn't supposed to be an option. But she had made up her mind. Her decision was final.

Anguish rushed in and filled his being. His heart continued to thunder and rage as tears streamed down his face and soaked the pillow. Both of their cats briefly came in to check on him, but quickly went their own way to leave him in his grief. He cried until dawn. There was weeping and gnashing of teeth.

So there was nothing he could do. He wanted her to be happy, and regardless of his own happiness--for if she didn't want to be with him making her stay wasn't going to make either of them happy--he let her go. In fact he did more than that. He rented the U-Haul truck, helped her load up what possessions they had agreed upon she got, drove the damn thing, and helped her move into her new apartment on the other side of town.

Funny thing was they had two cats, one male and one female. He kept the male and she took the other. Within two days she brought the female back saying that the cat would not stop crying and looking for the other one whom they both thought she didn't really care for. Apparently their feline bond was more than they had thought, more than what the female cat led on. So now he still had both cats which were antisocial and currently hiding in the bedrooms, hiding from his guests.

"Yep, a 'dear john' letter," Daniel said bringing himself back to the present conversation. "She didn't want to be married anymore, at least not to me...so I let her go. A month later we went to the courthouse, she said we had 'irreconcilable differences.' The judge asked if I agreed...." Daniel paused for a long time, lost again in remembrance. "I damn near said 'No.'"

"Aw, duuuude!" Nevver cut-in, drawing out the "u" in dude for several beats for effect, "You totally should have! Just to fuck with her--you never get those chances back again! The judge probably would have made you guys go to counseling then!" He shouted it like it was a perfect plan, smiling from ear to ear.

"I couldn't do that," Daniel replied laughing. "It wouldn't have really helped, I don't think."

"You're too nice, man...Better than what she deserved by far...she's never gonna find someone as good as you," Nevver said. This in and of itself was a lapse in Nevver's hard exterior. It showed that he really respected and perhaps even loved his friends, more than he ever showed. "Remember that fucking time?" he continued after a drink of his beer. "You remember?" Nevver probed, as he sat near the edge of the couch and looked hard at Daniel, giving him a knowing look, then looking to Church and back at Daniel.

Daniel just nodded his head, looking off into the past. The memory flooding back to him at Nevver's mention of "that fucking time."

"I *do* remember."

CHAPTER TWO

t was some nine years prior, "that time." Daniel and Stacy had been dating for a little over a year and had been living together for about nine months. He was working at Sears at the time as a salesperson and the day started like every other work day. In the early afternoon Nevver had come to visit him, something he never did. What was even stranger was their short conversation that day.

"Hey, buddy," Nevver said in way of greeting as he walked up to Daniel in the store. Daniel was wearing his black sport coat, black pants, white shirt with a purple tie--his salesperson uniform and way too hot and overdressed for July, but the store was thankfully air conditioned. He was the only salesperson in his department--vacuums, computers, telephones, and microwaves--at the time so the conversation was more or less private. Daniel thought it was strange, Nevver's greeting, as it was polite. Not sarcastic or condescending or mean or belligerent, as they almost always were.

"What's up?" Daniel asked, puzzled, but still glad to see his friend.

"Stacy wanted me to come check on you," Nevver had said.

Now *that* was odd. Sure they knew each other, as Nevver, Church and a half-dozen other couples were part of their social circle. They even considered each other friends, if not acquaintances at least. But for Stacy to ask Nevver to come "check on him" that was just...weird.

"She wanted me to make sure you're okay."

What the fuck did that mean? Daniel had thought. His mind quickly raced, trying to figure out what the hell Nevver could be talking about. Nothing came to mind. Everything was fine in their relationship, he was working two jobs, here at Sears and still a part-time manager at Little Caesars along with Nevver and Church. All good.

"Yeah, I'm okay. Why was she asking you to ask me that?"

"Not sure," he replied, looking around the store, avoiding eye contact. "She just said she was worried about you, wanted me to check on you...see if you need anything...You need anything?" Nevver asked, genuine concern in his voice. That was weird too.

"No, I'm good," Daniel told him.

"All right then. I better let you get back to all of this hard work," he quipped as he looked around at the deserted department. "I'll check you later. Call me if you need anything," Nevver had said as a way of good-bye.

Daniel didn't think much more about it, until he arrived at his apartment after his shift later that night. Stacy's car was gone, which was a little strange because she wasn't at work. But, *No big deal,* he had thought. Until, that is, he walked into the apartment.

It was cleaned out. Well, not really. All of *her* stuff has been cleaned out. Panic set in quickly. His mind screamed, *what the hell is going on!?!* Now Nevver's visit made sense, not good sense, not rational sense, but he knew why--at least why Nevver had shown up at work. But all of Stacy's things being gone, that made no sense. He didn't know why.

His heart pounded and raced, blood rushing into his ears, blocking out all sounds of the passing cars on the busy street, the wind in the trees outside, the drone of the aging refrigerator. He quickly ran to the bedroom, opened up the dresser drawers that were hers. Empty.

He ran to the bathroom and opened up the medicine cabinet. All of her stuff has gone. The pictures she had on the wall--gone. Then he saw it, a piece of paper on the cheap black coffee table. In three strides he was there and snatched it up. He read it quickly, trying to gain the knowledge of what was happening as fast as he could. Then again more slowly.

Dan,

I don't think things are working out for us. I need time to figure out what I want, and you need to do the same. I'm staying with Theresa for awhile.

I had Nevver check on you because I want you to be alright. I think this is   for the best.

Stacy.

"You gotta be fucking kidding me!" He screamed. He couldn't figure out what had gone wrong. Yeah, they argued about stupid things, but what couple didn't? Theresa? Her boss at that drive-thru burger joint? He knew they were friends, but moving in with her? Something else that didn't add up.

He was panicked...and angry. He didn't cry, not this time. He was mad. Things didn't make sense, and his mind *needed* them to. He called Nevver. Luckily for Daniel he was home and picked up on the third ring.

"Dude! She fuckin' moved her shit out!" Daniel shouted into the phone as soon as the call was connected. He didn't even wait for a "Hello."

"I know, I know....I'm sorry, man. She told me she was moving out, that's why she wanted me to check on you," he explained.

"What!?! She told you? You *knew* she was moving out and you didn't tell me, what-the-fuck, man?" Daniel was incredulous. *One of my best friends aligned in the fracture of my life with my girlfriend?* His mind reeled from the information.

"Well...it was obvious you didn't know, and I wasn't going to be the one to tell you. Not at work. To have you freaking out at work, lose your job? How would that help you? I was looking out for you, dude," he rationalized.

Daniel knew he was right. That not telling him then was the correct decision. But, it didn't calm him any. Didn't make him feel any better. "Did she tell you why?" Daniel asked hoping that maybe he would get more information than what the note had said.

"Just that you two weren't getting along and she needed to move out," Nevver told him.

Nothing more was said. What more was there to say? It was the next day that became "that time."

Daniel didn't work, which was fortunate as he couldn't sleep at all the night before. After talking to Nevver he had changed out of his hot work clothes and put on just a pair of shorts. He opened a can of beer, sat on the black vinyl sofa in front of the box fan and half watched Star Trek Deep Space Nine on VHS as he tried to figure out his life.

In fact he stayed up drinking beer all night, and when he had tried to sleep he couldn't. He could still smell her on his pillow. There was just one now. Her scent was still on his, and the sheets, and the thin, summertime blanket. Plus it was hot, and the box fan in the window did very little to dissipate the heat and humidity of the mid-Michigan summer night in the upstairs apartment.

It was afternoon before he had picked up the phone and dialed Stacy's grandmother's house. He was in good terms with her grandmother, they both stayed overnight there a few times helping her out with various things. Keeping her company mostly. Daniel told her what Stacy had done, what her note had said.

"Ohh, I am soo sorry," she had said, drawing out her words. "Lord knows what's gotten into her."

"Is she staying with you?" Daniel asked, hoping that was the case, that the note had lied.

"No. She's staying down on Fifth St., as far as I know. That's what she told me."

Fifth St...Got it... Daniel didn't know where Theresa lived, but now he knew what street she was on. He cut off the conversation as quickly as he could without being rude.

He got in his car and drove across town, over the bridge to Fifth Street. It had taken him 15 minutes to get there from his apartment. As he didn't know where on

Fifth Street she was, he started at the river and drove slowly past the police station, past the low income apartment complex, slowly down the residential area. Only a few cars past him: a yellow Ford Festiva with a woman driving, her hair teased up 80s style; an old, brown Dodge pickup driven by an elderly man wearing a tall red trucker-style cap that read: Say YES! to Michigan; a new hatch-back style, black Camaro Z-28, rear window covered with louvers, radio blaring a song he didn't recognize, engine rumbling from the dual exhaust as it passed.

All the houses on the street were older, built in the 40s and 50s. Nearly all of them were in some state of disrepair or another. People on this side of town seemingly didn't take care of their things.

The lawns were mostly overgrown, needing a mowing badly. The majority of the houses needed to be repainted, or resided. The sidewalks and driveways were cracked and pushed up at odd angles by the large roots of trees that were planted in the yards decades before. Grass grew out of the cracks. The air smelled dirty down here: the smell of rotting fish from the Saginaw River wafted in the air; the Chevrolet plant a few blocks away gave off the pungent smell of machined metal and stagnant coolant; even the cloying, rotting smell of sugar beets from the Big Chief Sugar factory on the south side of town could be tasted on the air. The spindles on the porches, the ones that remained anyway, had thick white or brown paint that was chipping off in long strips. All the windows seemed dirty, their wooden trim the same as the porches. Some driveways even had old cars up on jack stands, partially or totally covered with gray canvas tarps. Someone's dream in progress.

Daniel drove slowly down the street scanning for Theresa's or Stacy's vehicle. After the fifth block he saw it: Stacy's car. It was a little silver Citation, four-door, 10 years old with a loud exhaust, a plastic crystal pendant hanging from the rearview mirror. It was parked on the street, more or less in front of a brown two-story house with peeling white trim. He drove slowly past, scanning, looking at all the houses to either side of the vehicle and across the street from it. He didn't have an address. He didn't see Theresa's tan Buick anywhere. But he *did* recognize a pick up truck. The sight of it made his heart beat faster, his breathing come in shallow gasps.

It was one of the smaller S-10 models, blue and badly rusted. Dented and dinged. Various stickers on the back window: STP, SNAP-ON and KLM, even a NASCAR. Daniel recognized it as one of the vehicles parked at the burger joint she worked at. It belonged to one of her coworkers. One Daniel thought *she* didn't like at all, someone who picked on her and she complained about often. *Son-of-a-Bitch!* he thought.

Puzzled, he decided to park down the block with a view of her car and the house with the blue pickup truck in its driveway. He watched, with the window down, the radio on--the *Frogstomp* cassette from Silverchair--for what seemed a very long time. He was hoping Stacy would come out and go for a drive, so he could follow her and they could talk somewhere else. *That's all*, he though. *Just talk*. It had been 20 minutes and so far no movement. His adrenaline was pumping now, his heart beating fiercely in his chest. Fear and anxiety assaulted his mind. He had the sinking suspicion that this wasn't Theresa's house.

You know it's not, his mind told him. Daniel shook his head in an effort to clear that thought and try to erase what thoughts would follow.

After another slow ten minutes of waiting he couldn't take it any longer. He drove around the block and came back the opposite way and parked directly behind Stacy's car. He got out of his black Ford Tempo and slowly walked up the aging steps and rang the doorbell with a trembling hand, his heart racing. He struggled to keep his breathing even.

An older woman opened the door, and it wasn't Theresa. Puzzled, Daniel looked past her, trying to see if Stacy or Theresa, whom he knew, was indeed in there. All he saw was a man, looking to be in his 40s, sitting on a weathered couch. The living room was a little cluttered, with papers and a dog bed, a fat television sat on a wall-sized entertainment center adorned with pictures and potted plants. The smell of boiling hotdogs and ketchup wafted out as the woman asked, "Can I help you?"

"I'm here to see Stacy," he managed to croak. "Is she here?"

The woman looked puzzled, if not a little pissed off at the question. "Yes, she is," the woman said defensively almost like she was protecting Stacy somehow.

What was the attitude for? Daniel wondered. *What the hell had Stacy told them?*

Stay cool, his mind warned him. You don't want to do anything you could go to jail for. Daniel took in a deep breath as he waited for a response from the woman before him.

"And who are *you*?" the woman asked, her gaze piercing, her tone demanding, she almost spat the last word. The man seated on the couch, presumably her husband or boyfriend, glanced their way, then continued to watch television, though Daniel could tell he was listening to them.

"I'm her boyfriend," Daniel said with more anger than he intended. With that the woman's eyes widened and her facial expression went from annoyance to confusion.

"Her boyfriend!?" she exclaimed. "My *son* is her boyfriend," she said angrily.

His world tilted. His heart sank and seemed to hit the pit of his stomach then bounced straight into his skull, smashing into his brain and blurred his vision. Before she could continue, Daniel countered the ridiculous statement with, "Well, I'm the one she's been living with for the last year!"

With that statement the woman's eyes softened toward him, but immediately hardened again as she took a step back, still blocking the door, and looked at the man on the couch who was now looking straight at them both, a look of concern on his face now, too. Though he seemed to be more worried about the woman asking him to get off the couch and do something than he was with the current situation. "Wait here," she told Daniel as she shut the heavy, wooden door.

Behind the now closed door he could clearly hear the woman yelling, "Stacy! Get up here, *now*!" It seemed odd, as if they knew her well and were scolding her like a child. Like a child of *theirs*.

Daniel paced on the porch, his mind racing, not really able to focus on one thought. It was a jumble of feelings mostly: anger, confusion, anxiety...fear. All were wrestling and battling for mental supremacy, trying to control his mind and therefore his body. His breathing came in short, nearly gasping breaths. Then the heavy wooden door creaked opened.

Stacy walked out onto the porch, closing the door behind her. She was wearing a t-shirt he had never seen before. It had a pair of boxing gloves on it and "Everlast" scrolled across the front. *A new shirt? Someone else's?* he thought.

"What are you doing here?" Stacy said in a low, but angry voice. Her eyes blazed with anger and what Daniel read as embarrassment. He quickly guessed that she had lied to these people and his very unexpected arrival had brought upon her a situation she didn't want to deal with. *Well, too fuckin' bad for you, bitch,* he thought.

"What am *I* doing here, what are *you* doing here? Who's fucking house is this?" Daniel spat. She walked passed him, down the porch steps toward his car that was parked in front of the house on the street. He followed her. "This obviously isn't Theresa's house, so who's is it? You're with that asshole you work with," Daniel searched his memory for the name. It came to him as he recalled many stories of how he would pick on and torment Stacy at work. He was one of the douche bags she had to endure. "James? I thought you *hated* him because he picked on you at work all the time!"

She looked at him and simply replied, "No, his brother."

What!?! Another punch to the gut. "When did this happen?" he asked. It was all he could think to ask.

So, she's hanging out with people from work and hooking up with their brothers? Ask her how she met him, his mind quickly prompted him.

Reluctantly, Stacy answered him. "A bunch of us started hanging out after work. TJ works there, too...I smoked pot for the first time...and I liked it!" she said with a sort of glee in her voice. "You're not happy with me, anyway," she said, like it justified her actions.

"Just come back home. We can work on it...on us," he said. He was pleading now.

No, don't do it! His mind yelled at him.

"I can't," she replied. Her gaze was hard, still angry.

"Why not?" He asked. *Whatever it is, we can fix it,* he thought.

She hesitated for a few heartbeats then said, "Because I'm pregnant."

WHAT!?!

Anger won the wrestling match.

"Are you fucking serious!?" he yelled. Thoughts of her having sex with someone else, while they were living together no less, sent his mind into a frenzy. Standing next to his own car's rear driver-side door he thrust his elbow into the window. It hit with force, but the glass didn't break. His anger swelled into rage: something was going to break!

Rain that elbow on her face, not our ride! His mind told him, but he ignored it.

"Dan, stop it!" Stacy yelled as she watched his elbow hit the glass a second, then a third time in quick succession. Third time's the charm.

His right elbow finally broke the plane, shattering the glass. Even though it was "safety glass," it still was glass. As his flesh forced its way through, broken shards cut deep into his skin in several places. The concussion of the impact followed by the sound of the glass shattering a split second later filled the air of the quiet street. A dog barked.

"Oh my God!" Stacy shouted. "Dan, your arm!"

The door to the house opened and the woman peered angrily out, shouting "Stacy, you alright?"

Daniel turned his neck to look at her, giving her an almost evil look. "We're *fine*!" he yelled, his look and tone of voice conveying: *Don't you fucking get involved, lady!* She got the hint and closed the door.

Daniel quickly took off his white t-shirt and wrapped his right elbow with it. The blood was flowing, soaking the shirt immediately. He tightened it, in an effort to stop the bleeding. The sharp, slicing pain was now radiating from the wound, up his arm and down to his wrist and hand.

That was stupid, his mind said. Now we have a broken window to deal with and no girlfriend! Daniel ignored the admonishing thought.

"Your arm," Stacy repeated, pointing at it, looking at the broken window. She had never witnessed him in such a state. Yes they yelled sometimes and argued, but never physical violence. This was a side she had never known was there. And it frightened her.

"I don't care!" Daniel shouted, speaking of is arm. "How long has this been going on?" He demanded, still searching for answers. *Pregnant? What the fuck!?!*

"Dan, I'm sorry. I didn't plan on this...but it happened...we're done," she told him. Her eyes and voice were icicles in his heart. Her lips were tight, brow furrowed. There was a coldness in her eyes that he had never seen before. He was taken aback by it. At that moment as she looked at him with anger, sadness, (and was that disappointment?) he felt alone, abandoned. Betrayed. "I gotta get back inside," she said as she started to walk toward the house. "You should go to the hospital."

"I don't need a fucking hospital," he said angrily as he watched her walk away from him. "Like you give a shit anyway," he said aloud to himself. Panic began to set in. Not wanting the woman, who was now peering out of a window at them, to call the police, he decided he'd better leave. There was still much to say, to discuss. But that would have to wait. She obviously wasn't going to do it now, not here.

Still boiling with anger, Daniel got in his car, slammed the door as hard as he could, started the engine and popped the clutch on the four cylinder to squeal the tires as he sped away.

"Fuck, fuck, fuck!" he yelled into the air, pushing the words with as much anger and force as his voice allowed.

The adrenaline was starting to wear off, and the pain was becoming more noticeable. He couldn't tell if the bleeding had stopped, but he could feel each heartbeat in his fresh wounds. He sped across the Veterans bridge toward Nevver's apartment, which thankfully was only five minutes away. He noticed the drivers of the oncoming vehicles: one lady driving a new, blue Ford Escort was putting on eye makeup; an overweight man in a red and white Chevy K5 blazer was eating a fast food hamburger; a teenaged boy in a rusted, dented 1983 silver Mustang was singing along to the stereo; another teenaged boy in an orange Volkswagon Rabit was picking his nose. Daniel's mind registered these things almost as an afterthought, he saw them, knew what was going on, what the vehicles' makes and models were, but it was a passive exercise. What occupied his mind mostly was the pain not only in his right elbow and arm, but the pain he felt in his heart.

He pulled quickly off the one-way street into the driveway. Nevver's dark blue Pontiac Trans-Am was there. *Thank God, he's home*, Daniel thought. The thought that Nevver should get the firebird air-brushed on the hood oddly occurred to him as he walked past it.

The summer sun was starting to set, though the temperature was still hovering around seventy, but falling with the sun. Shirtless, with heart still racing, Daniel got out of his car and went to the back door--none of his friends went to the front dooor--and knocked.

In less than a minute Nevver opened the door. "Hey, Dan-O," he started, then he saw the bloody shirt wrapped around the middle of his friend's right arm. "Holy fuck, dude, what happened to your arm?" He said this as he moved back from the doorway and let his friend enter.

Anxiety now filled Daniel's mind. The adrenaline had all but dissipated now. The anger had subsided, replaced with sadness, fear, and uncertainty. "I smashed out my car window," he told his friend. As they locked eyes Daniel saw concern and puzzlement on Nevver's face. "I found Stacy," he began, but was unsure how to articulate the rest. So he just said it, "She's *pregnant* with some asshole's kid!" he said angrily.

"Fuck, dude! Are you serious?" Nevver was incredulous. "That bitch!" he said in punctuation. "Come on, we gotta clean that and see how bad it is," Nevver said, referring to the still bleeding arm.

The two went into the bathroom and Nevver turned on the tub's faucet. No sense going to the kitchen or bathroom sink, the wounds were over too large of an area for the smaller sinks, and the greater pressure from the tub faucet would be helpful in flushing out any remaining pieces of glass. Daniel knelt down and leaned on the cool porcelain of the old tub. He carefully untied the t-shirt and pulled it from the wounds. The blood had begun to clot and was sticking to the shirt.

The act of pulling it off reopened the barely closing cuts. Daniel gritted his teeth as he used his left hand to rub at the cuts, feeling pieces of glass and gingerly trying to dislodge them from where they had been embedded by the impact. Fresh pain shot through his arm as he cleaned. It served to focus his anger and he almost welcomed it, as it momentarily took his thoughts off of the unexpected turn his life had just taken.

He turned his arm in an effort to see the damage. He counted three large gashes and four or five smaller cuts all around the elbow and a little higher toward the triceps. The water flowed hard on the wounds, washing them, sending the blood in a torrent down into the tub, pooling momentarily, then circling down the drain. Nevver returned with a large dark blue bath towel and held it out for his friend. "Here," he said.

Daniel turned his head and looked at it and hesitated. "I don't want to ruin your towel," he said.

"Who cares?" Nevver said. "It's only blood....so what the fuck happened?"

As Daniel's mind brought to focus the event that had just happened within the half hour he began to cry. He tried not to show his friend his weakness, but after a vain attempt at stifling it he gave in. He didn't care. As he shut off the water and wrapped the clean towel around his arm and put pressure on the wounds, Daniel began to recount as best he could to his friend what had just happened. What she had said. What she had done. What he had done.

"What the fuck am I gonna do now?" Daniel asked rhetorically.

Nevver felt the need to say something. He wasn't much for compassion or encouragement, and this scene made him uncomfortable to say the least. But it also made him angry. This was a friend of his. And no one fucked with his friends.

"Don't worry...that fucker is *done*," Nevver reassured him. "You say he works with Stacy?" Nevver asked. "What does he look like....and when does he usually work?"

*   *   *

It was after eleven-thirty on a Wednesday night, weeks after Daniel had broken his car window. The sun had long set and the night air was cool. The small parking lot of the drive-thru only burger restaurant was empty except for the two vehicles of the closing employees. One of them was a dirty, rusted, blue Chevy S-10.

Nevver and a friend of his, Brian, waited patiently behind the dumpster enclosure next to which the S-10 was parked. The enclosure was at the very back of the parking lot, about a hundred yards from the building. There was a large light on a pole on the side of the enclosure on the opposite side from where the pickup was parked. It threw yellow light on the dumpsters but only a fraction of the truck was lit. They waited in the shadows, keeping watch on the back door of the building.

Brian was a large man. He was over six and a half feet tall and pushed the scale at nearly two hundred fifty pounds. He had long, bushy black hair and thick matching sideburns that ran to his jawline. Brian was one of those individuals that went to the bar to get *drunk*. And to fight. And he almost always won.

They were alerted when light spilled onto the parking lot from the door opening. A gangly twenty-year-old white kid, with his work-issued baseball cap cocked to the side walked out. Alone. He was carrying two large, transparent bags of garbage, evidently heading directly to the dumpster. Brian looked at Nevver and whispered, "That him?" Nevver just nodded.

As the unsuspecting man sat the trash bags down and threw back the black, plastic lid of the dumpster he heard, "Hey, TJ!" yelled from behind him. Close behind him. That was his name, and it startled him. He turned, but that is all he would remember.

Nevver's right fist connected with TJ's left temple just as he turned fully around to see who was calling him. TJ dropped like a sack of sand to the pavement. Dazed but still conscious and moving, he was less prepared for what followed.

Brian stepped up and kicked the downed man square in the balls with his steel-toed boot.

Like a pro Soccer player executing a corner kick, or how one kicks off the hardened snow/slush that collects and hangs off of their vehicle's wheel wells in winter. Not once, but no less than four times, Nevver counted. Cries of pain, then whimpering could be heard meekly emanating from TJ's throat. Brian then knelt directly on the downed man's chest, pushing his bulk into him, making him gasp for air.

He then quickly delivered thunderous blows to the man's face in a right, left, right, left, right, left rhythm that reminded Nevver of pistons firing in a two-cylinder engine. In a few short seconds the man's face looked nearly pulverized by the onslaught. Nevver tapped Brian's shoulder twice and the huge man stopped, pushed up off of the now unconscious and bleeding man. They quickly checked their surroundings and didn't see anyone, leaving the scene as quickly and silently as they had arrived.

TJ's mother would later find him in the hospital with a broken jaw, in three places; broken nose; three dislodged teeth; and a cracked left eye socket. He pissed blood for two weeks.

CHAPTER THREE

Daniel finished recounting the story, with Nevver interjecting some details that were missing, putting his usual flair into the telling. Church sat there almost dumbfounded. He looked to Nevver, "*You* did all that?"

Nevver shrugged, "Hell yes! I had Dan-O's back!" He said as he finished the beer. "I'd do the same for you...but you'll never have anyone," he said almost offhandedly, but he meant it.

Church was asexual. In high school he'd had a few girlfriends, but nothing serious. Then after high school he even had a few boyfriends, but nothing serious. Church decided he didn't really care one way or the other. Sex really didn't matter to him, it wasn't something he needed or desired. Having companionship or a family was a nice thought, but not something he worked for, something he thought he needed to complete his life. He focused instead on himself and his career. He was a good friend and had many friends and acquaintances, and that seemed to be enough for him.

Nevver, on the other hand, was a total man-whore. It was his mission in life to sleep with and defile as many women as he could. He was a misogynist through and through. He liked women a lot, but to him they were just objects, things to be enjoyed, used, then discarded when he became bored or was just finished with them. He liked to think of himself as the quintessential bad boy. He liked to fight, drink, smoke almost anything, narcotics were also enjoyed, though lately he'd seemed to keep that to a minimum and usually only as bait for his next conquest.

Daniel was somewhere in the middle. He believed there was "one" person for him, and he spent many thinking hours on the subject. He was never one to sleep around, and he had never had a one-night-stand. Which wasn't saying much, because Stacy was the first woman he'd had sex with. Through his adolescence, Daniel had pined and longed for the companionship he saw his friends enjoy, even if it was just "puppy love." He had a few girlfriends, for a short time. He had quite a few girls that were friends in his circle, ones that he would "wait in line for," so to speak. But those relationships never seemed to materialize.

"So you went through all of that," Church asked, "and you guys somehow *still* got married?" He gave both of them in a very puzzled, confused look.

Daniel sighed. "Well...The best way I can explain it is...She was *mine*." He said the last word very strongly with the possessiveness that neither one of his close friends had seen in him very often.

"Maybe I shouldn't have gotten back with her...Looking back now, I probably...*definitely*...should not have...But at the time, she was what I wanted. And because of my beliefs, my faith, I thought that was what was expected of me, that it was what I was *supposed* to do--be with one woman. I forgave her for what she had done. I actually even forgot about it after a time. We had moved on from that, and I thought we were building a life together. Apparently I was wrong."

Because you're a dumb ass who doesn't listen to me, his mind scolded.

"Dude," Nevver began, and as he said the first word, Church winced as his mind anticipated what would follow. "You should've left that bitch down on Fifth Street with the rest of the White Trash. Woman does you like that, she *deserves* the shit storm that's in her future...The future *she* created," Nevver concluded as he got up, shook the empty bottle of beer and walked towards the kitchen for a fresh one. "After you patched up your arm that day, you should've patched up your heart and kept on moving," he added as he walked into the kitchen.

Good advice. Hmmm...did someone else say that to you, I wonder? Daniel ignored the berating thought.

Church lowered his voice and leaned in and asked, "So what happened to the baby?"

Daniel replied, "There was something in Stacy's pH system that basically aborted the fetus within the first couple months. That was one of the main reasons I stayed with her. If she would've had the baby, I don't know what I would've done."

"So, now she's gone, for good this time?" Church probed.

"Looks that way," Daniel said.

"So, what now? What are your future plans, now?" Churched asked, concerned.

"I got a general manager job at this brand-new restaurant, I will focus on that. There's a lot of work to be done, and the current general manager whose job I'm taking is being demoted to assistant...and she's not taking it very well, to put it mildly. So I got that to deal with as well," Daniel told him.

"So how's that going so far?" Nevver asked as he returned with three Michelob Ultra bottles, handing one to each of his friends before retaking his spot on the couch. He dug a big hand into the bowl of peanut M&Ms and munched as he listened to the reply.

A warm blast of summer air flowed through the window brining with it the smell of cut grass and sunshine. Daniel closed his eyes for a second and took in a deep breath, trying to fill his being with the calming scents before answering.

"Pretty good. There's a lot to learn, a lot of rigid rules and specifications, being a corporate franchise restaurant. We're in the middle of moving to a brand-new location. We currently only have sixteen employees, and the new concept restaurant will require fifty-two according to my boss. And in the meantime the woman whom I'm replacing as GM is still the GM of the current location, and she's pregnant. And she's pissed," Daniel told them.

"That's a raw deal for you, though I can't say I blame her," Nevver said.

"Yea, but doesn't she realize that it's not *your* fault? That it was the upper management's decision to have her replaced?" Church said.

"They gave her a shot," Daniel explained. "We both took a third-party independent test to see who was ready for this dual-brand concept. I tested 'ready now,' she tested 'ready in six months plus.' But people being what we are, that doesn't really matter to her. And she has it in for me."

"Details," demanded Nevver.

"Well for starters, she's telling everybody that works there that I am homosexual," Daniel said. His friends laughed and Church shook his head.

"That's funny," Church said. "Why would it matter if you were?"

"Exactly," Daniel said. "It really wouldn't. But the fact remains I am *not*, never will be, but I don't need stupid rumors like that undermining my authority and ability to do my job."

"She's just jealous, and being petty and vindictive," offered Nevver.

"Not only that, from what I gather she's convinced nearly all of the current, trained employees to *not* move to the new location. So that means as I'm learning these new procedures and policies and how to cook the new menu items and everything else, I have to hire and train fifty new crewmembers, and three assistant managers. All in three months time. Starting two weeks ago," Daniel said, and laughed before taking a long drink from his beer.

With that, Church raised his beer bottle and said, "To Daniel: May your future be blessed and brighter than your past."

As the three bottles clinked together to complete the toast, Nevver added, "And let this tribulation harden your heart, and your cock, and may your balls grow big so that you will forever become the fucker and not the fucked!"

"Amen to that," Daniel said and smiled. Church just shook his head and laughed.

"So let's fire up that grill, man" exclaimed Nevver. "I'm starving...Church! Get on the phone and get those women over here, pronto! Dan-O, rack the balls on that oversized pool table you got over there...I'm gonna take you to school, boy!"

CHAPTER FOUR

Daniel sat in his car, a black Toyota Matrix, all-wheel-drive, windows blackened. It was illegal in the state to have the front windows tinted. He didn't care, it looked cool. Drops of moisture fell heavy from the sky, running down the windows and obscuring his view of anything. Again he didn't care. He wasn't trying to see what was outside at the moment, or for several hundred moments that had past. It was night, a half past nine in the middle of October in Northern Michigan. It had been dark for nearly four hours.

The night was a wet bowl of ink. It was cool, the outside temperature currently hovered at fifty-three degrees and dropping every few minutes by a quarter degree. The heater was on low, the audio system playing a compact disc burned from his computer. It was a mix of current Christian Contemporary music supposed to be uplifting in message and tune. It wasn't working. The rain streaked the windshield and scattered the rays of light that were broadcast by the sodium-vapor lights of the Wal-Mart parking lot where he was parked near the back of the lot, away from the late evening shoppers' vehicles that were understandably huddled together as close to the entrance as possible because of the weather.

His focus was on the second-generation cell phone. A very small, silver thing that cost fifty bucks and that got spotty reception at best. He was texting her, and all too eagerly awaiting each response. The blood was rushing in his veins and pounding in his ears, obscuring the songs playing over the speakers at low volume.

But what started out as excitement had now become an ordeal. He had been there in that spot, headlights off, engine running, then not, then running again to stay warm, for a few minutes shy of two hours.

"What am I still doing here?" he asked himself out loud, shaking his head, still looking at the greenish one-by-two inch screen of his cell phone, mentally urging the next response to come quickly, and with the anticipated reply. He knew the answer to the *why* question: Pussy. *Give her a few more minutes,* he thought. He had been telling himself that for over an hour.

Every eight minutes or so he would activate the windshield wipers on the Matrix to shed the water from his view. He would look up toward the backside of the enhanced Pizza Hut restaurant some three hundred yards away up on the hill from where he was parked. From his vantage point the could see the back door clearly and the employees' vehicles parked there. He could also see the delivery driver's vehicle parked in a premium spot, ready to speed away with the next set of orders so he could hurry back and cash out the tickets. They had 39 minutes from the time the order was placed until the driver had to be *back* from the delivery, completing the transaction for them to have had a "successful" delivery.

He knew this because he was the new General Manager of that restaurant, having been with the company since May of that same year. It had been a trial of his will and skills as a restaurant manager the past few months. Opening a new restaurant with a brand new staff was hard enough let alone his newness to this particular concept. He had worked earlier in the day and managed to get the evening off. He hadn't had a full day off in over six weeks. *The mantle of leadership...the curse of making salary*, he thought.

Bleep The cell phone sang out. *A new message*, he thought with lustful excitement. He pushed the button that opened up the messages folder and began to read the text.

Still waiting for her to get back from the store, was all it said.

Daniel's fingers worked the keypad. He hit the number four twice, the number six three times, nine once, repeating the exhausting ritual of changing the letters to spell out a word, then a phrase: How much longer??? Three question marks to convey his frustration. No immediate answer. Several minutes crawled by, the windshield obscured again with yellow backlit streaks of rain.

The woman he was electronically communicating with was named Faith Collins. The *her* the text referred to was Faith's friend Dawn who apparently was having some issues with her kids and Faith was helping her out, blah, blah, blah. He didn't care. Not one bit.

Faith was cute, had a large Native American nose, but that was the extent of the obviousness of her father's heritage. She was pale skinned, wore her black hair short and choppy, highlighted with deep purple and sometimes maroon streaks. She was a size 6, he guessed, and walked with a slight wobble because of back surgery she had when she was a teenager. Somehow she managed to turn that wobble into a strut. She always smelled nice, a mixture of body spray and two different colognes, he would later find out. Faith had a nice smile, and always seemed to be giggling and laughing, joking around with the other crew members and the customers. She was a hard worker and a good server. One of Daniel's best. And he liked that. He found it very sexy.

With all the stress and the chaos that he was enduring, when she was scheduled he relaxed a little bit. Because he knew she would help others, the weaker servers, and in turn help him run the restaurant better.

With that being said, she had a lot of baggage. She was going through what amounted to a bitter divorce, even though they were not technically married. From what he gathered from conversations with her and other crew members, Faith had four children, the oldest had a different father than the younger three. He had heard rumors that her "ex" had smashed up her van, called the police on her a few times, and had her arrested. Most recently he had kicked her out of their house and refused to let her see her kids. All in all it was a shitty situation for her, and he felt bad for her and wanted to help her if he could.

Aside from that, there was something about her that was very alluring. He guessed for the most part it was her smile, her laugh, and she seemed to be bubbly and happy most of the time. It was a refreshing change from Stacy who was dour and unhappy most of the time. Faith would also flirt with Daniel, winking at him, flashing a certain smile. She would also say certain things when others weren't around. Things like, "I don't wear any underwear," and asking him, "Do you sleep naked?" And there was something in those blue-green eyes of hers. He couldn't quite pinpoint it, but something about her made his heart stir and flutter. That coupled with the fact that he hadn't had sex in what seemed a very long time made him want her. But it was forbidden.

The Franchise had a policy that managers could not date any subordinates within the same location. It made sense, and he knew the reasons why. In fact, in all of his years in management, Daniel had never acted upon any of these desires before. It wasn't professional. And Daniel prided himself on being professional. Still...

As the windshield wipers cleared the rain from the glass again, Daniel stared toward the restaurant. Memories of how he'd gotten here, right then, filled his thoughts.

CHAPTER FIVE

Faith was a server, one of the better ones, that worked for him at the restaurant. She was one of only five employees of the "old" location that elected to work at the brand new location with the new concept. All of the others had bought into the gossip and rumors that had been spread by the woman Daniel was replacing as General Manager. Her goal was to sabotage the new location and Daniel, so that when she returned from maternity leave she could step back into her position. Her rightful position, and "save" the day and be the hero of the Franchise once again. Though her plan mostly succeeded, Daniel wasn't about to lose. He gratefully took the five trained employees and pushed ahead toward the goals set before him.

With the help of two of his bosses and some managers from other stores, Daniel hired and trained 44 new employees which was shy of the 52 that were needed. His boss had asked him, "Dan, we don't really have enough employees for the opening, which is in one week. You want to postpone until we get more people hired?"

Daniel thought about it (and actually had been thinking much about it in recent days), before replying, "We've already got flyers and advertisements out stating the date of the grand opening. It's too late to push it back--we'll look amateurish if we do. The show must go on," he told his boss with a smile. "Push forward. We can do this." And so they had.

The mantle of leadership has its pressure and stress, even for a lowly restaurant manager. Though Daniel had been doing this work for years, it never got easy. There was always something that needed to be done. Something that needed to be attended to: some maintenance problem, some bill that needed to be paid, something that needed to be cleaned, some employee or customer problem that demanded attention.

The bane of his existence was the schedule: going through all the requests for time off, who could and could not work certain days and shifts, trying to ensure you have the right amount of people for the flow of business, but didn't have too many where labor costs would be too high. Then there were the severs, a special bunch of employees filled with ego, self-centeredness, greed and selfishness. And drama. Too many servers on any given shift and none of them made much money, as they were paid $2.65 and hour plus tips, which didn't amount to much some days.

The bitch of it was that for this franchise the managers were pooled together with all the other workers to calculate one labor percentage. Therefore, Daniel and his team of managers were doing not only manager duties--food ordering, scheduling, training and managing crewmembers, handling cash and customer issues, sales projections, quality control, food prep pars--they were also doing all the other tasks that needed to be done--food prep, cooking, putting deliveries away, cleaning, running food, busing tables, shoveling snow off the sidewalks in the winter, watering the plants and the trees in the summer, even delivering pizza in their personal vehicle. It was a delicate balance trying to keep the employees happy--at least to the extent that any employee was truly happy to be at work--to keep them wanting to work and productive, and trying to meet expectations of customers to keep them coming back.

It was after midnight, the restaurant had been closed for an hour and a half. The last crew member had just left. Daniel was by himself at the back desk area in front of the DOS-based computer system. Inputting the schedule. He had to finish the paperwork and prepare the deposit, but that could wait. He had to get the schedule finished and posted.

Two hours passed. It was nearly two A.M. when he sent the finalized schedule to the printer. It was as good as he could get it. He gave the better employees, the better workers with good attitudes, as many shifts as he could, and the lesser ones the most the store could afford, according to the home office-determined percentages based on the sales projections he calculated.

Time for the deposit. As Daniel made his way to the electronic safe he glanced at the clock on the wall. *Shit!* It was five minutes after two in the morning. He knew it was futile, but he did it anyway: he jogged to the safe, dug out his set of store keys, and pressed the magnetic master GM key to the reader on the safe, and input his code. The cold black steel box with its red, digital readout mocked him: Time Locked.

"Son-of-a-bitch!" He yelled, his anguish echoing throughout the deserted restaurant.

The safe was locked. From 2 AM to 8 AM the safe was electronically time locked, and nothing short of a diamond tipped drill bit or a small ribbon of C4 would get it open during that time. Daniel cursed himself for his lack of time management right then. Which meant instead of being able to sleep in and coming in at 2 P.M. the next day, he would have to be there at nine or ten AM to complete the deposit and take it to the bank. *Motherfucker*, he cursed himself. As if working 85 hours a week wasn't enough he had just brought more grief and frustration to himself.

Another day in the life, he thought. "God," he prayed aloud, looking toward the ceiling, through the roof and into the sky beyond and hopefully up into Heaven, "When will this get easier?"

He heard no immediate answer.

*   *   *

It was a couple days later. Daniel opened the restaurant, worked and managed the lunch and early dinner shifts. It was late September, the temperature hung around 65°. It was warm with a very slight breeze as the sun started to set. The dinner rush had ended as quickly as it had started. Daniel took the opportunity to tell his assistant manager that he was leaving for the day. But before he left, he cut the six servers that were on down to three. He made a point to tell Faith personally that she was off the floor, meaning that she was not to take any more tables, get her side work done and then was free to leave.

In the preceding weeks he and Faith had talked more. She had become a little more brazen in her conversation, and it was obvious that she was interested in Daniel. He had made some sexual comments and innuendos, playfully getting her excited, or so it seemed. It was playful banter that helped him cope with his long, stressful days...and his loneliness. Faith's smile and laugh and the way she played and teased back electrified him. He hadn't felt that in what seemed like a very long time.

That night before clocking out, Daniel waited until Faith was in the walk-in cooler stocking items for the salad bar. He quickly went in where they could be alone and have some privacy, if only for a few moments.

"What are you doing after work?" He asked her, looking into her eyes and smiling.

"Ahh...Nothing," she answered after an awkward pause.

"I'll be in my car out back. Come find me when you're done," he instructed her as he reached out and brushed his hand along her bare arm.

She smiled that smile, and gazed into his eyes. "Okay," she replied. He held her gaze and she his for a few long moments. Then the cooler door opened and another crew member stepped in. Daniel quickly withdrew, grabbed his coat, said his good-byes, and went to his car to wait.

As Daniel sat in his car with the engine off his mind raced. His heart was beating fast contemplating what lay ahead.

You know you shouldn't do this, his mind told him. There are so many reasons why this is wrong.

And Daniel knew it. But at that moment he was powerless to fight it, because he didn't care. He had been alone for too long now. Alone with his thoughts, with his stress, alone inside his mind. *It's only going to be one time*, he told himself. *Okay, maybe a few times. But what's wrong with that?* He reasoned.

Daniel knew that he would be in trouble if anyone found out, anyone they worked with that is. And Faith did have a psycho ex-boyfriend/baby daddy that wanted her back. But Daniel wasn't thinking clearly. In fact his brain wasn't thinking at all. His dick was in charge now, at least for the rest of the night.

Twelve minutes later, Faith emerged from the back door of the restaurant. She stopped quickly just outside of the large steel door, took a Newport menthol cigarette out of her jacket pocket and lit it with a green Bic lighter, which took her several attempts and a few shakings to get the flame to light. She took two long drags, exhaling slowly as she scanned the parking lot for his vehicle. She found it, smiled and wobble-strutted over. She quickly took three more drags on the cigarette on her way, then dropped it to the ground, crushing it out under the sole of her black, ankle high work boot before opening the passenger door of his car and slipped into the seat next to him.

"So what did you have in mind?" She asked in a sultry voice, a slight giggle adding to her smile.

He leaned in towards her. The smell of her cologne and body spray mixed with the menthol of the cigarette smoke filled his nostrils. He kissed her slowly then, pressing his lips against hers. His right hand gently grabbing her left arm by the elbow, pulling her closer towards him. He felt her body react, leaning towards him. Her right hand laid on his right thigh.

He kissed her harder, feeling her lips part, her tongue darting into his mouth. His met hers, swirling, sliding back and forth against one another. Her breathing became heavier and a soft, quiet moan escaped her throat. It was their first kiss. An organic electricity flooded his body and his mind swirled as he tried to concentrate on his kissing. He poured his emotion into it, tried to let his longing take over the mechanics of it. She tasted like cigarettes and peppermint. He tried not to think how he tasted to her.

After a few long, intense moments he pulled back from her. When she opened her eyes he held them with his gaze and smiled. She smiled, too. "So," Daniel began, his heart pounding, his breathing heavy, his mind wanting more. "Your place, my place...or a motel?" He asked.

Faith smiled and let out a giggle as her right hand, still on his thigh, squeezed gently. "Ahhh...motel," she answered after a thoughtful pause. "But first, I need to go to Wal-mart and get some wine."

He thought about it for a second and thought *Some alcohol would be good right now...and I should probably get some condoms.* "I'll go with you," he said.

*   *   *

After their shopping, with Daniel and Faith both hurrying and wary, not wanting to run into anyone they knew, or worse yet someone they worked with, they met at the Days Inn motel located less than a half-mile from the restaurant. There were several motels on that strip, but that had been the closest, and he had stayed there a few nights on the Pizza Hut's dime during their first two weeks of opening.

The motel had two buildings separated by a parking area on either side of both buildings. The second building was a two story structure with outside walkways. Daniel went into the office and asked for a room on the second floor. $79 later and Daniel had the plastic key-card to a room located towards the back of the building, away from the restaurant. Faith parked her vandalized, green Ford Windstar minivan (one of the seemingly ongoing gifts from her ex-boyfriend, and the father of three of her children, had given her during a night of argument and rage that had gotten out of hand) several spots away from his vehicle, and backed it in, in a vain attempt to conceal her obviously recognizable vehicle.

With plastic bags containing their purchases, they climbed the stairs quickly together. He scanned the lot for anyone watching, for any recognizable vehicles. There were none. The sun had set now, the shadows of the night, created by manmade lights and the Moon, were blossoming and spreading their tendrils in hard angles across the parking lot, through the iron railings, and onto the cement walkways. Daniel read the descending numbers on the doors and found the one marked 214.

On the third try swiping the key-card they heard an electronic click and a small green light blinked four times rapidly. Daniel opened the door, flipped on the light, and they went inside. Once inside, he closed and locked the door and secured it with the flip-latch. He went and pulled the heavy curtains across the lone window, shutting the world and everyone and everything else in it out of their life. If only for a few hours.

Within a few minutes they were both sitting on the bed sipping their drinks. Faith had a four pack of small Woodbridge, screw-capped bottles of merlot. Daniel was drinking Michelob Ultra from a bottle taken from a six pack that he had awkwardly jammed into the mini-fridge. The room smelled of dust and cleanser. The room was partially warmed by the yellow light emitting from the wall sconces on either side of the television. Vehicle noise from the busy road could be heard clearly. Daniel got up off of the bed, leaving the rough, floral patterned comforter for a minute and went to the combo heater/ac unit mounted under the window. He set the controls to a neutral warm setting and turned on the fan. The noise filled the room and drowned out the sounds of the world outside. He smiled at her and sat next to her on the bed.

Daniel looked at her, gazed into her greenish blue eyes. He couldn't help but smile at her, as he watched her drink directly from the small bottle. Her full lips painted with deep maroon lipstick wrapped around the small opening of the bottle, the way her neck was smooth and rippled slightly as intoxicating liquid ran down her throat. She caught his eyes and pulled the bottle from her mouth. "What?" She said with a smile and a giggle. That smile that sent a lightning bolt of anticipation and desire from the small of his back up through his torso and directly into his heart.

"I was just admiring your smile," he told her. With that, she smiled even more and reached a hand out and touched his leg. It had been so long since someone had touched him. His breathing became more rapid, his heart rate began to quicken. He quickly took a drink of his beer.

"Umm..," She said, hesitant, unsure how to form the next words. "I want to take a shower, get the Pizza Hut smell off of me," she told him.

"Okay," Daniel replied. It wasn't what he had expected, but then again didn't really know what he expected.

"Would you like to join me?" She asked after a moment, her hand and squeezing his leg just above the knee.

Shower sex? he thought. He wasn't a big fan of it. Seemed like one person always hogged the hot water, while the other tried to stay warm in the meager overspray, then the awkward dance to change places in an effort to share, all the elbows and handing one another the proper soaps and shampoos, neither one being able to shave...The showering part of it was not enjoyable.

Though, embracing under the hot water streaming down over two bodies as they were intertwined, kissing lips and tongues exploring, hands moving, imagining that you were under the stars and moon of a far off tropical island, luxuriating in the warm rainfall from the heavens, just the two of you, no other worries, no time schedule, nothing but the long moments punctuated by your beating hearts and passionate kisses...that part he did like.

"Yes I would," Daniel replied. Faith got up from the bed then, grabbed his hand and, flashing a smile, she pulled him from the bed and led him toward the bathroom.

They watched each other undress. He noticed that as she removed her tight, black work pants that she wore no panties underneath. Faith must have read his facial features as she said, "I don't wear underwear. It's uncomfortable. After I had my daughter I don't like the feeling of it," she explained.

"Okay...that's kinda hot, though I do like thongs," he admitted. Faith smiled and let out a small laugh, shaking her head.

"Have you ever been with a woman who's had children?" She asked in a serious tone.

"No."

"Well, I don't really like my body," she began. "I breast-fed all my children, so I don't like my boobs, and my stomach won't tighten up," she told him with obvious embarrassment in her voice. "But I do like my legs and my butt," she said with a grin, her eyes lighting up.

Daniel smiled at that, "I like your legs and your butt, too," he told her as he took two steps to close the gap between them, pulled her close and kissed her gently, pressing his lips into hers. Their lips parted, mouths opening a little wider. Faith's tongue pushed into his mouth, probing and flicking his own tongue. As they kissed passionately he became erect and he pulled her body closer to his so she could feel it through his underwear.

"What's this?" she asked him as she grabbed him firmly in her right hand, tugging a little.

Daniel smiled and said, "It's a present for you."

Faith let out a slight laugh and replied, "Oh, yea?" Then she bent over, pulled down his underwear and took him into her mouth, working the tip with her tongue and kissing it gently. Daniel's mind was racing now, he was watching with great anticipation, urging her with his mind to take him in her mouth. Which she did. Gently and slowly she sucked alternately caressing his shaft with the tips of her fingers of her right hand. But only for a few short seconds. Faith quickly stopped and stood up.

She looked him in the eyes and said, "You'll have to wait." She cocked her head gave him a devious smile, and winked. She then turned to the shower, bent over slightly and turned on the hot water.

Daniel couldn't resist, he slapped her on the ass playfully. She bolted upright, turned and said, "Hey!" She unhooked her bra and let it drop to the floor with the rest of her clothes. Completely naked now, she stepped into the shower and pulled the curtain closed. "You can join me anytime you're ready," she said. Daniel quickly removed the rest of his clothing and stepped into the shower.

The metallic-smelling water was warm and inviting, Faith's body equally so. She was facing towards the shower head, so he gently grabbed her and turned her towards him. With the water cascading and splashing onto them, he kissed her again. He had to bend forward and she had to stretch her body upwards to compensate for the difference in height.

Almost naturally now their mouths and tongues hungrily engaged one another. He pulled her body close to his, the warmth of her body against his was exhilarating and caused him to kiss her hungrily. He pushed his erection into her so she could feel him, he wanted her to want him. As they kissed he reached down between her legs and felt her vagina for the first time. He caressed and probed it with his finger tips, gently swirling and rubbing as the warm water poured over them, their mouths still embraced in a dance of discovery.

She pulled her mouth away from his as she let out a gasp of pleasure. She smiled up at him, and their now opened eyes locked onto one another. Still looking deep into her eyes, Daniel pushed his middle finger into her, watching her facial expression change to surprise, then quickly to desire. Simultaneously he pushed his mouth onto hers and reengaged the passionate tongue battle while curling the finger inside of her, rubbing against the front wall of her vagina. Her tongue was strong and took command. He in turn tried to match her rhythm and level of force. It was a sensual fencing of the mouth muscles. He felt her hand on his cock again, gently pulling and tugging. His mind was racing as fast as his heart. *This is really happening!* his mind shouted as tingles exploded throughout his entire body. Faith was moaning softly as they continued to kiss and pleasure each other.

Daniel leaned in and began kissing her neck, sucking and tickling with this tongue. He began to bite gently as her body seemed to quiver as he continued to rub and caress her. He used his palm of that same hand to rub against her clit in a rhythmic fashion, matching in a way the movements of his tongue and mouth across her neck. Faith moaned as her hand gripped him tightly, then suddenly let go of him and pushed his hand out of her, using her other hand to push his shoulder backing him up a step. "Wow," she breathed. "How do you know how to do that?" She asked.

"I don't know," was all he said as he pulled her close and kissed her neck again.

She seemed to melt for just a second, then pushed away. "You gotta wait till were done showering," she told him. It was a statement. A command.

Daniel laughed, "Okay."

In a few minutes they were done showering, Daniel had finished before Faith and had gotten out and dried off while she finished. Still naked, he helped himself to another Michelob Ultra from the mini fridge and laid down on the bed and waited.

It took Faith another 10 minutes, a long 10 minutes to Daniel, for her to emerge from the bathroom. She was wearing a thin, green tank top and nothing else. Her short, punk-style haircut had been styled, she had put on a eye makeup and lipstick, and had sprayed that glorious combination of cologne and body spray all over herself. The perfumed air seemed to proceed her, filling his senses and locking in the smell of desire.

She smiled at him with that inviting, intoxicating smile. Her eyes glistened with a mischievousness and wanting. She lay down next to him, and he put his beer on the side table. Lying on their sides now, he picked up where they left off, lips and tongues probing, exploring, fencing. He gently grabbed her ass as they kissed, then slid his hand slowly down her upper thigh and then between her legs again. He rubbed the outside of her vagina slowly and softly, just on the verge of tickling.

She reacted by breathing heavily and saying, "Yes, I like that...touch me softly." Which he did for a few moments, and he inserted his finger began twirling and rubbing the erogenous zone inside of her. He continued the rhythm, tongues, hands, exploring. Faith's breath quickening, her breast heaving under the tank top, her hips gently bucking against his hand.

He gently rolled her onto her back, still kissing. Then, with his finger still inside her, still moving, he slid his body downward on hers until his mouth hovered above his fingers where one was inserted into her. He began to lick hungrily at her clit.

"Not so hard," she scolded, and he stopped. "Lick it gently...like, tickle it," she instructed.

Daniel had never had instruction from a lover before, but he didn't mind it. In fact, he wanted to give her what she wanted, what she liked. Obeying her command, he licked her slowly, teasingly up and down, tasting her. "Take your finger out," she told him. He did so, without stopping with his mouth. He presses entire mouth onto her now, though still licking as she wanted.

She ran her fingers through his hair and pulled her knees up towards her chest. Daniel took this opportunity and grabbed her ass with both hands and pushed his mouth onto her more firmly, now inserting his tongue into her. He continued this for what seemed a very long time, but in actuality was only a few minutes, before Faith pushed his head back and told him to kiss her.

Daniel climbed back up and laid on top of her and kissed her passionately, pressing himself onto her. He was totally erect now, throbbing and pulsating with desire. He awkwardly reached for and grabbed the condom packet from the side table that he had placed there while she was still in the bathroom, tore it open and rolled it onto his erection. He then looked into her eyes as he guided himself into her slowly. She gasped as she looked into his eyes, her mouth open, her breath coming heavily. The wetness of her enveloped him and he pushed himself fully into her. He started thrusting in a rhythm, matching with kisses, while her hands grasped his lower back and his ass. This he continued for several minutes, luxuriating in her body, in her warmth. In the intimate contact with another being who wanted to be with him.

He felt that feeling, his body began to tingle, and pulse, his breathing became heavy. He tried to control it but he knew it was only a matter of seconds. "I'm really close," he told her, as he began to thrust harder.

"No!" She said loudly, almost yelling at him. "Stop! Stop!" She demanded. "Control yourself!"

What the fuck? He didn't expect this, he had never had someone telling him to stop before. But he obeyed. Using his muscles to tense himself to keep himself from climaxing. He pulled himself from her, as he looked into her eyes. She looked at him sternly, yet still with wanting desire. He let out a laugh, *Unbelievable*, he though. And she smiled at him.

"I'm not ready yet," she told him in way of explanation. "I'll give you a minute or two to relax," she said, as she got up off the bed after he rolled from and lay next to her.

Daniel watched her walk across the room, her naked form wobble-walking the short distance to where her bottles of wine were. She took one from the small carton, turned her head and asked him, "Do you want a beer?" as she cracked the screw top and took a small drink.

"No, thank you," he replied as he pulled the condom off of his shrinking erection. He lay there in wonder. This was a surprise to him, he had never experienced anything, or anyone like this before. He watched her drink the wine as his heart rate slowed, and his erection continued to fade.

She walked back to the bed, took a long drink from the small bottle and placed it on the side table. Daniel was still lying on his back as she climbed onto the bed and positioned herself between his legs. He smiled at her, and she at him as she began to slowly stroke his penis, and took the tip into her mouth. As she began to slowly suck and stroke him his erection came back full and hard. She smiled at him and looked him in the eyes as she drummed her fingers along the shaft, almost as if to say: "Hmmmm, what should I do?"

He was immensely turned on and fascinated as he watched her technique. *I can't believe this is happening!* His mind screamed in ecstasy and excitement. She tried to put him fully into her mouth and she started to gag a little. She took him out of her mouth and said with a breath of laughter, "You have a big dick, Daniel."

He didn't know what to say, so he just let out a nervous laugh and said. "Thank you," thinking: *I'm sure you say that to all the guys.*

She played with him for a while, sucking and teasing and pulling, then stopped and said to him, "I want you to get behind me." He smiled at her and just nodded his head.

After they repositioned he began rubbing her tight ass as she kneeled before him, bent over on the bed, and he on his knees behind her gently stroking himself to keep his erection. He spit a little on his hand and rubbed it on the opening of her vagina before inserting himself into her, slowly. He didn't bother reapplying another condom, the heat of the moment engulfed him and he didn't think about anything else. Just the two of them, becoming one.

He gave her just the head at first, then slowly and methodically more of him, sliding in and out in a steady rhythm. Faith was moaning and pushing herself back into him. Their bodies were in sync now, becoming one, sliding onto and into one another. He reached up and began massaging her shoulders and her back as they continued the rhythm.

"Harder!" She yelled after a couple of minutes.

With that instruction, Daniel grasped her shoulders firmly and pulled her body back into him as he thrust forward. This he did over and over again as Faith wailed and moaned, yelling his name.

Within a few seconds, she began saying, "Oh fuck, oh fuck...Oh my God!" Her right hand slid to her clit and began rubbing furiously. Her body shuddered as she climaxed. She pushed her face into the pillow and let out a half moan, half scream, her left hand clutching and pulling at the bed sheet. It was too much for him to handle, and he climaxed into her, still thrusting, still pounding for a few seconds more for he collapsed on her and she fell forward onto the bed. Both breathing heavy. Wide smiles across their faces.

He slid off of her and laid next to her with his arm wrapped around her and his legs still intertwined with hers. He kissed her gently on the neck, smelling her sweat and perfume, the scent of their sex filling the air. His heart was racing, his body tingling from the explosion of hormones.

They lay there for a few minutes, just enjoying each other's body, listening to each other's breathing. Daniel could feel her heartbeat though it was faint compared to his own thundering pulse. Faith rolled over and embraced him. Daniel was on his back now, his head on the pillow, his eyes closed. She was playing with the hair on his chest and the line of it that ran down his belly to his groin.

"It's a happy trail," she said referring to the line of hair. He had his arm around her, her head lying on his shoulder and chest. Her warm body next to him, her hand touching him lovingly, her leg wrapped around his... It all seemed right. He missed this. The touch of another, the embrace of one who wanted his. The smile. The look in her eyes. The taste of her minty breath. The smell of her.

No, she wasn't perfect. Her body had flaws. She had flaws. She had baggage. She had children. They worked together. She had a psycho ex-boyfriend who was the father of her children, one that wanted her back...But he wasn't perfect either. And he wanted to help her. He wanted to show her that there was a better life. He could sense and he felt that she was a good person, that she deserved a better life.

As they laid there in each other's arms, Daniel began to fall asleep. He had a smile on his face, not because he had just been satisfied physically, though he had to admit that was part of it. But because for the first time in a long time he felt like he was wanted. Like he was desired. He felt like he had something else to look forward to, besides getting up every day and going to a stressful job. He wasn't sure what his future held, but for now, for that night, he didn't care. He didn't worry about it. He just enjoyed the embrace, her smell, the way her body felt against his, the warmth of her skin. He dreamt of better days. For both of them.

CHAPTER SIX

She had ran from the living room, down the hall as fast as she could to her room, slamming and locking her door in one quick, practiced motion. Her heart was racing. That was almost 10 minutes ago. Ten very long minutes. They seemed like hours. She could barely hear the sounds from the other room. The sounds of her mother yelling. She couldn't tell exactly what her mother was yelling, just that she was. Yelling at her little sister and her baby brother. Well, he wasn't really a baby anymore, he was six. Six. That's how old she was when her stepfather had moved in. That's when the long nightmare started. When everything changed. When her life as she knew it had changed forever.

Her dad had died that year, when she was six. She remembered him going away on vacation, but she couldn't go. Not that time. Her mother would not let her. Her parents had just divorced and they were still fighting. She was her dad's little girl. He was her life. She did not know why, could not understand, why she couldn't stay with him. Why she couldn't live with her dad. Her mother kept her from him. She didn't want her oldest daughter to spend any time with her father. And she did not know why. Couldn't understand why.

She still remembered the way he smelled, like Irish Spring an Old Spice, like a man smelled. She still saw his face, strong and handsome. She still knew his smile and his laughter, though she would never hear it again. He would lift her up and put her on his shoulders. So high up, so far from the ground below. They would run around the yard. She would feel the warmth of the sun on her face and the slight breeze brought on by his running as she giggled and she heard her daddy laugh. Those were good times. The best times. She was happy then. Before she was six.

That all changed when her dad did not come home from that trip. It was an accident, they said. He had fallen off the boat, had hit his head, and drowned. She wasn't sure how that could happen, as her dad was a good swimmer. He was strong. He won every fight. He was a good man. And good men shouldn't die. Not when they had little girls that needed them. And she needed him. He said he was coming back.

He said he was coming back for her. She waited. She waited for her daddy. But he never did come home.

The brass door knob to her room rattled. The wooden door began to shake violently. "Young lady open this door, right now!" Her stepfather yelled.

Panic filled her entire being. She began to shake with fearful anticipation. She didn't want him to do those things he did to her. But this would not be like the other times. She had a plan. This time when he came for her she would hold on to the leg of the bed. And when he grabbed for her he would not be able to pull her out. He would tug and tug, she thought, but she would hang on so tight, so very tight, that he would not be able to pull her free. And he would give up. He would get tired and give up. "Please God," she prayed, "let him give up...just this once."

Then the door flew open with the sound of splintering wood and wrenching metal, and banged against the wall. The light to her room flipped on, casting a sickly yellow glow and she could see his bare feet standing on the carpet. She could see his yellowish toenails staring at her like the eyes of a spider. Her stomach churned. They quickly walked toward her. "Where are you?" He yelled. Then in an instant his face was at floor level looking under the bed. Looking at her. She could smell his putrid breath, a cloud that smelled of ground bologna and whiskey. A drunken hand shot out and grabbed her by the ankle and began to pull. She could feel his long fingernails digging into the thin flesh of her ankle. She held onto the leg of the bed as tightly as she could. She screamed, "Mommy! Mommy! Mommy!" She needed help. *Can someone, anyone, please help me!?!* Her mind screamed, as tears ran down her face, as whimpers escaped her throat.

But there was only his laughter. A horrible, malevolent cackle. "She can't hear you little one," he said as he gritted his teeth, grabbing her ankle with both hands and pulled with all his strength. Her hands were ripped from the bedpost and her body was dragged across the carpet--the fibers burning her soft, young skin--and out from under the bed into the harsh light. His hands grabbed her roughly and her body was pulled upright, inches from his face. His yellow teeth snarled at her for an instant. She repulsively focused on his smile, like a jack-o-lantern with missing teeth; black holes in his mouth. Then she felt herself being hurled backward through the air. In her mind she wished that he had pushed her so hard that she was flying, that she had been pushed far, far away, to some place else. Some place safe. Somewhere where monsters were only myth and folklore. To a place where dark spaces to hide in were not necessary. Then suddenly she cracked her head on the wall and fell onto her bed, her mind was focused abruptly on the reality of where she was. Where she always seemed to be.

She began crying from the pain and from the knowledge of what was coming next. She wished, she prayed, that the stuffed lion, the stuffed husky dog, even the stuffed dolphin would come to life, come to her rescue! But they remained silent and dead-eyed. All the love that she had poured into them could not bring the cotton and polyester to life when she needed them most. Through tear-stained eyes she saw him close the door to her bedroom. Since it was broken now, it would not shut properly. So he kicked at it and pushed it, and made it stay in place. Then he turned and dropped his dirty, denim shorts to the floor.

Bile rose up in her throat. She knew what was coming next. She was 10 now, and this had been going on since she was six. At least once, sometimes three times a day. Every day. But she did it to protect her sister, and her little brother, she told herself. Because he told her that if she didn't that he would do it *them* instead. And that she should never, ever tell her mother.

But she *had* told her mother. But her mother did not believe her. Her mother told her to quit lying. Mother told her that she was a bad little girl, that she needed to be a good girl and listen to her mom and her new daddy. And so it continued. Oh how she wished her dad was still alive! She would've been safe with her dad. This would not have happened to her if he had come back from that trip and had taken her away to live with him as he promised. But he died--he had fallen out of the boat and dirty water had filled his lungs, and he did not come home. And a part of her died that day as well. And ever since she was six and her stepfather had moved into the house, another part of her died each day. She had toys, and dresses, even a house for her dolls. But those meant nothing when the sun went down, and her mommy was sleeping on the couch and couldn't hear her screams. Because her daddy was gone.

She felt his hands tear the Strawberry Shortcake pajama bottoms off of her. Felt his rough skin on her naked body. He pulled her waist-length hair hard and wrenched her head back. She cried and screamed with all her might, "NOOOOOOOOOO!"

Faith woke up with a start, her heart pounding in her chest. She was sweating, trying to catch her breath. Her head hurt and throbbed with each beat of her heart. She wasn't sure where she was. She looked around the strange room and then felt somebody next to her. In a panic she quickly pushed herself away and blinked her eyes. The dim light from the bathroom allowed her to see the man lying next to her, shirtless. Then she recognized him. She breathed a sigh of relief. She remembered now. She wasn't 10 years old. It was a dream. Well, it was a memory in the form of a dream, that had become a recurring nightmare. The man beside her was Daniel. Her boss. Her new friend. Her lover? They were in the motel room. She remembered now. She was safe.

She lay back down next to him, put her arms around him, and intertwined his leg with hers. She kissed his shoulder and tried to go back to sleep. She smiled. She was safe. For the night, she was safe.

CHAPTER SEVEN

He sat in his car in the rain in the Wal-mart parking lot remembering...and waiting for the next text. It was over two hours of waiting. He was getting angry. Angry with her. Angry with himself.

You need to let this go, his mind told him. You had your fun, you got away with it. It's time to move on, and focus.

Daniel looked at the little display on his phone. He waited for the series of beeps, for the little envelope icon to appear signifying that she had sent him another text. Hoping--needing--that it would be the text saying that she was finally on her way.

Another 10 minutes rolled slowly by as Daniel fought off his own mind, and the advice that it was giving. He was thinking with his dick again. Still.

He switched on the windshield wipers one last time as he turned over the engine and kicked up the heater. His phone bleeped, and instantly his heart rate accelerated. A smile involuntarily spread across his face as he quickly flipped open the little phone. There on the small, green illuminated screen was the envelope icon. Daniel quickly pushed the button with his thumb and opened up the message.

His smile faded just as quickly as it had arrived. The short text said that she wasn't able to make it. That she was sorry. Nothing she could do about it.

Fuck! He said to himself. No sex tonight. Maybe not ever again with her. The thought of their night being a one-night-stand frustrated him. He had never had a one-nighter, and didn't want to start now. *Maybe just one more time*, he thought.

Daniel's conflicted anger continued to burn slowly. But he was still wanting. Still wondering. Still hoping for more. For *something* more.

Just then, sitting there listening to the rain, Daniel's thoughts transported him back to another time. Another time of waiting.

      *   *   *

He was 17, behind the wheel of his first car, a faded silver 1976 Chevette four door, hatchback. He had upgraded the radio and speakers. He'd put on black and gray seat covers over the two front bucket, and rear bench seats, covering up the yellowish tan upholstery. He tried to wax it once, tried to make it shine. But the paint was too faded, too old. All his effort just seemed to put swirl marks on the dull, gray-looking surface. It was his first car. His grandfather gave him that car. And he appreciated and loved it. Many of his friends did not have a car of their own yet, so it was something to be proud of. No more taking the bus to school. No more riding with your older sisters. No more waiting for mom to pick you up. It gave him freedom and responsibility.

He was parked with the engine running in a stranger's driveway. He'd only been in the house a couple of times, never venturing further than the living room or the entry. Hadn't even used the bathroom. The house was a small, rundown one story, with no basement or crawlspace, the foundation was just a slab of concrete. The times he had been inside he could smell the earth, the dampness of the ground coming up through the concrete floor even through the carpeting that was laid on top of it. The smell reminded Daniel of something old, something discarded.

It was late April, just over a month of school left. He had been driving this way, waiting for her every morning, waiting for her after school, and driving her home every school day since the previous autumn. He considered her a friend. Her name was Jennifer. She had long, dark brown hair, a cheerleader's body, wonderful smile and a quirky laugh. She smoked cigarettes, Newport menthol. For her birthday the previous year Daniel had bought her a carton of them. He didn't smoke, but he allowed her to in his car. He would've done almost anything for her.

Her house was some 10 miles in the opposite direction of the school. She was not on his way, it was not convenient to pick her up and take her home. Just the opposite. He never asked her for gas money. Never asked her for anything, really. But in his heart and in his mind was trying to get her to like him more than a friend. He'd actually asked her out once, but that hadn't worked out as he planned...as he dreamed it would.

When he called the night in question to ask what time she wanted him to pick her up for their date, she was not at home. Her dad had answered the phone, said she wasn't there.

"Do you know where she is?" Daniel asked.

"Yes," was the gruff answer. No elaboration. No more information was given.

"Do you know when she'll be back?" He asked, his mind questioning, searching for answers. His heart was aching and his breathing heavy. Confusion and disappointment draining his energy.

"Don't think she'll be back tonight," was the curt reply.

"Please tell her that Daniel called," he said.

"Yep," was all he heard before the click, and the dial tone.

That was a Friday. She had not returned his call.

The following Monday, Daniel got ready for school, as usual. He got in his car and backed out of his driveway, the same time, as usual.

Don't you do it, his mind told him. She's using you. You are getting nothing out of this relationship. It can't even really be called a relationship.

Daniel's sat at the stop sign. Right was the way to Jennifer's house. Left was the way to school. He sat there for long minutes, as he waged a war in his mind.

He had not had sex yet, had not even had a real girlfriend for longer than a couple of weeks. He was the insecure type of person who would stare longingly at a girl until she would sense him looking and she would look back. Quickly he would avert his eyes, and look down or away. Avoiding. A couple times he had mustered the courage to ask an attractive girl to dance, only to be told, "No thanks." Those instances only added to his indecisiveness.

Jennifer was his current "dream girl," the object of his infatuation. He had been watching her in a few of his classes over the previous year and a half. A couple of his good friends had dated her a few times, as far as 14 and 15-year-old dates went anyway. He wanted to be next. He had befriended her and had put in a lot of time talking with her, showing her how caring and giving he was--with rides and cigarettes, and just being nice and decent to her. He wanted to show her that he was different. That he was better. That he would treat her better than all the rest. But he wasn't sure how to do that, exactly. "Just be yourself," was what they had said. So he was. And so *here* he was.

Part of him knew he was being used, was tired of it. Another part didn't want to let go of what little he had. For having little was better than having nothing. And he felt that he didn't want to give up, he didn't want the time he had spent, the effort that he had put in so far to be wasted. *She had to come around soon*, he thought. *She must have a good reason for Friday*, he told himself.

Daniel gripped the steering wheel tightly and rotated it to the right and pressed the gas pedal. *One more time*, he told himself. *Maybe this time will be different.*

     *   *   *

A truck drove by, its headlights flashing yellow through the rain-streaked windshield, the brightness of it making Daniel's eyes involuntarily close and his head turn to his right. It also brought him back to the present. He hadn't thought about Jennifer in a very long time. He laughed at himself and shook his head at the memories. He never did go out on that date. A few more weeks of him following her around, a few more weeks of rejection, and Daniel had finally had enough. He quit picking her up for school, he didn't speak to her for quite a while. And she seemed not to notice. Or care. *What a waste of time and effort*, he'd realized. Anger had replaced the infatuation. Anger with himself. Anger at her.

Now, as it was then, Daniel wasn't ready to give up on Faith, on this woman that obviously had interest in him and he in her. Not yet. Especially since he had the intense feeling that for some reason Faith needed his help, and he needed to help her. Help her out of her situation. Help give her, and perhaps her kids, a better life. He felt there was a reason they were brought together, and he intended to find out what that reason was.

Right then he was disappointed--he felt slighted, let down...abandoned. He felt like his loneliness was *not* at an end, that the night spent with Faith was going to turn out to be just a one-night-stand. And the thought of that being true frustrated him. That was the only thing he was really sure of right then. That, and the fact that he had to get up and start his workweek all over again in nine short hours.

CHAPTER EIGHT

The alarm's cacophony jolted him from his sleep. Too soon it was time for work. Daniel grudgingly and angrily rose from his bed and readied himself, going through the daily routine, keeping a watchful eye on the clock. Once readied, he drove to work taking his usual route. The sun had risen for a couple of hours by now and its harsh light made it impossible to drive without sunglasses.

Daniel looked at passing vehicles and thought briefly where they were off to. A young woman in a white GMC Jimmy, four door, rusted, displaying a butterfly sticker on the rear window; a silver haired elderly man in a pearl white Cadillac Deville wearing extremely large sun "goggles" over spectacles; a black Toyota Matrix similar to his passed him going the opposite way, a woman driving, *There I go*, he thought to himself. He noticed that it was not an all-wheel-drive XR model as his was, and the windows were not tinted. These things he noticed and briefly thought on, though in his mind he was reliving the previous night of waiting. He was still angry, still unsure of what to do. What to say to her. If anything.

He decided to focus on what he had to do that day, to get the restaurant ready for the day. He had time, as Faith did not work until 3 o'clock. That fact lessened his anxiety. He was working nine until whenever the dinner rush slowed down, which meant about eight o'clock. Faith was the first server to be cut from floor, meaning she should be done working about the same time as him. So maybe... Just maybe.

     *   *   *

The lunch rush had come and gone without much fanfare. He and his crew of five others handled that well and without incident. Thank God. It was 2:30 PM now and Daniel's heart began to quicken its pace as he anticipated the first meeting with Faith since the letdown the night before.

He did not text her after the last one she had sent. Not last night, not today. She had not texted him either. Though they weren't supposed to have their cell phones active and on them during work, Daniel had his back at the small manager's desk and he checked it periodically throughout the day. Nothing. He wasn't sure what that meant. The lack of communication only added to his anxiety.

He busied himself by getting ready for the dinner rush: Having the correct number of the various sizes and types of pizza dough pulled to meet the pars for the evening, proofing the correct amounts, ensuring the right number of backup items were ready at a moments notice to refill the make tables. Six different kinds of pasta were ready. Three types of backups still had to be portioned, but he delegated that. Salad bar backup items were ready, fresh herbs were cut, sandwich buns prepped and ready. All was ready to go.

None of the servers nor cooks had called in sick. Yet. That was good. One of his assistant managers, the one he had nicknamed "Girl," was scheduled to arrive at three and worked the closing shift. She was a cute, bubble-headed, strawberry blonde. He felt that she was kind of lazy, didn't really take her job seriously enough. She just didn't seem to care. *Probably because of her age*, Daniel thought. Most of the young adults, it seemed, had a very poor work ethic these days. No, the pay wasn't great, but as a manager the potential to get promoted to make more money and bonuses were there. But you had to work for it. It didn't come easy. He knew it was only a matter time before this one quit. Such was the way of things.

He heard the loud wrenching of metal on metal that signified the back door was being opened. Sunlight and a blast of warm, spring air blew in, carrying with it a familiar smell. It was a mixture of Lucky brand perfume, strawberry body spray, with a hint of the smoke of a cigarette. When the scents entered Daniel's nasal cavity they triggered in him memories of that night. His heart immediately quickened, his mind quickly ran through what had happened, what they had done to each other. For each other. He smiled as he heard Faith greet her coworkers as she clambered in with that wobble-walk of hers that was a side effect the spinal rods she had fused in her back.

The rods were a result of a scoliosis-correcting surgery when Faith was fifteen. The wobble came from the fact that her left leg was about an inch longer than the other, due to her back not being able to bend and twist normally. She had told him once that the rods in her back were supposed to be adjusted and lengthened to allow for growth, but after the initial surgery her mother never took her back for any subsequent follow-ups. Consequently the rods could not be removed, could not be adjusted. They were permanently fixed to her spine, the vertebrae bones growing around the hooks of the composite alloy rods, fusing them together.

And though it straightened her spine, it did not allow her free movement. She could not bend or twist normally. Because of all that, chronic pain assaulted her body on a daily basis. The bones and her muscles fought against the foreign intruder that had become a part of her over the past 17 years, more than half of her life. She was prescribed painkillers, basically a super dose of Tylenol, and went monthly for cortisone injections to try to manage the pain. She was also prescribed Klonopin for anxiety. This he knew directly from her from the many conversations over the previous weeks.

The anxiety attacks Daniel had witnessed firsthand several times. If she did not have the medication it seemed a minimal amount of work-related stress would set her off to where she couldn't function properly. She began to shake, needed to sit down. Once he'd seen her breakdown into tears over some picky customer yelling at her because they perceived they had waited too long for their food. Mostly though the anxiety came from outside the restaurant. All too frequently she had come in stressed, worried, frantic over something that had happened in her home life.

Today, however she seemed to be in a very good mood. That was a good thing. No matter what happened between them after work, Daniel breathed a sigh of relief over the fact that he could count on her to be on her "A" game and help, in her own way, run the restaurant with him. And hopefully she would make some decent money as well.

After making her rounds, putting her things away and clocking in, Faith made her way toward Daniel, who was now in the back prep area putting frozen discs of dough into oil-sprayed pans. She walked in close to him and rubbed his back gently with one hand. "I'm sorry about last night," she told him, all sincerity in her eyes. "I tell you about it later," she told him, a hint of frustration in her tone.

"It's okay. I understand," he lied. But he smiled at her to reassure her. He kept working, though he breathed deeply and took in her smell. He wanted to touch her, to grab her. To take her right then, right there on the prep table. The thought of it aroused him, and he looked into her eyes trying to convey what he was thinking. She smiled at him, the twinkle in her eye seemed to affirm that maybe, perhaps she was thinking the same thing.

"Do you have plans for tonight?" He asked. The words just came out. He had not planned on asking her again, had wanted to leave it up to her. He wanted to see if she was really interested. Wanted her to make the next move. *Too late now, dummy,* he thought to himself.

She hesitated. Looked away from him. *Dammit!* He shouted to himself. The small ball of anxiety that lately was ever present in his being suddenly burst and he felt a shockwave of fear radiate through him. His body temp spiked and he felt his face redden. Daniel wasn't exactly sure what he was afraid of. Afraid of her saying no...afraid of her saying yes?

Don't go down this road, Daniel, his mind told him. Did waiting for three hours in the rain teach you nothing? His mind asked.

He did not respond, pushed the thought away. She was so close, his desire and his lustful need overrode his sense of right and wrong just then.

"Ummmm," she began after what seemed like a very long pause. "I'll have to let you know, okay?" she said as she rubbed his back again. The sensation of her touching him shot a bolt of exhilaration through his body. And the anticipation of what *might* happen again riveted him to her. Her touch, her reassurance, though slight, gave him hope. He felt his anxiety relax and compact.

Daniel smiled and nodded. "Sure," he began. "I'm working through dinner tonight, and you're first off the floor, so I can make sure we're out at the same time," he told her.

"Cool," she replied. Just then another server walked up, and Faith quickly removed her hand from Daniel's back and took two steps away from him.

"Faith, you have a table," the young woman told her. And with that, Faith turned and walked away without another word.

     *   *   *

Daniel sat in his Toyota Matrix. His back and feet were aching from work. Long shifts on hard surfaces without much time to sit down were taking its toll on his body. But though the pain was present his mind was focused not on his immediate state, but on the very near future.

He wasn't in Petoskey, wasn't at the restaurant. He'd gotten off of work some 30 minutes before and was now waiting for Faith. He was in the next town across the bay: Harbor Springs. He was parked in a designated lot for carpoolers or some such other thing. But it was a safe spot, away from the prying eyes of coworkers. Even though it was a mere 3 miles away from where his boss, the District Manager, lived. Daniel still felt this was the best place. The best place to meet, and leave Faith's vehicle. Neither of them could risk her vehicle being spotted parked in his driveway, or even down the street from his place. They were not supposed to be together.

I've been telling you that since you started this thing, his mind told him. Daniel ignored the words in his head.

He was listening to the radio, well it was on anyway. He kept looking up the street. Looking for the green van. The one with the cracked windshield, and the dented hood. The telltale front headlights and grille of the Ford Windstar. Faith's minivan.

Then he saw it, and his heart's pace quickened. She put on her blinker and slowly pulled into the lot next to his car. It took her some long moments to get out. Daniel wondered what the hell she was doing, what was taking so long. He scanned the street to either side, and toward the main road perpendicular to where they were parked, looking for any recognizable vehicle. Looking for anyone who might know their vehicles, and wonder what was going on. The sun was setting quickly now, and Daniel welcomed the oncoming cover of night. Shadows and darkness would mask their union.

Part of the excitement, part of the thrill of being with Faith was not only that they were "not supposed to be together," but also the looming threat of them being caught together. Of what would happen then. But those things, those questions could wait for another time. Right now, what was set before him was all that really mattered. Savoring the moment.

Faith finally climbed out of her vehicle, locked and slammed the door. Daniel leaned over and opened the passenger door for her, pushing it open. She got in quickly and shut the door behind her. She had with her a large, black leather purse and a small duffel bag that she stowed on the rear seat before sitting. Instantly he could smell her perfume, and the unwelcome tinge of the cigarettes. But that was part of who she was. And right then he didn't care. He was looking forward to learning more about her. Exploring her world, and letting her into his.

He was still leaning towards her side of the vehicle when she climbed in. She smiled at him and leaned in for a kiss. It was not a quick kiss. As soon as their mouths met, their lips parted and their tongues intertwined. Daniel reached up and grabbed the side of her face, cupping her jawline and her right ear. He pulled her closer to him, their mouths making love.

When they finally pulled away from each other they each smiled. It was a reflex, not forced. "Are you ready?" Daniel asked.

"Yes," she replied. "Sorry I'm a little late, I had to stop and get something," she explained as she held up a small four pack of Merlot. He put the car in gear and began to drive the 20 minutes to his place. As they drove she cracked the screw cap on one of the small bottles of wine and began to drink. *I wonder if she's an alcoholic?* He thought to himself.

Go ahead and ask her. She what says, his mind prodded him. But he didn't. He let that thought die. But he did ask another nagging question.

"How many men have you been with?" He asked, not wanting to know the answer. From what he gathered she was promiscuous. The question came anyway, whether he really wanted to know or not.

She looked at him and was silent for just a moment before answering, "Not as many as you probably think," she said. No elaboration. No direct number. Though the answer really didn't satisfy him, he decided he really didn't want to push the issue. Wasn't sure why he asked in the first place.

"Have you been cheated on before?" She asked him after a few moments of silence.

Daniel remembered that time. He remembered Stacy. He remembered all the turmoil and heartache...The taking her back... Almost *begging* her back...Their subsequent marriage...Their divorce...The sleepless nights...The weeping and gnashing of teeth.

"Yes," he told her. And before he could process it, before he could think better of it, he blurted out, "And that is the *one* thing I *cannot* forgive...If you cheat on me," he told her.

And there it was. It was the truth but for some reason he regretted saying it. He didn't know her well, and had been warned away from her by more than one person because of who she was, what she had done in her past.

Should have kept that to yourself, his mind scolded him.

I want her to know that I am serious about relationships, he thought. But there was instant regret in telling her that.

"Don't worry," she reassured him. "Even though I've been with several men, I've never cheated on any of them. I wouldn't do that to you." She said the last as she reached out and grabbed his hand in hers and squeezed, looking him in the eyes.

He smiled at her. He didn't know if he believed her, but he would take her at her word. *Why would she lie?*

Faith pulled out her server book which contained her writing pad and the money she had earned that night. She began counting the cash she had. She counted three times, flipping bills around so the heads were facing the same way. He could tell by her expression she was not pleased.

"Not a good night?" He asked, glancing at her and looking back to the road. The two lane highway was a curvy line with deep woods, state owned land, on each side. The sun was setting, and with it the temperature was becoming colder. Daniel reached over and grabbed Faith's thigh gently.

"I needed to make $120 tonight for rent," she told him. "I only made $70." She let the last just hang in the air. No elaboration, no more information.

Don't you do it, his mind warned him. It's not your problem. It's not your burden to carry. You got your own bills to pay.

"How much is your rent?" Daniel asked, hoping for more information.

"Six hundred a month, includes utilities," she said. "My landlord's a real creeper, though," she told him, as she looked at him. "He's come into my apartment, let himself in, while I was sleeping! Fucking weirdo woke me up standing over my bed!"

"Are you serious!?" Daniel asked, incredulous. "Why don't you call the cops? He can't come in there, as a landlord he has to give you 24 hours notice."

"He seemed nice at first. I told him my situation, about trying to get away from Scott, trying to get my kids back through the courts. He said he would help me, didn't charge me a security deposit. But then a week or two later he was asking me out, coming in the apartment when he knew I was alone. He's let himself in there even when I had my kids there. My two-year-old daughter was there!"

"So have you called the police?" Daniel asked again.

"No, he's friends with the cops. So is Scott," she told him. She was silent for a few long moments then added, "I don't want to think about it right now. I just want to enjoy this time, with you," she said as she reached across and grabbed his thigh and rubbed it gently.

Daniel smiled, and nodded his head in agreement. He continued to drive, a little faster now. The speed limit was 55, he pushed his car near 10 miles an hour over the limit, which was more reckless than he usually drove, but he was eager to get her home.

$$* \qquad * \qquad *$$

The rest of the drive was uneventful. They talked about work, laughed as they discussed their coworkers, vented about the bullshit that each of them had to deal with throughout the day. Their conversation seemed to strengthen the bond between them.

Daniel pulled into the driveway, shut off the engine, and walked around to the passenger side. Faith was already getting out.

"Do you need help carrying anything?" Daniel asked. Faith shook her head no and smiled.

Daniel led the way to the side porch and quickly opened the door, scanning the surrounding areas for anyone who might recognize them both. Searching for any cars that he recognized. He found none. The sun had almost set now. Shadows were beginning to lengthen and deepen. The colorful pink, light purple, and orange of the early autumn sunset was fading to black.

Once inside, Daniel shut and locked the door, closed the vinyl blinds on the windows, and turned on the floor lamp that lit the living room. He went over to the stereo and put in a Nickelback CD, and queued up one of Faith's current favorite songs.

They both sat on the couch, Faith was drinking wine out of the small bottle, and Daniel had gotten a bottle of Michelob Ultra from the fridge. They were both enjoying the song that was playing.

"I really like this song," Faith said as she got up and began to dance.

Daniel smiled as he watched her gyrate and move. He was turned on by her lack of inhibition. Even with the rods her back, Faith moved her lower body seductively as her arms moved in time with the song. Daniel was not a dancer, wasn't about to start then. He just watched, and enjoyed. While Faith continued to dance she smiled at him, would lock eyes with him for a few seconds then would close them and continue with her fun.

When the song ended, Daniel rose from his seat, took a few steps toward Faith. He grabbed her around the waist with his right hand and pulled her close to him so that their bodies touched. He kissed her hard, her mouth opened and returned his kiss with matched passion. He slid his hand down and grabbed her ass while he continued to kiss her.

She was still wearing her tight, black polyester work pants. She did not wear a belt with these, and the access was a zipper in the back in the middle. He grabbed the tab of the zipper and unzipped them. "Whoa, wait a second," she told him as she backed away and broke their embrace. "I want to go have a cigarette first," she explained.

"Okay," Daniel replied as he smiled at her. He kissed her again, gently, passionately. "Don't be long."

She giggled, smiled as she grabbed another small bottle of wine, her cigarettes and lighter, walked through the kitchen and stepped outside. She did not close the door all the way but left it ajar so that she could still hear the radio, a sliver of light from the kitchen spilled from the doorway and illuminated the porch.

Daniel, still smiling and giddy with excitement, sat back down on the couch, the leather was cool and inviting. The song playing now was about a couple going through strife, and the man wanting to give her a better life, that he would make things better, though not "right now," that they would have to wait. But he wanted to rewrite the ending of their story. The song brought up in him emotions that he had pushed down and stifled for too long.

Lately, his spirit felt like it was floating on a black sea in a small boat with no motor, no sail, no oars. No water to drink. The sky was overcast, dark and gloomy. Threatening rain. Thunder rumbled in the distance. He was being rocked and battered by the dark crashing waves, carried by the current, hoping and praying each day that he would reach his destination...find his destiny. Fulfill his purpose...be happy.

She is not your destiny, Daniel, his mind told him. Don't take this too far.

The thought ended there, no elaboration, no explanation. No nugget of hope for what lay ahead. No hint of the direction he was supposed to go. No urging on what he was supposed to do, only of what he *wasn't* supposed to do. No joyful alternative to what was presented to him right at that moment. He'd been waiting for so long that he didn't want to wait any longer. We was weary and tired. Tired of being lonely, tired of working so much, tired of hoping...tired of doing the right thing.

The song's lyrics made him pause from the thoughts of his own life and current circumstances and he thought of what Faith had been through. What she was going through now, what she had already endured. He knew he could give her a helping hand, if she only chose to accept it.

He got up from the couch and walked to the kitchen for another beer. Just then, Faith came back in, bringing with her a blast of cold, fresh autumn air mixed with the stale, harsh smell of burned menthol tobacco. She turned and locked the door. Before she could turn back around Daniel was right behind her. He pressed his body against hers putting his hands on her hips. He leaned in and began to kiss the back and side of her neck, just below her short hairline. He moved his mouth up and down her neck, down to where her shirt collar blocked him from going further. Small moans escaped her mouth as she began to breathe heavy. Taking that as a good sign, Daniel began to suck and even nibble on the muscle cord of her neck. With that action, Faith seemed to explode with passion as she let out a yell, and her body jolted and shivered beneath his hands that were still on her hips.

He reached for the zipper on her pants again and pulled it open, loosening the tight fabric. She did not stop him this time. The island of the kitchen was directly behind them about five feet away. He slowly spun her and stood her next to the island, she placed her hands on the countertop for support. She was facing away from him as he gently pulled her pants down and let them fall to her ankles. She was not wearing any underwear.

Daniel quickly moved closer and started kissing her neck again, while undoing and taking off his own pants and underwear. Faith reached back with her right hand and grabbed some of his hair as he continued to kiss her neck. She felt his erection pressing against the exposed skin of her bare ass. She reach back with her left hand and began to caress and stroke him.

Daniel gently pushed her forward, she bent at the waist and rested her arms and upper body on the counter. She was still standing though bent over now. He spit on his right hand and rubbed the saliva on himself then reached forward and rubbed some on her vagina as well. He inserted himself into her slowly. Faith moaned and said, "Oh you feel so good."

"You feel amazing," he told her. The hot wetness of her coated his skin. His heart was racing fast and he thought that he could feel hers as well. He was almost certain that she could feel him pulsing inside her as he slowly pushed and pulled himself in and out in a fantastic rhythm. The hard rock music was still playing. To Daniel it was a bit of a distraction as his consciousness, his focus, was being split between the song lyrics and the lustful, intimate action. He also had slight anxiety, as he desperately wanted to perform well. Mainly for her pleasure and satisfaction, so that she would want more. Maybe even crave more. But part was his own ego as well.

He reached up with his right hand and grabbed a handful of her short black hair, and pulled. Not hard, but not gently either. As he did so he thrust into her, hard. Faith yelled, "Oh God!" Daniel pounded himself into her a few times, then reached up simultaneously with his left hand and grabbed her by her left shoulder. As he thrust and he pulled back on that shoulder adding force, and depth. He was pushing and pulling harder and faster now, but keeping a steady rhythm.

Faith cried out, "Fuck me, Daniel! Fuck me hard!" *I thought that's what I was doing?* He thought. Taking her direction, Daniel intensified thrusting and his pulling of her shoulder and her hair, though he was careful not to hurt her.

She was making loud noises now, they too were almost a distraction, but he just concentrated on the pleasure, on how she felt against him. On how he felt in her. After a few short minutes of this, Faith yelled out, "Ohh fuck! I'm gonna get off! Don't stop!"

Daniel continued until he felt her quiver under him, more yells and moans escaping her throat. Her voice was at such a volume he knew the neighbors could probably hear. He smiled to himself. He finally let go of her shoulder and her hair, putting his hands on her hips, and continued to thrust. He was close now. He closed his eyes as he listened to her now softer toned moans. He could feel the pressure and tingling sensation building within him. He felt his erection thicken, like a Ballpark frank over a hot flame. Faith could feel it too, he was sure, she was now thrusting herself back into him and the volume of her moans increased once again. Seconds later he exploded into her, still keeping up the rhythm. He yelled her name as he grabbed her ass tightly, squeezing. He collapsed forward onto her, so they were both slumped over the counter. He was still inside her. They remained as one.

They lay there nearly motionless for several moments, just listening to each other's breathing and the beating of their hearts. He kissed her gently on the neck.

"Okay, time to get up," she told him.

Daniel complied and stood up, simultaneously pulling his shirt up over his head and off his body. He quickly used it as a makeshift towel and put it between her legs as he pulled himself out. He helped her stand up straight, and she almost toppled over as her ankles were still bound by her pants. They both laughed. Daniel bent down and pulled her pants back up for her so she could walk. She thanked him, grabbed her duffle bag from the floor beside the coffee table as she made her way through the living room toward the bathroom.

Daniel put back on his underwear and pants, walked to the fridge and grabbed another beer. He went back to the living room and changed the CD. Maroon Five, *Songs about Jane.* He queued up *She Will Be Loved* and waited for Faith to return.

Daniel looked at the digital clock that sat under the television and calculated how much time before he had to go back to work. He didn't want to think about that now. He did not have to open the restaurant the next day, he was the closer. So that meant he could sleep in, his body intertwined with Faith's. *Today was a good day,* he thought. *Tomorrow will be a good day.*

CHAPTER NINE

It was January. A Wednesday afternoon. He was walking back to school for wrestling practice. The walk was just over 1 1/2 miles from his house. When he could he would ride his bike, but this week the snow was too deep, the sidewalks too icy. He attempted it once, riding his bike on the ice and snow. Not a good move. The tires just spun, no traction. He dumped the bike a couple times, almost hurt himself in the process. In frustration he ended up pushing his bike the remaining mile to school. Luckily for him one of his older teammates gave him a ride home, put his bike in the trunk.

From the time school ended and he got off the bus he had roughly an hour and a half to eat something, maybe relax, do some homework--yeah, right--before having to leave to get to practice that lasted two, sometimes two and a half hours. He was a Freshman, but since the school was small and the district was as well, and the wrestling program was not large, Daniel was on the Varsity team, wrestling at 98 pounds. It was an honor to have the chance to get a varsity letter, especially in your freshman year. His win/loss record was at 10 - 8. Not bad, not great. Still time left in the season to improve that.

Daniel liked wrestling. It was physical, and you had to use your mind and your wits. It was just you against one other person. Wrestling was *not* a team sport. The team had T-shirts printed with the phrase "Wimps need not apply" on the back. And it was true. Some football players had tried out for the wrestling team, had come to some practices, but only a few stuck with it. "This is hell compared to football," was what one of them said, referring to the daily practice regimen, just before he quit the team.

The only thing Daniel wished the wrestling team had, that the football and basketball players had, where cheerleaders. Sometimes one cheerleading squad would share the upper gym with the wrestling team. Daniel would watch, and fantasize about some of them. That's all he would do. His coaches and nearly everyone on his team liked him. "He's a very nice kid," they said. He heard somewhere that "nice guys finish last." He didn't like that, was trying to change that, at least in his own life.

The wind was angry, bitter, and icy cold. It cut through his winter jacket as if it were a cotton T-shirt. His legs under his jeans felt numb, nearly frozen. He was wearing a stocking hat and winter boots, but no long underwear. Those weren't "cool." He walked along the uneven pavement of the sidewalks, past familiar houses and trees. He stopped briefly at the intersections to check to make sure the way was clear before proceeding quickly, yet carefully, across the ice and snow covered pavement.

As he bounded up the next curb onto the sidewalk he passed a large maple tree that was growing on the street side of the sidewalk. Movement caught his attention and he stopped. Horrified.

Lying there, outstretched, one tiny, clawed paw grasping the root of the tree, was a brown squirrel. Its body was shivering, its mouth open, ragged breaths coming fast, small sharp teeth showing. Small gray clouds of its hot breath puffed from the open mouth, like a tiny steam engine, as its small chest expanded and contracted with each seemingly painful lungful of air. Daniel looked into its eyes. It was scared. Terrified. The look on its face and in its eyes seem to plead with Daniel, "Help me!"

Daniel looked and saw that at least one, maybe both of its hind legs were broken. The small animal was dragging them uselessly behind its body as it apparently tried to climb the tree to no avail. *Hit by a car*, he thought. His pulse quickened and a sadness overcame him. He wanted to help the poor creature, but he didn't know what to do. He didn't want to approach it, for fear that he might get scratched or bitten. He thought briefly about killing it, putting it out of its misery, because he knew there was no saving it. No one would care about one little squirrel. There were thousands of them in the city alone. Still, Daniel wanted to help it. Wanted to save it. Or help it die.

He looked around for something, a shovel, a heavy tree branch. But there was nothing. He thought about walking up to it and stomping its head in with his boot. He shook his head at that, *No way I could do that*, he thought. *It may be suffering, but I can't do that.* Out of options and needing to get to practice, Daniel said a prayer for mercy for the creature. "I'm sorry," he said to it as he turned and walked away.

    *   *   *

There was a violent pounding at the door. It was loud and raucous, the visitor was not just using their fist but also some sort of metal, a flashlight or their keys, to amplify the knocking against the steel of the door. Daniel bolted up as his mind registered what was happening.

He was panicked. The dream of the dying squirrel still fresh in his mind. No. That wasn't right. It wasn't a dream, it was a memory. But why did his subconscious bring that to mind? He didn't know. The pounding on the door seemed to intensify.

Faith was awake now as well. She seemed just as confused, just as startled and panicked as he was. *Was that her ex?* He quickly thought. *One way to find out.*

Daniel quickly and quietly got off the bed. He took a deep breath as he pulled on his pants, but left his chest bare. He quietly made his way toward the kitchen, toward the sound of the pounding. He knew the blinds were closed and was thankful for that. He carefully lifted up one slat of the vinyl blind and peered out. There was a green Jeep Cherokee parked in his driveway. *Oh, fuck me!* He thought and his panic increased. "It's fucking Cindy," he whisper-yelled to Faith who was slowly walking up behind him. "Go back to the bedroom," he told her. "I'll find out what she wants."

The pounding was coming from the front door as Cindy had never been there before she assumed the front door was the main entrance. Daniel quickly pulled the leather chair away from the door and prepared to open it and confront her, find out what she wanted. His heart was beating fast and he was filled with apprehension.

Cindy was one of his assistant managers. Well, not technically. She was an assistant manager at a store in another city, but she was tasked with helping train his staff, and Daniel as well, during the first few months of the new store's opening. Currently she was one of the managers running shifts at his restaurant. He didn't know why she was there, though she did live in the same city.

He was afraid that somehow, someway she had found out about him and Faith. That she was there to bust them in the act. He took a deep breath, grabbed the knob of the door with one hand while twisting the lock open with the other and pulled it open.

The pounding abruptly stopped as the door was pulled inward away from her fist clenched over her keys. "Ah, Hi," she managed to say as she looked at Daniel, trying to avert her eyes from his half-naked form. She obviously wasn't expecting Daniel to answer the door in such a fashion.

She was a heavyset woman, long black hair that she usually wore in two braids, parted down the middle like a Native American. She had large, round breasts and a large, round butt to match. Daniel and her got along very well. They would joke around at work, but she was good at her job, and so was he, and when it was time to get things done they worked well together. She was tough and capable, but she had a playful side. She was well-liked by most of the team. She had told Daniel that she was impressed by how quickly he learned and by his leadership abilities. Daniel also guessed that she liked him more than a friend, but he didn't feel that way about her. He tried to picture it once, fantasize about it, but he couldn't wrap his mind around it. She wasn't his type sexually.

"What's up?" He asked.

"Jim tried calling you, but all he got was your voicemail. So he calls me, *wakes my ass up*, so I can come over here and wake *your ass up*!" She said in explanation using playful sarcasm. Jim was the district manager, his boss. Daniel knew he didn't have to work that morning, therefore he purposely shut his phone off. Plus, Faith was over and he didn't care who would be calling. Apparently that was a mistake. his job demanded a lot from him, and this was another example of that. "Josh had a heart attack last night," she continued.

"Holy shit, are you kidding me?" Daniel blurted. That wasn't good for many reasons. Josh was one of his newly promoted managers, and he'd become a good friend. He was young, but overweight, which apparently was the cause of his heart attack.

"Would I be here if I was shitting you? I don't think so, my ass would be sleeping," she countered. "So, poor Josh obviously is not at the store right now," Cindy continued her explanation. "Old Jimmy wants you there ASAP, Mr. General Manager, sir," she said, saying the last condescendingly but also playfully.

There wasn't anything else to say, really. It was part of his job, to fill in, to work. To be the dependable one. To be the one holding everything together. *Fuck me!* He yelled in his head.

"Okay, I'll be there in about an hour, in time to open the store...*and* close the motherfucker tonight too!" He said, trying to be playful but it came off dripping with his exasperation, frustration and stress.

"You're the man," she said. "I'll let Jimbo know," she told him. She took another long look at his naked torso and said, "Ohh my!" Mostly to herself as she turned and walked back to her vehicle.

Daniel quickly shut the door and was startled to find Faith standing in the kitchen by the small desk just on the other side of the partial wall left of the front door. "So, you gotta go to work?" She asked, having overheard most of the conversation. "I thought we were busted!" She said with a smile, relief in her voice.

"Me too," Daniel said as he leaned in and gave Faith a bad breath morning kiss, reaching around and grabbing her ass as he did so. He was fully awake now, adrenaline surging through his system. There was an excitement to what they were doing: the danger of being caught, the rush of sneaking like spies at rendezvous points, the carnal act when they were alone, the pretending while they were at work...all of it made it more exciting. To Daniel it was intoxicating, and though it added to his stress level, it gave him a welcome release from his mundane life. It gave him something to look forward to. Something to dream about. Something to hope for.

"So, I have to get in the damn shower and get my ass to work," he told her. What made the day even more disappointing now was that Faith had the day off, so he could not even look forward to seeing her later, look forward to her help at the restaurant. At the realization of this his stress level rose and threatened to stay there for the duration.

Welcome to management, welcome to leadership, his mind told him. *Fuck you self. Fuck you very much*, he thought.

CHAPTER TEN

She was kneeling on the floor of the living room in front of the Christmas tree. It was a six-foot artificial tree, supposed to be a blue spruce. There was still the scent of pine and cinnamon in the air, though they came from a scented candle that was burning on the coffee table. Her and all the kids put up the tree and decorated it the night before. Her ex had even participated and put the lights on. Faith was rearranging the presents that had already been wrapped, preparing to wrap the ones that hadn't been. She had her Scotch brand tape, scissors, a roll of various colored ribbon, a bag of multicolored bows, and four rolls of wrapping paper. This was a good day for her, even if it was a little strange being back in the house. *I'm not really back*, she told herself. And she had to keep telling Scott that as well. She was staying over just for the holiday weekend, sleeping with her daughter in her "big girl bed," a twin size with *Dora the Explorer* bed sheets and comforter.

They had been officially broken up for well over a year. Well, their relationship had been over for a long time before that, Faith knew, but she had moved out and stayed out for that length of time. She had left a few times before, but always came back for the children. *Her* children. And since they did have children together, they would never totally be able to separate themselves. And he didn't want to. In one way or another they would forever be part of each other's lives.

Scott used that fact to his advantage at every opportunity. He desperately wanted her back and was doing everything he could to make it so. She wished he'd have another heart attack and just die already. *Why did the good men, like dad, die young, and pieces of shit like Scott keep living?* she wondered. Life didn't make sense to her most days. *Best not to think too far ahead*, she reasoned.

Her little girl, Tara, who was nearly 3 years old, celebrating only her second Christmas, was playing on the floor a few feet away from her. She was scribbling in a *Dora* coloring book, singing "Jingle Bells" to herself. Faith was humming along, trying to match her daughter's disjointed rendition. Her three boys, ages five, seven, and eleven, were playing outside in the snow. They were each making a snow fort and preparing for an epic snowball battle. Inevitably, one of them would be coming in crying and screaming about what the other two had done to him. But they hadn't yet. Just a part of motherhood, she supposed.

As she wrapped, Faith smiled to herself as she thought of Daniel. Her Knight in Shining Armor. It was his generosity that had helped make this a good Christmas for her kids. It was just a few days ago and they were shopping at Wal-mart. Faith made her way back to the layaway department, Daniel went with her.

The attendant seemed pleasant and smiled at them as they approached. "How much do I still owe on my layaway?" Faith asked, digging in her purse for the receipt with the total.

The cashier collected Faith's information, tapping on the keyboard and looking at the screen for a few minutes. "The last payment was $25 a week ago, which brings the total due down to $320."

"How can I still owe that much?" Faith asked, her voice rising with panic.

The cashier rolled her eyes and listed the total amount put on layaway, and the dates and amounts of all the payments that were made. "And it has to be picked up in three days, or it all goes back on the shelf and you lose all the money you put on it," they were told.

"How much shit did you buy your kids?" Daniel asked, more harshness in his voice than he had intended.

"Well, I promised the boys remote control cars, and I have to get all of them one, or they will fight. And I got Tara some coloring books, and some cute little outfits, and a couple of toys. The boys I got each some clothes, because their asshole dad will let them wear the same thing all week long, he doesn't care how they look. And I wanted to give them all a good Christmas this year, since this would be the first year I'm not with them," she told Daniel, frowning. "I just thought I would have more time," she said, sadness in her eyes as they began to well with tears.

Daniel stood silent, thinking.

Faith turned back to the cashier. "Can I take some items off, put some things back?" She asked, the sadness evident in her voice as it cracked when she spoke. She imagined how her kids would react to the lack of presents from their mother. They would be disappointed, not getting what she had promised them. Their dad would look like the hero, once again. And she would look like the piece of shit mother he was making her out to be. The thought gave her anxiety and sadness. *Will anything ever be easy? Will anything ever go my way?* She thought.

Daniel's heart broke as he watched this woman crying over some toys for Christmas. He'd never gone through it, but he could imagine how hard it was for a woman who loved her children to be forced away from them, no matter what the circumstances and mistakes that were made.

Before the cashier could respond to Faith's question, Daniel said, "How much does she owe?" He pulled his wallet from his coat pocket, and the debit card from that as the lady was speaking. Faith looked at him with confusion, but then realized what he was doing when he handed the cashier his card.

"Daniel, you don't have to do this," Faith told him with all sincerity. "I'll put some things back, my kids will be okay," she told him.

"It's okay, I want to," he said as he leaned in and kissed her on the mouth. As he pulled away she threw her arms around him and hugged him tight. He returned the embrace and kissed her on the neck.

"Here's your card back, sir," the cashier said holding out his card, cutting off the public display of affection. "I'll be right back with your gifts," she said smiling before disappearing into the back room.

"Thank you so very much," Faith said. "You still don't have to do this, we can return some things up front, if you want."

She said it, but Daniel knew it would be hard for her to choose what to put back. Even though to him it was a lot of money, he was doing it for kids that might not have a Christmas. He was doing it to help the woman he loved.

"Nope, it's done already. I want you and your kids to have a good Christmas," he told her.

"I love you," Faith told him as she got on her tip toes and gave him a kiss, then wrapped him in another strong hug. Daniel smiled at her. She loved his smile, the way he looked at her. It made her feel good that a good man wanted her and was supportive of all of her bullshit. *One day we'll get through this*, she thought. *Then we can be happy.*

Sitting a few feet away in the well-worn, almost worn-out, fading blue upholstered recliner was Scott, her ex, the father of her children. Well, three of them anyway. Her oldest was from her previous marriage when she was emancipated from her mother at 14 years old. She had finally escaped her stepdad and her mother with the help of a somewhat older boyfriend. But those were memories better left for a different time. Today was a good day.

"Hey Princess," he said condescendingly. "I've been trying to talk to you." He called her Princess, as if he treated her like one. In his mind he probably thought he did, having paid her bills, given her a roof, "allowed" her to mother his children, gave her the satisfaction of doing his laundry and all of the house and yard work, even gave it to her good and rough whenever *he* was in the mood...even got her high. Supplied all her needs. She was ungrateful, and his mind. Never appreciated what he did for her. Yea, maybe he smacked her a bit, but she didn't get more than what she had coming to her, what she was asking for with that smart mouth of hers. She thought she was so tough, thought she was a fighter. Maybe with the other bitches she was. He'd seen her get into many a scrap, and had usually came out on top. But not with him. Not with a real man.

"Princess!" He yelled again, this time throwing a cork coaster at her as if he were throwing a Frisbee disc. The object hit her square between the shoulder blades. The hard corner cracked into her spinal bone.

"Ow!" Faith screamed, immediately trying to massage the spot with her hand, her arm contorted, but she couldn't reach it. "Scott, you fucking asshole! Why did you do that? I'm just wrapping presents for *our* kids!" She yelled as she turned and glared at him. "You know I'm here for the kids, not for you! Just leave me the fuck alone," she demanded of him, giving him a glare that she wished would kill him. *Why did he have to be such an asshole all of the time!* her mind screamed.

Just the sight of him now made her sick to her stomach. He was sitting there in loose, stained cotton shorts, no shirt. He was a big man, 6'3" tall and weighed well over 300 pounds. His skin was a pasty white, covered in coarse, black hair. He resembled a mutated black bear with mange. His belly was large and round, as were his sagging man-breasts. His facial hair was always scrubby, on the verge of a beard but never quite getting there. He was usually sweaty, his hair a matted, greasy mess. Like Bugs Bunny he took a bath every Saturday night, whether he needed it or not. Unfortunately that was still a couple days away. He fancied himself a hunter, a stock car driver, and a drug dealer. In truth he was all three, though not overly successful at any of them. It was the last thing that finally made her get up the courage to leave him for good. Though she had made some mistakes with that.

She made the decision to leave for her children, more than for herself. She could handle herself, she thought. She could deal with the bullshit in her life. She'd been doing that since she was six. *One day at a time*, she told herself. *Deal with today, don't worry about tomorrow, or the day after that. If it's a good day, enjoy it. If it's a shitty day, do what you gotta to make it through to the next.*

She was shocked when she found the drugs. She knew Scott was a Pot dealer, to her that was no big deal. Smalltime stuff. Even some of the Sheriff's deputies came by to buy it from him, or just collected from him as payment for something they had done for Scott, or one of his brothers or his father. As with larger cities, in small town Northern Michigan cops could be bought, judges could be bought. Lawyers were complicit. She found that out the hard way.

She had known that he had harder drugs around: cocaine, heroin, prescription meds of various kinds. But those were in small quantities mainly for personal use, for friends and family, though he didn't give anything away for free. *Nothing* in this life was free. She'd learned that hard lesson as well.

Everything came with a price weather it was a small price or a larger one. Whether it could be repaid in a one time event, or drawn out over several transactions. Even "gifts" came with the caveat of reciprocity. Favors weren't cheap.

Daily necessities like food, rides the store or to the doctor, cigarettes, a soft drink or a bottle of wine, these were lesser but when needed they still came with a cost. Cash was king, but sex was a very close second. And drugs came closely behind that. At least those were the commodities she had been taught were the most sought after. Those means of payment she had been brought up in. The one's she could not avoid. It was the way of things in her world, in the world in which she found herself living in. And could not escape from.

But when Faith found what to her looked like two kilos of cocaine stashed in the drop ceiling of the bathroom, she knew he was trying to go big time. That realization scared her. That would bring too much down on her and her kids. That she couldn't deal with. She had to do what she could to protect her kids. Like a good mother should. Unlike her own mother, Faith wasn't about to watch her kids suffer. Especially if she could do anything to prevent it. She had to do her best to keep the monsters away. That's when she went to the police. More specifically she went to S.A.N.E., short for Straits Area Narcotics Enforcement.

She told them that she just wanted her kids, and to get out of there, but she was afraid. She knew Scott would not let her go. She tried before, and had been severely beaten for her troubles. She told them that she would cooperate, even set him up.

"Don't worry," they told her. "You help us, and you'll get your kids, the house, everything." She believed them. She swallowed her fear and did everything they asked her to. She put herself at risk for her kids' sake.

For weeks while they built a case and coordinated based on her information, Faith's stress and anxiety levels were high. She had to be careful. Unfriendly eyes and ears were everywhere. Scott held all the cards, all the power. She was on Klonopin for anxiety, but it didn't seem to be working. Her doctor switched her to Xanax. Faith found that one was good, but not quite enough. It took the edge off, calmed her down a little bit. But not enough for what she was going through. She was still nervous, frustrated and scared. So she began taking two pills, three times a day. They helped her cope. Got her though to the next day.

When it came time and everything was set for the narcotics enforcement team to move in and make the arrest, what they found in the house was next to nothing. After an exhaustive search which included every place they and Faith could think of: in the ceiling, floorboards, in the shed and garage, in the freezer, the tank of the toilet, in old suitcases, even in the children's rooms, all they found was a small amount of marijuana apparently packaged to sell, enough to arrest and prosecute him for intent to distribute and for maintaining a drug house. But no cocaine. No prescription drugs. No heroine. No large amounts of money. Nothing that would equate to real time behind bars.

Scott had been tipped off by his Sheriff buddies. He knew they were coming, just not exactly when. But he was prepared. He moved the drugs. He even moved all of his assets into his father's name. On paper he owned nothing. The cops could still confiscate vehicles and even the house if drugs were being sold from there, but it was a harder case when the assets were that of an elderly man not directly associated with the warrants, and since only a small amount of drugs were actually found on the premises going after those assets was a stretch for the prosecutor. Even more devastating to Faith was the revelation that prior to his arrest Scott had paid off a lawyer and a judge to have custody of their children given temporarily to Scott's sister, effectively cutting Faith out of the chain of custody of her own kids. So in short order she realized she got nothing. Absolutely nothing. And Scott knew it was her who had informed on him.

He was out on bond. The court case was still ongoing. He had a good lawyer, who took cash and drugs as payment. On paper Scott just looked like a construction worker. Things would eventually go his way, as they always did. He was pretty sure of that. *Now the only thing that remains,* he thought, *is getting Faith back into my house, and into my bed. Making her life so miserable that her only choices will be that, or suicide. I'm good with either.*

With that goal in mind he pried himself up from the chair with visible effort and lumbered over to where Faith was sitting on the floor wrapping a Red Power Ranger action figure for one of her sons. Scott reached out a thick, hairy hand and rubbed it down her back. "I'm sorry, Princess," he said with mock sincerity. "You know I just want to make you happy."

"Get away from me, Scott," she demanded. She could feel his presence behind her, and it made her skin crawl. She could smell his acrid breath, feel the heat of it on her neck.

He quickly moved his hand to her head and pulled her backwards twisting her as he did so that her face landed in his crotch, and he held it there. "You're gonna do something for me, bitch!" He demanded as he grabbed her head with both hands and pushed her face into the front of his shorts.

Faith screamed, placing her hands on his large, sweaty thighs trying to push herself away. He started moving her head back and forth, rubbing her face on his growing erection beneath the fabric. She screamed again in frustration and anger, and using her long fingernails she clawed at the flesh of his legs, drawing blood. He yelped and took a step back, finally releasing her from his grip. She had time enough just to look up to see that he was advancing on her again. She swiped at him with her left hand, her fingernails scratching deep furrows across his stomach, the red of the blood trickling from the shallow gashes a stark contrast to the pale gray-white of his skin.

"Just leave me alone!" She screamed again. The baby was crying now. Faith went to her and picked her up, cradling her in her arms, hoping that the fact of her holding their baby daughter would be enough to keep him away. Scott smiled a malevolent smile and left the room. After Tara calmed down, Faith went out into the garage and smoked a cigarette, leaving Tara to play on the floor, though she could still see her from the open door.

Fifteen minutes later there was a knock at the front door. Scott got up from his seat, "I wonder who that could be?" He said in a lighthearted voice, followed by vile laughter. He opened the door and there were two Sheriff's Deputies standing there. They spoke with Scott for a few short minutes. Faith couldn't quite make out what they were saying. She did recognize them as having been to the house before. Buying stuff. This would not be good. Her adrenaline spiked and her heart began to race. Her mind quickly ran through scenarios of what might be happening, of what she could do. She thought about running, but why? She hadn't done anything wrong.

The fat man moved out of the way as the two officers entered. One was already taking handcuffs out of his holster. "Please stand up, Miss Collins. You are under arrest for domestic violence," they explained.

"For fuck-sake, Scott! It's fucking Christmas Eve! All of our kids are here!" She was ranting, screaming. She didn't know what to do. She was angry. She wanted to slit that mother fucker's throat. Emotions of sadness, anger, frustration all boiled to the surface and she could no longer contain them. "I didn't do *anything* wrong!" Faith screamed. "He attacked *me*! I was defending myself," she added, backing away from the advancing officers.

"We see no indication of that, ma'am, however we do see evidence of marks on *his* person," one of them said. "Did you scratch him?" he asked.

"Fuck you!" she yelled as tears streamed down her face. They quickly advanced on her, one of them grabbed her by the wrist and pulled her off balance. Her vision began to blur and her head swirled. She began to shake with anxiety, falling to her knees.

"I...need...my medication," she pleaded, her words gasping from her mouth with sobs of anguish. They just laughed at her as they wrenched her arms behind her back and handcuffed her, pushing the cold steel as tightly against her wrists as her flesh and bone would allow, causing immediate pain. They stood her up, and roughly shoved her out the door and toward the police cruiser.

The three boys were standing by the police car now, snow and wind whipped around them. They looked confused, dumbfounded. Then the two older boys, Martin and Kyle, started yelling at the cops as they dragged their mother out of the house. "You let my mom go!" the younger one screamed. "She's not the one you should be taking," yelled the older one. "Dad! What are they doing!?!" Kyle screamed as he launched himself toward the Deputy who had his mother's hands behind her back, pushing her through the snow, the bottoms of her pajamas becoming wet, her slippers now covered with heavy snow.

The other Deputy saw the impromptu attack coming and stepped in its path. As carefully as he could the officer restrained the young boy and allowed him to continue to rant while trying to calm him to no affect. "Let her go!" he continued to yell, tears now running down his face. The youngest, Isaac, stood mute, but with a malevolent smile stretching across his face. He thought it was funny. He was his dad's son.

"Boys!" Scott bellowed from the doorway. "Get in the house, NOW!" It was obvious they did not want to, but they complied because they knew what would happen if they didn't.

As the car slowly pulled out of the driveway, Faith watched through the rear window at the fat man standing in the doorway, holding her daughter. She could not hear him, but she could read lips enough to know what he had said to their little girl: "Wave goodbye to mommy."

Sobbing tears rolled down her face. Her body shook with rage and frustration. She wanted to curl up in a ball and die. "I didn't do anything wrong...I didn't do anything wrong...I didn't do anything wrong..." She wailed between the sobs.

CHAPTER ELEVEN

Daniel was home in his own bed. It was the day after Christmas and he was waking up from a restful sleep. He did not remember his dreams, if he'd had any. He rarely remembered them, unless they were traumatic in some fashion. But even then the thoughts or memories of the dream faded quickly and were forgotten. Most times.

He crawled out of bed, feeling the cold of the floor on his bare feet. He never slept with socks on, he needed his feet uncovered to help regulate his temperature during the night. Under the covers when he was cold, poking out from underneath them when he got too warm.

He quickly made his way to the thermostat and punched the Up arrow a couple times to kick on the forced-air heat. There was a rumble through the house as the furnace ignited the propane and began to push warm air through the vents. He continued into the kitchen and readied the coffee pot. Ten cups today, a bit more than he usually drank. But it was a good day, he was going to relax and enjoy it.

He told his family that he had to work that day, the day after Christmas. He lied. When he was in charge and had the option, he always took the day after Christmas off. He usually found that after visiting family, or being on a rare out-of-town vacation he needed an extra day just to recuperate and prepare his body and mind to go back to work. If he had told his family that he had that extra day off, they would expect him to stay longer. Which was a good thing, that they wanted him around, wanted to spend more time with him. And it wasn't that he didn't want to spend time with them, it was just that in his own selfish way he wanted and needed that time for himself. For his own brand of sanity. He didn't want to disappoint them, didn't want to let them down. So he figured the lie made sense. Better for everyone.

He fondly remembered the events of the previous day. It did his heart good to watch his family embrace, and smile, and talk to one another. Their whole family dynamic had changed over the years. Which was not unique to them, he knew, but Daniel did not like that kind of change. There was something to be admired about routine and tradition. To him it gave him something to look forward to, something to hold on to, something solid. A happy feeling. He could see the joy on his father's face as he laughed while embracing and talking to Daniel's sisters and niece. Daniel thought he could feel the happiness that was in the room then, as if emotions were tangible, could be more than felt, but touched and held. It was good for him to be with them in that moment.

In his line of work it seemed there were constant changes that he had to adapt to and be ready to adjust with at a moment's notice. No matter how much planning and forecasting he did he could not tell the future, no plans ever seemed to go off without a hitch of some sort. It was said that the best military plans did not survive the first thirty seconds of combat...Daniel thought the same could be said of the restaurant business. Some days it was all he could do just to make it through to the end of the shift, drive his weary body home, and try and recuperate and prepare for whatever the next day held. So, whenever he had the chance to enjoy his family and push the cares and worries of everyday life to the back of his mind he did so with happiness and peace.

Even though things were not as they once were, Daniel still enjoyed being around his family. Their distinct voices, their jokes, their unique and individual laughs. Their smiles and their welcoming hugs and handshakes, these things never seemed to change. And he was thankful for that.

In his mind he would always hold on to those things, along with the cookies and the meatballs and everything else that made this time of year so special, so memorable. He wished Faith had been with him to experience and enjoy what a good family was. From what he knew of her past she did not have that, though he felt that she desperately wanted it.

Hopefully I can change her outlook, show her there are good people and good families, he thought.

Life had never been perfect and never would be, he supposed. But he was thankful for the family and the upbringing that he had. For the love that was shared. If somehow he could pull someone else up into a better world than what they were accustomed to, and have that person to love and hold, then he thought, all the effort might just would be worth it.

As he prepared a pot of coffee, Daniel checked his cell phone for the fiftieth time in the last twelve hours. Faith had not called nor texted him. Had not replied to any of his texts: How was your Christmas?...Did the kids like their gifts?...When are you coming back?...Are you okay?

That was strange and a bit worrisome. She would occasionally wait some hours before texting him back, citing some dramatic catastrophe that was preventing her from replying earlier, but she never went this long. Especially when he would send an angry text demanding WTF was going on?

He was starting to get angry. *Why the fuck did I give her a cell phone if she wasn't going to use it to communicate with me?*

His mind raced. It began to conjure up images of her cheating on him, and worse with her ex, *BARF! You don't know that,* he thought. *Just calm down. She will contact you, and you will get her side of the story.* He prayed that nothing bad had happened to her. Faith seemed to be a magnet for several things...none of them good.

He was wearing sweatpants, a black T-shirt with a black Star Wars zipper hoodie sweatshirt with the insignia of the *Mandalorians*, the bounty hunter Boba Fett's kin, an abstract of a mammoth head screenprinted on the front. Brown, fuzzy bear claw slippers adorned his feet. The house was silent as he poured his coffee, put in a packet of Splenda sweetener and chocolate-flavored creamer. The metal spoon gave off a satisfying clink as it swirled the hot mixture in the 20 ounce Superman mug. Daniel figured if he was going to have a cup of coffee, he was going to have a *cup* of coffee. No sense getting up two or three times when one big mug would do. He took a first sip and savored it, feeling the hot liquid roll down his throat and warm his chest. It was then that the landline phone broke the silence with a shrill ringing.

He didn't use the house phone very much, and in fact he would not even have it at all if it wasn't needed for DSL-enhanced dial-up Internet. The phone was in the back bedroom that served as his office, complete with a desk, his computer, and Darth Vader-esque black leather chair. He almost never answered that phone, as it was mostly telemarketers and other bothersome calls. But for some reason he hurried to it, coffee mug in hand, and answered it.

"Hello?" He said. What he heard next was immediately puzzling, but then the realization sunk in and he quickly sat down in the chair.

"This is a collect call from the Charlevoix County correctional facility. If you accept this call, please say Acccept," the computer generated voice said.

Shit. This was not good. He knew Faith was in Charlevoix County, in Boyne City. He knew that she had been incarcerated before for fights and a recent DUI arrest. All of which took place in Charlevoix County. He quickly spoke into the receiver, "Accept," though he knew what followed would not be good news. *Here we go,* he thought, inhaling deeply.

"Babe, are you there?" A distant sounding voice said after series of clicks and a short silence.

Immediately Daniel knew it was Faith. Her distinctive raspy voice was unmistakable. Though he could tell it was tinged with sadness, fear, and regret. He knew that whatever had happened, it wasn't good. He tried to brace himself mentally.

"I'm here. What the hell happened?" He asked.

She recounted for him, the short version because of time's sake, the events that led up to her arrest nearly two days prior, on Christmas Eve. "They won't let me have my meds," she told him, pleading in her voice. "I'm shaking and freaking out!" her voice broke with anxiety. "They said I can go if someone posts bail," she explained, sobbing now. "I called my mom and my stupid, fucking brother, but they won't help me," she told him through tears and a thickness in her voice.

Hearing her words, the tone and timbre of her voice, Daniel's heart felt heavy. His head began to ache. *Why me, Lord? Why her?* He didn't want to deal with this today. Not at all, actually. But here he was, with a decision to make.

Let her stay. It's not your burden, his mind told him.

I can't do that, he thought. Anger and rage flared up in him. He was angry for the injustice that had befallen Faith. He was angry for the situation he was in. He was angry that his one relaxing day had become not so relaxing so quickly. *Mother fucking shit!* He thought angrily, his hand clenching the phone, knuckles white.

"How much do they need to get you out?" He asked, not wanting to hear the reply.

There was silence, obvious hesitation. He could feel the worry from the other side of the phone. "Ummm...They need $350--but you'll get that back once I go to court," she quickly explained, her voice strained with audible stress.

Fucking Hell! He Thought.

To Daniel it was a lot of money. Especially since he just spent about that much on gifts for *her* kids. He did not have it in his checking account, but he did have enough on one of his credit cards. He remained silent. Trying to think, trying to reason.

Don't do it, his mind told him. It's not your problem. You did nothing to create it, you're not responsible for trying to fix it.

He pushed that notion from his thoughts. *Okay*, he thought to himself. *If I do this, if I get her out and bring her back here, then I'll have some say in what she does next...how she proceeds in this other situation. I can keep her safe, keep her out of trouble. Help her right her life*, he thought.

"Where's the jail at?" He asked, not knowing where it was or how to get there. Faith explained it was in the city of Charlevoix one block off Highway 31 that bisected the small vacation destination. She told him where to go, and what to do, trying to make it as easy for him as possible.

"I'm so sorry, Daniel. I didn't want to bring you into this. I didn't want you to have to deal with my bullshit," she told him, her voice still thick with tears.

"Okay, just try to calm down. I'll be there soon as I can," he reassured her.

"Thank you so very much. I love you, and I'm sorry," she said.

Daniel was angry, and didn't want to say the words, but felt he had to. He felt it was the right thing to do. "I love you, too," he said before hanging up the phone.

He was angry with her for the trouble that she was in, whether she'd caused it or not. He was angry with himself for giving in, for committing to helping someone even though it really wasn't his problem. On the one hand he felt obligated to help her because of their relationship, on the other hand he felt like he should help her, just to show her that there was good in the world, that someone did love her for who she was. So the decision was made. The consequences were set in motion.

*   *   *

The sky was gray and bleak. The roads were snow-covered, and because of the low temperature, they were a little icy. The Toyota Matrix's all-wheel-drive was most helpful in such conditions, though Daniel still had to be careful. There were many cars traveling the highways today, people rushing into stores to spend their gift cards, or exchange gifts that weren't quite right. Even though he didn't like big crowds or chaotic shopping, Daniel would've rather been mingling with the hoards doing day after Christmas things than what he was doing now.

You don't have to be doing this, his mind reminded him.

He was fighting the urge to turn around, to just say *fuck it* and forget the whole thing.

Cut your losses, this is not your burden, his mind counseled him again.

I've committed myself, and I'm not going back, he thought. *She's had nothing but betrayal and heartache, and I won't be the one to add to that misery. I want to try and stop it,* he told himself.

He found the jail right where she said it would be. It was a blonde brick building, boxy and unadorned, almost nondescript. Brown signs announcing Charlevoix County Sheriff Department and Correctional Facility were the only overt signs of what the building was, aside from the half-dozen all white or all brown police cars parked in the lot.

Daniel felt some anxiety as he parked his Toyota and made his way toward the main entrance. He looked around, noting the police cars, the tinted windows of the building, the two story structure of it with bars on its windows. He knew he had done nothing wrong, but in today's society that meant little. One could be accused of almost anything. Someone could be stopped and searched and harassed for almost no reason at all. Guilt by association was what he was probably most afraid of at that moment. He knew Faith had a record, had been in jail before. And according to her all the cops in the town knew her, and didn't like her. Her family had a bad reputation.

Another reason to get gone, his mind told him.

Part of him wanted to heed that warning, and knew that he probably should. Another part felt that he should help this person, and he knew he was helping himself, even if just a little, in the process. *Just get through this day,* he thought. *Help her this time and see what happens.*

The few trees that were planted around the perimeter that during spring and summer and fall gave the place a welcoming feel, only now served to heighten his anxiety. They looked dead, their spindly branches reaching out like the bony hands of skeletons toward the sky. The sidewalk had been shoveled and salted, the snow thrown in haphazard piles to both sides. Fresh footprints could be seen in the snow, as it was falling softly covering the ground in a thin layer of white. There wouldn't be much accumulation today according to the forecast, but Michigan forecasts were fickle and could not always just be trusted.

He made his way through the heavy steel and tinted glass doors, looking around. The smell of cold cement and dust, mixed with just a hint of pine cleaner assaulted his senses. He saw a Sheriff's deputy dressed in traditional brown to his right behind the wall into which was set a sliding window. He walked up to the window and waited to be acknowledged. He felt like he was placing his order at the walk-up Dairy Queen, *"Yes, I'll have two scoops of Faith, to go, please,"* he though lightheartedly to himself, trying to ease his own anxiety.

"Can I help you, sir?" The deputy asked.

"I'm here to post bail," Daniel told him.

"For whom?" The deputy asked walking to the window. Daniel could feel the officer eyeing him, almost suspiciously. Perhaps it was just his imagination, or perhaps it was just the way all police were.

Daniel told the deputy who he was there for. The man nodded knowingly, almost as if he knew who she was by name, and he probably did. In a few seconds he was told, "Bail is set at $350. We do not take credit or debit cards or personal checks. Cash only."

Are you fucking kidding me? Daniel's mind raged. He rolled his eyes, let out an exasperated breath and told the deputy, "Okay, I'll be back in a few minutes. Gotta go to the ATM," he explained. The deputy just nodded his acknowledgment.

"Can you start the process before I get back with the money?" Daniel asked.

"Nope. Need the money first," he was told.

This news made Daniel even more frustrated and angry. The day that began so full of promise was turning out to be anything but. And it wasn't even noon.

Not being familiar with that town, it took Daniel nearly ten minutes of driving around to find a bank. He had never used his credit card for a cash withdrawal before and didn't like the idea of doing it now. The interest rate was way higher on a cash advance that it was for a purchase. He needed a PIN, and had one set up, but wasn't sure if he could remember it. Luckily the number in his head worked.

Still not too late to change your mind, rang the thought in his head as he punched in the numbers and waited for the machine to dispense the cash.

Daniel felt his anxiety rise as he listened to the cash flutter inside the machine into a neatly stacked pile. He grabbed it quickly, shoving the pile of money into his front pants pocket, looking around to make sure no one was near him as he did so. Cars drove by, the wind blew cold flakes of snow into his face, the wintry world continued on as normal. No one was watching, no one seemed to care. Ten minutes later he was back at the jail reluctantly handing the deputy $350 in cash, an amount that represented over half of his weekly paycheck. He felt a churning in his stomach.

He was given a receipt, told some things about the bail process and signed some papers. Daniel wasn't really paying much attention. He just wanted to get out of there. After the formalities were over, the deputy told Daniel to have a seat and they would bring Faith out shortly.

Shortly happened to be another 35 minutes. He sat in one of the hard plastic chairs staring at the cold, white cement block walls. He read through a couple of bail bondsman's pamphlets, looked at his phone a few dozen times, studied the discolored ceiling tiles. If he would've thought he would have to wait so long he would've brought a book to read. He thought about going back out to the car to sit in a more comfortable seat and listen to the radio, but ruled that out because when Faith did finally come out he would not be there, and she undoubtedly would freak out. Finally, Daniel saw movement through the small square glass window set in the heavy steel door. It clanked and was pushed open, revealing a disheveled looking dark-haired woman with tousled hair and rumpled clothing. Faith.

He almost did not recognize her. She had no makeup on, her hair was not fixed, and she walked like an elderly woman being led to the toilet, almost as if she had leg irons on. He got up from the hard plastic chair and walked toward her. She immediately threw her arms around him and gave him a big hug, resting her head on his chest. She felt bony and frail beneath his arms as he hugged her back. She smelled like incarceration.

"Thank you for coming for me," she told him, thickness in her voice.

"Do you need any paperwork, anything for court?" He asked her.

She shook her head no, "They gave it to me already," she said holding up some folded sheets of paper.

Daniel took the sheets of paper from her, knowing that she would probably loose them, and put his arm around her waist and led her out the door into the cold. She had been wearing a thin sweatshirt and her light blue penguin-adorned pajama pants, and worn sneakers when she was arrested, that was all she was wearing now. The wind and snow had increased in intensity, the cold blasting them both as soon as they crossed the threshold. The sterile warmth and shelter of the jail was almost welcomed in comparison. Almost.

Daniel thought about leaving Faith inside as he got the car and pulled it up to the curb, but rejected that thought as it came too late. They were already halfway to the car now, no sense her turning back now. He could feel Faith shiver under his arm so he pulled her body closer to his trying to shield her from the wind. He picked up the pace and they finally made it to the Toyota. He used the key fob to unlock the door before they got there and quickly opened the door for her. When she was seated, he shut the door and quickly made his way around to the driver side. He started the engine as fast as he could, but waited a few minutes for the engine to warm before he cranked the heater.

"Are you hungry?" Daniel asked, not really sure what to do or say just then.

Faith looked at him with tired, pleading eyes. The sadness they conveyed seemed to penetrate him. He'd never been in jail before, had never experienced or endured a fraction of the things she had in her life. But as she looked at him and he looked into those eyes he felt a deep sadness and pain that seemed to emanate from her soul. He felt a twinge of pain in his chest and sadness in his mind.

"Yes," she said reluctantly. She knew what he had to do to get her out and she didn't want to ask for more. But since it was offered...

He pulled into a Burger King half a mile away, knowing that she didn't like McDonald's, and in the small town there wasn't anything else to choose from that had a drive-thru. He ordered her what she usually got: a double cheeseburger, small fry. But he also wanted to make her feel better, so he asked, "What kind of shake do you want, chocolate or strawberry?"

She looked at him, surprised. She managed a smile and responded, "Umm, strawberry."

He smiled at her and patted her leg with his hand, giving it a squeeze of reassurance. They ate as he drove. Faith half unwrapped the whopper with cheese and bacon, no onion, that Daniel and ordered for himself and handed it to him, setting his fries in the cup holder so he could reach them. As he ate, Daniel was pushing the events of the day behind him, though he knew that the ordeal was not over.

Daniel waited for her to finish eating. She thanked him for the food, and again for coming to her rescue. He smiled at her and said, "I'm your friend, Faith. Maybe the only one you truly have." She looked down and away from him. He wasn't sure what she was feeling then, probably a multitude of mixed, maybe even confusing emotions, he thought.

"I know," she said, though Daniel doubted she really meant it. Doubted she actually realized it.

"So what the hell happened?" He asked her. He was going to wait until later, after she had a shower and time to relax but he couldn't help himself from asking. He felt he deserved to know what was going on.

She told him her version of events. She told him about the two days before Christmas when she arrived at her previous home. She told him of the events of Christmas Eve in great detail as she remembered them. She told him of every event of her booking and incarceration--how because of her agitated state and combative nature they had restrained her in the "Bam Bam chair." It was a wooden straitjacket-like chair that the police used to secure and completely restrain a combative and most times belligerent inmate. It was a way for the police officers to protect themselves, and to protect the inmate from injuring him or herself as well. It was also quite embarrassing, she said. But at the time, in the heat of the moment filled with anger and frustration she wanted to--needed to--lash out at someone. And so she had.

Faith told him of her phone conversations with her mother and brother from jail, and their unwillingness to help her. She told him how he was her last resort, that she regretted even having to ask him for help. That was the reason she sat in jail almost two days before calling him, not wanting to ruin his Christmas with his family. Daniel could tell she was embarrassed and saddened by the whole situation.

"I'm sorry you had to go through this," he told her.

She looked at him with puzzlement, but also with a sort of admiration. "It's not your fault. Any of it," she told him, and edge to her voice.

"I know. But it's still bullshit."

The words hung in the air for a long time, neither of them speaking. Both of them thinking, trapped in their own thoughts, in their own minds.

"So, what did they serve you for Christmas dinner?" he asked after a long silence, trying to lighten the mood.

She looked at him, incredulous with a *WTF?* look on her face, then laughed out loud, hard. "You're such a Brat!" she exclaimed, still laughing. He was laughing along with her, rubbing her thigh with his right hand as he drove with his left. "They gave us sliced turkey and mashed potatoes, which actually weren't that bad, if you must know...Brat," she told him.

He smiled at her. He was glad he was able to make her laugh after such an ordeal. He knew this wasn't Faith's first time to jail, and he was unsure just how many times she had been or what the circumstances were. But he was sure he didn't really want to know. He felt he didn't need to know, not really. Their life now demanded they had to deal with the consequences of the past, but it didn't have to be defined by it, he thought. *We can choose to move forward, hand-in-hand, into a brighter future*, he thought to himself. He desperately wanted that to become a reality.

In what seemed like a short time of silence--both of them pretending to listen to the music but being trapped in their own minds, fencing with their own thoughts--they arrived back at Daniel's house. Daniel quickly got out of the car and ran to the door and unlocked it, pushing it open. He then ran back to the car and helped Faith from it, helped her hurry across the frozen ground to the waiting warmth of the house.

"I think I'm gonna take a bath," Faith told him after they got inside. "I don't take showers there because they *watch* you! Fuckin' assholes," she explained.

"Sounds like a good idea," he agreed.

"In a few minutes will you bring me some wine?" she asked. She liked Merlot, and Daniel knew there was an unopened bottle.

"Sure thing. I'll give you a few minutes," he told her.

With that she went off to the master bathroom with the large garden tub, but no whirlpool feature. It took a few minutes for her to fill up the tub with hot water, to which she added some bubbles and bath oils. Before getting in, Faith put a *Wilson Phillips* CD in the portable radio. From the living room, Daniel could hear Faith singing along loudly to the songs. He laughed to himself while drinking a Michelob Ultra, cold, fresh from the refrigerator. He walked to the entertainment center and powered up his Microsoft Xbox and put in the EA Sports NHL hockey game. He figured he would have a good half hour to an hour before Faith was done with her bath. Maybe she'd like to play a game of pool when she was done.

Daniel's house was set up with two bedrooms and a bath on one side, and the master bedroom and bath and kitchen on the other. Separating the two "wings" was one large great room. On one half of this room was the television, leather couch and leather loveseat. On the other half of this room were the dark mahogany stained bookshelves filled with nearly 300 books that Daniel had acquired over the years. Of the many paperbacks and hardcovers displayed 85% were fiction, the rest nonfiction. Daniel had read most of them. These were arranged along one wall on which they were perfectly set, looking almost like built-ins. In front of this was an 8 foot, drop-pocket billiards table. Black with maroon felt.

Faith was an admitted bar scene pool hustler. She told Daniel several stories of times she hustled people, mostly men, at the bar, taking their money and their free drinks. He was sure she used her feminine, sexual allure to distract them just as much as she used her billiards skill to win. And undoubtedly she used her flirtation skills to get the free drinks. He didn't want to think about what else she might've done with them. So he didn't.

Daniel enjoyed the game, but wasn't that good at it. He played "slop" mostly, which was when the player did not call their shots. By playing in that fashion the player got credit for one of their balls going in, even if it was by accident and unintentional. It turned the game of skill more into a game of luck. To Daniel it made the game more fun and random. And easier. To hardcore players "Slop" was crap and an unacceptable way to play, as its very nature took a lot of the skill out and could make a mediocre player statistically even with a skilled one. In either case, it was his table and his rules. That was the main reason he did not like playing pool out in public, at bars. He liked going out and having fun, some drinks and some dinner, with someone like Faith, but inevitably some stranger would put some quarters on the table and say, "I got winner," and wanted to play for money, or just trying to hustle you or hit on your girlfriend. None of those scenarios did Daniel care for, and he wanted to avoid those types of bullshit confrontations if he could. So, he researched and bought a pool table online, assembled it himself, and they played happily at home. They played slop. And Faith didn't care. She liked playing. Enjoyed the competition and the activity.

She was more of a social butterfly, more outgoing and extroverted than he was. She probably enjoyed the interaction, the crowds, the random conversations. He was sure she even liked the attention she received from strangers. But it seemed in such places along with the compliments on her hair, clothes, jewelry there were the eventual scowling faces, the muttered comments, the "accidental" bumps and shoves. And of course the unwanted advances. All of these latter things led to an unhappy experience. Someone got angry, someone got in a fight--verbal or physical, or both.

Maybe that's what she wants, maybe that's who she is, his mind told him.

Ridiculous, he thought. He knew there were people that went to the bars to get drunk and pick fights on purpose. And he knew that she was a self-proclaimed fighter. But he had a hard time believing that was what she wanted, that it was fun for her.

As he turned events over in his head, contemplating, over the blaring radio from the bathroom he heard Faith's high-pitched yell, "Babe! Will you bring me my wine now?"

"Yes!" He yelled back so she would not continue to yell for him. He paused the game (Detroit Red Wings up 2 to 1 in the second period over the Anaheim Mighty Ducks), got off the couch and went for the bottle of wine. *It was a turning out to be a pretty good day*, he thought. *Maybe tonight will be better.*

After a relaxing bath and some wine, and then a couple games of pool, that was usually enough for Faith to become amorous. He would test the waters when he brought in her wine, see how she was feeling after the ordeal of the last few days. He did not want to think about court dates, fines and costs, repercussions, the waiting work days. Technically, to him it was still the Holidays and he was determined to enjoy them. He was going to drink some beer, play some games with the person he loved, and hopefully have sex like a porn star. A great end to a not so good day.

CHAPTER TWELVE

H is cell phone rang. He recently upgraded the tiny silver one to a larger, black LG flip phone with a larger screen and a camera. He bought Faith the matching one in purple. Daniel let out a sigh of relief as he saw from the readout it wasn't his work calling. It was a Wednesday, nearly three weeks into the new year, and his day off. The last thing he wanted was to deal with work-related trouble when he shouldn't have to. It was Nevver.

"What's up you skank bastard?" Daniel shouted as he flipped the phone open and connected the call.

There was the familiar laugh, nearly diabolical in nature, before the reply. "Well, if it isn't my favorite turd!" Nevver retorted. "Happy fucking holidays, asshole," he said cheerfully. "Thanks for the card, it must have got lost in the mail as I just got it a couple days ago."

Daniel laughed out loud. "Must have," he told him. In all actuality, Daniel had forgotten to send the card out. He bought it, wrote some cherry and sarcastic bullshit in it, licked the envelope flap, and let it sit on the desk in the kitchen for too many days before finally buying a stamp and getting it in the mail. A little embarrassed, Daniel quickly changed the subject, "Are you coming up this way anytime soon?" He asked.

Nevver still lived in Bay City and hadn't been up to the Petoskey area since the summer. Even though he could be a chore to deal with sometimes, Daniel missed his friend, though neither of them called very often. *New Year's resolution*, he reminded himself.

"Not for a bit, working hard ya know?"

"Yeah, I get it. Me too. It's good to hear from you," Daniel said with all sincerity.

"So call me more often, cocksuker! These hear cellular communication devices work both ways, meaning they receive *and* can send calls," Nevver scolded, his words dripping with sarcasm.

"I know, man. I apologize. I'll do better," Daniel said, much sarcasm in his own tone.

"So how are things? Still with that freaky chick, what's her name, Grace?" Nevver asked.

Daniel laughed, "Her name is Faith, not Grace. And yes, I'm still with her. Actually, she lives with me now."

"No shit? I never thought you'd get into the married thing again. Must be pretty serious...or you're dumber than I know you to be!" Nevver quipped.

Daniel went into an explanation of the past few months, and a little bit of Faith's background, what she had been going through, what she was still dealing with.

"I see," Nevver said, though there was much doubt in his voice. "She still the funny, happy, hard-working, sexy woman you fell for?"

"Oh yeah, things are great," Daniel lied. He hadn't really thought about it until his friend's words brought those things to the forefront of his thoughts. Faith was still sexy, still hard-working, but now she was only working part-time though she did most of the house chores, insisted on it, really. They still had fun, but her smiles and her happiness were not a daily thing. She seemed to be slipping into depression. Daniel was trying hard to pull her out of it, or at least give her some stability, some sort of even keel, to keep her from falling deeper into the pit.

She had lost custody of her kids, only had every other weekend visitation rights now. She had no say in their school, in their health, in anything really. And because Scott had custody, Faith was ordered by the Friend of the Court to pay *him* child support. It was a catastrophe, a fucked up mess, but Daniel still tried to keep her happy, to keep himself happy. None of this he told his friend.

"We get her kids every other weekend for a couple of days. They can be trying at times, but we're all getting along pretty well."

"Instant family man, huh? Never figured you for that. How many does she have, five?" Nevver asked.

"No, four," Daniel corrected him.

"Are you nuts? You go from divorced bachelor man, with no kids, not ready for kids, as far as I know, to some baggage-laden woman with four kids? What are you thinking? There's an easier life out there, man," Nevver told him.

The words hurt Daniel. He wasn't sure why, though. He knew his good friend wasn't trying to be mean, wasn't trying to belittle his situation. Daniel knew Nevver had his best interests at heart, even if he rarely showed it. There were darts of truth in what his friend had just said. But Daniel wasn't ready to face that truth. He was still looking forward to a day in the future where they would have some semblance of happiness every day, not just one or two days out of the week, or month. He was looking forward to the time when Faith would be the happy, smiling, playful woman he thought her to be. To a time where joy would reign, and sadness and hard circumstances would be few and far between.

"Yeah, I'm probably going a little nuts. Work is stressful, as always. Faith's issues add stress as well. But for the most part, we make each other happy and are helping each other get through the hard days. And we're enjoying the good times," Daniel explained.

"Sweet man. Good to hear. Just make sure you got more good times than bad," Nevver advised him. "Otherwise, what's the point?"

"I hear you," Daniel told him.

"We'll see, buddy. Listen, I gotta go just wanted to say thanks for the card and see how you were doing," Nevver said. "Oh, but one more thing! I may have a chance to move up that way in the next couple months. I'll let you know."

"Really? That would be awesome! Stay in touch. If you need help moving, I'm your man," Daniel reassured him.

"You better be! Later," Nevver said and broke the connection.

Daniel sat back down at the kitchen table and stared out the larger row of windows. What he saw looked bleak and desolate, as the landscape was covered in cold, white snow. The wind was whipping small snow devils across the yard. His neighbor's house across the way had a good eight inches of snow packed on the roof.

Faith was outside bundled up in her snow pants, winter jacket, new snow boots Daniel had bought for her, hat, scarf, gloves. If he did not know it was her he wouldn't be able to tell with all the clothing. She was shoveling the long driveway. Even though she had constant, chronic pain in her back she still struggled and managed to do chores, not wanting to give up and give in. And he knew that she did those things because it made her feel useful, and because it was her way of trying to pay him back for his generosity and kindness.

Daniel went back to what he was doing, balancing the checkbook. As he looked at the entries and made a few new ones the events of the past month came back to his mind. His new relationship moving towards their first holiday together, in helping her buy presents for the kids, and being able to spend time with his family. All were good things. But what had started out as a great and wonderful thing at Christmas time had turned into a horrible thing on Christmas Eve for Faith. Spending Christmas in jail was a cold, harsh thing for someone to do to another person. Especially when it was done out of spite, anger, and hate.

Daniel theorized that love could turn into hate. But he did not know what steps that took, how long the process was, what circumstances could twist one's feelings so irreparably that dark and destructive emotions replaced those of light. He laughed to himself as he thought the answer might be akin to the Tootsie Pop commercial where the kid asked the owl how many licks it takes to get to the center. The world may never know.

Daniel looked back to his checkbook and finished calculating all the expenses incurred over the previous months. *I hope February gets better*, he thought. He looked outside again, watched Faith struggle with the shovel, pushing it along the ground trying to get as much as she could on each pass. He was going to put on his gear and go help her, take over for her, but she was on her last pass. She did a good job. He was proud of her. The sun was setting fast now, most of the visible light came from the snow. It would be dark in less than fifteen minutes.

He got up from the table and started to make dinner. He liked to cook, liked to cook for somebody who appreciated it. Faith always appreciated it. Tonight it would be something simple. Spaghetti with meat sauce, and garlic bread, of course.

He just filled the large pot with water and placed it over a high flame on the stove when he heard the door open and sounds of boots, followed by a gust of icy cold air.

"Fuck it's cold outside," Faith said in way of announcing her presence as she began taking off her outerwear.

"I know. Thanks for doing that, babe. I appreciate it," he told her.

"You're welcome," she said. "I should've got out and done it earlier."

"Making dinner. Spaghetti with garlic bread."

"Yummy," she replied. "I'm gonna take a hot shower before dinner. Do I still have wine left?" She asked.

Daniel turned to her, knowing what was on the counter. "Yeah, you have one bottle and a little bit left in one from the other day."

"Awesome," she said. "Can we play pool after dinner?" She asked, her voice innocent, like a kid asking their parent if they can go out and play.

"Yeah, that sounds fun," he told her. A game of drinking and billiards was always fun. Especially since it almost always led to another nighttime activity.

He slowed down his cooking timetable, giving Faith time to do what she wanted to do. While the noodles were cooking and the meat sauce was simmering, Daniel pulled the vinyl cover off of the pool table, got the mahogany triangle rack from the pool cue stand in the corner and began pulling the balls out of the pockets and rolling them across the table to the end nearest the bookshelves.

The table he bought did not come with any accessories, therefore he had to buy pool cues and balls and chalk, etc. For the balls, Daniel didn't want just simple, ordinary found-at-the-bar pool balls. So after some research he went with an Aramith set called the "Stone Collection." The balls, both stripes and solids, had a speckled pattern within their colors that made them look like granite. They were unique and cool looking especially against the maroon felt of the table.

For cues Daniel had four standard, one-piece of various weights. He had a pair of two-piece cues of better than standard quality, one with a black grip, one red. For Christmas he bought Faith a two-piece aluminum cue made by Players, dark blue with a black grip. It had a cool black and silver pattern. For himself he wanted something unique. He searched for a white cue with a black pattern. Finally he found the one he wanted made by Scorpion. He even loved the scorpion logo.

So, they both had their own cue, and no one else was to use them. That was a rule. When the kids came over they could use any of the other cues, but not Daniel's or Faith's. He even had a little 24" cue made for tight spots, but was also well suited for Faith's daughter. It was fun watching the kids play, until they started arguing. When that happened Faith would give them two warnings before making them put things away and the game was over.

With the stone balls racked, Daniel went back to check on dinner. The pasta was nearly al dente, the sauce simmering nicely. He had a lid on the large pan so the spitting and popping of the sauce did not make too much of a mess. He slid the baking sheet with the loaf of garlic bread into the preheated oven and set the timer. Next, he turned the heat off under the pasta pan, letting the hot water continue to cook.

He went into the living room and turned on the stereo and powered up the five disc CD/DVD player. He loaded in some of their favorite CDs: John Mellencamp, Pat Benetar, Nickelback, Cry of Love, and Live. From the bathroom The Dixie Chicks was playing. Daniel did not like some of Faith's go-to music, but he tolerated it for a while anyway. If it made her happy, then it was worth it.

*   *   *

They had eaten at the large, wooden kitchen table, a match to the coffee table in the living room. After dinner, Daniel opened her bottle of Merlot and started the first CD in the player, and cranked up the volume to a loud, but not obnoxious level. While he did this, Faith went out and had an after dinner cigarette. She smoked Newport 100s which were menthol. He couldn't remember exactly when she had started smoking, but he thought he remembered her saying since she was twelve. But she was a courteous smoker, always smoking outside and away from other people who did not. She did not like the smell of it on her clothes or on furniture, so she was adamant about cleaning and using air fresheners, about washing her hands and using cologne or body spray afterwards to mask the sent.

As was customary Faith "broke." They used the 21 ounce, solid one-piece cue as a breaking cue. She did well, putting in two solids and one stripe on the break.

"Look at you, a pool sharktress!" Daniel teased.

"You're just jealous," she replied with a wink and a smile. She put in another solid with her next shot. She took a sip of wine, leaving dark lipstick on the rim of the glass. She sat the glass down and wobble-walked around the table, studying the formation trying to choose her next shot carefully. She came to a conclusion and readied herself. She leaned over the table, bending at the waist making a 90° angle. It was too much for Daniel to resist. Before she could make her shot he quickly moved up behind her and grabbed her ass with both hands and ground his pelvic region into her.

She began to laugh, "Stop it, brat! You have to wait," she told him, a playful edge in her voice.

Daniel backed away and slapped her ass as he did. She missed her shot. He laughed.

"See what you made me do?" She asked, feigning anger.

"Oh I'm so sorry. I guess it's my turn," he said smiling.

"Yeah, I can see your real sorry...Such a brat," she told him as she took another sip of wine, drumming her fingernails on the side of the glass creating a tinkling sound.

The playful banter and the game of slop went on until Faith finally sunk the eight ball. She went outside for another cigarette as Daniel re-racked the balls. The music and the night wore on, Faith's bottle of wine was nearly gone, six empty bottles of Michelob Ultra stood by the kitchen sink. Their playfulness had become more and more flirtatious and sexual in nature. It was fun, Daniel was having a good time he could feel that Faith was too.

Faith was outside again, smoking a cigarette and also talking on her cell phone. Daniel wasn't sure who she was talking to, didn't really matter. Until she had been out there for over 15 minutes. He had been standing looking at the configuration of pool balls, waiting for her to take a shot. He drank his beer and sang along to Bob Seger's *Against the Wind*. After three songs he finally sat down, becoming agitated and frustrated. He didn't like waiting, being kept waiting. *So damn inconsiderate*, he thought.

After a few more minutes of waiting he walked quietly through the kitchen to where the door was very slightly ajar. He leaned in close, trying to hear the words of her conversation in an effort to ascertain if his happy night was going to end good or badly because of some drama on the other side of the phone.

He could make out her voice, but nothing that she said. The wind made it hard to hear. *Was she whispering?* He thought. Strange. He opened the steel entry door and pushed the storm door open, still holding the handle to keep the wind from taking it. Frigid air blasted his body and face, instantly making him shiver.

"Faith, do you still want to play?" He yelled over the wind, though his tone was still warm and friendly.

She seemed startled, like he scared her with his presence. She must not have heard the door open. She whirled towards him, cell phone still pressed to her ear.

"Yes, I'll be right there. Can you pour me some more wine?" She asked.

"Sure," he said, then went off to do just that. And wait. *At least she still seems to be in a good mood*, he thought.

It was about five more minutes before Faith came back inside. She quickly took her jacket and boots off. "Is it my turn?" She asked as if she didn't know.

"Yes," Daniel replied, trying not to sound angry or frustrated but failing in the attempt.

Daniel's head was floating. He was up to his eighth beer, and any negating effect the spaghetti had was long gone. He noticed he was stumbling a little bit as he walked, had to brace himself on the wall behind the toilet as he stood to relieve his swollen bladder. He heard the crack of billiard balls as he flushed the toilet and washed his hands. He walked in the other room where Faith was standing, pool cue in her left hand glass of wine in her right.

"I missed," she said smiling.

He smiled back at her, trying to keep the moment light. Nickelback was playing in the background now. As Daniel stepped up to the table to take a shot, Faith started to dance to the music. It was a sultry, body swaying dance. Daniel didn't know if she was any good at dancing, he wasn't a good judge of that, but it did turn him on.

He sank his first shot and walked past Faith, brushing her body with his on his way around the table. She reached out and grabbed his ass as he went by. As Daniel lined up his second shot he noticed Faith was staring at him. She wasn't smiling, exactly. It was more of a smirk, like she was trying not to laugh. He missed the shot and she did start to laugh.

"Nice try, nice try," she said to him as she moved towards the table. Daniel stood up and backed away as Faith moved to the far end of the table where he was standing. She was chalking her pool cue and making a bit of a show of it, moving her hips and her feet to the music. She bent over the table for her shot directly in front of Daniel. Her baggy jeans were sliding down her hips, revealing the top of her panties. They were pink with white and purple polkadots, Daniel saw. *Enough waiting, I'm taking what's mine*, he thought greedily and quickly moved towards her.

Faith took her shot and missed, but before she could stand up and turn around Daniel was pressed up against her. He could smell her perfume and body spray mixed with the still lingering scents of cigarettes and wine. He grabbed her gently but firmly by the hips and leaned in and began kissing on her neck. He found the spot that made her twitch and moan as bolts of erotic electricity shot through her body. He tasted the acidic film left by the Cologne.

She gripped the edge of the pool table and pushed her body back into his.

He moved from kissing the right side of her neck over to the left, and with his right hand he reached up and grabbed a handful of her short hair at the back of her head. He didn't pull, he just made a fist while his tongue and lips probed her neck. He let go of her hair and moved his right hand back to her hip were his left still was. Quickly he grabbed the sides of her jeans and pulled straight down, yanking her pants to her ankles.

He was on his knees now, his face nearly directly in line with her ass now only partially covered by the polkadotted thong. He leaned in and slid the thin fabric to the side and began to probe and lick as he gently pushed on her lower back in an effort to get her to bend over the table. She did. She spread her legs as far as she could but her ankles were bound by the jeans. Daniel could smell her sweat and tasted her wetness.

After a few minutes Daniel stood and dropped his own pants revealing his erection. With Faith still bent over the pool table Daniel quickly inserted himself into her. She let out a cry and her torso came up nearly vertical. Daniel pushed her back down, trying to keep the angle the same. He was thrusting in a good rhythm now, almost to the music that was still playing loudly from the speakers. Faith was moaning as she reached back with her left hand and scratched Daniel's stomach, her long nails biting into the skin.

He pull his torso back trying to avoid the second swipe but failed. Again her nails scratched into his skin. The pain was more intense than he thought it would be, like the scratch from the super-sharp claws of a kitten. Unlike some people, Daniel did not equate pleasure with pain. He stopped thrusting though he was still inside of her as he grabbed her wrist and held tightly to it. She thrust back into him and Daniel took this as a sign that she wanted it this way. Still holding onto her wrist, Daniel bent her arm so that her forearm was laying across her lower back. He held it there with his right hand and slapped her ass with his left, thrusting harder now. She then swiped at him with her free right hand, catching him in the stomach again with sharp fingernails. Daniel grabbed that wrist and bent that arm the same way so that he had both of her forearms clasped in his hands. He thrust harder now, his frustration and pain now mixing with his lust and desire.

Faith let out a yell and thrust hard back into him, pushing him off balance. She stood up and quickly turned around. They stood facing each other, both half naked. Daniel was puzzled but decided to go with whatever this was, being in the heat of the moment. He stepped toward her and embraced her, kissing her on the mouth. She returned the kiss, reaching her hand down and grabbing his erection. He slid his hand down between her legs and curled a finger up into her vagina, working it side to side. He walked forward moving her backwards and pushed her back onto the pool table.

She was laying on it now looking up at him. He put both arms under her thighs and raised them up as he inserted himself back into her. Her wetness was hot and welcoming as he began to thrust again. He grabbed both of her wrists with his hands and pulled as he thrust, giving himself more force.

This he did for only a minute or so before Faith yelled out, "Stop it! Stop it!"

What? His mind yelled. Puzzled, Daniel stopped thrusting though he still had a hold of her wrists and held himself inside of her.

"Get off! I don't want to do this anymore!" She shouted, tears streaming down her face now.

What the fuck? Daniel didn't know what was going on, didn't know what to do. He didn't think that he was hurting her, it seemed like she was enjoying it as much as he was. He let go of her and backed away. He wondered to himself if he should help her off of the table but before he finished the thought she had already righted herself and gotten down. She sat on the floor and cried.

Daniel thought as if he might've slipped into the Twilight Zone. This didn't make any sense to him. He couldn't figure out what her problem was, if he had done something to hurt her. "I'm sorry, Faith. Did I hurt you?" He asked her kneeling down beside her.

"I...I...just don't want to do this anymore," she managed to say.

Confused and unsure of what to do or what to say, Daniel decided to just leave her alone for a few minutes. He pulled his pants back on and walked to the guest bathroom to relieve himself. When he had finished and came back out she was no longer on the floor by the pool table. He looked into the master bathroom and she was not there. He walked in the kitchen and noticed that the side door was left ajar.

He quietly walked over to the door to check on her, to see if she was all right. Again he found her outside smoking and talking on her cell phone. He couldn't tell what the conversation was but her tone was more agitated and the words he could make out were all swear words. He tried to hear exactly what was being said, but he couldn't. He decided it was best just to leave her alone for now.

Daniel went back into the living room and shut the music off. He then walked to the pool table and picked up the cues and put them back in the rack. Next, he pushed all the colored balls into the pockets and put the vinyl cover back over the table. He shut off some lights and went into the master bedroom and turned on the television.

He took off his clothes and put some sweatpants on and a black T-shirt and crawled into bed. He had to work the next day, though it was a closing shift so he could sleep in and sleep off the alcohol.

Maybe when she comes back in she'll tell me what the fuck is going on, he thought. He was angry now, deprived of sexual release, but more than that he was confused.

None of this made sense. The only thing he could think of was that their pool table sex had set her off somehow, maybe it brought back a bad memory. He didn't know if it had something to do with the previous and subsequent phone calls either. *Too many variables to figure it out,* he thought. *I'll just have to ask her.*

He flipped through several channels offered by the satellite company until he found something that caught his interest: a replay of the last days of World War II on the History Channel. His head was heavy with alcohol and his eyes were burning. He tried to fight his sleep and wait for Faith to come to bed, but his body had other plans. In four minutes Daniel was fast asleep. He didn't even stir when Faith came to bed thirty minutes later.

CHAPTER THIRTEEN

He was half drunk and sexually frustrated, which seemed to be his normal state as of late. He was talking to one of his female coworkers, a young woman whose name was Pamela. She was freshly 21 years old. She had a boyfriend, but things weren't going well and he thought it was a good time to stir the pot, see if he could drive a wedge in between them.

"Come on, girl," Nevver said smoothly, putting as much charm in his voice as he could. He pulled the cell phone away from his face as he took a drink from the 16 ounce can of Natural Ice beer. "You're a hot woman, and should be treated like one," Nevver continued after his drink. "He doesn't appreciate what he's got, and he never will. 'Cause guys like that never do."

Nevver strained to listen to Pamela's reply, but her words were just blather, he didn't really care what she had to say. He just wanted in those pants. He glanced at his watch and mentally calculated how much time he had before his live-in girlfriend, Melissa--whom he called Lissa--would be home from her job. *About 45 minutes*, he thought. Not enough time to actually get anything going with Pamela, but enough time to set more seeds of discourse into her mind and thus into her relationship. Enough time to play with her some more, to pull the conversation into sexual waters and see how she responded.

Truth be told, Pamela's boyfriend did not treat her well. He was jealous and controlling, as most immature and insecure men were, Nevver knew. Her boyfriend was kind of a scrawny punk, that thought of himself as a badass. Nevver wasn't afraid or intimidated in the least. Even if he found out and wanted to fight, Nevver could handle himself. *Man it's been a long time since I whipped someone's ass*, he thought. *That outcome might make fucking this chick even sweeter*, his drunken mind mused.

"I just want to show you a good time, girl. You'll never know what a real man can do with a body like that if you stay with a boy. I'll show you how you should be treated," he told her. "And don't get me wrong, I'm not just talking about sex. I'm talking the whole package of how a woman should be treated and respected," he continued. Pamela was a bit on the heavy side, but depending on which pants she was wearing her ass was inviting. Plus she had large, fat-girl tits, which Nevver liked. A lot. And she was pretty. And blonde. *Man, I would give my left nut to find out how natural that blonde is,* he thought. Her eyebrows were light colored, and just the thought of them hovering over her deep blue eyes, hinting at what lie under her panties, drove Nevver's lust-driven mind crazy.

Now she was saying something about how things weren't really that bad, about how he treated her well *most* of the time.

Nevver had to interject, "Pamsel," he began, calling her by the nickname he had given her. Pamsel was a play on damsel, like she was a damsel in distress and needed saving. She needed him to save her. Or at least have sex with her. *Hopefully more than once,* he thought.

"You can make all the excuses you want for that piece of shit, but it does not, and will not, change the fact that you deserve better, nor the fact that he will never change who and what he is. I just want to show you, so that you know beyond the shadow of a doubt, what that better could be. Plus, you don't want to wake up five years from now with three of his kids and realize you should've listened to Nevver way back when."

He let those words hang in the air to hopefully absorb into that blonde skull of hers as he took another drink of beer. He had a full buzz on now. He was sitting on his couch wearing his Detroit Pistons shorts and no shirt. It was his day off, and he was enjoying it.

SportsCenter was on the TV, volume low, closed caption on. He was almost paying more attention to that than he was to what Pamela was saying. His mind was focusing on her keywords, almost like he was a NSA data sweep program. The sentence and the content didn't really matter so much, unless she was saying what he was hoping to hear. Doubtful words, words that affirmed what he was saying to her, any sexual words, etc were what his mind was searching for. The positive thing, Nevver thought, was the fact that she was still talking, still carrying on with the conversation that they have been having over the past few weeks. That meant she was interested in him. *Seduction can be a slow game,* he thought.

Just then he heard a rattle and a key hitting the lock of the entry door. His drunken mind jumped, frazzled. He didn't know what to think, didn't know what was going on. Before he realized what was happening, Lissa came through the door.

Oh fuck me, he thought, his eyes widened. *I never get to do what I want.*

She looked directly at him as she shut the door and threw her keys on the small table next to it. "Hey, babe. Who you talking to?" She asked, politely no edge in her voice, but Nevver read a slight suspicion in her eyes.

"Dan-O," he said, not missing a beat. Then, speaking into the phone, "Hey, Lissa just got home. I'll catch you later. Think about what I said and let me know," he finished as he snapped his cell phone closed, ending the call.

He could smell the grease and food from the restaurant emanating from her clothes. The scent was not pleasant and it clung to her clothing so much that they had to wash her work clothes separate from their other things.

He smiled up at his girlfriend and said, "So, how was your day?" As she spoke his mind scanned her answer for keywords, for clues as to what he should be concerned, or not concerned, about, trying to accurately gage her mood. Same old, same old: Blah-blah-blah work's hard, blah-blah-blah my manager sucks, blah-blah-blah we were slow so I was sent home early.

"Nice, that you got out early. That boss of yours is never gonna treat you right," he said, not really listening, but he figured his response conveyed that he had been. "So, you want to fuck or have dinner first?" He asked in his playful, smarmy tone, hoping for the former.

Lissa rolled her eyes, then just gave him a glare conveying: "You wish." She looked around at the apartment. The living room was littered with presumably empty beer cans, a crumpled bag of cheddar and sour cream potato chips, a small pile of their clothes tucked under the secondhand coffee table. A glance in the kitchen told of dirty dishes piled in the sink and of an overflowing trash can parked next to the refrigerator. She could smell ammonia and the familiar perfumed gravel of the cat litter box located in the second bedroom of their small apartment, demanding attention. Nevver's hair was unkempt and he was shirtless which told Melissa that not only had he neglected the housework on his day off he also opted to not shower that day as well. The apartment smelled like dirty clothes, soiled cat litter, and slimy dishes. She grabbed the can of Febreze Air Effects off the table and sprayed as she walked around the apartment.

Nevver got a little angry by the look and the act of spraying the deodorizer, he knew what she was implying. According to his mental calendar they had not had sex for thirteen days. Which in his mind was about ten days way overdue. And part of the reason he was trying so hard with Pamela. *It's always good to have options*, he thought.

They had been living together, he and Lissa, just shy of three months. They had been dating for four months prior to that, the last two were exclusive. It seemed like a logical step in the progression of their relationship, and financially it was a no-brainer. But it seemed they were becoming more like just roommates instead of lovers, though they shared the same bed. But it was a king size which virtually guaranteed enough sleeping space where one could roll around as much as they wanted and did not have to even worry about touching the other. The cuddling had stopped as well. Not that Nevver was really a cuddly-type person, but in a relationship it was expected and in some cases, to some people, it was needed.

Nevver drained the beer from the can and pushed himself up off the couch and toward the kitchen for another. In a glass cake pan on the counter covered with cellophane wrap were two nice cuts of rib eye steak. Never was marinating them in Italian dressing. He planned on grilling them on the propane gas grill that evening for dinner. He was hoping it would be a great meal after some good sex. But it seemed more likely he would just have to settle for a good meal with mediocre company, and rubbing one out in the bathroom before bed. He thought maybe if he could get Lissa to have a drink or two she might loosen up, warm up to the idea of having sex that night.

"Babe, do you want me to fix you a drink?" He asked her, raising his voice from the kitchen so she could hear him.

"Ahhh...no, not right now," she answered.

Nevver rolled his eyes. *That's what I figured*, he thought. *At this rate I'll never have sex with her again.* But he still wasn't ready to give up. Maybe after she had a wonderful steak, expertly prepared by him, she would want that drink and would welcome his touch and the sexual release.

His mind drifted to Pamela. The curves of her body, similar to Lissa's...the way she smiled at him, with that *look* in her eyes...the longing? He hoped it was. He desperately wanted to satisfy that longing. Well, maybe it was *his* longing that he wanted to satisfy. And perhaps it was his lust that he was projecting onto Pamela. In either case he would not be satisfied until he had conquered her. But, unfortunately, that would have to wait. Tonight he would set his sights back on Lissa and try to seduce her.

*   *   *

The steaks were cooked to perfection, if he did say so himself. Medium for her, medium rare for him. Diamond patterned grill marks, slightly charred on the outside, the marbled fat sizzled and spat over the flames as it cooked. Smoke from the cooking meat rose in the air, the wonderful smell of charred beef filled his nostrils. Nevver drank another 16 ounce beer as he cooked.

To go with the steaks, earlier he had prepared a mayonnaise-based rotini pasta salad with fresh grape tomatoes, sliced black olives, diced green pepper, and a few slices of pepperoni for added spice, texture, and color. It was seasoned with his special blend of garlic salt, pepper, and a few other spices. A line from a Jack Nicholson movie came to mind: *Good times and noodle salad.* Nevver smiled at the thought. Grey Goose vodka was in the freezer and he contemplated switching to that, but he would wait and see what Lissa would be drinking after dinner.

If it were up to him a big fat, fully loaded baked potato with sour cream, bacon, and melted cheddar cheese would accompany the steak. But Lissa liked to eat healthy, and even though pasta salad wasn't really healthy, people thought it was a healthy alternative to a potato. Whatever made her happy. Whatever got her in the mood.

It was March 17 in Bay City, Michigan. He was still wearing his basketball shorts, but was forced to put on a hoodie sweatshirt over his bare torso as the early spring temperature was only 52°. The chill air was still, no breeze. The crisp, pre-spring smells of uncovered earth, damp pavement, and cool air filled his senses, promising warmer days to come. Dirty snow piles still littered the streets and yards, ugly punctuation on the brown-trying-to-turn-green grass. The sky was full of clouds, gray and dark, threatening rain, which would help erase the snow and feed the green. Keeping with the theme of his shorts, the hoodie he wore was licensed by the Detroit Pistons, white with blue and red. This was a standard, off-the-rack issue without customization. No "Nevver 69" emblazoned across the back.

The cold weather did not bother Nevver much. He was one of those individuals that could wear a spring jacket even when it was 30 below zero and not shiver. He was hot-blooded, he told those who asked. He could handle the cold, and the heat. Temperature was one of those things that he just didn't waste his mental and physical energies on. He had other things that consumed his mind.

Alongside the steaks--put on in the last few minutes of grilling--were butter marinated asparagus spears. Five apiece. He took his rib eye off first and set it on a plate on the side table of the grill. About two minutes later he pulled off Lissa's steak, then a minute later the asparagus. He turned the burners of the grill off, then tightened the valve on the propane tank beneath it. Satisfied that it posed no threat to the apartment, Nevver grabbed the plate with the two premium steaks and the asparagus stalks, steam rising from them, carrying their aroma towards the upper apartment. The smell of freshly cooked meat and the grilled vegetable made his mouth water. Almost as much as the thought of going down on Pamela did.

He shook his head and tried to clear the thought of Pamela from it. But it persisted. The thought of her lying in his bed, or spread across the back seat of his car, intoxicated him more than the beer.

He carried the plate to the small dinette just off the kitchen. Through the computer's MP3 player and the portable JVC speakers, Nevver was playing a mixture of songs from his library. Currently *Audioslave* was playing. One of Lissa's favorite bands.

"Babe, dinner is ready," he called, he forced the tone of his voice to be light and caring. He put a couple large spoonfuls of the pasta salad onto her plate, arranging it next to the rib eye and above the asparagus. Along with the Italian dressing marinade he had seasoned the meat with garlic salt and cracked pepper. Lastly, he took a small dish of melted butter and basted the steak and the asparagus one last time with it. Pure deliciousness.

He calculated that by the time Melissa sat down the steaks would have rested for the appropriate amount of time, perhaps even a little bit longer. When she tasted that first, tender, juicy bite it would almost melt in her mouth. He hoped that this near gourmet meal would melt that icicle in her vagina and allow him to give her dessert as well. He smiled at the thought. The thought of tasting her juices for dessert.

        *   *   *

She loved dinner. It seemed to calm her nerves and rest her spirit after a trying day at work. She accepted an after dinner cocktail: Grey Goose vodka mixed with 100% cranberry juice and a splash of imitation lemon juice. Nevver mixed it fairly strong, though when he sipped it, it tasted wonderful. He made two, one for each of them, in a 16oz glass nearly filled with ice. In hers he put a pink bendy straw and garnished the rim with a lemon.

She had changed out of her work clothes--tight black slacks and a revealing V-neck, long sleeved black shirt--and had put on more comfortable, couch potato attire: baggy pink sweatpants and a matching pink sweatshirt. He was definitely more turned on seeing her in her work attire. Nevver assumed she had no bra on, as she usually freed the "girls" when she got home. Lissa was overweight for her size, but she made up for it with large breasts, and her big ass was around and inviting. Or so Nevver thought.

After dinner they had moved into the adjacent living room. He took his usual spot on the loveseat, but she had opted for the armchair. *Not a good sign*, Nevver thought. With remote in hand, Lissa shut off the computer music and turned on the television. *An even worse sign*, Nevver thought.

She hadn't said too much since she had gotten home. And neither had he. He was letting her chill out while he cooked dinner. Now that dinner was over, and the after dinner drinks were nearly gone, Nevver thought it was time to make his move. *If I wait too much longer she's gonna be asleep*, he thought to himself.

He got up from the loveseat and walked over to the side chair where Lissa was seated. He reached for her nearly empty glass and asked, "Would you like another beverage, girl?"

To his surprise she smiled up at him and replied, "That would be great, thanks."

He took that as a very good sign. Not wanting to lose the moment, Nevver leaned in as he grabbed her glass and kissed her softly on the lips. He held his mouth to hers for a few heartbeats, waiting to see if she was going to just accept the kiss or would respond and kiss back. Again he was rewarded as she opened her mouth slightly and pressed her lips to his.

Nevver wanted to grab her then and take her on the chair, or better yet, scoop her up in his arms and carry her to the bedroom. But he resisted the urge. He didn't want to overplay it and ruin the moment and destroy the future. He'd done that before--acted too quickly and impulsively and ruined the mood. So, he pulled back slowly and smiled at her, looking her in the eyes. Silently he went and made two more drinks.

*   *   *

Lissa was finishing her third drink now. Never had not taken the third, since he was pretty much drunk before he started on the vodka. They had watched an episode of CSI New York, and now Nevver was waiting for the commercial break in between programs to make his next move.

He got up slowly from the loveseat and made his way to where Lissa was seated in the chair. He knelt down in front of her and gently pushed her pink sweatpants-clad legs apart and wedged his body in between them. He put his hands on her hips as he leaned in and kissed her gently on the mouth. He then moved his head to the right and began kissing and licking her neck. Lissa responded by running her fingers through his hair. Nevver continued kissing her neck, now moving to the other side to where he knew she was more sensitive. She began to breathe heavily and soft moans, barely above a whisper, escaped her mouth. The sound of it made Nevver's heart race.

After some long moments of this he kissed her on the mouth and her lips parted, their tongues darting into each other's mouths. As they kissed passionately, Lissa's hand gripped into a fist, pulling and tugging on Nevver's black hair. His left hand slid up underneath her pink sweatshirt and he grabbed a big, round breast. He cupped it and squeezed gently, then began to pull at her nipple, feeling it get hard as he did so.

His right hand was still on her hip. He grabbed a hold of her sweatpants and pulled gently, silently urging her to take them off. She pushed herself up and allowed him to pull her sweatpants and panties down along her thighs, over her knees, passed the ankles until they were just a pile of fabric on the floor.

Nevver hooked his arms under her knees and pulled her gently towards him so that she was now seated on the very edge of the chair, still leaning back. Blood pounded in his in his head as his excitement rose. He hungrily went down on her, tasting and smelling her sweat, feeling how her body felt pressed against his face. Her breathing and moans came louder now, as she caressed his skull with both hands, digging the nails of her fingers into his scalp, tugging the hair of his head, gently pulling his ears. In a few short minutes both hands gripped into tight fists as she grabbed handfuls of hair and pulled his face hard into her. She let out a yell as she climaxed, Nevver still continued to lick and suck, not wanting this moment to end. Not wanting her fulfillment to end.

To her it started to tickle. She pushed his head away while simultaneously sitting up, pulling her body away. Lissa kept her arms outstretched holding him back. "Give me a minute," she said.

"Okay. I gotta go the bathroom anyway. Be right back," he told her. He walked to the bathroom with a sense of satisfaction. He had pleased his woman and in a few minutes she would be pleasing him.

After relieving himself, Nevver walked back into the living room showing off his erection. But as he neared the chair his drunken mind had a hard time trying to figure out what had happened. The chair was empty. He quickly scanned the living room. Lissa was gone. The pink pile of panties and sweatpants were also missing. The television had been shut off. Puzzled, he glanced towards the bedroom. The door was closed.

Confused, he walked to it, turned the handle and slowly pushed the door open. There was a large, body-sized lump under the covers. *Are you fucking kidding me?* His mind raged. *In two minutes she went from the height of passion to sleeping in the bed. Un-fucking-believable!*

An adrenaline fire exploded within him. Frustration, sexual tension, and the feeling of betrayal fueled the fire of anger. Nevver's alcohol-laden mind went into standby mode. His baser instincts and his body took over his actions.

He grabbed the covers and yanked them back, tearing them from the bed and throwing them to the floor. Melissa lay there in a fetal position, again wearing her matching pink sweatpants and sweatshirt. Her long, blonde hair cascaded across the pink pillowcase. Just the sight of the pink pillowcases and the matching pink sheets infuriated him. To him, just then, the realization that he allowed her to girlify his world, that sleeping in a pink bed was glaring evidence of his recent pussyfication, brought his egocentric rage to bear.

His mind did not register if she was sleeping or awake. He did not wait for her to stir, to ask what was going on. He just acted and reacted. He jumped on her as she lay on her side. He straddled her body and pushed her over onto her stomach, using his strong thighs to clamp on the sides of hers, effectively holding her in place.

Nevver was naked. He had taken all of his clothes off before leaving the bathroom, having anticipated the continuation of their sexual episode. His large hands grabbed once again at the pink sweatpants and yanked them roughly down, exposing her bare buttocks. Now Lissa was definitely awake.

"What the fuck are you doing!?" She yelled as she struggled underneath his weight, trying to buck him off of her, but he was too heavy. Her arms were free so she reached down and grabbed at the top of her sweatpants, trying to pull them back up, anything to stop what was happening. Nevver grabbed her wrists in his hands and bent her arms at the elbows so her forearms were parallel to one another across her back. He grabbed both of her wrists in one hand and clamped down, using his weight to hold her arms in place. With his right hand he grabbed his erection and guided it between her legs.

"Get off of me!" Lissa screamed and squirmed as she felt the head of his erection sliding between her cheeks.

Nevver could feel her wetness and it spurred him on. The strong smell of sex was still in the air. He could still taste her on his lips. The sticky, slipperiness of her vagina begged him to enter. He pushed himself roughly forward and felt it slide into her. He was mounted on top of her, like some great Silverback Ape. He thrust and pounded with all his sexual tension and anger as Lissa still continued her demands for him to stop, to get off of her. She tried to clench her lower region, but that only served to heighten Nevver's sexual pleasure instead of lessening it.

With his free right hand he grabbed at the pink pillow from his side of the bed. He pushed it down over her turned head and face to muffle her shouts. He could feel her body beneath his, pushing and straining, the muscles tensing. She was struggling in vain, there was no way for her to break free. He was too strong. He was too determined.

Nothing in his mind was telling him that it was wrong, that he should stop. He was lost in the moment. His singularly focused mind could not be swayed from its goal. He was going to finish what they both had started.

After a couple short minutes Lissa quit struggling against him. Though her body was still tense, she did not push and rise beneath him. He let go of the pillow but kept it in place over her head. He could still feel her breathing beneath him as he thrust, the sounds of skin slapping mixed with his heavy breathing were the only sounds now.

As he was about to climax the distant thought of him not wearing a condom occurred in his mind. He had always done so, not wanting to get her pregnant. But this time he didn't care. His body tensed and spasmed as all of his sexual energy was let loose inside her. He let out a moan, then a yell, as he continued to thrust during his release. He straddled her for a few moments, still holding her down. He slid himself out of her and pushed himself back, wiping himself off on her pink sweatpants before climbing off the bed.

She lay there almost unmoving. Through drunken eyes he could see her body rise and fall with her breath. She slowly returned to the fetal position, not taking the pink pillow from her head. He watched for a few more seconds as her body seemed to quiver and shake. Then he heard it. Punctuated between large gasps of air were sobs. Though slightly muffled by the pillow, Nevver clearly could tell that she was crying.

Having been sexually satisfied, his mind was now more clear, able to think more rationally. Guilt and regret flooded his chest cavity and entered into his brain.

He started to fell sorry for her, bordering on remorse for his actions, but suddenly his ego suppressed those feelings and replace them with anger.

Well, fuck me, he thought. *That's not how I wanted this to end.*

He figured he could do the whole "I'm sorry, baby. I'll never do it again" thing, but he knew that this relationship was over, and probably had been for a while. There was no sense in pushing on. He had anticipated a bad end to the relationship, something that was common in his life, just not so soon.

He always had a "go bag" prepared for just such an occasion. Simply, it was a duffel bag packed with three day's worth of clothes, $300 in cash, a 9 mm handgun and ammunition, a sharp, tanto-bladed folding knife, and an emergency credit card with $1000 available balance. It was meant as a get-the-hell-out-of-there-quick safety net where he could gab it and "go" within a minute. Something he learned from movies and spy novels. *Useful information,* he thought.

He learned to travel light most of his life. He lived in his car for weeks at a time, once lived in a tent at the state park for an entire summer, couch surfed with friends and family until he wore out his welcome more times than he could count. He would survive.

He dressed quickly, grabbed his go bag from the hall closet and jammed all of his "Nevver 69" gear into a separate duffel bag. He also grabbed the laptop computer and power cord. This took him all of 4 minutes. He stopped by the bedroom and peered inside. Lissa had not moved, though she had wrapped herself up in the pink top sheet and her head now lay on top of both pink pillows.

"I'm sorry, Lissa," he started. But he didn't know what else to say. There was a lot he could say, perhaps even a lot he *should* say. His mind quickly wondered if he should stay. But he pushed that notion aside. It was time to move on. If he stayed she would just be angry and vindictive for days, weeks, maybe even right up to the inevitable end of their relationship, he reasoned. And he wasn't going to put himself through that hell--the cold shoulder, the bitching, the arguing, the animosity. She might even call the cops on him. *Might still call the cops on me,* he thought. The bottom line was damage had been done, and he did not have the wherewithal to try and fix it. He didn't care to.

Without saying another word, Nevver pulled the bedroom door closed, gathered up his bags and his computer and walked out of the apartment for the last time. *I'll miss the cat,* he thought absently as he walked down the stairs and out into the street. The sun was setting and it was growing colder, the wind picking up. *Fan-fucking-tastic,* he thought.

CHAPTER FOURTEEN

The death of winter had finally come. The long months of ice and snow and bitter wind were over. Spring had come quietly but hadn't seemed to stay long. Though it was only May, the summer heat was upon Northern Michigan. Unseasonably high temperatures were welcomed by most after such a long winter. The cold and snow had started in October, well before Halloween. The rain and warmer temperatures did not return until mid April. Though the spike in temperature was met--like seemingly every and any change in climate in Michigan--with a mixture of pleasure, disdain, and complaining of some sort. There was a saying: If you don't like the weather in Michigan, wait five minutes. And inevitably with the change also came the bitching and the complaining. No one in Michigan was ever completely happy about the weather. But, Daniel theorized, it was better to complain about the weather than about each other. At least the weather gave some common ground in all conversations.

Daniel and his restaurant staff had weathered the "slow season" of winter, and with Memorial Day fast approaching they prepared for the "busy season" of Fudgies who were on vacation and Snow Birds returning from their second homes in southern states, mostly Florida and Arizona. The multitude of servers in all Northern Michigan looked forward to the busy time, as it was an opportunity to make good money and hopefully bank it for the slow season. Making $2.65 an hour plus 10 to 20% off the gratitude of patrons made for an uncertain financial future at best.

Daniel was at the small desk that served as the manager's office looking over fresh applications, deciding on which candidates to call for interviews. He needed to add roughly a dozen people to his staff for the season. It seemed like it was a never-ending cycle of hiring, training, coaching, and retraining. In any given day there seemed to always be five things that needed to be done and someone that needed help. Or someone had a complaint. Or no one was answering the phone. Or someone had called in "sick." They usually were never really sick, they just wanted the day off to go to the beach, or whatever. Daniel would have loved to be able to call in sick, to have an extra day off. But that never happened. Too may people depended upon him and his not being there would create too much anxiety for others. He couldn't bring himself to do that to them. But, the work ethic was shit these days, Daniel realized, especially with the younger generation.

Daniel let his mind wander back a few months to when the store first opened. The chaos and stress he'd went through then was now minimized and things were running more smoothly. But he wasn't sure if they would ever be smooth, ever be easy. He missed Faith, working with her.

They had decided that they could not keep the relationship a secret any longer. And knowing the consequences they decided that she should put in her notice and quit. There were lots of rumors swirling about, and Daniel knew it was just a matter time before they were found out--before they were caught--and his career was put in jeopardy because of it.

He had contacts with other restaurants, other managers in town. Faith was a good server and he secured her a job at a family restaurant that served breakfast, lunch, and dinner, working night shifts mainly. She was well received as a new employee, being found friendly and capable. She made friends quickly, but Daniel was uneasy about those friendships. Wary about the kind of people that were drawn to her, and she to them. She seemed to be drawn to the more seedy elements. Those with questionable habits and private lives.

Faith was also still struggling with her kids, and her sanity, Daniel thought. The Klonopin she was on for anxiety seemed to have lost its effectiveness, and she was also having trouble sleeping at night. Her doctor prescribed her Xanax for anxiety, and also wrote her a prescription for Ambien for insomnia. The latter she had been on for just over a week and it seemed to be working, though a couple nights he heard her talking in her sleep, having conversations of which he only heard her side. It was strange, yet interesting. He listened intently to see if she was reliving a memory or her mind was replaying a recent conversation. He tried to glean any information from the ramblings. He was suspicious of her phone calls and relationships that he knew next to nothing about. In the pit of his stomach he knew that there was something not right about their relationship. But he didn't want to think too much on it. He had enough stress with work and paying the bills to have his mind consumed with phantom fears of her infidelity.

Her pain management was another story entirely. Her primary care physician had told her that she needed to find someone new, that he could not treat her any longer. He said the cortisone injections had become ineffective, and the high dosage of acetaminophen had also become ineffective on her chronic pain and would soon start damaging her liver. He was unable, or unwilling, to prescribe her higher and more severe pain management medications. He did, however refer her to another doctor who accepted her as a patient. This physician thought it best if she went on a

Fentanyl patch. It was an Opioid painkiller that was time-released through the skin for around-the-clock pain management. One patch would last up to four days, eliminating the need to take pills every four to six hours. It seemed like a great thing for Faith. She seemed happier, back to her old self. Though the long-term effects were yet to be determined, as she was still on her first month's worth of the prescription.

He had confronted her about the episode during their first--and last--time having sex on the pool table. Faith had said that at first it was great, but for some reason she became anxious and afraid. He asked her if it brought back some bad memory of her being raped on a pool table. She didn't say yes or no, exactly, just that it brought on an anxiety attack and she needed to stop. She apologized and said it didn't have anything to do with him. That he did nothing wrong. Daniel accepted the explanation and said he, too was sorry. They never brought it up again.

Daniel glanced at the clock and saw that it was 10:25 PM. Five minutes until he could lock the door. He set the stack of applications side, and made his rounds. The phone hadn't rang in more than 25 minutes, which was great because it meant that no new orders had come in. All of the touch computer screens were blank: no orders pending.

The conveyor oven had three decks, basically three huge ovens. The bottom conveyor was split into two tracks. Each track could be set at a different speed which allowed it to cook different items at the same time. Hot sandwiches needed to run through the oven at four minutes, while breadsticks and cheese bread sticks needed 6 1/2 minutes. The split track allowed items to go in at the same time and yet still cook at different speeds. The two upper, main ovens were set at the nominal 8 1/2 minute speed for pizzas.

The gourmet pastas were cooked to order on the infrared induction burners in large 14 inch, nonstick frying pans. All of the salads were also made to order by hand. The only thing in the oven now were a couple of employee pizzas.

Daniel contemplated on taking one home for himself and Faith, but decided against it. He was kind of sick of the pizza, and by the time he was finished working and brought it home it would have been sitting in the cardboard box for over an hour. The quality would be crap, and he would have had to reheat it in the oven anyway. And by that time it would be near midnight and he really wasn't up to eating then.

He walked out into the dining room and saw that, too was empty. *Thank you, Lord*, he thought. He quickly took the set of keys out of his pocket and using the Allen wrench he popped the push bar of the two entry/exit doors out, effectively locking them. He saw that the closing servers were tearing down the salad bar and cleaning it. The tables were being wiped down, the floors being vacuumed. He walked into the mens and then the ladies restroom making sure that they were stocked and cleaned and ready to go for the morning. The mirror in the mens room was spotted. Daniel splashed some water onto it and wiped it off in a circular motion with a clean paper towel from the dispenser. The mirror was clean and shiny.

He made his way back into the kitchen area and checked the nightly prep list, ensuring that everything was done and ready for next shift. Then he made his way into the dish room and started helping Matt, whom he nicknamed Dippy, finish the rest of the dishes and pans before moving on to the nightly paperwork and counting the deposit. He hated counting the money and balancing the books, especially so late at night where his mind was drained and worn out from the day. He often had to count the tills and the safe two and three times to make sure that he came up with the same number. One night, he remembered he had come up with a different number four times! He was infuriated and almost left it for the next day. But he took a deep breath and slowly and carefully counted again. The number he came up with matched one of the previous numbers and he figured that was close enough. Deposit done.

Thirty minutes after the last employee left Daniel was finally locking up, shutting off the lights, and setting the alarm. He jogged to his car, enjoying the warm night air. He breathed the spring freshness in. It was a bit humid, but the fresh air was welcomed compared to the hot, enclosed kitchen air and restaurant dining room air conditioning that he had been trapped in for the previous eleven hours. He was nearly exhausted when he climbed in behind the wheel of the Toyota Matrix and started the engine. He hoped that Faith would be in a good mood, maybe even be *in* the mood when he arrived home. He smiled at that thought.

As he drove home he absently noticed the same buildings, the same closed businesses for the night. A routine drive home. The same streetlights, probably the same cars passing him at the same time. He could usually tell by the headlights what car was coming towards him or driving behind him. Certain cars he could tell right away, like a Chrysler 300, a Ford Taurus, or a Chevy Monte Carlo. It wasn't just the lights themselves, but also the vague outline and shadow of the vehicle, of the grill, of the slope of the windshield, the position of the orange running lights. All of these things added to the picture that his mind recognized and remembered.

He was about a mile away from his house when he passed the small gas station/convenience store market. It was closed at that hour, only a few security lights on in the interior of the building. The large lights for the gas pumps were darkened. As he drove by, Daniel noticed a minivan at one of the pumps. *They're closed, you dumbass!* His mind shouted, and Daniel had to laugh out loud. *Stupid Fudgies*, he thought.

Five minutes later he pulled into his driveway and to his alarm he saw that Faith's vehicle was not there. *Where the fuck did she go?* Was his first thought. He was instantly angry. He knew that she still went out, still saw her friends, but he expected her to be home when he got there. Or at least call and let him know what she was doing. That was the courteous thing to do.

His mind flipped though various scenarios of where she was, who she was with, and what she was doing. His mind was not kind. The images were not good, not helpful to his current situation. His mind focused on the worst scenarios as he parked his car and got out.

He walked up to the side door and saw that it was open. Not just unlocked, but open. The kitchen lights were on as well.

He walked in the kitchen and called out her name, hoping that maybe she was there, and for some reason she had loaned her vehicle to her brother or one of her friends. The kitchen had two walls of windows and all six of them were open, the fresh night air blowing through the screens. The smell of summer night air somehow intensified his panic. It seemed to amplify the emptiness of the house. No other sounds were evident: no television, no radio, no one talking. Silence, except for the wind blowing the curtains--*flap, flutter, flap, snap, flap, flutter, flap...*

He heard no reply from his calls. Starting to panic, he quickly jogged through the house, calling out her name in each room he went to. No answer.

Faith was gone.

There was no note that he could see. All of her things were still there as far as he could tell. Her clothes were in the drawers and closet. She hadn't moved out. No sign of a struggle or a robbery. Everything seemed to be where it should be. Except one person was missing.

He pulled his cell phone from his pocket and hit the speed dial for Faith's number. When the phone connected and began to ring his heart sank and his adrenaline and fear skyrocketed. His world seemed shrink in that instant.

He heard her phone ringing from the kitchen.

He ran back to the kitchen, cell phone still held up to the side of his face. He was listening to her phone ring--a portion of the song, *I Alone*, by Live--his ringtone! On the small desk in the corner of the kitchen was a small, purple rectangle lighting up. In the tiny lit window the word *Daniel* could be read.

"Fuck!" He yelled in panic and frustration. *What the fuck do I do?* He thought to himself. He tried to think, he tried to reason where she might have gone at that late of an hour. With no note, no text message, no phone call explaining what she was doing. *Why wouldn't she take her phone?* It didn't make any sense. She *always* had her phone, even if she didn't answer it.

Then it hit him like an icy cold slap in the face. The blood drained from his head making him dizzy for a few moments. He stood frozen in the kitchen as the realization of the situation sank in. *The fucking van at the gas station!*

Oh my God! His mind yelled. He quickly put his phone back in his pocket and grabbed hers off of the desk. He jogged towards the door patting his pants pocket for the car keys. He pulled them free, unlocking the car door with the electronic fob button. He jumped in and started the engine, slamming the door and racing backwards out of the driveway. Gravel spat and spun out from under the tires as he raced down the short gravel road to the pavement. He didn't stop at the first stop sign, he knew nobody was coming. He raced the eighth of a mile to the major road and stopped at that stop sign, scanning left and right for any headlights. There were none. He cranked the wheel to the left and jammed on the gas.

That fucking van, that fucking idiot that was parked at the pumps when the station was closed! That was Faith's *van!* His mind screamed.

How had he not recognized that when he drove past the first time? Yes it was dark and he couldn't tell the color, but he knew the make and model, he felt it was something his mind should have picked up on, even if just subconsciously. But it was so alien of a thing, he didn't even think that she would be gone from the house, let alone at a closed market just over a mile from the house!

Something was wrong. Something was very wrong. *What if the van is gone when I get there? How the fuck will I find her? I have her phone! Why did she leave her phone?* Nothing made sense, and that fact increased his panic. If she wasn't there, he realized, there would be no way for him to find her.

He pushed his car up to 70, he dared to not go much faster than that. As he crested the hill, Daniel stared through the darkness at the empty gas station. There were no cars parked at the pumps. His heart sank for a split second and his mind raced, trying to figure out his next move. Then he saw the shadowy shape of the vehicle. It wasn't parked by the pumps where he had seen it the first time. Now was parked up by the building as if someone had parked there to go in and do some light grocery shopping. In the darkness the van looked just as alien and out of place parked by the side of the building as it had parked by the pumps.

Daniel quickly sped into the vacant lot and pulled up next to the van. No question it was Faith's. The color, the make and model, the dents. The van's engine was running, its headlights on. He jammed his car into park and quickly got out and ran around to the van. He stopped abruptly and walked slowly up to it, instinctively knowing something wasn't right. Faith sat in the drivers seat, her window was down, and she was talking. The radio played at low volume. Daniel peered through the back windows looking for whomever she was talking to. The van was empty. Faith was the only occupant.

He wasn't sure what was going on, or exactly what he should do. He listened to her talk for a few seconds. She was carrying on a conversation. He only heard one side of it: her side. But it was obvious by the way she paused, then continued speaking and by what she was saying that she was answering questions from some phantom passenger.

"Faith?" Daniel said her name as he walked up to her side window, trying not to startle her with his presence.

"Hey, babe. What you up to?" She asked, almost offhandedly. She didn't really seem surprised to see him. Though Daniel took it as a good sign that she recognized him and who he was.

"Who are you talking to?" He asked politely, trying to understand what was going on.

Faith twisted in the drivers seat turning her torso towards the back as she motioned and said, "My sister, and my friends, Melissa and Rachel," almost as if she was introducing them. "We're headed up to the bowling alley to play some pool and do some dancing." She explained.

Daniel got scared for a second. The bowling alley was about 20 minutes away, and it was closed as well at that time. He would not have thought to look for her there. *Thank you, God for helping me find her when I did.* "Um, there's nobody there," he finally told her.

He let the words hang in the air as he read the puzzled look on her face as she absorbed what he had just said. She looked back again. Daniel wasn't sure if she still saw whom she thought was there, or just the empty seats. "Honey, you're alone--no one else is in the van," he said as she looked back at him.

She just sat there with a confused look on her face. She looked at Daniel with questioning eyes, like someone who just awoke from a dream that was so real they didn't know what was really happening.

"Do you know where you are?" He asked her.

"Yes," she said quickly, no hesitation. "I'm at Mickey's," she told him, using the name of the grocery/convenience store. "We were getting cigarettes before we went to the bowling alley."

Daniel's heart skipped a beat. From the time he passed her and laughed at the person parked by the closed pumps until the time he searched the house, realized what was going on, and made his way back to the gas station at least 15 minutes had passed. That was way more than enough time for this imaginary cigarette shopping to have been completed and her and her friends to be on their way. *Thank you, God for small miracles*, he thought.

"Babe," he began, not really sure what to say or what to do. He thought about leaving her van there and coming back to get it the morning. But, he had to work in the morning and was sure they would not have time for all that messing around. And she seemed to be coherent now. "Do you see nobody's in the car with you?"

"Yes," she said though he could tell by the look on her face she was very confused and scared as well. "I don't know where they went--they were just here."

"I think you're having a reaction to your new medication," he told her. "Do you think you can drive home from here?" He asked.

Faith nodded her head in the affirmative, "Yea, I think I'm okay now," she said, but the tone of her voice and look on her face said that she doubted it as much as Daniel did.

"Okay. Were going to go *straight home*," Daniel told her, emphasizing their path. He was afraid that she would start driving and take off in some other direction. With no phone and no way to communicate with her, he would be at the mercy of her whim, watching and following not been able to do anything else. The thought terrified him. He then remembered he had grabbed her phone from the desk. He fished it from his pocket and handed it to her.

"Here's your phone," he said, handing it to her. He looked her in the eyes, trying to gain her undivided attention. "You got that? Straight home. I will follow you. Don't go fast, we're not very far. Okay?" He asked trying to ascertain if she understood what was going on and what was expected of her.

"Okay, babe. I got it. Straight home," she said and managed a smile.

The five minutes it took for them to drive home seemed more like half an hour. Daniel had his windows down and radio off. The cool wind blew across his face as he took deep breaths trying to calm his nerves and focus his mind. The humid temperature had dropped off considerably and it was welcomed. He watched the green van in front of him, focusing on the red taillights. She didn't seem to swerve, was driving at a good pace. And when they got to their access road she used her turn signal. All good signs. He followed her down the road and into their driveway. She parked the van and shut off the lights. Faith got out just as he was pulling up. She stood in the wash of his headlights waiting for him.

In the flood of the bright headlights, Faith looked more like a apparition than a flesh and blood person. Her facial features were gaunt and sunken. Her clothes seemed washed out like an overexposed photograph. Her eyes shown like snowflakes in the beams of light, blotting out their color, as she stared toward him. The expression on her face was nearly unreadable. She seemed to have no expression, just a blank stare.

As he came around the front of his vehicle and approached her she came forward and gave him a hug. Daniel hugged her back. It was then he noticed that she was in her pajamas with a zippered sweatshirt over top, and her white sneakers on her feet. He seemed to tower over her, as her head lay against his chest just below his shoulder. She squeezed him tightly, pressing her cotton-clad body against his. At that moment he pushed her back away from him ever so slightly and kissed her lips. She returned the kiss, pressing her body closer to his.

With reluctance, Daniel broke the embrace. With his arm still around her, he led her toward the still open side door. They walked inside together. She seemed to walk fine, managing the steps with ease.

As they walked into the kitchen Daniel said, "I think you've had a reaction to your new medication. I think you should not take any more of anything until we call your doctor tomorrow."

Faith nodded her head in agreement. "I don't feel well," she said.

That's an understatement, his mind said.

"Why don't you go lie down in bed. I will be there in a minute." *First, I need a beer*, he thought.

"Okay," she agreed, and walked off toward the bedroom.

He watched her walk away as he opened the fridge and grabbed a bottle of beer. He twisted the top off quickly and took the first, satisfying drink. *I don't need this shit*, he thought.

Time to back out, man, his mind told him.

But Daniel just shook the thoughts from his head. He couldn't abandon her now, not when she needed him.

He finished the beer quickly, trying not to think of the day that lay ahead of them. His mind swam with all the things that needed to be done, all the pressures and the stresses that were mounting. Not only his, but Faith's as well. He knew she wasn't capable of facing these problems on her own. And he knew her family and so-called friends wouldn't be there to help her.

He heard her calling from the bedroom. Daniel took a deep breath as he shut off the kitchen lights and walked toward the bedroom. As he walked and started to take off his clothes, he noticed that Faith was already in bed.

"Yes?" He asked.

"I just wanted to know if you were coming to bed now," she asked, her voice quiet and soft. Almost childlike in the way she asked question.

"Yes, right now," he reassured her.

He shut off the bedroom light and climbed into bed next to her. The sheets were cool against the exposed skin of his arms and feet. She immediately scuttled over to him and pressed her pajama-clad body against his. He noticed that she had changed into a different set of pajamas. He also noticed that her feet were icy cold.

"Damn! Your feet are freezing!" He said, in a teasing though serious way.

"Sorry," she said as she pulled her feet from him and worked some covers in between them in an effort to warm them up. She wrapped her arms around him, pulling herself closer to him.

"Thank you for coming to get me," she said as she nuzzled her face to his neck.

Daniel rolled toward her, careful to keep her arms about him. He faced her now. She instinctively wrapped her right leg around his left at the knees. He smiled. He loved how she used even her legs to hug him. It felt right, the closeness. He could taste her breath, minty, as she had brushed her teeth before bed. He kissed her then, softly and with passion. He felt her body and mouth respond to his as she kissed him back. He planned on just cuddling with her, but now, feeling how she was responding to his touch, his baser instincts took over and he kissed her with more force, more passion.

Faith responded in kind. Their tongues intertwined in a frenzy of desire. They melded together for long minutes, mouths hungrily enjoying each other. Soon, Faith's hand wandered down between his legs. She groped and massaged him to full erection.

They smiled at one another as simultaneously they slid down their bottoms. Daniel rolled Faith away from him onto her side. He slid himself close to her, feeling her bare ass against his skin. It was cool, soft, yet firm. He licked his fingers and rubbed the wetness onto her. She shuttered as she felt him slide into her.

She pressed back against him, arching her back. Daniel maneuvered himself so the angle was better where he could push himself all the way in. After a short minute or two it got uncomfortably hot, so Daniel threw off the covers. They both ground against one another in a spoon dance of the flesh. Their moans and heavy breathing spurring each other on.

"Will you get behind me?" Faith asked, looking back at him, still moving with his rhythm. Daniel replied by slowly taking himself out of her and struggling to his knees. Faith did the same. She pulled the two pillows to her and tucked them under her chest. Daniel slowly reinserted himself and they once again started their personal song of sex.

After a few minutes more, Faith cried out and bit at the fabric of the pillowcase as she thrust herself back into him. Daniel continued for thirty seconds more before he finally climaxed into her. They both fell forward, Daniel lay on top of Faith, their bodies still one. They listened to each other's heartbeat and panting for long moments, each lost in their own thoughts, neither saying a word.

After a few minutes, Faith groaned under his weight and Daniel laughed. "Am I squishing you?" he asked, knowing the answer.

"I need to go to the bathroom," she said. Daniel took is cue and rolled off of her. He lay there and let her use the bathroom before he got up and cleaned himself off. He could have used the other bathroom, but was too lazy, too spent. The smell of their bodies was thick in the air. Daniel smiled. He didn't know what time it was and right then he didn't care. In fact, all of his cares were gone just then. At least for that moment. *Happiness is...,* he thought as he fell asleep and drifted into a warm, dreamful sleep.

CHAPTER FIFTEEN

The Fourth of July had come and gone. Daniel had to work through it, as usual. The busy vacation season was in full swing. Daniel was still working long hours, still clocking over 75 hours a week, having to work six days for the past couple weeks. Not only was he under the burden of being the top manager of the store, he found himself stuck running a position every shift as well. The pay for hourly employees was mediocre and was hard to keep decent employees, though the turnover seemed to have stopped for the time being. Even assistant managers-- though paid decently because Daniel had insisted on a higher wage for a better caliber of leader--were still hard to keep motivated, and thus their performance could've been considered lacking on most days. Sometimes they were just part of the crew and not leading or managing, Daniel thought.

But today was his one day off for the week. And Daniel was enjoying it. *Not going to think about or care what happens to the restaurant or any of its people...not today,* he thought.

The sky was a light blue, punctuated by only wisps of white clouds. A jet contrail painted twin ivory arcs across the backdrop some twenty thousand feet above. The afternoon sun was hot and it continued to bake the already dry ground. He had two sprinklers running, in a vain attempt to water his lawn and the fresh grass seed and fertilizer he had spread earlier in the day. Daniel had been trying to turn his so-called lawn of field grass that was hard, scratchy, and uninviting into a real lawn of lush, soft, green grass that begged bare feet to walk upon it. So far his weeks of effort had been in vain.

He sat in a folding deck chair just off of the side door warming and coloring his pale skin in the rays, sweat beading on his skin and soaking into his t-shirt and shorts. A Michelob Ultra was in his hand, his fourth of the day so far. It was just past two in the afternoon. He wore a black baseball cap with a Superman logo embroidered on the front, black, polarized sunglasses shielding is eyes as he watched the breeze blow the leaves in waves through the forest some two hundred yards away. The breeze brought with it the smells and sounds of summer: fresh cut grass and the hum of a lawnmower in the distance, blooming flowers, the rustle of the leaves, the sun-garnished scent of clean air, kids yelling as they played.

He thought of building a much needed garage. He fantasized about having a bonus bedroom above it. Maybe for Faith's eldest son so he could have a private space away from his considerably younger siblings. He envisioned a paved driveway that would make snow removal immensely easier and cut down on the amount of sand tracked into the house. All of these dreams would cost money, however, and Daniel was strapped for cash and his available credit was shrinking as his credit card debt rose. Faith had a few recent court dates and fines she had to pay, mostly child support related, though some were because of the Christmas Incident, as they referred to it. Though it wasn't his obligation he paid anyway in an effort to keep what he had insofar as his love relationship with Faith was concerned. To keep her out of jail and thus incur more court debt and risk her health.

Faith was not working at all now, having filed for disability under her doctor's recommendation. Her condition would not get better, and probably would only deteriorate she was told. She had gotten a disability lawyer and they had started submitting the paperwork. But because of this she could not work at all, which left Daniel to pay for everything. And she was told it could take *years* for them to work through the system and get the desired outcome.

He shook his head, trying to rid his mind of these thoughts. It was a wonderful day and he did not want to waste it brooding over what had to be done, what should be done, and what he wished would happen.

He pulled his LG flip phone from his pocket and checked the time, while simultaneously checking to see if he'd received any messages. No messages.

Faith had taken his vehicle to run into town to pick up her prescriptions. Her van had quit running months before and was still parked in the backyard. Grass and weeds growing up around it. Her brother was supposed to come out and diagnose it, as he was a capable backyard mechanic. But he had not done so yet, and so the van sat. Daniel had given her $20 to pay for her three prescriptions, which were covered under her Medicaid insurance, which left enough money for her to get a pack of cigarettes and some Orange Crush soda. Her favorite.

She had been gone over two hours. That was way more time than needed if the prescriptions were ready to be picked up, that is. He had texted her over half an hour ago asking her what was taking so long. Her reply came back quickly and just said: waiting for pharmacy to process insurance.

He accepted that, though he still worried about his vehicle. From conversations they had, Daniel gathered that Faith had owned, or driven on a regular basis, four or five different vehicles. All of which she had crashed and destroyed. None of the incidents were her fault, however, she told him with much sincerity. Daniel doubted that. When he had ridden with her he noticed that she was a distracted driver, snaking within her own lane, hardly keeping a straight vector. *Scary*, he thought.

He was beginning to have his fill of the hot sun. Daniel took a few deep breaths of the clean, warm air before folding up his chair, placing it beside the propane grill, and going into the house. It was immediately cooler. Daniel's body welcomed the change in temperature.

Since he had some time before Faith returned he decided to watch a movie. He grabbed another beer from the refrigerator before going to the living room and turning on the entertainment system. He knelt down in front of the DVD cabinet and opened the double doors.

Stored within it on sixteen shelves were dozens of movies. Daniel wasn't obsessive compulsive so they were not arranged in alphabetical order, nor by genre. They were just stored, though he did manage to have most comedies together and his favorite action movies were grouped next to each other as well. He scanned shelf by shelf, mentally reading the titles and making a split-second decision whether that was the right movie for then or not. There were comedies, action movies, Science Fiction, a few dramas, even big screen cartoons like *Shrek*.

Daniel looked for *Hoffa*, starring Jack Nicholson and Danny DeVito, also directed by the latter. He couldn't find it. He scanned again and again, then a third time going more slowly thinking that perhaps he may have missed it. It wasn't there. The missing movie angered him, as he knew it was just there. Strange.

Planes, Trains, and Automobiles, the John Candy and Steve Martin comedy classic was the next title he searched for. Frustratingly he came up with the same result. The movie was gone.

"What the hell is going on?" He yelled to no one but himself.

He would have to have a conversation with Faith when she returned. *If she borrowed them to somebody, why wouldn't she tell me?* He thought. Their absence didn't make sense, and it frustrated him.

He settled on *Training Day*, the performance that finally won Denzel Washington an Oscar. He drained the beer that was gently sitting on the carpeted floor next to him as he put the DVD in the player. As the machine went through it starting cycle, Daniel went to the kitchen grabbed another beer. He thought about making some microwave popcorn, but decided he was too lazy to put forth the effort right then.

The humidity from the outside could be felt on the interior of the house now. In the master bedroom there was a small window air conditioner and a TV with a DVD player as well. Daniel briefly thought about moving his movie in there and turning on the air, but he knew that if he did that he would just fall asleep and he didn't want to do that. Not yet.

As he made his way to the soft, leather couch, Daniel pulled the flip phone from his pocket, glanced at the screen--no messages--and set it on the coffee table. He kicked back and put his feet up on the table as one of his current favorite movies began to play.

      *   *   *

The sun was in the last stages of its descent toward the horizon. Even with the evening breeze the humidity was high and the temperature was still hovering near 80°. Daniel had fallen asleep, though he did watch the entire movie and then another before the alcohol driven sleep overtook him. He slept on the couch with a fan blowing on him. He was wakened when Faith came home and announced her presence loudly. "Babe! Babe! I'm finally home!" She yelled in her smoky, crackled voice.

Daniel sat up, blinking the sleep from his eyes, trying to clear his head. The alcohol he had drank had mostly worn off. He grabbed his phone and checked the time: 7:47 PM. *Wow, I must have been tired, I slept for over three hours*, was his first thought. *Where the fuck did she go for eight hours?* Was his second. His adrenaline and anger spiked.

She's in a good mood and she just got home. Hear her out before you jump all over her shit. You don't want to get into a huge argument, his mind warned him.

"Hey," he called back, trying to keep his voice light and friendly.

She walked into the living room, smiling. She was wearing short jean shorts and a black tank top over a black bra, the straps of which were fighting for the same space between her neck and shoulders. Worn black leather sandals adorned her feet. The metallic blue on her toenails matched her fingernails, both seemed freshly painted. She walked over to where he was seated and leaned awkwardly over to give him a kiss. It was a peck on the lips, but Daniel still tasted cigarettes. He smelled her perfume and body spray and something in his loins stirred as he felt her closeness.

He quickly grabbed her around the waist and pulled her towards him and gave her a longer kiss, though still closed mouthed.

"What the hell took you so long?" he asked as she stood upright. He couldn't help himself, he had to ask.

"Oh, God, it took *forever* at the pharmacy. They said it wasn't time for me to get a refill, so I had to argue with them about that. So, then they had to call my doctor and of course they didn't answer the phone, so we had to wait until they returned the call. Then they wanted to charge me $280 for the scripts, so I flipped out on them over that!" she explained.

"What? You've gotten them before without a problem, why the hassle now?" Daniel asked.

"They said Medicaid don't cover the patches any more! After I waited over two hours to get things sorted out they told me this would be the last time I would get them without paying full price!" she told him, the anger and frustration in her voice conveying her distress. "Now, I gotta make a doctors appointment so they can reevaluate me to prescribe something that Medicaid *will* cover," she continued.

"That really sucks," Daniel replied. But his suspicion and anger was still not satisfied by her explanation. "But why were you gone so long? All that hassle doesn't explain the other hours you were gone," he scolded.

She walked away from him toward the kitchen as she began further explanation. Daniel followed her.

"I went to my brother's, cuz he had the money he owed me," she told him. "Then I went shopping and got some food and some soda."

"So, do I get the $20 back I gave you then?" Daniel knew the answer before he asked the question, but he wanted to see her squirm a bit.

"Ahhh....I did need it for my prescriptions, and for cigarettes, like you said. My brother didn't give me a lot, but I got us soda, and some hamburger for dinner tomorrow. I figured you could grill them," she said.

He ignored the comment of the groceries and asked, "Did you put gas in the car?"

Faith hesitated a moment before answering, "A little, but I used it going to my brothers and back."

Of course, he thought. *And whatever else you did being gone all day. My only day off! I should have written down the mileage before she left. Next time I will.*

He watched her put the meager groceries away, thinking. His mind wandered, making up scenarios of what she might have actually been doing all day. On his only day off. He wanted to spend time with her and hopefully have sex, but it looked like neither was going to happen. The day was over and the humidity was hanging heavy upon him. He was still tired. His mind was tired. The near constant frustration of work and Faith's drama was exhausting.

"I'm going to go turn the air on and lie down and watch some TV," he told her.

Faith stopped putting things away and looked at him. She had a look of slight confusion and he detected a hint of disappointment on it as well. "Oh, okay," she said. "I'll be in in a little while."

Daniel went into the bedroom and closed the door behind him. He walked to the lone window and switched on the air conditioner. The unit shook and rattled as it came to life, the fans whirring as it began to blow mechanically cooled air into the room. Daniel stood in front of it for a few seconds, his body wet with sweat, absorbing and enjoying the coolness.

He stripped down to his underwear and laid down on the bed. He grabbed the remote and turned on the television and the satellite receiver. He flipped through the channels and settled on a movie already in progress, *Ronin*, starring Robert DeNiro.

His thoughts drifted to Faith's explanation of where she'd been all day. It didn't add up, didn't make sense. He could've gone with her, he supposed. But since it was his only day off he didn't want to spend part of it in the car, at the pharmacy. *Maybe I should have*, he thought. *Then, at least I'd know the truth.*

The movie was nearing its end as Daniel's attention flipped between what was on the screen and what was playing through his mind. With the drone of the air-conditioner he could not hear anything in the other room. The sun was down now, and had been for a few minutes. For some reason that Daniel couldn't justify, he suddenly felt worried and overcome with anxiety.

His heart began to race and his breathing became heavier. *Should I go check on her?* He thought. It had only been an hour since she'd been home. He didn't want to seem controlling, or untrusting. He didn't want to give her a reason, or excuse, to hide things from him. He felt she was already doing that on her own. He lay there in the coolness on top of the covers, brooding. He let the thoughts battle in his mind for another 10 minutes before finally getting up off the bed and going to see what Faith was doing.

When he opened the door to the bedroom a blast of warm, humid air assaulted him. It smelled like wet cotton. He stepped through the blanket of heat and closed the door behind him. The sound of the air-conditioner was muffled now. "Faith?" He called once, then again. No answer.

The other side of the house, where the two bedrooms and guest bathroom were located, was dark. In the living room area the TV and stereo were off, no lights were on. The pool table had its cover on it and on top of that folded clothes. The kitchen light was on. Daniel walked into the kitchen expecting to find her there. The kitchen was empty.

Daniel quickly scanned the room and saw that her purse and phone were sitting on the large dining table along one row of windows that overlooked the driveway. From the light of the kitchen that spilled out those windows he could see his car was parked in the driveway.

That's good, he thought. *At least she didn't take off in the car again. She's probably just smoking a cigarette before bed*, he reasoned.

He walked towards the side door at the far end of the kitchen and noticed that it was ajar. The outside light was on. Daniel walked up to the screen and looked out before exiting. Just off the low, wooden porch on the sand and gravel between the house and the shed, lying there on the ground was Faith.

He stood there, his mind absorbing what he was seeing. She wasn't lying on the ground, exactly. She was more or less in a kneeling position, though her torso was folded forward on top of her thighs, and tilted to the side. Both arms were slack, her hands--one palm up the other palm down--rested back by her ankles. Her head lie directly on the ground, her right cheek planted in the dust. He couldn't see her face, only the back of her head. Her short black hair was coated with a thin layer of sand.

Daniel knew that her medication would sometimes knock her out, especially when she had just gotten a prescription. But this was something different. This was odd. His mind snapped back and his body lurched forward, pushing the door open. He jogged the few feet to her and knelt down beside her. He was in bare feet with only his underwear on. The stones of the driveway dug into his feet and then his knees. The pain only seemed to intensify his growing alarm.

He nudged Faith in an effort to wake her. She did not respond. He bent his head closer to hers. In the darkness awash by the small light on the side of the house and that of the kitchen that bled through the windows, Daniel could see that Faith's mouth was open. Her lips were pale, though he couldn't tell if that was from the sand and dirt or because of lack of oxygen.

Adrenaline and panic spiked through his body.

His heart began to race fast as he yelled, "Faith! Faith!" Trying to wake her.

There was no response. He pushed on her back, rocking back and forth with one hand as he continued to say her name. Her body was warm, though it felt heavy, like trying to roll a 40 pound bag of dog food.

You have to get her inside, his mind instructed him.

Daniel got up quickly and positioned himself behind her. He straddled her and bent over at the waist and the knees. He grabbed her under the armpits and hooked his hands around her shoulders. He pulled upright, straining against the limp weight. He had no problem picking her up and playfully carrying her around, usually on the way to the bedroom, but this was different. With no help from her muscles she seemed twice as heavy. Daniel grunted as he struggled to unfold her body to a half standing position. The heels of her sandals made furrows in the dirt and dust as he walked backwards, pulling her towards the porch and the house.

He hesitated, uncertain of how he was going to open the door. *Fuck it*, he thought as he let her fall as gently as he could to the wooden porch. He quickly went to the storm door and opened it, sliding the small metal catch to hold the cylinder and the door open. He then went back to her limp body, grabbing her underneath the arms as he had before. He pulled her into the doorway, past the washer and dryer and into the kitchen and lay her down on her back next to the dining table.

He heard a ragged gasp come from Faith. She took in one large, deep breath. The sound was almost a moan and it terrified him. It was strange and unexpected.

That's a good sign, sort of, his mind told him. At least she's breathing.

Daniel saw that though she was covered in sand and dust, her skin was pale and her lips were a bluish-gray. *Oh fuck me*, he thought in panic. *She's O-D-ing on me!*

Daniel watched and listened, his mind flipping through options of what he should do.

Maybe it's time to let her go...You didn't create this problem, but it may be a way for you to get out of the mess you're in, his mind reasoned.

No! I can't just let her die! his thoughts screamed in his head as he tried to think clearly. The adrenaline had burned off any remnants of alcohol or sleepiness that lingered within him, but his mind was now foggy with alarm, anxiety and uncertainty. His world seemed to shrink and only this moment and the next few mattered.

She did not seem to be breathing now. He quickly knelt down beside her, trying to remember the CPR training he had in high school. He traced a hand up her stomach to her rib cage then positioned a palm on her sternum. He began compressions. He pressed with both palms five times, then with his left hand under her neck he gently pushed her forehead down with his right to open her airway. Just before he was about to pinch her nose and blow into her mouth her body rose up slightly as she took in another large, ragged breath.

The sound again unnerved him. It sounded like a wild animal wailing in panic. His mind reasoned that it was a sound a body makes when it fights for life, as Faith's desperately tried to drag in life-sustaining oxygen. He calculated that she was only breathing once like this every minute.

Not good, man, his mind told him. If you're gonna save her you better get on the phone and get some help quick!

With his mind's prompting, Daniel got up quickly and ran to the small desk on the other side of the kitchen and grabbed his cell phone. He quickly dialed 911.

The operator came on and asked what his emergency was. A male voice.

"Ah, my girlfriend is unconscious and she's not breathing," he began. "Well, she's breathing about once a minute," he explained.

"Where is she?" The operator asked.

"I found her outside in the driveway, but I brought her in the house. She's on the floor in the kitchen," Daniel told him. As he was speaking Faith's body again drew in a ragged, ghostly breath.

"Is that her breathing?" The operator asked. He could hear the haunting sound through the phone.

"Yes. She's doing that about once a minute is all."

"What is your address?" The operator asked. Daniel told him. "Is she on any medication?"

"Yes," Daniel replied. He was trying to keep his voice calm, though he knew it was cracking and that worry and sadness were bleeding into his words. He didn't know if she was dying right before his eyes, and he was having a hard time processing what was going on.

"I'm dispatching an ambulance to your location...What kind of medication is she taking?" The operator asked. Daniel could hear clicking of keys as the operator typed.

"Ummm, she's...she's on a Fentanyl patch," he began, his voice cracking and breaking. "She also takes...Xanax for anxiety...and I think something for blood pressure," he managed to say.

Faith's body again pulled in a large lungful of air, the sound like a gasping, drowning person struggling to stay alive. Daniel looked down at her, her skin was pale, her lips still blue-gray. Her eyes remained closed. He knelt down beside her and grabbed her hand. It was cool to the touch, clammy.

"The ambulance should be there within a few minutes," the operator told him.

Time seemed to stop as he looked down at her. He noticed the slackness of her face, how the lines and wrinkles seemed pronounced without the facial muscles active. Her makeup which she applied heavy looked even more so against her pale, oxygen-deprived skin. He imagined this is how she would look in a coffin.

She was motionless, expressionless. Though as Daniel looked at her he did not get the impression of peacefulness that one hopes comes with death. He thought that perhaps in this teetering between life and the afterlife there was no peace, that peace only came after you were totally on the other side and had let go of this world completely.

The 911 operator was speaking to him, asking him how Faith's condition was, if there was any change. Daniel absently answered the questions with one-word answers, not really focusing on what was being asked.

Then Daniel saw the lights. Red and white and his eyes detected orange as well. They spun and flashed, signaling the paramedics' arrival. The big truck pulled in behind Daniel's vehicle. He got up from beside her and watched through the kitchen windows as two men got out and approached the side door that was still open.

"They're here now," Daniel said in the phone.

"Would you like me to stay on the line with you?" The operator asked.

Daniel wasn't really listening, his mind was still lost in the fog of fear and confusion. "No," he managed to say.

"She'll be okay. She's in good hands. Don't worry," the operator assured him before breaking the connection.

The two paramedics entered with equipment in hand. One had what looked to be a fishing tackle box, and the other a canvas tool bag. They struggled to find a place to set up, one on each side of Faith as where she lay there was not much room between the wall and the table. Simultaneously they began to rummage through their equipment cases. One grabbed a sealed syringe and tore open the package and prepared an injection of something. The other grabbed scissors and immediately began to cut Faith's shirt and bra off.

What the fuck? Daniel yelled in his mind. *That's a new fucking bra, she's gonna be pissed! I could've took her clothes off of her, you assholes didn't need to destroy them!*

He watched as the fat, hairy EMT with the scissors pulled the fabric from underneath her and away from her, exposing her breasts and bare torso. Daniel detected a leering glint by both of them as they looked at her half naked form. A flash of anger filled him. He wanted to say something, but he bit his tongue.

The syringe was filled now. The EMT found a vein in her right arm and administered the dosage. Daniel cringed as he watched the needle slide into the bulging vein in the crook of her arm opposite her elbow. Within seconds Faith awoke and tried to sit up. Her eyes were open and fluttering, trying to adjust. Her mind was awash in confusion, trying to figure out what was going on, who these men were. Daniel noticed her breathing seemed to be back to normal and she was speaking, though it was unintelligible, like she was talking in her sleep. Daniel breathed a sigh of relief as he watched as Faith was pulled back from the edge of death.

The fat EMT urged her to lay down and explained who they were. Movement suddenly caught Daniel's attention. A figure appeared in the doorway, walked into the kitchen and stood next to the EMT that was putting the syringe in a red plastic bag. Daniel was confused, almost scared. The late arrival was a Michigan State Trooper.

He was tall, clad in the dark blue and gray of the state police, the large cop hat sitting on his head. "Mr. Gibson, has she gotten any prescriptions lately?" The trooper asked.

"Yes, just this afternoon," Daniel told him.

"Could you get them for me?" The trooper asked, all business. The officer's cold, blue eyes seemed to bore into Daniel's.

"Sure," Daniel said as he left the kitchen and went toward the guest bathroom where Faith kept her meds. *Why the fuck did they send the cops?* He wondered.

Daniel quickly found the box of the Fentanyl patches and returned to the kitchen, handing the box to the trooper. The trooper examined the box and looked inside.

"You say she just got these today?" He asked.

"Yes, this afternoon."

"Why are there two patches missing?" The trooper asked accusingly.

"What? What do you mean?" Daniel asked, confused, his mind was teetering between dread and frustration. Just a half hour before he was ready for bed, hoping for some sex, but not planning on it. Ready to put this day behind him and try to prepare himself for the work day that lay ahead. But now he was forced to deal with this: his girlfriend was apparently overdosing on her meds and was near death when he found her. And to top it off it seemed like this cop was looking at him like he did something wrong!

"I mean this box contained five patches, but there are only three left," the trooper told him, as he tilted the box to show Daniel only three sealed packages remained.

"I don't know...Why would she use two?" Daniel asked even more confused.

The trooper just looked at him, then to the EMTs, then back to him. It was like he was being assessed, but the trooper remained silent. Then after a few seconds he asked, "Where does she administer the patches?"

"Usually on her lower back, or on the back of her upper thigh," Daniel told him.

With that information one EMT asked Faith to roll on her side, which she did reluctantly. They examined her and only found one patch on her lower back. Her shorts were high enough that they could see her bare legs and upper part of her thighs. A second patch was not found on her body.

"Could you bring me the trash from the bathroom, to see if it contains the packaging of the patches," the trooper asked him. Daniel did as he was instructed and came back the trash. It had been changed very recently, so the only contents were a few cotton swabs, a couple pieces of discarded tissue, and two white plastic wrappers that had recently contained Fentanyl patches.

The trooper eyed Daniel suspiciously as he and the EMTs talked in low voices with Faith. She seemed coherent and aware of what was going on. Daniel could tell she was embarrassed being naked in front of the strangers. She crossed her arms and covered herself as best she could. Finally, the thinner EMT seemed to notice her discomfort and dug a hospital gown from his case and laid it over top of her.

"What was wrong with her?" Daniel asked no one in particular.

The cop seemed a little puzzled, like he was in the presence of an idiot. "Her body was shutting down due to a narcotic overdose," he said matter-of-factly, a hard edge to his voice.

Daniel looked at the EMTs, puzzled, not accepting--not wanting to accept--that answer. They all read the question on his face. "We know this because when I administered Narcan she came right out of it," the EMT explained. "Narcan is a drug that immediately stops and counteracts the effects that an opiate has on the body."

Daniel couldn't argue with the results. He witnessed how once the drug was administered within a few seconds she was awake and breathing normally. As Daniel's mind processed that information one EMT left only to return a few minutes later pushing a gurney. The trooper walked over to the EMT and the two had a quick discussion. Daniel could not clearly hear what was being said, partially because the blood thumping through his head with each beat of his heart obscured his ability to hear, and because the two men were purposely talking in low voices, *And probably code as well*, he thought. Then the Trooper left. Daniel watched him walk to his cruiser and drive away.

"We're going to take her to the hospital and have her checked out by a doctor," he was told. With that said, the EMTs helped Faith onto the gurney, covered her with a blanket and strapped her in. They proceeded to push her awkwardly through the doorway and out to the ambulance and loaded her into the back.

Daniel watched in silence, his mind reeling. It felt surreal standing in his kitchen, the flashing lights of the ambulance signaling to everyone who could see that something was wrong. The strobe lights were hypnotizing. He imagined then that they were programming his mind like some Manchurian Candidate.

We should be so lucky, his mind commented. Unfortunately, you are stuck making your own decisions my friend.

One EMT walked back to the house after a few minutes. "Mr. Gibson?" He said getting Daniel's attention. "She is worried that you're not going to go to the hospital and get her."

Daniel was puzzled. *Of course I'm going to the hospital to get her*, he thought. He was not sure why she was afraid that he wouldn't be there for her. He was always there for her. He wasn't like the rest of her so-called friends who abandoned her when she was in real need. He told the EMT to assure her that he would be there, that he would follow the ambulance to the hospital.

Daniel suddenly realized that he was nearly naked. He had to laugh at himself. *No wonder they're acting a little weird*, he thought. He quickly dressed and grabbed his wallet, his keys and his cell phone and headed out the door. The ambulance was already on its way. Daniel climbed into the Toyota, started the engine and headed off after the ambulance.

The night air was thick and warm. Daniel pressed the buttons for the electric windows and rolled all four down. The wind was welcomed for more than the cooling effect it had. The sound seemed to help massage his mind and calm his thoughts.

I need a drink! he thought.

No time for that. A stress headache was pulsating in his brain now. He looked at the radio for the time: seven minutes past ten pm. Thankfully he didn't have to work until noon, but it was going to be a long day. He pushed those thoughts away as he focused on trying to catch the ambulance. He didn't really need to, he knew, as he was looking at sitting in the ER for probably a couple hours before Faith was released, if she wasn't admitted.

Few cars passed him as he trailed behind the big, blocky ambulance. It rode with only its running lights on, no emergency lights, no siren. They drove the speed limit. It was no longer an emergency. They were now little more than an expensive taxi ride. *This is one of the worst days!* he thought.

Time to decide what's best for Daniel, his mind told him.

"I can't abandon her now," he said aloud. "That's not who I am."

Maybe it should be...echoed in his head in reply.

"Maybe I am supposed to help her. Maybe God wants me here because she needs me," he spoke to his mind.

Maybe...Maybe she doesn't want to be helped...Maybe you're better off alone...

Maybe, he thought to himself. *Maybe a lot of things.*

There was too many variables, too many things to think about. Daniel closed his eyes for a few seconds, trying to will the battling thoughts away. He kept both hands steady on the wheel, picturing the road awash in his headlights, how the big, square taillights of the ambulance looked in the near distance. He tried to slow his heart rate. He opened his eyes and saw that he had maintained his speed and distance, and drove accurately for those few seconds. He managed to smile at himself.

There was a three-way battle raging between his heart, his head, and his penis.

He felt that his heart was telling him to stay his course, to keep on moving forward in the relationship. Keep trying to give Faith a better life, show her that there was good in the world and a better way could be had.

He heard his mind telling him it was way past time to let her go her own way. He heard that she was pulling him down in several ways, that the train was bound to crash one day and he'd better get off of it before it did.

His dick, on the third hand, was urging him to stay with her for the sex and companionship. Even it wasn't living together, he should find a way to keep her close and intimate.

It seemed, like most of his gender, the part of his body with the least amount of mass usually won the arguments.

Daniel tried to numb his thoughts by concentrating on the back of the ambulance, as the wind continued to blow and whistle through the open windows. The temperature and humidity had dropped now, and Daniel was a little chilled. He thought of rolling the windows up, but figured the discomfort he felt was probably a good thing at that point.

He watched from a quarter mile back as the ambulance pulled into the hospital emergency parking. He pulled in shortly after and found a place to park. He sat in his vehicle, in silence, as he rolled the windows up and shut the engine off. He listened to the ticking of the engine as it began to cool.

Fuck! I don't want to be here right now, don't want to deal with this shit! his thoughts raged. He thought of punching his dashboard in frustration and anger, but dismissed the action as he didn't want to hurt his hand or damage his car. Neither thing would help his situation, only give him more grief to deal with.

He took several deep breaths, trying to calm himself before he mustered the fortitude to get out and go into the hospital. "In for a penny, in for a pound," he said to himself.

Yea, but the *pound* is a fist slamming you in the back of your head, his mind commented.

*   *   *

2 1/2 hours of sheer boredom almost drove him mad. Daniel hated hospitals. He hated the smell, mostly. It smelled of disinfectant. It smelled of old age. It smelled of sickness, and death. He was always slightly worried that he would become ill or infected just being in a place filled with so much sickness. By their nature, hospitals were nearly void of happiness and joy. He could not see himself working in a hospital, ever. In fact, Daniel very rarely went to the doctor.

I'll probably die from a curable disease, he thought to himself as he looked around at the white walls punctuated with colored pictures of various types: a summer scene of Little Traverse Bay from the Petoskey side looking towards Harbor Springs; an abstract water-color painting of what seemed to be an oak tree ablaze in autumn splendor; a tasteful advertisement for the Gas Light District on a snowy night. The pictures had the desired affect of calming as well as promoting the local area. Daniel appreciated them for the first hour, then they became an annoyance, like everything else he looked at in the ER waiting room.

He was tired. Tired of sitting in the uncomfortable chair. Tired of smelling the mingled, cloying scents that seemed to coagulate into a singular, gagging assault on his sinuses. He was tired physically and wanted to sleep. He was tired mentally and desperately wanted to *stop* thinking about everything. Because of his innate need to have control, to have things make sense, Daniel's mind was constantly working out scenarios, thinking of solutions to the various problems. In his mind's eye he would create possible paths and take them to a probable conclusion, then determining whether that path was truly possible and should or should not be taken. Daniel's frustration and stress levels had spiked and had stayed there for most of the time he was waiting, and thinking. Then he hit an invisible wall.

All he wanted to do then was collect Faith and go home and sleep. Right then he wished he could sleep for days, weeks if possible. He didn't want to think about Faith's drama...about work...about the bills that were due...about the cat litter that needed to be cleaned...about the laundry that needed to be done...about if he had energy drinks for the week ahead...about the next day, the next step in his life.

Almost as abruptly as the stress and anxiety had filled him, it subsided, leaving him drained and spent. His body felt like he had just worked a 14 hour day, and his mind was thick and unresponsive like pudding left on the counter to congeal and thicken beyond the point of rational consumption.

He pushed himself up from the chair and began to pace the floor. His body was stiff and sore. His feet and ankles ached. It took concentrated effort just to lift his foot up and allow it to fall back to the floor, one foot after the other. Within a few minutes a nurse came through a doorway and stood, catching Daniel's attention.

"Are you here with Faith Collins?" The woman asked. She was dressed in pink scrubs, wearing pink sneakers. Her dishwater blonde hair pulled back in a ponytail. Daniel noticed that she, too looked tired.

Daniel smiled at the question. *I hope I haven't lost my faith*, he thought to himself. Before his mind could ponder that notion he answered, "Yes," hoping that she was being released.

"Did you happen to bring any clothes for her?" The nurse asked.

Daniel stood frozen. He felt like an ass. *Nope, sure didn't!* He thought. *Why would I do that? I only watched the EMTs cut all of her clothes off her before they stuffed her into the back of the ambulance. Why would I think to bring clothes? Stupid.*

"No, I guess I didn't think about it. I should have." He let his words hang in the air, not saying anything more.

"It's all right, we'll find something for her to wear home. She'll be out in just a few minutes," she reassured him.

"Thank you," Daniel replied. *Yes, finally! I can go home and get some sleep.*

A few short minutes later, Faith came shuffling out of the doorway. She was stressed in a baby-blue hospital scrub bottom and an oversized white T-shirt presumably from the lost and found. She looked like she had just gotten up from a nap, her hair was unkempt, her makeup smeared. But her features were drawn, her eyes tired. She looked anything but rested. Without saying a word she walked up to Daniel and wrapped her arms around him. Instinctively he hugged her back. Her hair smelled of the hospital.

"Thank you for coming to get me," she said, still clinging to him.

"I'm sorry for not bringing you clothes," he told her. "It didn't even occur to me."

"It's okay, they had these for me. I just want to go home, okay?"

With that he helped her walk out of the emergency room and to the Toyota. He awkwardly helped her get into the passenger side. *It's like helping a 90-year-old woman*, he thought as he felt her frailty beneath his hands as he guided her down into the seat. *What is she going to be like in another 10 years?* He thought.

They drove in silence back to the house. Daniel had questions, but he knew she wasn't about to answer any of them yet. He focused on the fact that she was okay, that she had survived the accidental overdose.

Holy shit! he thought as the realization of what had happened hit him once again. *She almost died, right in front of me! What if I had fallen asleep?*

He let that thought float for long minutes as his mind went down that path, the one that was not taken. He imagined finding her dead body in the morning, still laying in the dirt of the driveway. He conjured images of a police investigation, maybe even an arrest. He thought of the funeral and her children and their fathers being there, her mother, sister and brother...They were not good thoughts. He shook his head to erase the images in etch-a-sketch fashion, focusing on his driving as he neared the house.

Once there, Daniel again had to help her out of the vehicle, up the steps and then back in the house. He helped her shuffle-walk to the bedroom and she immediately crawled into bed.

"I'll be back in a couple minutes," he told her. Daniel went to lock up the house and shut the lights off, but he stopped at the refrigerator for beer first. His head still hurt and his mind was still flipping through all of the things that he was worrying about. *I gotta get some sleep. None of this shit will be settled tonight*, he thought as he drained the beer quickly and joined Faith in bed.

As he pulled the covers over him, Daniel could smell the hospital scent wafting from Faith's now sleeping form. Ignoring the smell he rolled onto his side towards her and put his arm around her. To try and calm his mind he focused on a blank, white sheet of paper, pushing all other thoughts out. Within a few minutes his mind finally shut down and he drifted into a deep sleep.

CHAPTER SIXTEEN

H e unzipped the flap to the small, four-man dome tent and stuck his head out into the warm, late morning air. The smell of summer sunshine carried by the warm breeze mixed with the scent of dirt, the earth, the bark of the trees, and the harsh charred smell of lingering campfires from the night before. The campground was alive with motion and activity. Families and couples, old and young, even some babies could be heard as the man crawled on all fours out of the tent.

He was wearing long, basketball style blue shorts. He stood in his bare feet feeling the ground between his toes, feeling small twigs and pine needles poking him in the dry flesh of his feet. He was bare chested, which was normal for him during the warmer months. He began his stretching routine trying to loosen his aching muscles. *Sleeping on the ground was not meant for humans*, he thought. His hair was disheveled, his face sporting thick, black stubble since he had not shaved in several days. As he put his arms over his head to stretch them he caught a whiff of his own body odor. It was not pleasant. He turned quickly, knelt back down and crawled back into the small tent.

A minute later he reappeared with a small duffel bag. In the bag were a fresh change of clothes, sandals, and toiletries. Including a razor and shave cream. In it was also his 9 mm handgun. He knew he probably would not need it, but he didn't want to leave it unattended in his tent either. Better for everyone if he just kept it close by.

He had been living at the state park in the small tent going on six weeks. It was cheaper than renting an apartment and though it was a bit inconvenient and he had no luxuries to speak of, he had peace and solitude. And anonymity.

He knew he only had about another six weeks of tent living available to him before the state park started to shut down for the season. A month and a half to figure out what to do, where to go. His life and future were in limbo. He quit his job back in March after he left Lissa's apartment and what he had done behind him. He didn't know if she filed any complaints against him. He didn't know if the cops were looking for him. He didn't want to know. The cell phone he had was a prepay, and he let that lapse even before he set up shop at the state park. Friends and family couldn't contact him if they tried. For all intents and purposes he was "off the grid." The only electronic device he currently had was an MP3 player that had 600 songs stored on it. To charge it he just needed a USB port, and for that he could usually talk someone into letting him plug his device to their computer for a couple hours, or go to the cell phone store doing the same thing and just playing with the new devices while it charged. He was personable enough so it never seemed to be a problem.

Living at the state park was pretty great, he thought. Aside from waking up stiff and feeling bruised every morning, he had a bathroom, a shower, people to talk to when he felt like human interaction. And solitude when he didn't. He could usually bum cigarettes, a beer or two, even shots of whiskey from the partiers and other like-minded individuals. Most times he was offered those things, didn't even have to ask.

He caught some smiles, glances, and even some hard stares, from the various people as he walked the winding path towards the cement block building that housed the bathrooms and the showers. Most of these looks he ignored, but to some he would give a slight wave and a smile and a nod of his head in greeting. Almost exclusively, everyone that he chose to interact with in that manner were women.

He tried to ignore the small rocks, twigs, and pine needles assaulting his bare feet as he walked looking about, taking in the sights. He mentally took note of the various women. He would categorize them by age, height, weight, color of their hair. What they were wearing, how those clothes fit--either hiding or accentuated their features--how that made him feel. He noted if they smiled at him and held his gaze, or looked away quickly, some even had a horrified look before looking away. A few would even grab their children and pull them away from him in a gesture of protection. These he laughed at. And though it was not his goal, Nevver also took note of the other men in the campground. He took special note of the ones that looked dangerous and the ones who seemed to accompany the women he was more attracted to. He was sizing up the competition in a manner speaking. It was something that he instinctively tended to do, mostly without conscious purpose. It seemed like his mind just did it automatically, this cataloging.

However, on this morning Nevver was looking for one young woman in particular. The one he had seduced the night before. She had told him she was with her family, though Nevver did not know if that meant husband and children, parents and grandparents, or a variation of many possibilities. He didn't really care, but it would've helped him narrow down his casual search of the campsites. Though trying to find her probably wasn't the smart thing to do, especially if she was vacationing with her husband, or baby daddy, or whatever.

They had met on the beach as the sun was setting. They were walking towards one another across the wet sand and splashing surf of the beach that was quickly becoming deserted, as the families and couples gathered their belongings and headed back towards the campground proper to build their fires, have their dinners then their smores, or just roast marshmallows. Conversations muffled and some not carried up with the smoke from the fires. Louder, alcohol-fueled voices filled the air with laughter and shouting in spurts as well. The smell of the burning wood complimented the sound of the crackling and popping as the flames consumed their fuel completed the camping experience for most of those who gathered here on the lazy summer weekend.

As he reached his destination and quickly found an empty shower stall, Nevver set his duffel bag on the floor in the corner nearest the shower. He took out his combination shampoo and body wash and reached in and turned the water as far toward hot as he could. Jane. That's what she said her name was, Jane. He told her his name was Xavier. Whether she believed him or not, she didn't let on. They talked and walked briefly as the sun set into the waves. Nevver had some OxyContin that he was saving for just such an occasion. Through their short conversation he ascertained that she was interested in getting high and screwing around. Within a few minutes they were back at his tent, sharing a pint of strawberry flavored vodka. A few minutes after that they were kissing passionately. A few minutes after that, Nevver pulled her shorts off and took her doggy-style, pushing her face hard into a pillow to muffle her moans and screams as he roughly had his way with her. He grabbed her wrists and held her down, not asking, not caring if she was enjoying it.

It was angry sex, if he was truthful about it. He didn't do it because he really liked the woman--though he did have an instant lust toward her--he didn't do it because he wanted her to feel good just as he wanted to. It was all selfishness on his part. He did what he wanted to do, and through coercion seasoned with some lies, she let him, maybe even wanted him to. He wasn't sure whether she enjoyed it or not. It seemed like she had, but he couldn't be sure. And he didn't care one way or the other. But if that were true, why was he looking for her just then? He wasn't sure. He had a burning nugget of regret lodged in the pit of his stomach. But that could have been from any number of things he'd done in the recent past. Jane was just a means to an end. She was recreation. A pleasant distraction from his life. If she found him and offered, yes he would do it again, for as many times that she would let him. But if he never saw her again that was just fine with him as well.

The hot water cascaded down over him. He stood under the stream letting it soak in his long, black hair for a few long minutes before he applied the shampoo and started cleaning the sand, dirt, and grime from his body.

Then, without any warning he felt something crashing to the side of his head, right next to his left eye socket. The pain was instant and intense, almost as if he had been hit by something sharp. It had been proceeded by a quick gust of cool air. His head and face were full of soap, his eyes were closed. Though the floor of the shower was wet and slippery he managed to hold his stance and not slide or lose his balance. As he turned his body to face the showerhead and clear the soap from his eyes something smashed into his nose, not once but twice. Hard.

The first blow he seemed to absorb quite well. The second rocked his head back and cracked the back of it against the tile of the shower wall, while simultaneously his right foot slid out from under him. He slid down to the floor, landing hard on his tailbone. His eyes tearing from the multiple points of pain. Several parts of his body were radiating in alarm from the unexpected attack. He felt blood pouring from his nostrils as the water continued to beat down upon him and run across his naked body. Then something hit him, something larger than a fist, slammed into his chest. Twice. Nevver gasped in pain as the air in his lungs was forcefully released in a rush. He gasped for breath and started choking as he inhaled hot water from the shower. He still couldn't see, still did not know what was happening, except that he *did* know.

He knew he was being attacked, but he did not know by whom or why. But he knew he had to get up, he knew he had to do something. With water still streaming across his face and obscuring is now slitted eyes, Nevver quickly pushed himself up with both hands into a kneeling position, then in a smooth motion he braced his right foot against the back of the shower wall, putting himself roughly into a runner's starting position. He could make out a shadowed figure directly in front of him, that's when he launched himself at it.

Nevver jumped in the air as he pushed himself off the back wall, bringing his right knee up in front of him, while simultaneously bringing both arms down hard, his hands balled into fists. His knee attack did not seem to hit anything, his attacker must have backed up as he saw his opponent launch himself. But Nevver's long arms as they came down hit their mark. At least one of them did. His right fist hammered down and hit something solid. Never thought he heard an exhalation coinciding with the impact. Quickly he brushed the hair away from his face to try to focus his vision while continuing the rain of hammer blows with both fists.

His attacker seemed to gain his composure quickly and the next thing Nevver knew his attacker had grabbed his right arm and he was being thrown to the side towards the wall next to the row of sinks, his wet feet slipping across the wet cement floor. He fell hard, hitting his right elbow and right knee as he slid the short distance, his head cracked on the tile wall next to the sink. He was dazed and disoriented from the impact. The coppery taste of blood filled his mouth. He absently thought he might have bitten his tongue. Pain was emanating from several points on his body, but he knew he couldn't focus on that now.

He rolled onto his buttocks, his head and back resting against the tile wall. Again he tried to push himself up with both arms, but in that instant a foot came rushing in and crushed him in the genitals, twice. Nevver involuntarily let out a scream of pain as he doubled over, falling to the floor in a fetal position. The next thing he knew his head was wrenched back by his long, black hair. A face pushed close to his and growled, "That's for drugging and fucking my girlfriend, asshole," the man said. Nevver could almost taste the stale, hot breath. He smelled coffee and cigarettes. He could feel the anger and hatred in the words. He did not say anything. He did not move. He did try to brace himself against further blows that he was sure would follow. His assailant grabbed his head with both hands and threw it towards the tile, bouncing it like a basketball. Nevver's vision swam and he felt sick to his stomach. He vaguely was aware that the man was walking away.

He lay there, half conscious listening to the sound of the shower continuing to spray hot water toward the floor drain. With every beat of his heart his ears thundered, and all of his battle wounds throbbed and ached. It had been a while since he had been kicked in the nuts. And he couldn't remember a time when he had been naked during a fight, at least a fight with a man. He lay there for long moments trying to regain his strength and reassemble some shred of his dignity. Eventually, he was able to push himself up off the floor and he stumbled back into the shower.

I should've got my gun and shot the mother-fucker, he thought angrily. But he quickly dismissed that as an actionable thought. He didn't blame the guy--he'd do the same thing if their situations were reversed. *Maybe it is true,* he thought, *that you reap what you sow.*

Thankfully, the water pouring from the shower head over his bleeding and bruising body was still warm. He stood underneath the spray of water on wobbly legs and wished he was somewhere else. His battered mind briefly wondered then what it would be like to be someone else.

CHAPTER SEVENTEEN

Daniel mentally went through all the closing tasks, checking off each one ensuring everything was complete. The equipment was shut off, clean utensils set out on the food preparation stations ready for the openers; prep lists filled out; the server station was full of glasses, the ice bins, straw and napkin stations were full; all the trash can liners had been changed, the trash taken to the dumpster. He had a rule that the closing manager should have everything set up and ready for the opening people: Set up the next shift for success. In his mind, there was almost nothing worse than walking into a mess, to where you had to clean and organize for a period of time before you could start getting to the daily work tasks. All that did was set you back and make you hurry, where mistakes could happen. And you were angry for most the day because of it, at least that seemed to be how his mind functioned.

Being the general manager, Daniel could have worked mainly opening shifts. The easier shifts. But, because the majority of the employee problems occurred on the night shift he felt that he needed to be there to correct those problems and to lead the less experienced staff. So, for most of his restaurant management career, out of a sense of duty and obligation, Daniel always seemed to give himself the crappy schedule.

He was alone, and had been for the past 15 minutes. He was supposed to have, according to the corporate policy, at least one closer stay with him so they could walk out together for safety. But, Daniel usually had a few more things to do being the top manager, and he thought it was unfair to make someone sit and wait for him. So he let them punch out when they were done and get back to their lives.

Tonight, he allowed Faith to drop him off at work as she had some errands to run and a doctor's appointment. She was to get evaluated for her new medication. Her overdose episode had just been 10 days prior. Daniel would've liked to have gone with her to the doctor to ask questions, and maybe get some answers. Faith had told him that the first patch did not seem to be working after the first hour, so she took it off and put a second one on. That didn't make much sense to Daniel, but it did loosely explain the reason for two patches being missing from the package and only one found on her body. It was puzzling to Daniel, because he was under the assumption that the patch was a way to help stop abuse of the drug. He would have to find out more information from her doctor, eventually.

He had called her forty minutes earlier, letting her know about what time he would be done so she could be waiting for him when he got out. Daniel set the security alarm and quickly made his way out the front door pulling on it, making sure it was secure. The night was warm, but a breeze was blowing through Petoskey from Little Traverse Bay and it was welcomed. As he looked around, Daniel noticed the parking lot was deserted. No cars, and no Faith.

Daniel's stress and agitation rose as he stood outside the darkened restaurant and looked around. His mind took in the details of the night: the harsh glow of the streetlights, the blue and white lights of the Wal-mart down the hill, the sound of a lone dog barking, and the pounding of his blood through his own head thumping in his ears. He pulled his cell phone from his pocket and checked the time. *Where the fuck is she?* He thought angrily. He flipped the phone open and depressed the number two for several seconds, speed-dialing Faith. She picked up on the second ring.

"Hey, baby," she said in way of answering, her tone warm. "I'm on my way," she assured him.

"Where are you at?" He demanded, a hard edge to his voice. "I let you use my car all day, and all I ask is that you pick me up on time," he scolded.

"I know, I'm sorry. I'll be there in a few minutes," she said and then she disconnected.

He waited impatiently, checking the time on his phone seemingly every few seconds. Every time he heard a car approaching he looked expectantly to see if it was her. The sudden feeling of relief--that she had finally arrived--was suddenly replaced by a sinking feeling of disappointment as the vehicle he heard approaching drove past. Suspicious thoughts ran through his mind as he waited. Thoughts of where she had been, who she was with all day. In *his* car.

To try and stop these unproductive thoughts, Daniel sat down on the curb. The cold cement of the walkway leaked through his polyester pants, chilling the back of his legs. In his mind he pictured his Toyota winding its way towards him. Twelve minutes had passed since he had spoken to her. *She should be here by now*, he thought. He flipped open his cell phone again and called her. She answered on the fourth ring.

"Babe, I'm almost there."

"That's bullshit, you should've already been here by now," he shouted. He couldn't contain his anger any longer. He wanted to reach through the phone and choke her. Not so much because she was late picking him up--though that was disrespectful and the catalyst for his anger--but it was more because of what he thought she had been doing coupled with the fact that he did not want to be at work any longer. He just wanted to get home and relax. Well there's not much chance of *that* happening if you don't calm down, his mind warned him.

"I stopped at the gas station for some cigarettes and a soda real quick, and I think the place is being robbed 'cuz some cops pulled up and blocked everybody in. They're not letting anybody leave just yet," she told him.

What the hell is this shit? He thought. "You are not making any sense. Which gas station are you at?"

"The Holiday in Bay View," she said.

Daniel knew the gas station, passed it every day going to work. It was only about six minutes away depending on how slow the traffic was on the two lane, curvy highway. He briefly thought about walking there, but dismissed the idea. His legs and feet were aching and throbbing. And he knew that if he forced himself to walk the five or so miles he would just get angrier and the already deteriorating situation would only get worse. *Besides,* he thought, *as soon as I start walking I'll get about a mile down the road and she'll pass me and not see me.* So he decided to wait.

"Whatever," he finally said. "Just please get here soon as you can."

"I will, I will, babe," she told him and then disconnected.

Daniel paced the cement curb, thinking. He thought briefly about going back into the restaurant and doing some work, but he dismissed that thought. He didn't want to work anymore, he just wanted to go home.

Another agonizing seventeen minutes passed before the black Toyota Matrix rolled into the parking lot and stopped next to Daniel. He stepped off the curb and walked to the driver's door. Faith did not make a move to get out or even roll the window down, as she assumed that he would get in the passenger side and they would leave. Daniel stood and glared into the window until Faith finally rolled the window down.

"I'm driving," he told her, barely able to control his anger.

"Babe, just get in and we can go," she protested.

"I'm not in the mood, Faith. Get in the passenger side. *I'm driving!*" he shouted the last and she reluctantly got out and wobble-walked to the other side and got in. Daniel adjusted the seat and side mirrors and slammed the car in gear as soon as Faith was buckled in.

As she closed the door, Daniel could smell the strong odor of cigarettes mixed with her body spray. The mingled scents would usually have sent a thrilling sensation through him after a day of work, but tonight it seemed to fuel his anger. The smell of cigarettes was heavier than usual. She usually didn't smoke in the car, or at least had the windows rolled down to try and air it out. But today the smell of burnt tobacco was much heavier than normal which irritated him even more.

They drove in silence for the first few minutes. Even though Daniel was angry he still kept his speed to within 5 miles over the limit. As they neared the curve to where the Holiday gas station sat, Daniel slowed a bit and looked hard at the station.

All the lights were on, there were two cars at the pumps and one parked beside the building. The building lights were on, they were open for business. No cop cars could be seen.

"Strange," Daniel began. "That if they got robbed why would the cops not still be there, why would the station still be open?" He asked her.

Faith was quiet for only a couple seconds before responding, "They didn't tell me what they were there for. I just assumed that maybe they were being robbed or something. All I know is that I couldn't leave right away because they had the driveway blocked. They didn't come over and talk to me about anything. I just sat there and smoked a cigarette until the one car moved out of the way and they motioned that I could leave. I don't really know what happened," she explained.

Daniel wasn't sure if he believed her story, but it seemed plausible. Though it did little to lessen his frustration and lighten his mood.

"How did your doctor's visit go?" He asked her, trying to get more information.

"It was okay. I had to fill out all the paperwork again, go over all my medical history. I hate changing doctors, such a pain in the ass," she told him. Then she sat silent.

Daniel was waiting for more elaboration, but after a couple of minutes he knew that wasn't going to be the case. "What did they do about your pain prescriptions?"

Again, Faith seemed hesitant to answer. "He put me on methadone."

"Methadone?" Daniel nearly shouted it. He didn't know much about drugs, but he had heard about that. "Isn't that what they give people to break them away from heroin addiction?"

"That's one use, yes. That's because it's an opiate, which heroine is. The type he gave me is a wafer--I'll show you when we get home. I can break it into four pieces, so I don't have to take a whole large dose unless my back is really going into spasms," she explained.

"There is no way for you to go back on the Fentanyl patches?" He asked.

"Yeah, only if I want to pay full price for them!" She said sarcastically, though not aiming her frustration at him but at the medical system.

The conversation and the drive was starting to have a calming effect on Daniel. As he concentrated on the road and the passing cars, his mind focused and disseminating what Faith was telling him, he seemed to relax a little.

As he drove the Toyota Matrix down his driveway he noticed that most of lights in the house were on. It was a little odd, but he didn't think too much of it. He got out of the car and walked to the side porch and as he went to put his key in the side door to unlock it he turned the handle to find that it was already unlocked. Daniel just shook his head and decided not to scold Faith for not locking the house when she left.

Following his usual routine, Daniel took off his shoes as he entered the kitchen. He walked across to the room and sat his keys and his wallet on the desk in the corner. As he entered the great room with the 8 foot billiard table commanding the space he noticed that the black vinyl cover was on, though he detected something wasn't right.

On the leather side chair clean clothes had been folded and sat upon it. One of the pool cues, not his nor Faith's custom cue, but one of the solid wood house cues was laying across the vinyl cover. Evidence that someone had been playing pool, who most likely was not Faith. Or at least not her by herself.

As Daniel stood there surveying the room looking for other clues, other things that were out of place, he wondered where his cat was. Every day, like clockwork, as he arrived home from work his male cat would come running up to greet him and demand some attention. He had personality attributes that resembled that of a dog sometimes. He would come when you called his name, he would play "fetch," and he always greeted Daniel when he got home by licking his face.

Either the cat was not feeling well, which sometimes happened when he was not greeted, or he was hiding. And he only hid when strangers were at the house.

On instinct, Daniel walked towards the back of the house to the two spare bedrooms. The one on the left was currently his office. He had a computer desk with a tower PC and a 15 inch monitor and printer. He had a small bookshelf against the wall, on it sat some of his favorite books, as well as his superhero knickknacks and some prized comic books from days gone by. Also in the room was a standalone punching bag, the base of which was filled with 25 gallons of water to help hold it in place.

Admittedly he did not exercise and use the heavybag as much as he had intended, but as soon as Daniel had flipped on the light he noticed the bag had been moved from its usual spot across the room by the closet. Daniel then noticed that other things had been moved. *Someone was in my fucking room!* His mind raged.

Instinctively he knew that his home had been violated. He could feel the strangeness. Nothing like this had happened to him before. He could walk into a room of his and know, feel, where things were. He was able to find things in each room in the dark most times: light switches, night tables, desks, items on the dresser like the knife and flashlight. Yes, he'd bumped knees and even shocked himself once by missing a power outlet and putting his fingernail in it when attempting to plug in a lamp, but he learned from these mishaps. Corrected his mental map.

As he scanned for other items, he specifically looked for the case that held his laptop computer. He bought the laptop a few months ago so he could take it to and from work so he was not limited in his ability to get work related tasks done, such as scheduling and modifying prep lists.

He searched the room quickly, knowing that the computer wasn't there. He found an empty two liter bottle of Coca-Cola on the floor next to a coffee table that he had positioned under the window.

He stormed from the room towards the kitchen where Faith was. "Who the fuck was here, and where the fuck is my computer?" He demanded, his words hard, his volume loud.

She just looked at him with puzzlement, as if she didn't understand his words. "What?" Was all she said.

"Where's my computer? Someone was in my office, shits moved all around, and I found an empty bottle of Coke on the floor!" He said holding up the empty container.

"I don't know how things could have been moved in your room, but your computer is in the car," she said matter-of-factly, quickly answering.

"What do you mean, 'it's in the car'?"

"When I came to get you I noticed it was in the back of the car. I thought you put it there, that you wanted to take it to work, but that you forgot it," she explained.

Daniel could not believe what he was hearing. He knew she was hiding something. It was obvious to him, and there was proof that someone else was in the house while he was at work. He shoved past her, grabbed his keys from the desk in the kitchen and jogged out to the car. His heart was pounding, his adrenaline and anxiety had spiked once again. His breathing came in heavy gasps. His anger was building as his mind wrestled with all the clues and evidence before him. He knew something wrong had happened, but didn't want to believe it. He didn't need the added stress right now. But things had happened, and his brain was straining to try and figure things out. He needed more information.

He unlocked the vehicle with the key fob and looked inside. Through the tinted windows in the space of the hatchback behind the rear seats he saw a silvery object lying next to a darker bag. He opened the hatch and there not only was the bag containing his laptop, but also a fairly expensive socket set that had been a Christmas gift from his mother and stepfather. *I most definitely did not put that in the fucking car*, he thought angrily.

He grabbed both items, one with either hand and pulled them from the vehicle. He looked up to see faith standing in the doorway one foot on the threshold the other on the porch, looking at him. He held items up "What the fuck, Faith!" He yelled. *Something is going on and that bitch is going to tell me*, he raged.

He set the silver case containing the socket set down on the driveway as he slammed the hatch closed and locked the car using the key fob. He grabbed the tool case and stormed towards Faith who was now retreating back into the house.

"Why were these things in the car?" He yelled, his voice loud.

"I don't know why," she replied.

His anger swelled at that non-answer. Daniel had to force himself to control that anger, as he desperately wanted to strike Faith just then, knock her to the ground and make her tell him what was going on. What she had done.

"Faith, you're fucking lying to me! You better tell me the truth or you can pack your shit and get the hell out right now!" He warned her.

"Okay," she said, diverting her eyes from his harsh gaze. "I had my cousin and his girlfriend over and he brought a couple of his friends," she began. "They came over to play pool and listen to music. We were just hanging out, that's all."

She was quiet and didn't say anything else.

This angered Daniel even more, as he knew that was not even close to being the entire story.

"Okay, so why was stuff moved around in my room? How did my computer and tools get in the back of the car?" He asked.

"I know you're mad, but if you just calm down and listen to me I will tell you the whole story. But you need to just be quiet and listen, okay?" She said.

Daniel just nodded his head as he tried to rein in his anger and frustration.

*   *   *

Faith had dropped Daniel off at work a few hours before. After her doctor's appointment and getting her new prescription filled at the pharmacy, she invited her cousin, Mike and his girlfriend, Rhonda who happened to live a few miles away, to come over and play pool. Mike told her that Rhonda had some good shit--60 mg tablets of morphine--that she could bring, that pleased Faith. She couldn't waste any of her newly acquired methadone wafers, couldn't afford to get high on those, otherwise she would run out way before the prescription was to be refilled. At least not until she had a chance to determine how they affected her and how long the high lasted above and beyond the pain killing effects they provided. She'd have to experiment a little in the next few days.

She got so bored sitting in that house alone, not working. No real friends around. All of her friends and relatives were in the East Jordan and Boyne City area, a good 35 minute drive from where she was at in Alanson. And she had no vehicle, as her brother still had not come out to fix her van, or to see if it even could be fixed. She needed some interaction, something to take her mind off the trouble with her kids and her ex. Something else besides her medication to dull her mind and her pain of the past and present, both physical and mental. She was living for now, couldn't see what her future would bring. Though, she knew it would certainly be more pain and anxiety. *Things always get worse before they get better*, she thought. It was good to have people over for some fun again.

They were running late, as usual. She wanted them to come over earlier, she had been waiting for nearly two hours past the offered time for them to show. She was out on the porch having a cigarette when the old white, Ford Escort slowly pulled into the driveway. Well, it still tried to be white. It was yellowing around the massive rust spots that plagued the body and had all but devoured the front and rear bumpers. The seats were ripped and cracked, the headliner had fallen down and was torn away many years ago. But it still ran, albeit grudgingly. It was transportation one step up from a moped that could only do 26 mph with the wind behind you. But the sight of it gave Faith a thrill, as for the next few hours she would not be alone, and it was party time.

*   *   *

Rock music boomed from the speakers as the four played pool in teams of two, while the fifth person sat out and just watched, waiting for their turn. Rhonda and Mike had brought two of their friends, Justin and Greg.

Mike was thin and tall, about six foot. He had shoulder length brown hair that was messy, he had a mustache and goatee. He was missing a canine and a bicuspid on the right side of his mouth, so he tried not to smile. He was laid-back, and didn't talk a whole lot. He and Rhonda were currently ahead in the game of eight ball.

Rhonda was about 6 inches taller than Faith and 35 pounds heavier. She had long, straight black hair and she wore all black, usually baggy clothes to hide her figure. She smiled and laughed a lot, and liked to talk and carry the conversation. She used the F word as an adjective, even a noun, and usually used it as punctuation in nearly every sentence.

Faith was teamed up with Greg, who she did not know. He was one of Justin's friends, who she did know but only from hanging out with Rhonda and Mike previously. Greg was short, only about 2 inches taller than Faith. He was stocky, clean-shaven, his hair cut short and spiked on the top. He had several tattoos down both arms, and a flaming skull forever inked on the left side of his neck.

Faith seemed to get along with him right off the bat, asking him about his tatts. She showed him the ones she had: the small blue butterfly on her calf, the black cross on her left shoulder, she even lifted up her shirt and pulled her shorts down a bit so he could fully see the large, black and purple tribal dragonfly on her lower back that went from the top of her buttocks all the way up to her shoulder blades. She didn't flinch or pull away when Greg traced the outline with his hand from the bottom of that tattoo all the way up to the top. She did however, push him away when he grabbed her by the hips and pulled her next to him.

"Hey! None of that," she scolded with a smile.

Justin, the odd man out for this game, was sitting at the coffee table carefully crushing the morphine pills into a coarse powder. He was thin, about five foot nine, his hair was a disheveled, curly dishwater blonde mess. He had three day's growth of razor stubble covering a swarm of acne on his face.

As Faith bent over the pool table to make her shot, Greg ran a hand up the back of her bare leg and grabbed her ass. "Come on, girl. You know you want some," he said as he pulled her towards him.

Faith quickly turned and put her pool cue in between her and Greg, she then thrust it towards him, using it to push him off and away from her. "I said no, and I meant it!" She said pointing a finger at him.

"Hey fuckhead! Leave her the fuck alone, you fucking asshole!" Rhonda said in her defense.

Mike walked over and whispered something into Greg's ear. Whatever he said made Greg smile and nod. "Sorry, Faith. Just playin'," he told her.

"Whatever," she said. "Just keep your hands to yourself." *I don't need this kind of shit right now*, she thought. *I just wanna have fun, relax, and get high. I only have a few hours before I have to get Daniel.*

"We're ready to go people!" Justin announced from the leather sofa in the adjacent room. "How do you want to do it?" He asked them.

"I don't have any syringes," Rhonda said. "Anybody got any?"

"I got one," Greg said. "But I don't want to share, unless Faith wants to." He looked at her with lustful, predator's eyes.

"Fuck no!" Faith said quickly. "I don't like needles, there is no way I'm doing that shit," she explained. Her brother was a needle user, and she had vowed to herself that she would never be like that. Plus, any idiot new you didn't share needles, especially with strangers. Faith now had a bad feeling about Greg. He seemed cool at first, but now he was getting way too personal. She was going to have to talk to Mike about not bringing him over again.

"Suit yourself, girl," Greg said and he walked up and took his portion of the pulverized drug. It was in a small square of aluminum foil. He picked it up carefully and closed his hand around it, and walked off towards the kitchen.

"Lines?" Justin asked.

"Guess so," Rhonda said.

Justin removed the small cardboard protective sleeve from a razor blade. Out of the small bag he had brought with him he took out a dirty and badly smudged mirror approximately 6 inches square. Onto it he dumped the remaining four pill's worth of pulverized morphine. Using the razor blade, he separated the small pile into four equal lines. He then took a small piece of plastic straw, held it up to the powder and then brought his face down towards the mirror. He plugged his left nostril with his left index finger and put the plastic straw into his right nostril. He inhaled deeply while simultaneously moving the end of the straw up the line of powder. Almost instantly, Justin could feel the effects of the morphine. He had a head rush and then a feeling of floating euphoria. He sat back on the couch and held out the cut piece of straw for the next person.

Faith watched intently as Rhonda, then Mike duplicated what Justin had just done. Faith had never snorted before. Well, that wasn't quite true. She had snorted cocaine a couple of times years ago at a party with her ex. But she didn't like the effects that cocaine had, as it seemed to rev her heart rate too much and sped up her mind and her thoughts. It also increased her anxiety and combativeness. She vaguely remembered getting in a fight with some girl, almost ripping her hair out and kicking her in the face. Most of the details came from onlookers the next day. She preferred and enjoyed the effect that opiates had, as they just made her super relaxed and mellowed her out, letting her mind float on a cloud and all her stress, cares, and worries just weren't there anymore.

Faith took the piece of straw from Mike and snorted her line. Within a few seconds her mind and body felt numb and fluffy, like it was floating on a cloud.

"I need a cigarette," Rhonda said. She slapped Mike in the shoulder to get his attention and motioned for him to go outside with her to smoke. He struggled to get up off the floor and followed her out. Faith got up off of the couch where she had laid back after snorting the line and followed. Justin stayed on the couch.

Greg was in the kitchen, pulling the needle from his arm as the trio walked past him.

"Hey! Don't leave any of that shit in the trash," Faith told him as she walked past.

"No...worries," Greg managed to say as he wobbled a bit, trying to stand upright as the drug flooded his system. In a few seconds he regained his composure and followed the others outside.

They were sitting on the porch, lighting cigarettes. Greg sat next to Faith and slid close to her. "Hey, girl, can I bum a cig?" he asked.

Grudgingly, Faith pulled one from her pack and handed it to him. "Slide over, dude!" she said as he took it from her, letting his hand linger on hers before withdrawing it. He did not slide over. She noticed this and slid away from him.

After a few minutes Mike and Rhonda stood from the porch and headed toward the Ford Escort. "Hey, we're going on a run to my place real quick...we'll be back," Rhonda said as they got in their vehicle.

"What?" Faith asked, confused. She wasn't totally comfortable being alone with two guys who she barely knew. Being a fighter she figured she could handle herself, but she didn't want to deal with confrontation if it could be avoided.

"We'll be right back, Faith," Rhonda reassured her.

"You should probably go with them," Faith said to Greg.

"Nah, they'll be right back. Come on, let's go play some pool," he said as he flipped his cigarette into the driveway, got up, and walked into the house.

Normally, Faith would've been anxious and irritated over the situation, but the morphine had fully enveloped her system and her body was too relaxed to even care. She finish her cigarette and went back into the house. She stopped at the refrigerator and pulled out a 20 ounce bottle of Orange Crush. As she took a drink, Greg came around the corner from the living room.

"Hey, you get any more soda?" He asked as he walked over and stood right next to her, his hips brushing hers.

Faith took a step back away from him, "Ah, there's a two liter of Coke in there, I guess you can have some of that," she offered.

"So we gonna play some pool or what?" Greg asked. As he opened the fridge and removed the bottle of Coke, he eyed the bottles of beer, grabbed one.

"Hey! Put that back!" Faith scolded. "You can't have any of those beers. Daniel counts them, he knows how many there are."

"He won't miss one," Greg argued.

"Yes he will, besides I said you can't have it!" Faith yelled. She was becoming agitated now.

Justin came into the kitchen after hearing her shout. "What's going on?" He asked both of them.

"Greg's harshing my buzz, bringing me down," Faith said.

"Greg, leave her alone, man. Show a little respect would you?" Justin said. "Faith, I didn't get to play pool yet. I challenge you to a game."

"Okay. One game," she said.

Justin racked the balls as Faith chalked the breaking cue.

"Where's the bathroom?" Greg asked, holding the large plastic bottle of Coke like it was his own personal beverage.

Faith pointed towards Daniel's office and where the spare bedroom was, "Through there, to the right. You'll see it," she explained.

Faith hammered the white cue ball with the breaking cue, the sound of the hard resin balls smacking into one another almost sounded like a gunshot. She managed to sink the solid turquoise colored number two and the purple striped number twelve on the break, which meant she had her choice of being "solid" or "stripes." Faith studied the table and declared that she chose "solids." With that she chalked up her custom cue and made her next two shots.

"Very good, girl," Justin said. "I'm glad I'm not playing you for money."

Faith let out a slight laugh, "Yeah, you might lose what little you have," she said.

"Although," Justin began as Faith missed her third shot. "We could play like we did last time..." He let his words hang in the air, not explaining. Waiting for her reply.

Faith stood up and looked at him, puzzled. She wasn't sure what he was talking about, she was trying to remember what happened "last time."

This wasn't the first time that Justin had been over with Rhonda and Mike. And he had come over unannounced, and uninvited, twice. "Which time are you talking about?" Faith asked, her mind still fogged with the opiate. It was as if she was half out of her body, almost like she was watching the interaction and this conversation as she looked at it while she floated on a cloud, a third-party observer and not a participant.

"You know, last week. When I stopped by during the day," As Justin began to explain, he moved around the table and got close to her and lowered his voice. "I brought you a pack of smokes...a pint of rum...and those Oxys. Remember? We played...Strip pool."

Oh fuck, her mind snapped back to the memory of the day he was talking about. She hadn't remembered it at all until he reminded her of some of the details just then. She saw bits and pieces of it in her mind now. But it was not a complete picture, not a complete memory.

She remembered him coming over. She remembered him showing her how to smoke the crushed tablets of OxyContin. It was the first time she smoked it. At least she thought it was. She remembered that it was powerful, that it almost knocked her out. She remembered playing pool, barely. She remembered him taking his shirt off. Then, to her confused horror, she remembered Justin pulling her shorts down and bending her over the pool table as he fucked her from behind. She didn't remember it being a game of "strip pool." She didn't remember wanting it, or giving consent. She didn't remember it at all, until just now. Still, it was like remembering sequences from a nightmare, only bits and pieces. *Faith, what the fuck did you do?* She screamed at herself in her mind. Her heart began to race and her adrenaline spiked as Justin grabbed her by the hips, pulled her to him and kissed her on the mouth.

The kiss was so unexpected, Faith froze for a second. Then, instinctively, she brought her right knee up and connected with Justin's groin. At the same time she shoved at him with her right arm, pushing him away. He fell to the floor, both hands grasping at his injured body part.

"What the fuck was that for?" He shouted.

Greg came from the other room at the sound of the commotion. "What the hell you guys doing?"

Faith looked at Greg, then down at Justin. "You guys need to leave. Now!" She demanded.

Greg helped Justin up to his feet and said to Faith, "I don't think so. We're waiting for Mike to get back, he's our ride."

"I don't give a fuck," Faith yelled. "You guys need to go!"

"Nope, not 'till were ready," Justin said.

Anxiety and panic flooded Faith's mind. She didn't know what to do. Neither Mike nor Rhonda had cell phones, so she couldn't call them to come back. *But I could drive down there, could give these two assholes a ride down there*, she thought.

"Okay, get in the car. I'll give you a ride to Rhonda's," she told them.

They laughed at her. "Not gonna happen, unless you blow us first," Greg told her.

"Well, *that's* not gonna fuckin' happen! So, you can either get in the car and I'll give you a ride, or I'll call the cops," she threatened.

The two looked at each other for a quick second. "I don't think you're gonna do that. They'd get here and see that you're all fucked up, you'd be in more trouble than us. And we'd be long gone 'for they got here, so it would just be *you* that they would be looking at," Justin said.

Faith didn't have any intention of calling the cops. Even though it was a good way to get them out of the house, she hated cops and didn't want to deal with them. And she may get in some sort of trouble if they came to the house. It seemed that every time the police were called she was the one who got arrested.

She tried one last time to reason with them to get them out, "Please just get in the car and I will take you to Rhonda's," she said politely.

"Not until you blow us," Justin said this time.

Faith rolled her eyes. "I already done told you that's *not* gonna happen!" She yelled, frustration boiling into anger. Then she had an idea.

"Well, I'm gonna run up to Mickey's and get some smokes. You can come with, or not. I'll be back in a bit," she told them. She was hoping that the offer of cigarettes and a ride to the store would get them into the car.

"We'll be here when you get back," Greg said.

"Yeah, hopefully you'll be in a better, friendlier mood," Justin added.

With that, Faith quickly grabbed the keys to the Toyota and hurried out to the car. The sun was setting, but the air was still warm and heavy. She sped away and drove as fast as she dared towards Rhonda's. Her heart was racing, and her mind was scrambled. All she wanted to do was have a little fun tonight, and here she was dealing with other people's bullshit. *Why does this shit always happen to me?* she questioned.

She had to focus and really concentrate on her driving. She could barely feel her legs or her hands as they manipulated the steering wheel and the pedals. She managed to light a cigarette and rolled the window down. The warm air blasted in making the smoke from her cigarette dance erratically. It was only about five miles to Rhonda's. She was there in less than ten minutes.

As she pulled into the driveway, to her horror she saw that the white Ford Escort was not there. She quickly parked and got out. She wobble-walked as fast as she could to the door and pounded on it with her fist. "Rhonda! Mike! Open the door!" She yelled, still pounding. There was no answer.

Where Rhonda lived was a little shack of a place. It was in a compound that used to be small, one-room cabins for rent on the Crooked River. They were old and now dilapidated, rented out by a slumlord. There were five identical, square buildings haphazardly arranged on what was basically two city lots' worth of land. They were in close proximity to one another, cars parked randomly in front of and in between the buildings.

Faith had an idea and walked to the neighbors. She knocked more politely on that door, hoping someone would answer. Someone did. It was an older lady, looking to be in her late 50s. She , was wearing a thin tank top that showed off her cleavage, and baggy, lime green sweatpants. Her hair was pulled back in a ponytail showing the wrinkles that lined and defined her face.

"Hi, do you happen to know Rhonda?" Faith asked, pointing over her shoulder towards the small, square building that Rhonda rented.

"Yeah," was all the lady said.

"Well, she was hanging out at my place up the road and said she'd be back in a few minutes. She's got no cell phone, so I came down here to see if everything was okay, and they're not here. You know where they are?" Faith rambled.

"Her and Mike left outta here about 20 minutes ago," the lady told her.

"Do you know where they went?" Faith asked, mentally praying that she could find them soon.

"Nope, I didn't talk to them. I just saw them drive away."

"Okay, thanks," Faith said as she turned around and walked down off the small porch. "Fuck!" She yelled. "Fuck fuck fuck fuck shit fuck!"

Think, Faith, think! She thought. She was trying to keep herself from panicking. She knew she only had a couple hours before she had to pick up Daniel, she knew if she wasn't there on time he would be pissed. It was obvious that those two idiots were not going to leave willingly. She knew she should probably just call the cops, but she wanted to try one more thing first. Ryan.

Ryan was a new acquaintance as well. She met him through Mike and Rhonda a few weeks before. He was brown skinned, just barely 21 years old, with deep brown eyes and black hair he wore short, but the bangs were long and hung over his eyes. She had his cell phone number and knew he lived in the area, about 10 minutes away.

She went back to the Toyota and lit another cigarette. She pulled out her cell phone and dialed Ryan's number.

He answered on the third ring, "Hello? Faith?"

"Yeah, it's me Ry," she said.

"What's up? I don't have anything, if you're looking," he told her before she could even answer the first question.

"No, I'm not looking. But I need you to do me a favor," she said in her sweetest, alluring voice, given the circumstances and her anxiety that is.

Ryan was silent for a minute, trying to guess what she could want if it wasn't to get high. "What is it?" He finally asked.

In a rambling, unbroken paragraph, Faith explained to him the circumstances and the situation, with the F word being used frequently.

"So Justin and Greg are at your house and won't leave until you fuck them? Is that right?" Ryan asked.

"Basically, yeah. And I don't want to have to call the cops, 'cuz that's trouble none of us need. I just want them to leave. Please, they'll listen to you," she implored him.

"Well, I'd like to help, but none of those idiots has a cell, that I know of. I don't have a ride, you know that," he said.

"I'll come get you!" She said, excited now that he might help. "I'm at Rhonda's right now, I can meet you at the corner by your house, where I picked you up before. I'll take you to my house and you can get them to get in the car and I can drop you guys off wherever. "

"I don't know," he said. "Sounds like a bunch of shit, I don't really want to get into a fight."

"Please, Ry! They will listen to you, you gotta help me! I don't have anybody else, I don't know where Mike and Rhonda are, and they don't have phones either," she pleaded.

Ryan was silent.

"I'll do whatever you want, Ry, you just gotta help me!" She begged.

"Well...how about we do what we did a couple weeks ago? What you said we could never do again?" He asked.

"Oh for fuck sake, Ry! You're just as bad as those assholes! Why do guys have to be such fucking pigs!?!" She yelled. "I told you that was *a one time thing*. Yeah, I really liked it but I can't keep doing that shit, Dan is going to find out!"

"Just once more, and I'll help you out," he bargained.

"Fine," Faith said, obvious anger in her voice. "I'm coming to get you right now, you better fucking be there when I get there!" she said and she snapped the phone shut, disconnecting the call.

She let out a scream that seemed to rattle the windows of the Toyota. She was so angry and frustrated now. If it wasn't for the heavy drug that was in her system, she knew she would be shaking and having an anxiety attack. "God, why can't my friends just be *friends*!?!" She yelled her question to the heavens. She got no immediate answer. *Just because I said I'd fuck him again, doesn't mean I'm gonna*, she thought angrily. *Fuckin' assholes, all of them!* She let out another scream of frustration.

She slammed the car into gear and spun gravel as she sped away. She didn't know where Ryan lived exactly, as she had picked him up down the road from his house. She met him a few weeks before when Mike brought Justin and Ryan over to the house to play pool and get high. He was bigger, about 6 foot tall and stocky. She thought he was sexy, but didn't think much more than that at the time. As they played pool and talked they found they had things in common and that they were attracted to each other. They exchanged phone numbers. She texted him the following week, had picked him up and brought him back to the house just to have someone hang out with. She was so bored. Most of her life she had more guy friends than girl friends, so she didn't think there was anything wrong with it.

Ryan brought his acoustic guitar, and also some Oxys that they crushed and snorted. They played a couple games of pool, then Ryan said he wanted her to listen to a song he just wrote. Shortly after that they were making out. She felt his hands caress her breasts. She kissed him harder, their tongues angrily fighting for dominance. He reached up and grabbed the back of her hair, pulled hard as he then bit her on the side of the neck. Faith let out a moan as he continued to squeeze and bite. Her hand moved to his groin and felt his erection through his shorts. She began stroking it through the fabric, massaging it with her palm and her fingers, scratching the denim with her long fingernails. He was moaning now as well.

"Let's go to the bedroom," she said to him as she grabbed his hand and led him to the other room.

They fumbled with the closures of their clothes, each person taking their own clothes off as quickly as they could. They stood, naked and embraced, pressing their hot, warm bodies against each other's as they passionately kissed. Faith's mind and body swam in a cloud created by the opiate. She could still feel everything that was going on, everywhere Ryan touched her, but it was a surreal and almost dreamlike sensation. Her nerve endings seem to be enhanced, but her emotions dulled at the same time. Her rational, thinking mind was essentially set aside, and ignored. What she was doing now was just visceral and primal. There was no emotion, no love, no real desire attached to the actions. It was pure physical, animal lust and want.

He took her from behind, her on her knees. He roughly pushed her face into the pillow as he thrust hard and fast, yelling and swearing as he spanked her and pulled her hair with each jolting motion making her yell in a mixture of pleasure and pain. In less than six minutes he pulled himself out of her and climaxed, spraying her tattooed skin. They both lay on the bed, panting, trying to catch their breath for long moments afterward. Neither saying a word. They did not cuddle, they did not embrace.

Afterward she dropped Ryan off where she had picked him up, told him in no uncertain terms that it was a one time deal. She then went back to the house and cleaned it and changed the sheets and washed the comforter. She then took a shower and used a Summer's Eve feminine wash to clean out her insides. All with plenty of time before Daniel got home from work.

But she didn't want to think about that now. Couldn't think about it now. She knew she shouldn't have done it. But she did. *What he doesn't know, won't hurt him,* she reasoned. Faith knew she was treading a thin line between her two worlds. She had her emotional problems and her addictions, and those people in her life shared many of the same things. But those things and those people were far removed from the world Daniel knew, from the one he grew up in. She loved him, didn't want to lose him. Couldn't stand the thought of losing him. Besides her kids, he was the only good thing in her life. *Then why do you treat him as you do?* Her mind prodded her. "Fuck you, I'm doing the best I can," she yelled at herself.

Right now she had to get those people out of her house and cover up any evidence before she had to get Daniel. Which was soon. Too soon.

She sped away down the paved side road towards the spot where she told Ryan to meet her. She looked far ahead, past the headlights, trying to spot him before she actually arrived. There, by a large maple tree a man stood. It was Ryan. She breathed a sigh of relief.

She pulled over and stopped on the shoulder of the road and electronically unlocked the door. Ryan didn't hesitate in getting in.

"Thank you, Ry," Faith said as she reached out and grabbed his thigh. She wasn't trying to start anything, rather she was trying to reassure him that what she had promised would actually come to pass, if only to get him to do what she needed him to do right then.

"My pleasure," he said as he looked into her eyes. She looked away from him and put the car in gear and did an awkward three point turn and headed back towards Daniel's house.

They were there within eight minutes. As Faith pulled into the driveway, she saw Greg standing out by the shed, he was smoking a cigarette. The shed door was ajar. As she stopped and both her and Ryan got out, Justin walked out of the shed.

"What are you fucking idiots doing in there?" Faith yelled.

"Nothing, just checking shit out," Justin replied.

"Come on, guys," Ryan said, not wasting any time. Faith was thankful for that. "She needs you to get out of here before her old man comes home. Let's go, she'll give us a ride back to my place."

"She's gonna blow us first, we told her that," Greg said.

Ryan didn't waste his time with more words. He walked up to Greg, grabbed Greg's right hand that was holding the cigarette with his left at the wrist, and with his right palm struck Greg in the throat and clamped down in a viselike grip.

"Time to go, asshole," Ryan snarled. He turned his head to the right and glared at Justin, conveying *you don't want any of this.*

Greg, gasping for breath, dropped his cigarette and his left hand went up to Ryan's wrist at his throat and tried to pull it away.

"Okay, geez, man! We'll go! Just let him loose," Justin said as he grabbed at Ryan's right hand trying to pry it from Greg's throat. Ryan released him and Greg gasped and gagged for air.

"I have to use the bathroom, be right out. Get them in the car, Ry," Faith said as she headed into the house. The trio watched her enter.

"Why you guys such dicks?" Ryan asked. "You know if you're nice to her and get her high, she'll do whatever the fuck you want," he told them.

"She's a fucking bitch!" Greg yelled.

"Yeah, well, you fucked that up. Better luck next time. Now, get your asses in the car," he told them.

Ryan watched Greg walk directly to the car, as Justin walked back into the shed. A minute later he came back out caring a plastic silver case and a thinner, black duffel bag looking thing. The pockets to his hoodie also looked overloaded. He watched as Justin got in the back seat and put the two cases behind the seat in the hatchback area.

About five minutes later, Faith emerged from the house. She saw that Justin and Greg were in the backseat already. "Thanks, Ry. I owe you," she told him.

"Yes, you do. And I hope to collect very soon," he told her. She just smiled at him and gave him a wink.

"Where do you want me to take you guys?" She asked as she got in the driver's seat and Ryan climbed into the front passenger seat. She was starting to panic a little, as she needed to be on her way to pick Daniel up from work. He left her a message saying what time he would be done from work, and that he expected her to be there. The message came through nearly twenty minutes ago.

"You can take us to my place," Ryan told her.

Thank God, Faith thought, as it was only about eight minutes away on the way to Daniel's work. *I might still be able to pull this off*, she thought. *I don't have time to clean the house, but at least I can pick Daniel up on time so he won't be mad about that.*

She started the engine and backed quickly out of the driveway, heading towards Ryan's house.

Almost in unison the four of them lit cigarettes and rolled their windows partially down as they smoked. When Faith had gone to the bathroom she took a couple of her Xanax to help with the anxiety that was building and threatening to consume her. Her left hand shook as she smoked the cigarette. Her mind was a whirl of chaos.

Too many things were going on right now, too many things she had to worry about, try to figure out. She knew there was evidence left behind that she had people over, but she didn't have time to find what that evidence might be, let alone time to clean it up and cover it up. One part of her brain was trying to figure out a good, plausible lie to tell Daniel. She'd done so in the past, so many times. He believed her every time. Though usually not right away, there was always skepticism and suspicion and yelling and explaining. She would turn on the tears, that always seemed to help. Either Daniel accepted her explanations, or he just dropped it and let it go. Either was good for Faith. Tonight she knew there was going to be an argument, though. And she desperately did not want to deal with that. But she knew she had no choice. It was going to happen. She needed more time, and she didn't have it.

Headlights cut through the darkness. As the anxiety medicine kicked in she began to feel a little lightheaded. The cloud she was floating on suddenly became heavy. She flipped her lit cigarette out the window and put both hands on the wheel, straining to concentrate on the road.

"Hey! That's my road!" Ryan yelled as he backhanded her leg lightly, trying to get her attention.

Faith jammed on the brakes, the tires squealed and the car skidded. She jerked the wheel to the left and stomped the gas, sending the Toyota fishtailing slightly as she corrected her trajectory and roared down the side street. The passengers were yelling and screaming, telling her what a shitty driver she was, asking her what the hell she was doing.

"Hey! I used to be a fucking race car driver, just chill out!" She shouted at them.

They continued to comment about her driving and the perceived near miss accident that they could've been in. Two minutes later, Faith was roughly applying the brakes, sending all her passengers forward as the Toyota screeched to a halt.

"The last stop, fuckers. Get out," she commanded them.

Justin and Greg said a few choice words to her as they opened their doors and started to get out of the vehicle.

Just then her cell phone rang. It was Daniel. *Are you fucking kidding me?* her mind screamed. *Not now!* She focused her mind, tried to calm her stress-laden body, desperately needing to calm her voice before answering the phone.

"Hey, baby," she said in way of answering, her tone warm. "I'm on my way," she assured him. She held her hand up, signaling for them to be quiet. They could hear a man's voice on the other side, couldn't make out what he was saying, but his tone sounded angry.

"I know, I'm sorry. I'll be there in a few minutes," she said and then she disconnected. "Fuck, I gotta go," she said to no one in particular. "Get the fuck out, now!"

"So, be sure you text me someday soon," Ryan told her as he leaned in for a kiss.

Faith quickly slid away from him, leaning her torso towards the drivers door, smacking her head on the window as she avoided Ryan's unexpected advance.

"Not in front of the guys," she whispered to him. As she said that she looked to her right over the driver's seat to where Justin was bent over the rear seat and pulling things out of the hatch area. In the wash of the dome light her mind struggled to process what he was doing as he swiftly backed out of the car, kicked the door shut, and started walking quickly behind the car and up the small gravel road towards Ryan's house.

Mostly on instinct, Faith opened her door, got out of the car and ran around the front of it towards Justin. In the darkness cut by the headlights of the Toyota, she could see now that he was caring Daniel's tool case and what looked to be his computer bag.

"Oh, fuck no you don't!" She yelled as she took off running towards Justin. He stopped, and turned towards her. As soon as she reached him, Faith grabbed for the computer case with both hands, pulling it towards her. "You fucking thieving asshole!" She shouted as she tugged on the case. Justin let go of it, sending Faith falling backwards. She landed hard on her tailbone, the gravel of the driveway stabbing her in twenty different places. She winced as she struggled to get to her feet. Justin turned and started walking away with the tool case. Faith began to panic. "Stop!" She yelled. He did not stop.

Then a dark figure ran past her up the incline of the driveway towards Justin. It was Ryan. Faith watched as Ryan chopped at the wrist of the hand holding the tool case. Justin let out a cry of pain as he dropped it. She could hear them yelling at each other. She was standing now, holding the computer case, hugging it to her chest. She started walking towards them to collect the tool set. Ryan had picked up the case now and was heading back down towards her with it. He held it out for her and she took it. When both of her hands were full, Ryan made his move and leaned in and kissed her on the mouth. Faith returned the kiss for a few long seconds before she took a step backwards.

"Thanks, Ry. I gotta go!" She said as she turned and jogged as fast as she could towards the Toyota. She sat both cases on the ground by the rear bumper and opened the hatch. She then laid both items in and slammed the hatch shut. She quickly looked around to make sure that Greg or Justin or Ryan weren't trying to get back to the car, weren't trying to pull some other shit. Satisfied that she was finally alone,

Faith climbed in the still running car, slammed the door, made a three point turn, and headed towards Pizza Hut.

She sped down the road hitting 70, pushing the car 15 miles an hour over the speed limit in an effort to make up for lost time. She did this only for about three miles before she got stuck behind a slow-moving pickup truck. It was an old Chevy, rusted with one tail light dimmer than the other. The two lane highway was curvy and had only one, maybe two places were once could pass safely. But it was usually full of traffic going either way, making passing nearly impossible. Her speedometer now read 50 miles an hour, 5 miles an hour below the speed limit.

As her car seemingly crept along she tried to lower her heart rate and relax. She took deep breaths, then lit another cigarette, hoping the nicotine would do its job and calm her nerves. Her body was numb from the Xanax and OxyContin, but her mind seemed to be going a thousand miles an hour. Even so, she had not come up with a good lie, yet. As she tried to focus on that burning question her cell phone rang. She threw her cigarette out the window and fumbled in the console, trying to find the purple phone. She answered on the fourth ring.

"Babe, I'm almost there," she said in way of answering. He was yelling and swearing at her. *Oh shit, here we go*, she thought. He wanted to know where she was, what was taking so long.

"I stopped at the gas station for some cigarettes and a soda real quick, and I think the place is being robbed 'cuz some cops pulled up and blocked everybody in. They're not letting anybody leave just yet," she told him. The lie just blurted from her mouth, but she thought it sounded pretty good.

"You are not making any sense," Daniel said. *Okay, maybe not such a good lie*, she thought.

"Which gas station are you at?" He asked her.

"The Holiday in Bay View," she said. Faith figured that was a pretty safe gas station to tell him where she was, as it was close to his work. The timeframe to the gas station seemed plausible, and the added confusion with the cops would also buy her some time, she reasoned. Daniel was quiet, hadn't said anything for a few long seconds. Faith pulled the phone away from her face looked at it to make sure that they were still connected. They were.

"Whatever," he finally said. "Just please get here soon as you can."

"I will, I will, babe," she told him and then disconnected. She lit another cigarette. She had just passed Crooked Lake, driving through the tiny villages of Conway and Oden, nearing the outskirts of Petoskey. With every passing minute and every passing mile, Faith became more anxious. She knew she was going to have to tell at least part of the truth. There was too much that she wasn't able to cover up this time. *He may be naïve, and believes a lot of your bullshit, but he's not stupid*, her mind told her. "I am convincing. He will believe me. He knows only what I tell him," she said aloud to herself, giving her reassuring confidence.

      *   *   *

She had to be careful as she told him a clipped version of what happened. She had to leave out a lot of details, especially those of the drugs and the sex. She knew Daniel would never forgive her for the sex. She wasn't so sure about the drugs, but she didn't want to take that chance. Faith knew that if the topic came up again, and she was sure it would at some point, that she had to tell the exact same story. The details mattered and omitting certain details mattered more, she knew. She told him that she had people over to play pool and listen to music, and have a few drinks. She told him the part of Mike and Rhonda bailing on her, leaving her with Justin and Greg. She told him how she felt uncomfortable being there alone with them, and how she tried to get them to leave. She told him how she picked up Ryan and how he was able to get them to leave. Because they had stolen and attempted to steal things, Faith told him the truth about that, as far as she knew, anyway.

"I don't understand why you didn't just call the cops," Daniel said. He was drinking a beer now, his second. The story she was telling did not quell his anger. In fact, it was increasing it.

He listened to her explain how she was afraid of calling the cops, blah blah blah. He was furious that she had other guys over, and even more so that she left them alone in the house.

"You should be thanking me, if it wasn't for me you wouldn't even have a computer and tools right now," she was saying.

What she was saying broke through his own mental fog as he struggled to fit the jagged pieces of her story together. "Wait, what? I should be *thanking* you for getting my computer and tools back? If it wasn't for you having those dirtbag assholes over here they wouldn't have gotten stolen in the first place! So, yeah, thank you very fucking much for that, Faith!" Daniel shouted.

She was crying now. Sobs and tears, her eye makeup running. "I know you're upset. But I didn't do anything wrong! I just wanted to have friends over," she said.

"Well, get a better class of fucking friends!" He shouted.

She glared at him, biting back a rebuttal, "I need a cigarette to try and calm down," she said instead.

Daniel glared back at her. "I need to go through the house and see what else they fucking stole."

With that, Faith went outside to have a cigarette and Daniel went into his office to do a more thorough examination to see what was missing.

After only a couple minutes, Daniel found that his replica Rambo: First Blood part II bowie survival knife was missing, his professional 35mm camera with extra lens was also missing, his gold and diamond wedding band was gone as well. Those were the major things that he noticed right away. The room had nearly been ransacked so it was hard for him to discern what had been stolen from what had been moved, especially in his agitated state of mind. He left the office to go talk to Faith some more. He wanted to know who these dirtbags were, where he could find them.

He walked through the kitchen to the open side door and looked out. Faith was not there. He could hear her talking almost in a whisper. It was coming from the front of the house. Daniel's heart rate increased, the blood thundering in his head as he quickly made his way to the front door by the pool table. There was a small porch identical to that of the one on the side out the front door. The front door was barely used, as everyone came to the side door off of the driveway. Daniel pressed his ear to the metal door, straining to hear Faith's conversation. He could only hear very few words.

She's cooking up some shit, his mind told him. She's spinning a web of lies, trying to get her friends to go along with it in case you want more information.

What the fuck is going on? The thought screamed in Daniel's head. His anxiety was reaching its maximum level, he had to concentrate on taking deep breaths to try and keep from freaking out and losing it. His hands were beginning to shake.

He quickly went to the kitchen and grabbed a small glass tumbler. He returned to the front door and quietly placed it to the steel, then placed his ear to the bottom of the glass. It was apparently an old spy trick that he'd saw in several old movies and TV shows. To his surprise, he found that it did amplify and focus the sound coming from the other side of the door. He tried to calm his breathing and his thunderous heart, as the blood pounding in his ears from anxiety and adrenaline was drowning out what he was hearing.

Faith was talking in a low voice. It was hard to discern what she was saying. He heard: "...might...talk to you...tell him...you up at...Indian gas station...knowing where you live...gotta say Indian...station...I know...you too...just...for me...I promise...to you...Thank you."

He couldn't hear anymore after that. He guessed that she had hung up. He quietly moved away from the door and replaced the glass to the kitchen cupboard. He grabbed a bottle of Michelob Ultra, twisted the cap off and took a long drink. His heart was thundering in his chest. The hand that held the bottle of beer was twitching with anxiety and anger. He squeezed the bottle in an effort to control the involuntary action. He was so mad he felt that he could shatter the bottle just by squeezing a little harder.

You can't trust her. You know that, his mind told him. You caught her in her biggest lie yet. Who knows what all she's hidden from you.

I Need to find out the truth, he thought. *But I'm probably not going to get it from her.* Daniel knew that currently he was her lifeline, without him she didn't really have any place to go, would not have access to her kids, unless she moved back in with her ex which was a situation he didn't want to contemplate. It was a point of pride. He thought of Faith as "his" now. And if he let her go, or sent her way, because of her lack of options, he knew the most likely scenario would be her going back to the place that she sacrificed so much and tried so very hard to get away from. The very place that he was trying hard to keep her from being drawn back to, and all the stress and chaos that the place contained.

He did not want to be the reason she had to go back there. And he did not want to think about her going back to him. *All of my efforts will have been for nothing if that happened,* he thought. He felt it would be the same as losing. Losing a game. Losing a contest. Losing a piece of your life. Losing something that you wanted, something you found precious. It would be a crushing loss, like losing the Super Bowl by one point in the last few seconds. Of all the human emotions, Daniel had come to think that *loss* was one of the very worst to accept and to deal with.

You deserve better, his mind told him. You're settling because you were alone for too long. You're being used, and you know it. Stop this before it gets worse. If you compare the moments of happiness and joy to the ones of stress, anxiety, and misery the latter outweighs the former.

Daniel refused to acknowledge the voice in his head. Part of him knew there was an awful truth being hidden, but he couldn't clearly see what it was. Wasn't ready to see it, desperately wanting his suspicions to be proved false. That protective part of him was slowly turning the tide of the battle, though Daniel's ego was still propelling him forward down the shadowy path that it had chosen, denying obvious clues that would lead him to realize he was in a different reality than that which his mind, and his emotions, were projecting.

Daniel took his bottle of beer and walked out the side door and around the front of the house to where Faith was smoking. He tried to brace himself for the oncoming confrontation in the continuation of the night's drama. To his surprise she was still on the phone. *I wonder who she's talking to*, he thought. *The same person or someone else?* He got his answer.

"Ryan wants to talk to you," she told him.

Daniel stopped and just looked at her. *Strange*, he thought. You know that whatever he says is going be mostly bullshit, his mind told him.

"Why would he want to talk to me?" Daniel asked her, accusingly.

"He wants to tell you what happened, since you don't believe me," Faith offered, an edge to her voice.

Here we go, time for some bullshit, he thought. "Hello?"

"Yeah, ahh...Faith wanted me to tell you that she called me just to get those guys outta your house for you. They're not really friends of mine, but I know them through her cousin Mike. I didn't want to get involved, but Faith was panicked and said she didn't have anyone else to call. That she didn't want to bother you at work, so, you know, I helped her out. I kind of felt sorry for," he was told.

Daniel thought he'd play along a bit, test what he'd heard through the door a few minutes earlier. "So she came and got you? Where'd she pick you up at?" Daniel asked him.

"The gas station," Ryan said.

"Which one?" Daniel asked.

"The Indian gas station," Ryan answered.

The answer confirmed what Daniel suspected. Faith had coached him on what to say, and how to answer the questions. The *Indian gas station* was a term Faith used for one particular BP station on the way to Petoskey. It was owned and operated by the Odawa Chippewa tribe of Native Americans that also operated the local casino. As far as Daniel was aware, no one else besides Faith and her circle used that term to refer to that particular convenience store and gas station.

"And what time was this?" Daniel asked.

"Ahh, couple hours ago."

"Have you been to this house before?" Daniel questioned.

Ryan was silent for a few seconds. Daniel looked at Faith as he asked this question. She was smoking a cigarette, but she did look away averting her eyes.

"Um, a couple times--you know, just to play pool, and hang out--there was always someone else there, we were never alone," Ryan stammered.

"Did you know they were stealing shit from me?" Daniel asked, changing the subject, trying to get more information.

"No, I wasn't there long enough to see what they were doing. But I wouldn't put it past them, they're kinda asshole's," he offered.

Daniel without saying another word handed the phone back to Faith.

"Ryan?" She said in the phone as she took it back from him. "I'll talk to you later," she said and snapped the phone shut.

"Why the fuck would you talk to that person later?" Daniel asked, anger flooding every word.

"'Cuz he's my friend! We didn't do anything wrong! We're trying to help you!" She shouted.

"He's your friend...," Daniel said barely able to control his anger and frustration. "These other guys are your friends too, huh? You leave people that you hardly know in my house alone and they steal from me, from us, and you think that there's nothing wrong with that?" Daniel shouted. "You have these secret relationships with these people that I don't know, and you think there's nothing wrong with that?"

"I just wanted to have friends, okay! I didn't know they were going to steal from us! They wouldn't leave the house, I didn't know what else to do! I tried my best," she said tears streaming down her face now.

There was too much information for Daniel's mind to process. Among all the explanations threaded with lies and misdirection he had a hard time focusing on what was really going on, and what he should do next.

"I'm calling the police," he finally said.

"If you do, I'll probably be the one who gets in trouble and goes to jail," Faith said.

"Maybe... Maybe you should," Daniel told her.

"Maybe I should just leave," she offered, defensive.

"Maybe you should," Daniel said, turned and walked back into the house.

CHAPTER EIGHTTEEN

D aniel was on his third bottle of beer. Faith had walked across the street to the neighbors house. He watched her go. The lady who lived there, Noreen, was a single mother of one small boy. They were acquaintances. Faith would go over there and talk to her once in a while, but Faith said that Noreen was kind of boring and they didn't have much in common. So they didn't interact much, though they were on friendly terms. He wanted to call the police, but sympathy for Faith was holding him back.

You need to do this for yourself, his mind told him. She's probably done way more stuff behind your back than what she just let on. She goes to jail, so be it. Maybe she was controlling all of this, maybe all those things that have come up missing were her doing.

Daniel took another drink of beer as he contemplated the next few seconds of his life. I really just don't want to deal with this bullshit, he thought. I just want to have a decent life, and right now I just want to go to bed and try to forget about today so I can go to work tomorrow. But, he was angry and wasn't about to let his home being violated go unchallenged. Some of his suspicions had finally come to light and he wasn't going to look the other way, not this time.

Daniel pulled out his cell phone, preparing to dial 911. Just then the phone rang. The ring tone startled him and made his heart jump. Just by the sound he knew who was calling, but he looked at the small screen to verify the name anyway: Faith. He stared at it for a few seconds, listening to it ring a third time before he flipped open the phone.

"Yeah?"

"I called the cops, they should be here in a few minutes," Faith told him.

"You over at Noreen's?" Daniel asked for confirmation, his mind having absorbed her information immediately.

"Yes," she said. "I'll be here, 'cuz I'm sure they'll want to talk to me."

Faith was then silent. Daniel didn't know what to say, so he remained silent as well. Finally, Faith said, "Okay then," and hung up.

About 10 minutes later, a blue Chevy Suburban with a big red gumball light on its roof pulled into his driveway. The light was not flashing, no sirens were on. They were here just to log a complaint.

There were two troopers that got out of the vehicle, which was odd because Michigan State troopers usually worked alone. One was tall, nearly 6 1/2 feet including the big hat, the other seemed nearly a foot shorter, fat and stocky. Daniel stood in the kitchen and waited for them to come to the side door.

They approached the door together. The taller officer knocked loudly five times on the storm door. The interior steel door was open and the banging on the exterior aluminum rang through the quiet house. Daniel walked over to the door, nodded to the officer, pushed the latch and opened the door for them to come in.

"Mr. Gibson?" The officer asked. The second, shorter officer moved around behind him in the kitchen, looking around. There were few lights on besides those in the kitchen which was well lit. The house was mainly gloomy and dark.

"Yes," Daniel said, awaiting further response from the officers. Daniel eyed them both, sizing them up as they were him. His sense of smell was assaulted by the mingling of their colognes, clean and sickly sweet smelling.

"Tell us what's going on," the taller one said.

Daniel took about five minutes to explain the situation as he knew it. He added that he was unsure of Faith's truthfulness of the events, but he assured them that things had been stolen and people had been in his house without his knowledge or consent.

"Where is Faith now?" The shorter one asked.

"She's across the street, at the neighbors house," Daniel said pointing towards the neighbors house.

The shorter trooper rolled his eyes and looked exasperated, "Go get her," he told Daniel.

Daniel stood there for a second. He assumed the cops would go over there and question her, but apparently not. The two troopers followed Daniel outside and waited by their vehicle while he walked across the gravel road up to the neighbors front door. Once there, Daniel knocked on the door and waited for Noreen to answer, which she did in less than a minute.

"Is Faith here?" He asked.

"Yeah, she's here," Noreen said.

"The cops want to talk to her back at the house," he told her. She walked away from the door, presumably to get Faith, leaving the door ajar. Daniel waited for a minute before Faith appeared in the doorway.

"They want to talk to you," he told her. He turned and started walking back towards the house and she followed.

They walked in silence across the street and down his driveway, Faith staying a dozen feet behind him. Daniel was anxious, not knowing what to expect. He knew he hadn't done nothing wrong, but he was a little afraid for Faith, knowing that she was afraid to talk to them, most likely because she was hiding something bad and didn't want him to find out.

Don't feel sorry for her, his mind told him. She's done this to you, you're not doing anything to her. Even so, Daniel could not help but feel a sense of dread and sadness.

As they approached the police vehicle, the shorter Trooper said he wanted to talk to Faith alone outside, while the taller one wanted to speak with Daniel in the house.

Once inside, the Trooper asked Daniel if he knew what items had been stolen. He went through the short list of the more expensive items that he knew had been stolen, and added the information about the computer and the tool case. The officer made notes in a small, flip notepad.

"Can I see your office?" The Trooper asked. Daniel led him back past the pool table to the side section of the house where the two spare bedrooms and the guest bathroom were located. He flipped on the lights to his office and explained to the officer how the punching bag had been moved, where the stolen items had been located, and the things he had noticed that were moved.

"Okay, sir. I'm going to confer with my partner and see what we can find out for you," he told Daniel.

"Thank you," Daniel said as he followed the officer out of the room. He stayed in the kitchen as the Trooper walked outside to talk to his partner. Faith walked in the kitchen then.

Daniel could tell she was angry. The look on her face, and the coldness in her eyes seemed to bore through him. Her lips were tight in a scowl that hung on her face.

"I should probably pack a bag," Faith said.

Daniel nodded, "Probably a good idea, I guess." He would've been more sympathetic towards her, if he wasn't so angry at the fact that she had brought this upon him. *And she expects sympathy from me?* He thought. He could feel the anger and animosity she was projecting towards him. He didn't like it, he knew he didn't deserve it. *Fuck her*, he thought. *She's gonna treat me like I did something wrong?*

She's mad that she got caught, his mind told him.

Daniel wasn't sure, still, of what to make all of it all. His mind was battling with his emotions. His heart, his head, and his dick were fighting, once again, for dominance. He loved Faith, knew she had her faults but was still trying his best to help her, to show her that a better life was possible. But, he knew he could not stand being betrayed and lied to. His mind conjured thoughts of her having sex with these other guys, not that it was true, but that's what he thought, that's what he had suspicions of. It angered him.

Just then, Faith came into the kitchen with his small, rolling suitcase.

"Can I use this?" She asked. Her voice was soft, he could hear, and almost feel, the coldness in it.

"Yeah, sure," He told her. He looked into her blue-green eyes. He didn't like what he saw. He wanted to see love and sadness, but instead he saw anger and blame. Icy animosity.

Before either one of them could say anything else, the side door opened and the taller Trooper entered.

"Miss Collins, please step outside for a moment while I talk with Mr. Gibson," he said. Faith didn't say a word, she just walked outside, Daniel presumed she was going to have a cigarette while she waited.

"I have some information for you, Mr. Gibson. We know who Justin and Greg are, and Rhonda is a known person to us as well. Justin and Greg are wanted for questioning in some burglaries and vandalism at the local golf course, among other things. You are the victim here, Mr. Gibson," the trooper told him.

"Yeah, I know that," Daniel said. "So what does that mean now?"

"Have you had much to drink tonight, Mr. Gibson?"

"I've had three beers, but I'm fine," Daniel said.

"If you feel like you are able to drive without impairment, we'd like you and Miss Collins to take us to this Ryan's house so we can interview these guys. She said she picked him up earlier and knows where he lives. Then we'd like to go to Rhonda's so we can interview her and Mike as well," the trooper told him.

"Okay, let's go," Daniel said..

He grabbed his keys and his wallet, walked out the side door where he found Faith smoking a cigarette.

"They want to follow us to this Ryan's house. They said you told them you know where he lives," Daniel said. Faith looked at him with disdain and a slow burning anger in her eyes. Without a word she got up, still smoking a cigarette and walked towards the Toyota.

Daniel and Faith got in the car and he backed out of the driveway around the Trooper's vehicle. Faith told him to turn left once they got to Highway 66. She sat in silence, smoking a cigarette, which angered Daniel because he did not like it when she smoked in his vehicle, though he knew that she did. It was an inconsideration that he overlooked normally, but tonight it just made him more aware of how badly she was treating him. As they neared Mickey's gas station, Faith told him to make a left at the next road.

"So how is it you know where this guy lives?" He asked Faith.

"I don't know, really. I'm not even sure it's down this road. I think it is, but it's dark and I only got vague directions, I've never been there," she told him.

"So you don't know if it's down this road?" Daniel asked her, skeptical.

Faith was silent. Daniel looked at her, waiting for further direction. "I don't know where he lives," she finally said.

"What do you mean, you don't know?" Daniel demanded.

Faith turned in her seat and glared at him, "I mean I don't fucking know where he lives, and I won't take you there even if I did," she spat. She did not raise her voice. It was low and cold, almost reptilian. It startled Daniel for a few seconds as his mind processed this new side of her.

Exasperated and frustrated, Daniel pulled his car to the side of the road and stopped.

"But you told the cops that you do, and they're following us so they can question these guys and try to find out what the hell is going on," Daniel said. Faith shrugged her shoulders and gave him a look as if to say, "Oh, well...asshole."

Just then one of the officers walked up to Daniel's window, which he rolled down.

"What's going on?" The Trooper asked, a hard edge to his voice.

"Well, now she says she's not sure where this Ryan lives," Daniel told him.

The Trooper rolled his eyes and let out a sigh. "We don't have time to screw around here, folks," the Trooper told both of them as he leaned down and looked in the vehicle. After a few seconds of contemplation the Trooper said, "We know where Rhonda lives. Follow us there," he instructed Daniel.

The police vehicle did a U-turn and Daniel did the same, following them out to the highway. They turned left, going past the gas station.

"So, the police know who Rhonda is, know where she lives?" Daniel asked Faith. "That doesn't sound good. I thought she was your cousin's girlfriend?" Daniel asked. Previously, Faith had told him about Mike and Rhonda and how she found out that they were living up the road a few months back. She told him a little bit about each of them. *But apparently not everything*, Daniel thought.

Faith turned in her seat and gave him a cold, hard stare. *"You only know what I tell you,"* she hissed. The tone of her voice was so cold, so hard he could feel the hate and pain they contained. Daniel could feel that the words were supposed to cut him deeply. Which they did.

The words hit him like a revelation of clarity. *Oh, I see how it is*, he thought angrily. *You tell me whatever you like and I'm supposed to believe it all.* The sad thing was up until then that was the truth, he *did* believe mostly everything she told him. Because he *wanted* to believe it. With what she had just said it made Daniel question everything she had been telling him from the very beginning. *What is the truth, is it all lies? Sometimes ignorance is bliss*, he thought ruefully.

Ignorance is *not* bliss, my friend, his mind told him. The truth will set you free.

Daniel ignored what his mind was telling him. He was still having trouble accepting all of these dark revelations. His heart still not wanting to believe them. His dick not caring, still wanting and lusting her.

Daniel's anger flared at her words. She was mad at him, and he was the victim. *This is her doing, she created this mess, now she is mad at me because of it? Ridiculous,* he thought. He realized, though, that her admittance that *he only knew what she told him* was the sad, hard truth.

They were silent for the next three minutes as Daniel followed the police vehicle around the next corner to where the small enclave of ramshackle cabins sat next to the Crooked River. He pulled in next to the Troopers' vehicle. He and Faith remained in the vehicle as the officers walked up to one of the cabins, their flashlights out, illuminating the area as they walked between the trees. They checked the vehicles parked around as they slowly made their way through the compound.

The Troopers disappeared on the far side of one cabin. Daniel guessed they found which one they were looking for. Even though his mind was full of questions he remained silent. Faith opened her door, activating the dome light, and swung her legs out as she lit another cigarette.

She smoked for a full minute before turning towards him. "I will *never* forgive you for this," she spat, her anger and near hatred palpable.

Daniel was taken aback at her words, and the force with which they were said. The look in her eyes conveyed the sentiment as well. They were icy cold, squinted into angry slits as she spoke.

You'll never forgive me *for this?* He thought. *That's a laugh, what bullshit.*

Once this night is done, my friend, you gotta let this go. Let this be the last straw, his mind told him.

Daniel couldn't help himself, he had to respond. "Faith, you can get mad at me all you want. But, this is all you're doing. I'm not doing this to you. If anything you're doing this to me!" He said angrily.

He knew that she already had her bags packed and was planning on leaving.

Good. She needs to, his mind told him.

Over fifteen minutes had passed before the Troopers reappeared. Daniel and Faith had sat silent and brooding over their own thoughts the entire time. Neither said a word. Daniel wanted to say things, ask questions, but he couldn't sort the thoughts out. And he knew that she wasn't about to tell him what was going on, not after what she had already said to him.

The taller Trooper came over to the vehicle and said, "We'll follow you back to your house, Mr. Gibson."

With that, Daniel started the car, waited for Faith to close the door and put on her seatbelt before backing out of the strange jumble of cabins and headed towards his house.

They rode in silence. The hum of the highway beneath the tires was a welcome distraction. Faith rolled her window down as she lit yet another cigarette. The cool air gave Daniel gooseflesh as it poured in through the open window. Faith would cast sidelong glances at him every minute. He could feel the daggers.

Daniel was curious to find out what information, if any, the police had gathered from Rhonda and whoever else had been there. As he pulled into his driveway, with the police vehicle close behind, he was soon to find out.

Almost as soon as Daniel stopped the car, Faith had her door open and was getting out. She walked directly into the house through the side door. Daniel got out and stood by his vehicle, watching her through the large kitchen windows. She disappeared from view for a couple minutes, then the Troopers approached him.

The taller Trooper went into the house and stood in the kitchen. When Faith reappeared, he began talking to her. They only talked for a few short minutes before the Trooper returned back outside.

"Mr. Gibson," the shorter Trooper began after conferring in guarded whispers with his partner, apparently talking about what Faith had just said. "We were able to question Rhonda and Mike, as well as Justin and Greg on this matter, and the other investigations. As far as your situation here we have to tell you that these people she had over here are not good people. They appear to be into prescription drugs and other thefts in the area"

That figures, he thought. Daniel tried to brace himself for what came next. His blood thundered in his head, making it difficult for him to hear. He had to concentrate on every word.

"According to them this was definitely *not* the first time they had been to your house. They've been here roughly half a dozen times, and according to them, Faith was paying them the aforementioned items that have come up missing in your house to have sex with her," the officer said.

What!?! That's ridiculous! He thought. *Of course those assholes would say that they had sex with her, why wouldn't they? They're obviously dirtbags that can't be trusted, trying to pass blame back on Faith so they don't get into trouble*, he reasoned. But something in him was stirring. He had anxiety and a deep, foreboding feeling in the pit of his stomach. Like a knotted fist that was on fire, it was radiating pain and anger throughout his body. He felt sick to his stomach suddenly. *But her paying for sex doesn't make any damn sense! We have good sex, all the time. There is no reason for her to need or want it from somebody else.*

Daniel struggled to concentrate on what was being said. He had to focus and deliberately shut his thoughts off as he absorbed what he was learning. He then formulated a question, "What did Faith have to say about that?" Daniel asked, though he could guess the answer already.

"She's sticking to the same story that she gave you. She denies having sex with them, denies being involved in any of the alleged theft. But, I have to tell you we questioned each of these men separately, and their stories all matched."

Listen to them, Daniel, his mind told him. They're trying to help you.

The officer seemed to read the question and the doubt on Daniel's face. "You're the victim here. She's lying to you. My advice would be to let her go and don't let her come back," he recommended.

Just as he finished saying that, the side door opened and Faith came out with the suitcase. She had the handle extended and was using the rollers as she pulled it awkwardly across the gravel. Slung over her left shoulder was a duffel bag that seemed overstuffed as well. She didn't say a word, she just walked down the driveway and across the street to Noreen's.

Wave goodbye and be done with it, his mind told him.

I am done with it, he thought. At least for tonight.

The officers gave him a complaint number and said that they would file the complaint on the theft. Daniel thanked them and walked back into the house as they got in their vehicle and drove away.

Daniel shut and locked the door. He went to the refrigerator and grabbed another Michelob Ultra, twisting the top off and taking a drink even before he shut the refrigerator door. It may have been the cold from the refrigerator being open, but Daniel felt a chill run through him, one that seemed to stay with him. The house itself seemed colder. He began to shiver as he walked through the house. Thinking. Brooding.

He shut the lights off as he made his way to the bedroom. He turned on the satellite receiver and the television before taking his clothes off and getting under the covers, with pillows propped up against the headboard for comfort. His heart rate had started to slow. The adrenaline was seeping out of him now, his body and his mind were starting to crash. There had been too much chaos, too many startling and disturbing revelations for one evening. He had difficulty processing and sorting all of it. It was surreal and hard for him to believe that this was actually happening. It felt like a dream. A bad dream. The definition of a Nightmare come to life. Daniel wanted to wake up then. But he knew he was awake. Knew he wasn't dreaming, no matter how much he wished that were the case. Because when one woke from a nightmare there was a welcomed sense of relief that came from the realization that whatever horrible thing had just happened wasn't real, that it didn't really happen, that life went on normally. That everything was okay. He would find no such relief from the events of the night.

Daniel's emotions had been built up and pulled in so many directions over the last couple of hours his body and mind didn't know what to think, or what to do. Uncontrollably he started to sob, he couldn't stop it. He was feeling sorry for himself. Feeling sorry for Faith. He felt that he had failed her in some ways. He knew that she didn't have many friends--a lot of acquaintances but no real friends--but he thought, and hoped, that his friendship was enough for her. But obviously it wasn't. And for some reason she sought to befriend those who were not worthy of friendship, as they, more often than not, proved themselves to be users. Takers. Abandoners.

As he cried for himself--as Daniel's mind wrestled with everything that he'd been through, everything that he learned, the suspicions he still had, and what lay ahead of him--he fell into a sleep filled with angry, unsettling dreams.

CHAPTER NINETEEN

I t was like a colony of spiders running up and down her spine, her being in that house again. It literally made her skin prickle and seem to crawl. Certain smells, especially *his*, brought back memories that she thought had been left behind for good. It made the bile churning in her stomach rise into her throat. The moment she stepped through the doorway she was assaulted by that particular smell.

Each and every dwelling has its own distinctive set of smells depending on a lot of different variables: the age of the structure, the type of detergent used to clean the clothes, the brand of carpet or solid surface floors, the air fresheners used, the type of heating system, the kinds of foods regularly cooked, the type of soap and cologne used, if they had cats and cat litter boxes, if they had dogs in the house, if they smoked cigarettes, cigars, or marijuana, whether the foundation was on a concrete slab or had a crawl space or basement, these among a multitude of other factors made up the distinguishing scent of any given household. It was barely perceptible to those living in that environment, as it became "their smell." But to outsiders, the unique smell was immediately obvious and identified as foreign to their senses, their brains automatically processing the alien odors, trying to place and categorize them, consciously and subconsciously, in an effort to identify and label the myriad of scents so that they made sense to the newcomer.

Instantly, she was transported back and while she initially rebelled at it, a small part of her welcomed the smell of the house. The memories of her third son and daughter being born came to mind. Then, though, like a slide show flipping rapidly through the captured events, the odors brought back the horrors of what she had to deal with, what *he* had made her endure, until she found the courage to leave.

It was bittersweet being back there again, as it had been *her* house for over half a decade. She had picked out the furnishings, the curtains, the appliances, the dishes, the shower curtains, the bedding for the kids. It was surreal being back. Part of her felt like she was home, that she belonged there. Another part felt like she was back in a prison cell, a place where her actions and movements were controlled and dictated on a daily basis. There were rules and stipulations in that house. Her freedoms were curtailed and limited, almost as if she were a child living under the rule of a possessive parent.

But Faith had few choices on where she could stay after the events at Daniel's house some weeks before. Her brother and sister were not an option. Her mother could have been, *If she were any sort of real mother*, she thought. But she wasn't. All of her cousins and friends denied her a place to stay longer than a night or two, and not even that if she didn't have anything to "share."

So, against her better judgment, Faith swallowed her pride and asked Scott if she could stay there until she found another place to stay. He readily agreed, hoping that he could convince her to come back for good. For the kid's sake, he said. And so she did. For now.

Day by day she struggled to try and get some sort of routine going, as odd as that was. She was back to doing laundry in the old, familiar washer and dryer. The metal was dented and pitted, starting to rust in some places, but they still worked. She was again cooking dinner in the same aging pots and pans, mainly for herself and the kids, though she would save Scott a plate for when he got home from work, out of a sense of duty and obligation. But she refused to serve him, and so far he had accepted what little she was offering him.

But, he was still himself, which meant he was still hitting on her, would still brush up against her or smack her in the ass as he walked past. The touch of his body against hers really did make her skin crawl. She had a hard time remembering what she saw in him, why she was there for so long. But then in the next instant her mind would remind her, *you did it for your kids.* He was trying to buy her back as well. He offered to get her a vehicle, get her some new clothes, *if* she moved back in for good. And started sleeping in their bed again. Those were the stipulations, for starters, and with those came consequences she was not ready to accept.

Her children seemed less angry now that she was back in their house. She was sure Scott was telling them that she was back for good, that all was going back to the way it was. That all was right with the world. But it wasn't. Faith was struggling with her decisions, both past and present, which led her to where she was in life. She had too many regrets, too many missteps, too many people were trying to hold her down, she thought, to ever get out, to ever truly make things right for her and by extension for her kids. *One day at a time, Faith*, she told herself. That was her outlook now. She wasn't looking to any sort of future. She was living for the day.

We may not be here tomorrow, girl, her mind told her. So, do what you gotta do--whatever that is--to get through and enjoy *this day* as much as you can. Someone around you gets hurt along the way, that's their problem.

To deal with her situation, and to hide and run from it, her only refuge and her most faithful companion had become the Methadone wafers she was being prescribed, that and any OxyContin or Morphine Scott or her circle of so-called friends could score for her. She did need them for her chronic pain, so she was taking some orally as prescribed for that pain, but then she got used to snorting crushed up pills for an instant high that sent her on the cloud ride that made all her troubles float away. It seemed to capture all of her mental pain and anguish, wrapped it up tight and pushed it down to where she could no longer feel it. Until she came down and crashed from her high. Then she became irritable and angry. She fought verbally and sometimes physically with anyone and everyone. She felt she was losing control some days. She struggled to see past the moment she was trapped in, though she found it was too hard. There were too many clouds...too much fog, to see clearly the path ahead.

In those lasting moments of despair she thought of Daniel. She missed the life she had there, even though it wasn't perfect and she was bored and lonely. At least she was with somebody who treated her well. But she didn't have her kids, and she needed them. Faith felt regret for having to deceive Daniel, but she thought that what he didn't know truthfully would not hurt him. *And I have to put myself first,* she thought. *I gotta do for me first, because no one else is going to do it.*

She wanted to text him a few times, but then deleted it before she actually sent it. She wasn't sure what to say, or how he would react. She did check her phone periodically, hoping that he would reach out to her. But so far that hadn't happened. The drugs helped to numb her emotions and that was definitely something she wanted, and needed. She fought against thinking about the past. Couldn't allow herself to think or dream about a better future. Even the present posed obstacles and questions she passionately avoided.

She felt like she was trapped in a black box with all six sides showing her a different path, a different future. But the pictures changed too rapidly for her to see clearly what was happening on each path, they were all so different. Her mind hurt as she tried to concentrate, tried to make sense of the pictures and thoughts presented to her. She tried--Oh, how she tried!--but all the confusion just made her seek out the cloud of opiates that made everything okay. *Just get though the day...*

She heard the telltale sound of brakes squealing and hissing, and a large engine rumbling outside on the street. She looked up from folding the laundry out the window and saw the big yellow school bus in front of the house. Her sons were home. From the other room she heard her daughter waking up from her nap, the arrival of the school bus usually did that. It was a signal to her, and for Faith as well, that the after school chaos was about to begin.

CHAPTER TWENTY

H e wasn't sure how he got there. There were three of them, he knew that much. It was dark and rainy, he knew that much as well. The pavement and the multiple-story buildings that surrounded him were wet, the smell of wet brick and soaked asphalt mixed with that of the cold, oily rain that fell upon them. The droplets of rain that fell fast and hard were illuminated by a nearby yellow-hued sodium vapor light mounted high on a utility pole. He didn't recognize the men, not a single one. They all wore hoodies, the hoods pulled up and forward, their faces hidden in the shadow of the fabric. They surrounded him in a triangle formation. Daniel had to keep swiveling his head and turning his body, trying to keep them all in view. They were close, but with each passing second they were decreasing the attack triangle. He knew they were about to pounce on him, most likely all at once. He had to do something. Quick.

His arms were down by his sides, his hands balled into fists. He tried to bring his fists up in front of his face in a protective stance, but he couldn't lift them. Panic set in his mind then. He concentrated and tried to will his fists up, his arms to move, but they were lead, they felt like dead weight. Daniel seemed to have no control over the muscles in his arms.

His legs and the rest of his body seemed to be working fine. He didn't know what was wrong, his mind couldn't solve the puzzle.

Before he could ponder his situation any further, the man to his right lunged in with an attack. Daniel saw a blur in his peripheral vision, he quickly swiveled his body in that direction, bringing his right knee up close to his body, then striking out with his leg and foot, timing it so that he caught the assailant on his right knee as he advanced. The man let out a yelp as his leg buckled and sent him to the wet pavement.

In Daniel's mind he knew the others were probably advancing on him, though he did not see them. He swiveled quickly, but not quickly enough. His own leg buckled at the right knee as one of the other attackers struck him hard in the leg.

Pain flared throughout his body as the third attacker connected with something--*a fist?*--to the left side of his jaw. Daniel's teeth clacked together hard as his vision blurred and he fell to the wet pavement. His deadweight arms did nothing to stop his fall. His face slammed into the hard surface, just as if his hands were stuffed into his pant's pockets.

Daniel tried to move his arms, tried to push himself up to his feet, but they would not move. *Move, damnit!* He yelled to himself. *You gotta get up!* But he couldn't. No matter how much he willed them to move, tried to get his muscles to respond, his arms remained limp and useless. His breathing was rapid and shallow as he struggled to pull in oxygen. The air seemed hot and thick.

A flurry of booted blows thundered down upon him. Crushing stomps and splintering kicks landed everywhere on his body. Because of his useless arms he was unable to protect his face and his head. He felt his bones breaking, teeth forced from the gums, skin splitting and blood pouring from several parts of his body. His pain and frustration radiated through him.

"Yyaaaaahhhhhh!" He let out a scream as he absorbed another boot to the mouth. It was the only thing he could do. There was no stopping the onslaught.

His own screams pulled him from the nightmare.

Instinctively, Daniel pulled the blanket from over his head, feeling the cool bedroom air hit his face, his breathing heavy. He looked around him, confusion dominating his mind. It was dark, he was sweating. He blinked his eyes, trying to focus on his surroundings, desperately trying to figure out what was going on, where he was. What had just happened.

A dark figure leaped at him. Before Daniel could react, the creature began licking his face.

Almost instantly, Daniel realized he was lying in his bed, in his own bedroom. The creature licking his face was his cat. Daniel pet his soft companion as his heart rate began to normalize. The sounds of the feline purring soothed his raw nerves.

The nightmare was still fresh in his mind. He moved his arms freely, flexing the muscles. He breathed a sigh of relief as he realized that it was just a bad dream. He'd had the dream several times now, well variations of it, anyway. In each dream he was in some sort of fight, and he could not move his arms. He wanted to punch, to swing, use them in defense and attack. But they would not move, would not obey his mind's command. The dream was frustrating, as he seemingly knew what to do, he knew how to fight and protect himself. But he was unable to do so. The feeling of defenselessness led to a sense of hopelessness, then despair. He woke each time with a cloud of depression hanging over him, one that kept those feeling raw in his spirit even if his mind couldn't recognize them. Sometimes it would take days for him to shake the feelings. To feel normal again.

But what is *normal?* he wondered.

Through the closed blinds of the bedroom window, Daniel could see that the early autumn sun was rising. He twisted and leaned towards the side table and grabbed his cell phone. The time on the small display read 7:30AM. Too early to get up. It was his day off and he intended on resting his body and hopefully his mind as well. He rolled back over and pulled the covers back over his head, effectively blocking out the light of day. He fell back into the land of dreams that were powered by emotions and his unsettled subconscious mind.

This time Daniel dreamed of sitting on a grassy hillside bathed in sunlight. Beside him was a woman who held his hand as she smiled. They were on a hillside in northern Michigan, near Mackinaw City, a place he spent many hours playing as a child and adolescent. A happy place that only held fond memories. She squeezed his hand in hers as she told him she loved him. Daniel couldn't make out her face, as it was a blur in dreamy sunlight. His heart sang and leaped within him as her face seemed to shine as the sun was, warming his body and soul with her love and adoration.

*   *   *

Daniel made a pot of coffee and scuffled through his morning, wearing black sweatpants, a gray sweatshirt, socks, and a pair of black slip-on shoes. The house, which was just under 1600 square feet, seemed huge and cavernous when he was alone. Just having another person there, having Faith there, made it seem smaller, more homey and inviting. When her children were over, it seemed downright small. It had been weeks since she had left. He hadn't spoken to her since, and had only texted her twice in that time.

At first, Daniel was so angry, he was glad that she was gone. He hoped that she was having a really bad time where she was living and that she regretted what she had done to put herself back in that situation. But, as the days passed and he had no contact with her, his mind fought with his heart, and his genitals. There was a constant, ever-present battle, a war that waged in his head between his thoughts: What he should've done, what he should've said, what he wished would have happened...In his mind he saw things as he wanted to see them, as he hoped that one day they would be. He held onto that vision of the future, believing that it was just around the next corner. But, it seemed that his fantasy utopia with Faith was not to be, that their relationship was over.

Good. About damn time, his mind told him. You need to move on, cut your losses. Let your wounds heal.

As Daniel filled his cup with coffee, then added chocolate creamer and a packet of Splenda sweetener, he choked back feelings of remorse with each stir of the spoon.

What do you have to feel sorry about? His mind asked. She did this to you, lied to you. You did not send her away, she chose to leave. She knew she did you wrong, and she knew that she had to leave. Except it. Embrace it. Move on with your life. What you had is done.

These thoughts flowed through his consciousness, but even so something within him resisted.

He didn't like being alone. He felt empty, and hollow. Daniel realized that part of this feeling came from the knowledge that he had been betrayed, whether it was intentional or not on Faith's part. He felt violated. And used. In his heart he knew that he should accept what his conscience was telling him. But there was a piece of him that stubbornly refused.

One of the hardest parts of his life was sleeping now. Daniel had become accustomed to the warm body next to him. Even if they were upset or angry with each other, their bodies would still tend to gravitate towards one another. She would still grab his arm or his hand, still wrap her calf and ankle around his. He slept better with her warmth and her presence next to him.

Her scent, her essence, was all but gone from the sheets and the pillowcase now. He had washed them and in effect had washed her scent out of them. It made him sad in a way. It was a gradual separation back to reality from the fantasy utopian relationship his mind had been projecting. What it had been zealously wanting and striving for.

Daniel kept thinking, kept dwelling, on the good days, the fun times they had together. His body longed to be pressed against hers. To be one with hers again.

She was mine, he thought angrily. *She* is *mine!* His internal being raged against the thought of her being with her ex again. It struggled to deal with the assumption that what they had was gone, and that she had gone back to that which she had tried, that *they* had tried, to get her away from so very hard. Daniel didn't like losing. He didn't like the feeling of loss.

So call her and ask her to come back, he thought. *You know she will in a heartbeat.*

The day before in a drunken state of weakness he almost did just that. But, no. He knew that he couldn't do that. She had wronged him, and she needed to realize that. She needed to sincerely apologize for what she had done. He wasn't sure if she ever would. He wasn't even sure if she thought that she did anything wrong.

Since her departure his days had been filled with going through the motions of life. He went to work and did his job, endured all the stress and chaos that it threw at him. He did his laundry, cooked his own meals, and cleaned up after himself. He was capable and it didn't bother him doing these things. What did bother Daniel was a that he didn't see much point to doing these things.

What is life if you do not have someone special to share it with? He thought. He realized then why it was that couples who had been together, every day, for decades would die within weeks, sometimes days, of one another. They no longer had a purpose to live. A large part of their life was gone. Forever. Everyone needs a reason. Something to look forward to, even if it was just a kiss good night.

God, please help me find my reason, he silently prayed.

As he sipped his coffee, his cell phone rang. Daniel was startled by the ring, as he instantly recognized the ring tone. His heart rate accelerated instantly at the sound. It was assigned to Faith. A mixture of excitement, apprehension, and anxiety filled him with each quick thundering beat of his heart. The conflicting emotions made his mind whirl as he tried to sort them out.

He stared at her name on the small display for a few seconds, debating whether he should let it go to voicemail or if he should answer it. After a second of hesitation he flipped the phone open.

"Hello?" He said, waiting for her to speak.

"Hi, Daniel. How are you?" Faith asked. In her voice he detected a tone of sadness, but also apprehension. He thought she seemed afraid to be talking to him. *I bet she's going to ask if she can come back*, he thought.

"I'm okay. How are you?" He asked. He did want to know how she was, how she was doing. But, at the same time he did not want to know. Actually, he wanted to hear her say that she was miserable, that she was so very sorry, that she wanted to come back desperately. But even if she felt those things, he was sure she would never say that to him. She was too proud. Too stubborn. Saying those things would be an admittance of guilt. Daniel knew she was probably far from that point, no matter what she was presently enduring, what she had done.

"Well, the kids are happy that I'm here. But, the reason I called is that I have to tell you something. You're probably going to get mad, but I feel that you need to know, so you can do something about it," she told him.

What is this now? He thought. He remained silent, his mind spinning and whirling, trying to anticipate what she was going to say. His heart rate immediately sped up even faster, he sat his coffee cup down, anticipating the worst. His mind came up blank, not being able to conceive of what she was calling to tell him after weeks of silence. The fast rhythm of his pulse thundered in his ears made it hard for him to hear. He turned the volume up all the way on his phone and pressed it to the side of his face as he waited for her to speak.

"Umm...I went to my doctor and during some routine checks they find out that I have Gonorrhea," she told him.

Gonorrhea? The fucking CLAP? His thoughts were instantly tangled in a rage. "Wait, what?" He managed to say, still not really comprehending what was being said.

"I wasn't feeling right, and with what the cop told me what those assholes said we did-- and honestly I don't remember everything that happened, because of my meds, you know that I get confused and don't remember some things--So anyway, I had them check and they found out that I have an STD. So, I wanted to let you know that you need to go and get a shot to have it cleared up, okay? I don't know how I got it, but I do, well I did have it, but I got a shot. So I'm sure you probably have it, too," she told him in a rambling explanation.

Daniel couldn't believe what he was hearing. He never had a sexually transmitted disease before. And before the events of the previous weeks he had thought he and Faith were in a monogamous relationship. That it wasn't even a possibility.

"Are you fucking kidding me?" He yelled into the phone.

"I know you're mad, but Daniel I honestly don't know how I got it. I've never had sex with those assholes, I don't know why they're saying that. The only thing I can think of is that my friend Teresa stayed over a few nights--remember?--and I found her using my sex toy. She must've had something nasty, and I didn't wash it correctly, and I used it on myself and that's how I got it. That must be the reason," she said in another rambling, nonsensical explanation. "But, I didn't want you to get hurt, you should know about it so you can go get it fixed."

Daniel didn't know what to say. He didn't know how to react. What she was saying didn't make much sense to him. Though he did believe what she was saying about the disease. He knew that she would not have called and told him if she wasn't sure that she had something. His mind balled into a tight, flaming fist of fury. He wanted to reach through the phone and choke her.

"That's just fucking great, Faith! Thanks a lot for all you've done for me. I really, really appreciate it," he said coating his words with as much sarcasm as he could manage. "I hope you and Scott have a wonderful life together. Fuck you very much," he said as he snapped his cell phone closed, ending the call.

Daniel closed his eyes and gripped the edge of the counter tightly with both hands. He was so angry he pictured himself ripping the countertop from the cabinets and throwing the hunks through the windows, smashing them to bits. But he knew wrecking his own stuff wasn't helpful. He focused on taking long, deep breaths in an effort to calm himself.

That's just wonderful, he thought. *I gotta spend money on the doctor to get rid of a fucking disease that this bitch gave me.*

His emotions were locked in a wrestling match. Anger, frustration, and self-pity twisted and turned over one other, like a pit of vipers scrambling for warmth or scraps of meat. Daniel suddenly felt very ill and tired, and just wanted to go back to bed.

*   *   *

It was three in the afternoon when Daniel arrived at the clinic. It was a combination of urgent care walk-in clinic and a primary care physician's office. It was Faith's primary physician. Daniel parked the Toyota and walked across the small parking lot towards the entrance. The trees were just starting to turn colors. Mostly yellows and some orange, no reds yet that Daniel could see. A few leaves had already fallen and were starting to litter the green grass and the pavement. The air was crisp and chill. The smell of autumn was distinctly different than that of spring. To him, it had a tinge of death foreshadowing an end. Whereas spring smelled fresh and was filled with the promise of newness, new beginnings. There were only two other cars in the lot, so Daniel hoped that he would not have to wait very long. He hated going to the doctor.

After entering, Daniel walked up to the counter and waited for the receptionist to acknowledge him. It took her nearly three minutes to do so. She asked him the reason for his visit. Daniel hesitated, embarrassed. He could feel his face flush red, knew that she could see it as well. He didn't want to tell her. But he did anyway.

"I need to get treated for an STD," he said matter-of-factly and in as low a voice as he could without whispering.

To his relief, the receptionist did not ask any more questions. She handed him a clipboard with several pieces of paper on it and asked him to fill them out since it was his first visit. She asked for his drivers license and insurance card so she could make a copy of them. Daniel handed her both and then found a chair away from the other two people who were in the waiting room and began the process of reading the papers and checking off the appropriate boxes about his medical history. He filled out the first page with name, address, etc. It took him about thirteen minutes to fill everything out, after which he returned the clipboard and the pen to the receptionist she told him that he would be called shortly.

Daniel flipped through a few of the uninteresting and outdated magazines that were laid out on the table before the row of chairs. He looked at *Newsweek* very briefly before exchanging it for a *Popular Mechanics*. That kept his attention as he skimmed a few articles before putting that down and picking up a *Car and Driver*. The seat was uncomfortable and Daniel kept fidgeting in it trying to get comfortable. He started with his right foot and ankle on his left knee, then switch to the left foot and ankle on his right knee. Both feet on the floor, his knees bent, then his legs out with ankles crossed.

Finally, a solid wooden door to his right opened and a pleasant looking nurse, her dark blonde hair pulled back in a ponytail, wearing navy blue scrubs and blue and pink Nike sneakers walked in and stopped. She glanced down at her clipboard then said, "Daniel Gibson?"

Daniel quickly got up from his seat and walked to where she was standing. She led him through the doorway, closing it behind them, and over to a large scale and weighed him with his shoes on. She then led him into one of the examination rooms and told him to have a seat and the doctor would be with him shortly.

For the next nine minutes Daniel studied the anatomy poster on the wall, waiting for the doctor. His mind absorbed the terms and definitions, his eyes traced the different colored veins, arteries, muscles and tendons. He let his gaze wander around the room, taking in the small countertop and cabinets, the jars of sterilized equipment. The red Sharps container on the wall with the biohazard three blade insignia on the front. He briefly thought of bolting from the room and just leaving, wishing that he could leave this predicament and this bump in the road of life, his life, behind him. But he knew he couldn't do that. He had to get this taken care of, no matter how embarrassing and uncomfortable it was.

The door opened and a man in his late 40s with a mustache and thinning brown hair, wearing black slacks and a white lab coat over a light blue shirt with a stethoscope around his neck entered.

"Mr. Gibson, I am Dr. Thompson," he said as he offered his hand. The two men shook. The doctor looked at the clipboard before saying, "So, you think you have an STD?"

Daniel was still embarrassed, but that's what he was here for. "Yes. My girlfriend said that she was tested and treated for Gonorrhea," he told the doctor.

"Okay, well, there's a test that we have to perform to make sure that you have it, and if you do then there is the treatment," Dr. Thompson explained.

Daniel figured there was no sense in taking the test when the doctor probably already had all of the information he needed. "My girlfriend is Faith Collins," Daniel said matter-of-factly.

Dr. Thompson stopped and looked up. He locked eyes with Daniel for a couple of fast seconds, then asked, "*Faith* is your girlfriend?" With a name as unique as that, in a small northern Michigan town it really wasn't a question of who he was referring to, especially given the fact that she had just been treated a day or two before by this same doctor.

"Yes. She called me earlier today saying that she had been tested and treated, and that I should come and get treated myself," Daniel told him.

With that Dr. Thompson just nodded his head. He paused for a few long moments as if he wanted to say something, or had questions. But the doctor remained silent. Before the silence became awkward Dr. Thompson turned and walked out of the examination room closing the door behind him.

Daniel's heart was racing and his anxiety was building as he tried to push the embarrassing thoughts from his mind. He felt dirty. Used. Less than. He was hoping that for some reason the doctor would return and tell him that it all had been a big mistake, that he did not have an STD, that he treated Faith for something different, anything different....

The doctor returned in less than three minutes, carrying a couple of sealed pouches.

"Okay, Faith mentioned you might be in," Dr. Thompson began. "So, we can skip the test and go right to the treatment. Now, when I was in the Army they referred to this as *Rodding*," the doctor told him. "What I am going to do is take a long, cotton swab treated with ceftriaxone, and insert it into the opening of your penis and run it down as far as it will go. I will then give you one pill of azithromycin and that should take care of it."

You gotta be kidding me? Daniel thought. *How embarrassing!*

"I need you to stand up, and pull your pants and your underwear down to your knees," Dr. Thompson instructed. Daniel complied. "This will sting. It will not be pleasant, but it will only take a couple of seconds," he was told.

Daniel winced as the foreign object was pushed internally down the length of his dick. It was a hot, burning sensation, worse than he experienced as a child getting soap inside of it. But similar, Daniel realized. But much more humiliating.

Maybe that'll shut him up for a while, his mind said in jest, referring to the third internal opponent in their group whose arguments seemed to win out over the other two viewpoints on most occasions.

If it weren't for the stinging, burning pain and humiliation Daniel might have laughed to himself at the thought.

"Okay, we're done. You can pull your pants up," Dr. Thompson said.

You have to ask him, his mind prompted.

Fearing the answer, Daniel reluctantly asked, "Dr. Thompson, how do you get gonorrhea?"

Dr. Thompson stopped and looked at Daniel again. Daniel could read on his face that the doctor was reluctant to answer, being Faith's physician and having that medical relationship with her. "Through sexual intercourse," he finally said.

The words were like a slap to Daniel. His mind seemed to focus on the still burning sensation which seemed to match the reddening and the heat flaring in his cheeks at the embarrassment. *Why am I hear, Lord?* he asked silently. There was no immediate answer.

"Could you get it from a sex toy?" Daniel asked, seeing if Faith's story of sharing a dirty sex toy was plausible.

"No," the doctor began after another uncomfortable pause. "The bacteria cannot live outside of the human body, therefore you have to have direct genital fluid contact to transmit the bacteria from one person to the other."

No ambiguity there, Daniel thought ."Thank you, Doctor," he said. He felt broken. And hollow, like the essence of life that propels everyone forward, the force that allows them to get up after falling down, the internal drive that keeps them moving forward and moving on from life's setbacks, was leaking from is body and soul. He suddenly felt very tired.

"If you have nothing else, you're free to go. Just check out at the desk on your way out," Dr. Thompson said before turning and walking again from the room.

That fucking, lying bitch! Daniel thought, his anger flaring like that of gasoline being thrown on a campfire.

Now are you ready to let her go? His mind asked.

Maybe all those assholes were telling the truth, at least one of them must of had sex with her, he thought. The thoughts conjured pictures in his mind, and made him sick to his stomach.

Daniel's mind and body felt heavy, weighed down by the stressful events and by too much thinking. He wasn't sure what he was going to do next. But he was ready for a drink. As he got into the Toyota and turned the engine over, Daniel pulled out his cell phone. As he quickly backed out of the parking space and then sped out of the parking lot onto the highway, he speed dialed Faith's number.

His heart was racing, his anger building. He was vaguely focused on his driving as he listened to the phone ring, three, four times, before he heard her recorded voice announcing that she was unavailable to answer the phone. Daniel waited for the beep.

"Yeah, I just left the doctors office. And he said you're basically full of fucking shit! The only way you can get gonorrhea is by fucking somebody, you can't get it from a sex toy!" Daniel shouted into the phone, putting as much anger and frustration as he could into each word. "The cops said you were having sex with all of those dirtbag assholes you had over, I guess they were right!" With that, Daniel snapped his phone shut. He didn't know what else to say to her. He was thankful that it was her voicemail so that he didn't have to listen to her lame excuse or explanation. Though, he was sure that would come sometime after she listened to that message.

He wanted to punch some thing. Someone. He briefly thought about going over to Rhonda's, trying to find Justin and Greg and Ryan. He wanted revenge. He wanted them to feel the pain that he was feeling. He also wanted them to know that there was consequences to their actions.

That's not going to take back what happened, his mind said. And it was more Faith's fault than it was their's.

Daniel knew he couldn't argue with that logic. He knew the blame rested solely with one person. *Even if they somehow had forced her to have sex,* he thought, *she was still the one that put herself in a compromising situation. She was the one who invited them over. She was the one who would not call the cops on them. She was the one who was lying to cover everything up.*

He had a raging headache now. He wanted to get back home, take some ibuprofen and wash it down with a six pack of beer. He wanted to put this day, most of this year, behind him.

God, show me the way, he prayed. There was no immediate answer.

CHAPTER TWENTY-ONE

The music was loud. The DJ was playing a mix of classic rock and modern country, but once in a while he would throw in a top ten pop hit. There was a dance floor in front of the DJ station with his large floor speakers and an array of spinning and blinking lights, trying to add the effect of a dance party. The place was called The Keyhole Bar and Grille, but locals either referred to it as The Keyhole or just the Hole. Though they did have a small kitchen and offered a small variety of pub grub, they didn't serve much food. Partially because the prices were high and the quality was very poor. But, mainly it was because the people who went to the Hole went there to drink and get rowdy.

He liked to people watch, and woman watch mainly. From his vantage point he could watch the bathrooms, the bar, entry door, as well as the dance floor that was directly in front of him. Most of the people there were wearing jeans and T-shirts, having removed their denim jean jackets or their leather jackets because it was 30° warmer inside, especially with all the body heat, than it was out in the cold mid October night.

When he first arrived some 25 minutes earlier, Nevver grabbed a small two seat table along a side wall furthest from the door, but with a view of nearly the entire place. There were three bartenders, but only one server who was out on the floor. He was able to get a drink fairly quickly--double Maker's Mark on the rocks--but the server had not bothered to even look at him since then. As the song "Blue-collar Man" from *Styx* boomed through the speakers, Nevver made his way up to the bar, which was two and three people deep waiting for drinks. He thought about leaving, but since he didn't know the area well he wasn't sure he'd find another place, and just end up wandering around in the dark. So he decided to stay. *Besides*, he thought, *there are quite a few women in here, not all seem to be attached to someone else.* Not that that had ever stopped him before.

There were a handful of women that he kept his eyes on. One in particular had thick legs, but she wore tight jeans and something about how the denim hugged her large, round ass appealed to him. Plus, she seemed to have large round breasts as well. The real objects of his current lustful stares were a couple of younger blonde women, dressed the same in red and black flannel, tight blue jeans, and cowgirl boots. The flannel shirts were unbuttoned and nodded at the side, the sleeves rolled up to the elbows. One wore her hair long to the shoulders and had a black tank top exposed underneath, while her "twin" wore a red tank top exposed underneath, and her blonde hair was in two braids. Nevver was waiting for them to go out on the dance floor before he made his move with either, or both of them. Though he figured they might be a hard catch as they seemed to be constantly approached by men even in the relatively short time he was there.

There were a few others that he tried to keep his eye on as they walked among the crowds of people. But they seemed to be social butterflies and didn't stay in one place for too long. The lighting was dark and the bar was filled with cigarette smoke, which made it harder to zero in on specific females. There was a movement in Michigan to have all smoking banned in restaurants and bars, but the measure had had stalled in the Senate. So, things went on as usual.

He wedged himself in between two people a quarter of the way down the bar nearest the bartender that seem to be the fastest. The woman who is now pressed up against the front of him, or he against the back of her, was smoking a cigarette and she blew the smoke over her shoulder, directly into his face. The acrid smoke burned his eyes and he choked a little as he was just inhaling when the smoke assaulted him.

"Thanks for that," he said to her in a playful tone. "That's not my brand, but I did leave my cigarettes across the room."

The woman turned her body around and looked at him, puzzled. "Are you talking to me?" She asked.

"Yes, you blew your cigarette smoke in my face I was just telling you that I appreciated it since I don't have a smoke with me," he said again, the playfulness having gone out of it. She just rolled her eyes and turned back around.

Nevver focused his attention on the bartender. She was short, barely just 5 foot tall. She had dark brown hair with a couple purple streaks running through it. She wore cut off denim shorts that exposed large tattoos on both of her thighs. She also wore a leather vest that exposed her tattooed bare arms and shoulders, and was low-cut enough to show that she also had a tattoo across the top of her breasts. She had a diamond stud in her nose that caught the lights and glistened as she moved back and forth pouring drinks like a frenzied expert. As she finished mixing and pouring her current drinks and collected the money for it, Nevver caught her eyes with his.

"Double Maker's on the rocks, and two bottles of Bud Light," he shouted over the din. She nodded and went to work getting his simple order. He already had a ten dollar bill in his hand, which was for the Maker's and a tip, but at the last second he figured he better get a couple more drinks while he had the chance. He reached into his front pocket and grabbed his thin stack of folded up bills. From it he peeled off a five dollar bill. The bartender was back in a minute, setting a rocks glass and two bottles of beer in front of him.

"Eleven bucks," she said. Nevver handed her the fifteen dollars and smiled as he grabbed the glass containing the Maker's Mark with his left hand and the two bottles of beer at their neck in his right. The bartender seemed to be appreciative of the tip as she smiled and thanked him before moving on quickly to the next patron.

As he made his way back to the small table he noticed that there was a second room. It appeared to be a billiards room. A wry smile crept on his face as he thought of the thinning amount of money that he had, and the thought of double or tripling it with some of these rubes over a few games of pool. He collected his jacket and his cigarettes from the small table and made his way into the pool room.

In the room there were three seven foot pool tables with the standard bar-worn green felt and the coin mechanism built into the side. Two tables were currently in use, and the third was not. Six round, high-top tables with three chairs at each were spaced along the wall. Two racks of pool cues along with three or four well used chalk cubes were on the short side wall where the entry to the main bar was located. The table closest to that entry was the one not in use. Nevver grabbed the nearest round top to that pool table, set his drinks upon it, and settled himself in as he lit a cigarette.

The music from the other room could still be clearly heard, though it was slightly muffled due to the enclosed nature of the billiards room. But, thankfully, it allowed conversation to be had at near-normal levels, without shouting too much.

At the table furthest from him four redneck-looking guys played teams. They were all similarly dressed in jeans, rock band T-shirts, and sneakers. Their haircuts and facial hair varied to a man. They were all distinctive in that respect, Nevver noticed. They were laughing, joking and having a good time. And they all seemed to be fixated on the three women playing on the middle table.

Only two women were actually playing, the third sat at the round top and was nursing a bottle of Bud Light, though she did have a better-than-average personal pool cue next to her chair leaning against the wall. It was blue with black silver accents, definitely not one of the blonde and brown wooded house cues. *So, she's a player*, he thought.

The women were all very distinctive. One of the ones playing pool was tall, nearly six foot. She had long, dark blonde hair that was kinky-curly and flowed to the middle of her back. She wore black jeans tucked in to knee-high black leather boots with four inch heels. She wore a navy blue sateen blouse open down to third button, exposing a black lace bra. Over that she wore a short leather jacket that barely came to her waist, which was clad in a chrome studded black leather belt. She was a poor pool player, Nevver noticed, as she seemed to miss every other shot. She had a nice smile, and a loud, quirky laugh that somehow was alluring even though it was annoying. Her face was achne scarred and worn most probably by many years of cigarette smoke, and who knows what else. But she was attractive in a white trash sort of way, he thought.

Her current opponent was much shorter and also thicker than she was. About 5' 3" and stocky built, she wore a black fabric miniskirt stretched across an ample rear end and solid thighs, over black stockings tucked into ankle high, three inch heeled red leather boots. She wore a black leather corset laced with red that pushed up and out her breasts making them appear larger than they actually were. Her hair was pulled back into a tiny ponytail, being all one length. It was colored black with no accents. Her facial makeup was pale, her lips colored black, her eyeliner dark. That combination seemed to accentuate her dark eyes, and her straight, white teeth. She had a nice smile. To Nevver it seemed she was portraying herself as the vampire queen. She was obviously the better pool player.

But, for some reason most of his attention was drawn to the woman who was not playing. She sat with her legs crossed at the knees on the high stool at the table. She smoked menthol 100s, Nevver noticed. She wore tight, short, blue denim shorts that ended just a couple inches past her buttocks. She wore no leggings or stockings, her legs were bare and showed some muscle tone even though they were not tanned, though they were not overly pale. On her feet she supported bulky, black leather boots that went up mid-calf with a thick, high heel. Around her waist she, too wore a black leather belt that was studded with chrome accents that sparkled in the light. She wore heavy dark blue eye shadow, black eyeliner and he noticed her eyebrows had been shaved off and replaced with dark brown pencil-drawn replicas. She wore dark lipstick, though not black. A deep blood red. Her deep brown hair was spiked on top, though flowed to her neck, choppy. It reminded Nevver of Pat Benatar in a way. Not just because of her haircut, but also because of the look on her face. It had an edge to it, a hard, but sexy demeanor. Her voice was smoky, Nevver guessed because of the cigarettes and her drinking. But she seemed playful, and wild. She was lobbing comments and playful insults at her two companions as they played, punctuated by her own laughter. Something in his animalized brain wanted her. More than the other two. More than all of the other women in the other part of the bar. There was something about her that seemed to be drawing him in.

Nevver glanced down at the pool table closest to him, at the coin slot. He noticed that it was seventy-five cents per play. He dug three quarters from his right front pocket and jingled them in his hand as he took a swallow of the Maker's Mark. Noticing that the two women playing pool still had the better part of the game left to play, Nevver got off his high stool, grabbed one of the bottles of Bud Light and walked over to the woman seated.

"Hey there. We got an empty pool table, care to play game? My quarters," he said as way of introduction.

The woman looked up at him. At first Nevver detected annoyance in her blue-green eyes, but then they suddenly changed to playfulness, and maybe he even detected a sense of adventure. He liked that. Though, he sensed some apprehension on her part still.

He held out the bottle of Bud Light to her, "I'll even buy you a fresh drink. You can break. Unless you're scared, that is," Nevver said, baiting her on with a smile.

"Oh, really? We'll see who's scared," she replied with a smile and look in her eye that Nevver had hoped he would see. She accepted the bottle of beer and climbed down off the stool. She grabbed her personal pool cue and walked the few feet to the empty pool table. "Rack 'em," she commanded. Nevver complied.

     *   *   *

They had played two games of eight ball, each one calling their shots. Nevver won the first match leaving his opponent with four balls on the table. She took the next match leaving Nevver with six balls remaining.

"We gotta play a tie-breaker," Nevver announced.

"I'll rack while you go get us some drinks," she said, raising an eyebrow and smirking at him.

Nevver looked at her like she was out of her mind, but he smiled his best smile and said, "Okay, but let's make this one interesting. Twenty bucks to the winner."

"You're on!" she said as she got off of the high stool and put three quarters into the sliding mechanism that released the balls. Nevver greedily stared at her as she bent over and inserted quarters into the mechanism.

"We're done playing. We're gonna go dance," her taller friend told her as they both walked up to her. She looked up at her two fiends and smiled. Never leaned his pool cue against the table, turned and walked towards the bar to get the drinks. *Oh yeah, this bitch is mine*, he thought.

"I'll be there in a few minutes. That fuck is buying me a drink and wants to play again for twenty bucks!" She told them with a sly smile. "As soon as I win I will come find you. I wanna dance too--and *don't* leave without me!" she added quickly, as she had been in that predicament more times than she cared to remember, having to walk or bum a ride home from some stranger that either wanted sex or drugs for their "generosity," *Fuckin' sickos*, she thought. Her friends laughed and left her to rack the balls.

Just then her phone went off. The sounds startled her, even though she could barely hear it above the din from the music and the bar noise from the next room. But she had it set on ring and vibrate and it was sitting on the table top next to the ashtray. The purple phone vibrated and shook, making its way in an erratic pattern as the small display lit up. She grabbed it with her left hand, holding her cigarette in her right. She looked at the display and her mind absorbed the name. She debated whether to answer it or not. She wasn't sure what the conversation would be, but she could guess it probably wouldn't be good. She flipped open the phone anyway, curiosity getting the better of her.

"Hello?" She said with an exhale of cigarette smoke.

She listened to the words, to what the man on the other end was saying to her. But she didn't really care, not then. She was having fun, having a good time. "I can't...I'm with some friends, they're my ride," she told him. She wasn't ready to call it a night. She didn't get out as much as she wanted to, so she wasn't about to cut her night short. "I can't, I'm sorry. You know I would if I could," she told him and part of her meant it, but she knew that it wasn't possible so she didn't have to spin a lie to get out of her sense of obligation. She told the truth. It felt oddly refreshing. "I'll talk to you tomorrow, okay?" she said and snapped the phone shut. She thought about it for a second, then flipped the phone back open and depressed the power button, holding it down until the phone went dark, shutting it off. She tossed it into her purse which sat open on the stool next to her. She grabbed the bottle of beer and tipped it into her mouth only to find it empty. She slammed it on the table, disappointed.

From the next room she could hear the band beginning to play *FreeBird* by Lynyrd Skynyrd. She loved the song, but it made her think of her dad. It was the song they chose to play at his funeral, not *Amazing Grace* or any of the other typical funeral songs. She fought back tears brought on by hard memories. She wanted to go dance. She wanted a drink. She thought briefly about going to the bathroom and doing up one of her pills, but decided against it. For now. She wanted to win that money first.

Nevver returned twelve minutes later, as he had to wait at the bar for drinks, with four bottles of Bud Light. He wanted to get some shots of vodka in an effort to get this woman tuned up and more eager for some action, but he had to conserve his money, especially since he just bet her twenty bucks. She had the balls expertly racked tightly together on the table waiting for someone to break. He set the bottles of beer down on the table where she was sitting semi-patiently smoking a cigarette.

"Took you long enough," she said playfully as she grabbed one of the bottles and took a drink.

"Hey, if you can get drinks quicker you are more than welcome to get them yourself. And pay for them," he replied as he walked to the far end of the table, chalked his pool cue and moved the white cue ball just to the right of center as he aimed his breaking shot. He slid the cue once, then twice slowly aiming his shot. On the third stroke he used much greater force, slamming his cue into the white ball, sending it down the table smashing into the triangle of colored balls with a loud *Crack!*

Three balls were sunk on the break. Two solids, one stripe. "I'll take solids," he announced.

"Figures," she said in a sarcastic tone, playfully. "I knew you could not handle a real challenge."

Nevver looked at her and exhaled a laugh. "Oh, I can handle any challenge you got, girl."

With that, he lined up the cue ball and with a quick, forward motion of his right arm, slamming his stick into the white ball which then smacked into the dark red seven solid, sending it into the called pocket. He looked up, locked eyes with her, giving her his: *yeah, you know I got what you need* look. She smirked at him and took a drink in reply, all the while keeping her blue-green eyes locked on his.

Nevver made two more shots, then missed. It was her turn now.

She confidently got down from the stool, finished the half of beer left in the bottle, grabbed her custom cue and chalked it, all the while keeping her eyes locked on his. She was purposefully playing with him. Trying to get him excited, trying to get him thinking about-- focused on--her and not his pool game. She was trying to get his cock hard, and his mind numb. She wanted that twenty dollars. And whatever else she could take from him, without giving him anything in return, except a wink and an empty promise.

She called her shots well. She studied the table, not taking any overly risky shots. She sunk four in a row, then was eyeing up her fifth as the white cue ball slowly rolled almost into the perfect position. She looked at him, locked her eyes on his, and gave him *the I know you want my pussy smile*, as she lifted an eyebrow and drummed her long, painted fingernails on her pool cue. The trick was, though, not conveying the desired answer to that question. Leaving it a mystery. Leaving him wondering, his mind going crazy with anticipation...Wanting...Lusting.

She winked her left eye as she made her next shot, sinking the blue striped ten ball. She let out a giggle as he theatrically winced and swore. But, on her next attempt the green striped 14 just barely missed the side pocket, bouncing off the corner, ending her turn.

"Oh, fuck me!" She shouted, honestly pissed at herself for the miss. *I was so close to putting this asshole away and going dancing*, she thought angrily.

"Any, and *every* time you want," Nevver told her with a deviant smile. With a drink from his bottle of beer he walked up to the table and eyed his next shot.

The dark blue four, and the yellow one were both possibilities from where the cue ball had come to rest. He chose the more surer shot, calling out the four ball in the right corner pocket. He chalked the 21 ounce house cue theatrically as he looked her in the eyes and gave her a wink. With a swift *crack* of the balls--his eyes still locked on hers--the four banged against the rubber protector of the pocket and disappeared into the dark hole.

"Ugnh! Can you feel that!?!" Nevver said as he made several thrusting motions with his hips, dancing down the length of the table, celebrating his small victory. He had been watching her every time she bent over the table to make a shot. He wanted her. He wanted so much to violate her in so many ways. He wanted to see her look up at him as his dick slid in and out of her mouth, having her smile as she did so. Even if it took all night and the last of his money he was going to have her. At least, that was his goal. He wished he had some Oxys or Coke...he could tell she was into something, but he couldn't tell what.

She gave him a look like: *Ehh, I've had better, you really think I'm gonna let you touch me?*, conveying it with her eyes and her attitude that she was not impressed. Well, maybe a little, she had to admit. But, she wasn't out for that tonight. At least not yet. She just wanted to have fun, and that she was. *It's fun flirting and messing with this joker who sees himself as a Player and "God's gift to women"*, she thought. *It's not going to happen tonight, but it is still fun watching him squirm.*

The look gave Nevver more incentive, *I'm gonna fuck this bitch, hard!* He thought. He liked a challenge, but he liked conquering one so much more. He knew that he might only have one chance with any given woman. So, when he got the chance he always went for the most debaucherous, the most to degrading, the most dominating sex acts he could get away with. She was ripe for the taking, and he was not going to let this chance go to waste.

He chalked his pool cue like he was putting on a condom. He looked at her as he prepared for his next shot as if her little denim shorts were already in a pile of clothes on the floor, as he held her writs tightly making her yell and scream in that place between pleasure and pain....

CHAPTER TWENTY-TWO

He had been awake since the late October sunrise just shortly after seven-thirty. He lay in bed, thinking. The bed seemed too large, cold and empty. He found that he still slept on "his" side, not wandering over to "hers," not even in his sleep. Sometimes when he woke during the night he would reach across, searching for the warm body, only to find cold sheets. He pushed the pangs of loneliness down into his spirit. *Today was going to be a great day*, he thought.

He had the day planned out, though just tentatively. Food, *check*. He bought a massive pork rib, nearly five pounds of meat and bone that he and/or Nevver would grill up. Along with that he had large baker potatoes and fresh, uncut green beans. Garlic bread knots as an added bonus.

Drink, *check*. Daniel bought a case of Michelob Ultra and a case of Labatt Blue. He also bought a fifth of Maker's Mark and a fresh seven pound bag of crushed ice. Activities, *check*. Along with the billiards table and dozens of movies to watch, Daniel also had an Xbox and even an older Sega Genesis if they wanted to play some old-school games like *Sonic the Hedgehog 1* or *2*, *Madden 95* or *NHL 95*, he even had the *7-Up Spot* game and the head-to-head battle game *Herzog-Zwie*. The graphics weren't the greatest compared with the Xbox, but the games were still fun to play at times, and the three button controllers were definitely easier to manipulate than those of the Xbox.

To top it all off, Daniel in the late spring had spent $1500 on a two-seat go-cart. It had a 196cc Briggs & Stratton engine with a top speed of 31 miles an hour. It had large, knobby tires for off-road use was perfect for the private gravel road he lived on and for zooming around his acre of yard. He made a small track out behind the house, complete with curves, one small hill and plenty of mogul bumps that mother nature had seen fit to install in the ground previously. It was a short track that did not allow you to open up the engine fully, but the course made it challenging, and the bumps made it fun. He looked forward to doing some time trials with his best friends.

Even though Nevver usually insisted on having "women" in attendance at some point, Daniel was not about to try and provide any of that this time. Faith had been gone nearly two months and he had only spoken with her three times, once being when she told him of her STD, the second was her calling back to adamantly deny her having sex with anybody else, sticking to her false story of a dirty sex toy, or a blackout where someone might have done something to her and she was not aware. The third and last time was a short conversation just two days prior.

He had been drinking, feeling lonely and sorry for himself, and wanted some attention. After a few mental conversational battles his dick was victorious again, and he called her. The fact that she answered was a surprise in and of itself. He initially had a sense of anticipation, that she might actually take him up on the offer to come back, even if just for a night. Though, Daniel knew that if she came back for one night it would most likely lead to more and he might end up right back in the thick of things. But at that time, in that moment, he didn't care. Maybe that's even what he wanted. But, to his disappointment she told him that she was out with friends, didn't have a ride. She would not be coming over. He could tell by the noise in the background that she was at a bar, which made him feel even more sorry for himself. She was out having fun with God knows who doing God knows what and he was at home wishing and wanting for *her*. *What the fuck is wrong with me?* He thought to himself. But he did not take the time to try and figure out the answer.

So, today was not about women. It was about manly camaraderie and freedom. He had not spoken to Church other than to set up this event for more than six months. Nevver he had spoken to twice as much, though that was pretty lax when he thought of how much these two men meant to him. *I gotta do better to talk to these guys more*, he thought to himself. Part of the reason he didn't reach out to them was that he did not want to answer the question truthfully of "how are things going?" It was the same excuse he used to not talk to his family. He did not want to tell them that his relationship was horrible, that his job was stressful and he dreaded going to it every day, that he was fighting depression by drinking himself tired and taking sleeping pills to knock himself out at night so that his mind would shut down and his body could refresh for the next day in the grind that had somehow became his life.

No one wanted to hear that, he knew. When people greeted one another and asked, "How are you?" They didn't really want a twenty minute monologue on your aches and pains, your obstacles and stresses, or worse yet, a long recounting of every mundane thing you've done for the past several days. They wanted to hear how nearly everyone responded to that question with either "Good" or the less than everything is optimal answer, "Pretty Good."

Those answers let the asker and the answerer off the hook. It let them both move on with their daily business without either one having to divulge or listen to something that was best reserved for close family and best friends. And even then those conversations were best saved for specific times where hopefully actual solutions, or just healthy venting, could be attained.

All of these things rambled through Daniel's mind before he finally threw the covers off of himself and sat up in bed. The cold, crisp air assaulted his bare skin. He was wearing just a T-shirt and briefs. He quickly got out of bed and hurried to put on sweatpants and socks and a hoodie sweatshirt. He hastily and haphazardly made his bed and went to brush his teeth and wash his face before scuffling into the kitchen to make coffee. He had roughly four hours to wait with anticipation and to make any last preparations before his friends arrived around noon. *It's going to be a long four hours*, Daniel thought and smiled.

*   *   *

It was unseasonably warm for late October. By a sheer stroke of luck, a warm front had moved in and would be staying around for three days, or so the forecast had said. The temperature read 69°. *Nevver will be loving that*, Daniel thought. The wind was less than 5 mph, which made it seem warmer as the autumn sun shone brightly in a nearly cloudless sky. Most of the leaves had fallen from the trees, but a few brown, yellow, and dark orange still remained as if the trees held on to the fullness of life, not wanting to go dormant, resisting the onset of winter. *Me too*, Daniel thought.

He cracked a beer at 12 noon exactly. The icy cold amber liquid hit his taste buds as he closed his eyes, standing outside absorbing the warmth of the sun. With his eyes closed to Daniel it felt like summer. Though it smelled like fall, the sent of the earth was colder, harder than that of summer. And unlike the awakening smell of Spring, Autumn had the scent of decay. The scent of the dying leaves were apparent and in the distance someone was burning the dried leaves, the breeze carrying the pungent, acrid and unmistakable smell of the fire to him.

He was freshly showered, wearing jeans and sneakers with a black T-shirt screen printed with a red and silver Superman emblem. He looked at the black go-cart and thought about taking it for a quick spin, but he thought he'd wait for his friends to arrive, which should be shortly. He had it gassed up and had started it just the day before, so he knew it was in good running order.

The previous day he had worked a morning shift and had taken the empty propane cylinder from the gas grill with him to work so he could exchange it for a full one after his shift. It was warm when he got out that afternoon, so he did not wear a jacket and had taken off his maroon Oxford work shirt and just wore a black T-shirt with his black work pants. After exchanging the cylinder at the gas station he made his way from Petoskey back home to Alanson. He took a couple of back roads which saved some traffic headache. As he turned left at the top of the hill of

Division Street a State Police car passed him. To Daniel's dismay the car quickly did a U-turn and sped up behind him, the lights flashing.

"You gotta be fucking kidding me!" Daniel yelled to himself. Dutifully, Daniel pulled his vehicle over and immediately dug out his wallet and pulled his drivers license from it, and then pulled his registration and proof of insurance from the center armrest compartment. As the Trooper walked up to the window Daniel recognized him as one of the officers that had been to his house the night Faith had left.

"Do you know why I pulled you over?" The Trooper asked.

"Not at all," Daniel replied. And he didn't. He wasn't speeding, and unless there was something wrong with his vehicle, he knew he had done nothing wrong.

"I pulled you over because you were not wearing your seatbelt," the Trooper said.

Daniel was surprised and angered. "Not true, I *always* wear my seatbelt," Daniel stated matter-of-factly, his annoyance coating his words.

"I'm afraid you weren't. License and registration, proof insurance please."

Daniel handed the man the documents he requested. Daniel noticed that the Trooper had a booger hanging in his right nostril. He briefly thought of telling the man, but thought better of it. "You got some really good eyes as you could tell from 40 feet away, in direct sunlight, that in a black car with black seats and I'm wearing a black shirt that I did not have a black seatbelt over my shoulder?" Daniel asked sarcastically.

The Trooper did not reply, but took his documents back to the cruiser to run his information.

Daniel sat silently, fuming. *I always wear my seatbelt. I'll see that asshole in court. I'm going to fight this ticket*, Daniel thought. A blue Ford Taurus drove past in the opposite direction.

A minute later the Trooper came running up to Daniel's window, shoving his documents through the opening saying, "I wasn't positive about you, but I know that guy for sure did not have a seatbelt on," before running back to his cruiser and taking off at speed to pull over the man in the blue Ford.

Daniel smiled as he put his documents back where they belonged. *This is going to be a good weekend*, he repeated to himself.

As the previous day's memory hung in his mind, a pearl white Chrysler 300 crunched the gravel as it rolled slowly down his road and then turned into his driveway, bringing with it a cloud of dust. Daniel could see two occupants. His friends had arrived.

"Nice ride, Church!" Daniel yelled as he approached the vehicle while his two friends got out. They were similarly dressed in jeans, sneakers, but where Church wore a robin's egg blue polo, Nevver had on a home-blue Detroit Lions jersey.

"Thanks, I just got it a couple of weeks ago," he said. The two men hugged briefly, both smiling from ear to ear.

"Oh, geese!" Nevver shouted, feigning exasperated embarrassment, but he, too was smiling.

"Hey Dan-O, good to see you. Churchy and I already made out on the way over here, so why don't the both of you get over here and we have a three-way kiss?" Nevver sarcastically suggested as he held his arms out as if waiting for an embrace.

"Ah, has he been drinking already?" Daniel asked Church.

Churched laughed, "Something like that."

Nevver and Daniel shook hands and they followed him toward the house. Daniel stopped by the shed and pointed at the black go-cart. "That's for later. I don't have two so we can't race, but we can do time trials," he said.

"Sweeeeet!" Nevver said, drawing out the word as he went over and inspected the machine. "I got dibs on first!"

"I gotta use the bathroom," Church said.

"You know where it is. My house is yours," Daniel said.

Church went inside and Daniel joined Nevver at the small, off road machine.

"Can I take it out?" Nevver asked.

"Now? Sure if you want," Daniel said. "Buckle in and I'll pull start it for you."

Daniel showed Nevver where the kill switch was, other than that it was pretty simple. It had a gas and a brake pedal and a steering wheel. It started on the third pull. The small engine idled in a high-pitch, sending the smell of burning gasoline into the air.

"There's no gear shift, once you give it gas it will go!" Daniel shouted. Nevver nodded, gave a thumbs up sign and pressed on the gas pedal.

The vehicle took off, its large tires bouncing on the uneven lawn. Nevver apparently could tell where Daniel had made the course as he headed in that direction. Daniel watched as his friend accelerated, his cries of joy able to be heard above the engine's noise. Daniel laughed as he watched as Nevver leaned into the turns as the go-cart's rear end slid out throwing dirt and grass in its wake.

The next thing Daniel knew Church was standing next to him offering him a beer. "You kids couldn't wait, huh?" Church asked.

Daniel took the beer. He noticed that Church had brought one for Nevver as well. "You know him, he's an impetuous child." They clinked their bottles together at that true statement.

Nevver was on his third lap, really getting the hang of the turns and moguls. As he came around the final turn closest to where his friends were standing, he gave them a thumbs up just as the front tire hit a rut. It twisted the steering wheel and jerked the cart wildly to the left. Nevver quickly put both hands back on the wheel and applied the brake to keep the machine under control.

He then cranked the wheel to the right and drove at a moderate speed toward his friends, stopping abruptly in a cloud of dust right in front of them, showering them with a cloud of dirt and debris.

"Thanks, asshole!" Daniel shouted.

"You're welcome," Nevver said as he climbed out of the vehicle, leaving it running. He took the offered bottle of beer from Church. "Who's next?"

Daniel looked to Church and motioned for him to go ahead. Church handed Daniel his bottle to him before walking to the machine and climbing aboard. He took off apprehensively, testing the power and responsiveness of the vehicle before giving it more throttle. He took two careful laps at less than half speed, a wide smile on his face, as the cart bounced and jerked across the rough terrain.

"Open it up! You won't win the race driving like that!" Nevver shouted at him.

Church flipped him the middle finger in response, and they all laughed. Church then sped up and made three more laps as fast as he dared, then he, too made it over to where they were standing, sliding to a stop in a cloud of dust.

He unbuckled himself and used the rollbar as an assist getting out. "That's awesome!" He yelled over the din of the idling engine as he walked over and took the bottle of beer from Daniel.

"I'll go get the stopwatch, and you kids can time one another on five laps. While you're doing that, I'll get the grill going and put the ribs on. It'll take about two and a half hours for them to slow cook," Daniel told them. "Help yourself to beer in the fridge."

Daniel walked to the gas grill and opened the lid. He bent over and opened the valve on the propane cylinder stored beneath. Immediately his nostrils flared as they detected the mercaptan, the additive that was put in propane that gave it its distinctive smell. He then clicked the red igniter button three times before the spark ignited the propane, the flames appearing with a satisfying *whoosh!* Daniel closed the lid and adjusted the flame on both burners to low. As he walked the short distance to the house he watched Nevver taking off once again in the go-cart. "You need another beer yet?" Daniel asked Church who had found one of the folding deck chairs and had it positioned in the sun facing the makeshift go-cart track.

"You can bring one when you come back, no rush," Church replied.

Daniel smiled as he walked into his house. As he walked to the refrigerator and opened it the only sounds his ears detected was the whine of the small engine of the go-cart outside. The house was quiet. The TV was not on, the radio was not on. The washer and dryer and the dishwasher all remained silent. There were no kids running around, no fighting and arguing. No Faith singing while she folded laundry. Daniel enjoyed the silence, though part of him was struggling with it. But right then, he pushed that cold, empty feeling away and embraced the day.

Earlier, before his shower, Daniel had prepared the large slab of pork rib. It was not baby back rib, but the full grown style. He wasn't even sure it would fit on the grill. He had sliced it into two still large sections and seasoned both sides with a mixture of garlic salt and spices. He then wrapped them with large sheets of aluminum foil. He took these large foil clad slabs and carried them out to the grill. He opened the lid and was welcomed by a satisfying blast of heat from the propane fire. He placed the ribs onto the hot grill and closed the lid. Now he had to wait patiently as they cooked slowly.

He went back into the house and retrieved the digital stopwatch from the small desk in the corner of the kitchen. He then grabbed three more bottles of beer from the refrigerator. He noticed Church had brought out Labatt Blue previously, so he grabbed two of those and one Michelob Ultra for himself before joining his friends outside.

Nevver was still enjoying his time on the go-cart, and it seemed to Daniel that he was becoming more brazen and was pushing the cart faster as he became acquainted with the short course. He walked up beside Church and held out one of the bottles of beer for him. Church glanced up at him and smiled before taking the bottle and cracking the cap off in a smooth motion.

"He's looking pretty good out there," Daniel said.

"Yeah, he's definitely a risk taker. Look at that ass end bounce around on him when he's taking those corners," Church pointed out.

Daniel watched amusedly as Nevver drove quickly around the small course, the large pneumatic tires bouncing and jostling the cart and driver, its small engine whining. Daniel could tell that Nevver was driving two footed, one on the brake and one on the gas, applying the brake and letting off the throttle going into the turns, then stomping the right pedal as he exited the curve. As he completed the lap, Nevver once again headed toward where they were watching. Church and Daniel instinctively put their thumb over the bottle opening as the cart came to a crunching halt, trying to prevent the dust and dirt from entering their drink.

"Hot damn!" Nevver exclaimed as he unbuckled his seatbelt and got out of the cart. "You boys are gonna have to use all of your so-called driving skills to beat me," he said and laughed mock-diabolically.

"We'll see about that," Daniel replied. Nevver walked over to the porch and retrieved his nearly finished bottle of beer. Daniel walked to him and handed him a fresh, unopened bottle. Nevver took it with a smile. He finished the first, tossed the bottle into the grass beside the house, twisted the top off of the fresh one and took a drink immediately.

"Church, go get some practice laps in, then we'll start the time trials," Daniel urged.

Church drained his bottle and threw it underhand so it landed next to the bottle Nevver had discarded by the house. He then jogged to the still idling go-cart and got in. After buckling his seatbelt he took off in a cloud of dust.

Daniel brought out the stopwatch and clicked the reset button as Church entered the course. "We'll time his laps and see where we are," Daniel said to Nevver.

"Yea, you guys should've done that for me. You're gonna need all the edge you can get!"

Daniel started laughed as he walked over to the grill. Smoke was now pouring from the back of it in the smell of roasting meat filled his nostrils as he walked up to it. He could detect the spices and the juices cooking. He opened the lid, even though it only been a few minutes, but he wanted to check and make sure the flame was not too high, not burning the bottom of the meat. He used the long set of tongs that hung off of the shelf to the right side of the grill to lift up and examine each foil wrapped slab of pork. The silver foil was discolored, but not burned. He could hear the sizzle as the meat released its juices. He closed the lid and turned to see that church was just about finishing his second lap.

20.4 seconds. "He's just over ten seconds a lap," Daniel said to Nevver.

"It's different viewing it from out here, then it is from the drivers seat, but I think I was going faster," Nevver said.

"I think so," Daniel agreed. "But, you are one to take more chances. Church is always more careful."

"Well, obviously!" Nevver said as he plopped himself down in the deck chair. Daniel grabbed two more chairs and positioned them one to either side of Nevver.

"There you go, your highness. You can have the prestigious center seat," Daniel told his friend playfully.

"Damn straight. You'll make a good wife someday, but until then you're a fine court fool!" Never quipped.

"Thank you so much, my liege," Daniel said with a bow. Daniel finished his beer and looked to Nevver, "I'm going for another, you need?" he asked.

"I got half, but you can bring one. I'll want one in a few," he said.

Daniel left and returned with two bottles of beer and handed one to Nevver as he sat in the chair to his right. They watched as Church continued his practice runs.

Daniel smiled to himself as he briefly focused on what his senses brought to him. The browning of the landscape, the sounds of the small engine as it powered the cart, the smell of the cooking meat and the faint sound of it sizzling, the heat of the sun as it shown down upon him, how the canvas of the chair held him as he reclined, the perfumed scent of Nevver's body spray, the coldness of the bottle that made him switch hands frequently as he sipped, the taste of the light beer when it ran across his tongue, the buzz in his mind as the alcohol unleashed its effects on his body. He took in all of it and enjoyed the moment. He took deep breaths to calm and in effect unfocus his mind. He didn't want to think, to obsess over the stresses in his life. Those things would be there, he knew. He wanted to live and enjoy. And right then he was.

*   *   *

The ribs had been cooking over a low flame for over an hour. Just the smell of them was making them hungry. Daniel put three large baker potatoes also wrapped in aluminum foil on the grill as he flipped the ribs and closed the lid. The practice runs had continued for several rounds of half a dozen laps for both of his friends in order for them to get used to the course and the go-cart before they began racing.

On his first official run, Nevver had set the time to beat in their time trials: 8 seconds per lap average. They had settled on six laps, Nevver pushing the go-cart to complete his run in forty-eight seconds flat. Church was just finishing up his fifth lap, he was going to have to really push it to make up the lagging time. The cart was jumping and bouncing across the terrain and it seemed to Daniel that Church was having a difficult time keeping it under control while keeping it at a higher speed. Daniel glanced at the stopwatch as the digital numbers kept climbing. He had his thumb on the stop button as Church came around one of the final turns and into the final straightaway, as he rounded the final curve and crossed the start/finish line Daniel stopped the clock. He waited for Church to drive more slowly towards them and stop the vehicle, leaving the engine idling as he got out.

"Close, man, close!" Daniel shouted. Both of his friends looked at him in anticipation. "As we know, King Nevver had 48 seconds flat. Our good friend Church here came in at an impressive..." Daniel paused for long seconds for effect. "50.7 seconds. Close but no cigar!"

"Yes! Eat it, suckers!" Nevver shouted as he jumped up from his chair and did a short victory dance.

"Don't celebrate too hard just yet," Daniel warned. "It's my turn now, bitches!" With that, Daniel handed the stopwatch to Church and walked towards the vehicle.

"Hey, why does he get the stopwatch?" Nevver asked, feeling slighted.

"Because we all know Church can be trusted, you on the other hand would cheat!" Daniel stated matter-of-factly.

Nevver nodded his head in agreement, "True," he admitted.

Daniel drained his bottle of beer and flipped it over to where it landed clattering on the other bottles that were beginning to accumulate in the dying grass beside the house. He winced as he feared the bottles would break as it hit, but they did not to his relief. He couldn't remember how many he had drank in the last two hours. Four? Five? It didn't matter. He was feeling fine and having fun.

He buckled in and stomped on the accelerator, sending the black go-cart surging forward, bouncing across the rough lawn towards the starting point of the course. He knew what time he had to beat, his mind trying to tick off the seconds as the cart bounced and jerked, his body trying to move with the cart instead of against it, both hands gripping the steering wheel tightly as he used the brake and throttle to pilot the cart around the rough track.

The cool breeze brought on by the speed of the go-cart made his skin prickle as the dust and dry grass was kicked up and swirled about him. It was difficult at times to see through the debris and the swirling cloud of dust, and even harder to breathe as his lungs pulled in the fine particles which made him cough. But he was on a mission, and he could not let Nevver beat him, not on his own course, not with his own machine. Nevver would not let him live that one down. It was a matter of pride.

He was on the fourth lap now. Daniel pushed the cart faster, taking more chances with each curve, the rear end of the cart sliding out as he tried to compensate with the steering, the knobby tires biting into the ground. The cart was bouncing wildly as it hit the moguls on the straightaway. Daniel knew he was nearing the deep rut just before the last turn and tried to brace himself for that impact. He usually slowed down and took that sharp curve more apprehensively before accelerating again, but this time he felt that he should go faster, maybe the cart would skip over that rut. He knew that he might overshoot the turn and have to compensate, but he figured that at speed it would help and not hinder the progress.

The cart sped over the last mogul, Daniel held his breath as he accelerated the short distance before the rut. He tried to anticipate the curve just past that obstacle but something happened. He may have turned the wheel too soon, too sharply or too quickly. Maybe he was going too fast for what he was attempting. He wasn't sure what happened, or what went wrong. His mind was struggling with the fact that the cart had jerked violently to the right and was tipping over.

Hang on, don't let go of the steering wheel. The roll cage will protect you, his mind advised him.

Daniel thought he had a better idea. He imagined that if he could push off the ground he could right the cart again, keep it from tipping over. He only had a split second to act. The cart tipped, Daniel could feel the right side of the vehicle rising up on the two wheels of the driver's side. He tried to anticipate the timing of what he was attempting. He stuck his left arm out and pushed as the side of the cart came dangerously close to touching the ground and putting the go-cart entirely on its side.

But when his hand hit the ground, it seemed as if it was stuck in place. The cart did not move to right itself. Instead, it's momentum kept it moving forward, and the inertia of the cart tipping advanced as well. Daniel's hand was pulled behind the cart effectively stretching his arm out as the cart continued to topple. Too late Daniel realized his mistake. The black steel tube of the roll cage slammed into Daniel's left arm just below the shoulder, pinning it to the ground as the cart completed the fall onto its side. The engine was still running, the rear tires still moving.

Daniel was panicked now as pain and fear flooded his body. Still buckled in, Daniel tried to push the go-cart, push himself up with his pinned left arm, struggling to move the cart if not all the way back on its wheels, then just enough so he could pull his left arm free. But he could not. The go-cart was heavier than he thought, his position did not give him the strength or the leverage he needed to move it. He was trapped.

Frantically he looked back over his shoulder to where his friends were seated. He wasn't one to usually ask for it, didn't want to have to yell for it. But he needed it. "Help!" He shouted.

With that, both of his friends jumped from their seats and ran towards him. Daniel could feel something was wrong in his shoulder. He hoped it was just the pain of something heavy resting on it, or maybe that he had dislocated it as the cart had pulled his arm, stretching it out before it had landed on him. His breathing came in ragged breaths. Absently, Daniel reached up with his right hand and flipped the kill switch and shut the engine off. He then heard their voices, saw them grabbing the roll cage and without much apparent effort he was sitting upright in the go-cart. Instinctively his right hand went to his left shoulder and he held it close to his body.

"Duuude! You alright?" Nevver asked.

"Yeah, I think so," Daniel said as he carefully moved his left shoulder in a circular motion. The pain was intense, but not excruciating. He thought that maybe he had dislocated his shoulder. "I think it might have dislocated it," he told them.

Church grabbed Daniel by the right wrist and helped him from the machine. "Do you want to go to the hospital?" Church asked.

"Hell no," Daniel said. "I hate the hospital, and I don't think it's that bad."

Daniel allowed Church to assist him as they walked back to where the deck chairs were arranged, and Daniel sat down.

"Churchy, go grab Dan-O a beer and some ibuprofen, would you?" Nevver asked. Church nodded his consent and walked into the house.

"Damn, dude! That was some crazy shit! Sure you're okay?" Nevver asked.

"I'm okay for now. May need some help finishing dinner though," Daniel said with smile.

"Absolutely, man," Nevver assured him. "You be the chef, and I'll be your bitch. Tell me what you want done, and consider it done."

Church returned with a bottle of ibuprofen and a bottle of sodium naproxen and an open bottle of Michelob Ultra. "Which would you like?" Church asked.

"One Aleve and two Motrin," Daniel said. Without questioning the dosage, Church shook from the two bottles the requested amounts and handed the three pills to his friend. Daniel tossed the pills into his mouth and quickly reached for the offered bottle of beer, washing the pills down with two long drinks.

"You sure know how to bring the entertainment," Church said with a laugh as he sat down in the open chair.

"Hey, Dan, it's been almost two hours on those ribs. Do you want me to start prepping whatever else you need?" Nevver asked being proactive.

"Yeah. Follow me to the kitchen, boys. Let's get dinner going."

Daniel attempted to still be the host, opening the fridge and pulling the beans out, when Church grabbed them from his hands and instructed him to go sit down. Daniel took a seat at the dining table in the corner of the kitchen. He positioned himself so he could see Church and Nevver working. Nevver got out a baking sheet and preheated the oven, preparing the garlic knots. Church got out a large frying pan and started to sauté the green beans.

"So, Nevver how's the lady situation going?" Daniel asked, before the conversation was steered towards his love-life.

At the mention of it, Nevver's mind went immediately to Lissa. He hadn't told his friends how it ended, just that it had. He thought fondly on the time a few days after he left Lissa's that he actually got his shot with Pamsel. He snorted a laugh as he thought of all the things she let him do to her the night they were together, and then again the next morning. But that, too had ended even before it began. It was a one time thing, which was how Nevver actually preferred it. Well, he actually preferred several times with no commitment afterward. He thought about the woman at the state park over the summer, *what was her name?*, and a couple others he'd been with since then.

"Well, you know guys, I've added a few notches to the belt, but haven't found the right kind of crazy yet," he said while dusting the butter-basted dough with a garlic salt/powder mixture. "All women are nuts," he continued. "Most guys are too, don't get me wrong. Right Churchy?" Church just nodded his consent as he took a drink of beer. "We're all just going around on this big blue ball of shit, trying to find our way. Some of us just wanna have fun and live life, while others strive to do something important, leave a mark. Others just think it's their duty to enhance the human race by having multiple children and they struggle to not fuck them up as they raise them...some try to accomplish *all* of that."

"Nevver, what do you want out of life?" Church asked him.

"To have a buzz on all day, and fuck all night," he answered quickly as if it were a practiced answer.

"That's what you say, that's what you project. But, what do you really want out of life? Do you have any goals, aspirations?" Church asked.

"Well, dad," Nevver said sarcastically, "I don't really know." After a few moments of uncharacteristic introspection, Nevver continued, "I'd like to find the place where I feel I belong. Whether that's in a certain city, or a certain apartment or house, with a certain woman, having a certain job...All I really know is that I haven't found any of that, yet. I'm hoping that I will someday soon. But, since I don't really know what I'm looking for, it's kinda hard to spot it, right? Don't know if I believe in God, or fate, or in destiny. But if any or all those things exist, I'll get to where I'm supposed to be. One day. Until then, my first answer stands," he said with a wicked smile as he slid the loaded baking sheet in the oven and closed the door. He reached up and set the timer on the oven, turned and leaned on the counter and drained the rest of his beer. He held the bottle up and shook it quickly side to side. "Anybody need one?" He asked. Both of his friends nodded in the affirmative.

"That's almost profound, especially coming from you," Church said to Nevver. Daniel and Church laughed as Nevver gave them the double-middle-finger. "Dan, what do you want?" Church asked him as he accepted the beer from Nevver.

Daniel remained silent for a minute as he looked at his friends. He smiled and thanked Nevver as he took the bottled beer from his friend and sipped it. As the cold liquid ran down his throat he tried to gather his thoughts before answering. He took a breath and said, "I guess I'm looking for the American Dream."

"That's what I said! Sex, drugs, and rock 'n roll!" Nevver shouted. All three laughed at his answer.

"That's not a complete answer, Dan," Church scolded.

"Well, you know. I want a nice house, which I have. I want a nice car, which I have. I want a job that I enjoy, still looking for that. And I want a great woman to share those things with, to build a happy life with...I want a partner who puts into the relationship as much as I do. That's what I want out of life, but...I also feel that I was meant for something...*more*," he added after a long pause. "I should have died at birth, you know. So I feel that there is something that I'm supposed to do, but I'm not sure what that is...or how to figure it out," Daniel said, leaving his answer at that.

"What about children?" Church asked. "We all know that Nevver probably has a few bastards running around out there. How many do you think it is?" Church said in jest.

"Two that I know of. As for the official count, I have no clue. Nor do I want to," Nevver replied.

"Do you ever see them?" Church asked.

"No. I'm not even sure where they are. I don't think their moms want me around anyway," he said, with a slight hint of retrospection in his voice.

"So, you're okay with being a deadbeat dad?" Pressured Church.

"I wouldn't say that. What I am is doing humanity a favor. I am donating my superior genes to as many female recipients as I can. You know how much my sperm and my genetic code would be worth if I went to one of those sperm clinics? A hell of a lot, let me tell you. And these women don't have to pay a dime for that! Sure, they won't get any money from me to help raise the kid, but it's a give-and-take, situation. I *give* them the night of their life and a large dosage of my genetic material, and they *take* the kids and do whatever the hell they want with them...They're welcome," he said with his sarcastic, misogynistic brand of honesty.

Daniel and Church could not help but laugh at their friend. They knew he was a man whore and thought of himself as the epitome of the male species. Daniel could never see himself treating a woman as Nevver did. It was a foreign concept to him that what Nevver seemingly offered was what many women were looking for, even if it wasn't long-term.

"So, Daniel? Kids?" Church probed.

"I don't think so," Daniel offered. "I'm not really a kid kinda guy."

"What does that mean?" Nevver asked.

"Yeah, didn't your current, or ex, girlfriend have four kids? You seemed to do okay with them, didn't you?"

Daniel thought about that for a few moments. There were times that he did enjoy having the kids over. But if he was honest with himself there were more times when it just seemed stressful, with all the fighting and bickering and drama. It seemed like there were very few moments of peace and harmony. It was like no matter what he did it wasn't enough. But, on the other hand, Daniel knew that all children didn't behave like that, at least not all the time. And he realized that Faith's kids were dealing with a bad situation in more ways than one, and they probably didn't know how to deal with it.

"Well, I'll put it this way," Daniel said then took a drink from his beer bottle. "Babies. I don't find babies cute, or adorable...not at all. Baby animals, yes. But baby humans? No. Whatever it is inside of most people that look at a baby and find them precious and amazing, and want to hold it, to protect it...Whatever that is, whatever part of human DNA that is found in...I don't think I possess it. Not sure if that makes me a bad person or not, but that's how I feel. I'm actually kind of afraid of them, if you want to know the truth."

"Afraid of a baby?" Nevver yelled, almost spitting out his beer. "How can you be afraid of something that poses no threat?"

"Not afraid like it's going to hurt me," Daniel began to explain. "I'm apprehensive, because I don't want to hurt them. And the little kids, I don't know how to communicate with them. Some of them seem smart, and others not so much. Not sure if I should dumb-down my conversation, pretend to be interested in what they have to say...What really bothers me is the kids who just keep asking why, why, why, why, why, after every time you explain something to them. It drives me nuts. Maybe I just don't have the patience. And, you know how a parent has to be able to zip up coats, and tie shoes, and button shirts from standing, or kneeling in front of the kid? Yea, well I can't do that. For some reason I don't have the dexterity or the patience to do that. I don't think I'd make a good parent. A good role model, yes. But not a good parent," Daniel concluded.

"That doesn't make you a bad person," Church offered. "Some people with many kids should not be parents, at least you know that about yourself ahead of time. Or at least that is what you tell yourself." Church put the glass lid over the frying pan and turned the flame under the beans way down low. "I think you'd be a better parent than you realize. But, you are right--you are scared."

Daniel thought about it for a moment. "I guess, I'm truthful about it...It's not that I don't like kids, or I'm against having them. It's just that they take a lot of work, and a lot of time. And a lot of money. All things I really don't have much to spare. I do better with the older kids, I can relate and talk to them more. They understand better, you know? Probably if there were only two or three than it wouldn't be such an ordeal. There wouldn't be as much chaos. I've come to the conclusion that three or less is the right number. You see, two or three can play and get along just fine, until one starts picking on one of the others, which is bound to happen. But then, you can separate them. The two that are playing well together and stay together, and the instigator needs to be removed to go do something else. Same thing with two. They start to fight, separate them. But with four or more, there is never enough separation, there is always one stirring the pot and creating the chaos," Daniel said as he finished his beer.

"I hear what you're saying," Church said. "And since I don't have kids either, I can't really speak to that. All I'm saying is, that in your case, if you met the right woman you might change your mind. *She* might change your mind," Church said with a smile.

Daniel felt like it was time to change the subject of conversation, and he was nearly starving. "Well, that's enough girl talk. I'm going to check the ribs and baste them with Sweet Baby Ray's sauce for the last fifteen minutes or so," he told his friends as he got up from the dining table.

"I'll help," Nevver offered as he followed his friend outside.

    *   *   *

An hour later dinner was over. They had gorged themselves on pork ribs, large, fully dressed baked potatoes, green beans, and garlic knots. Piles of bones and some dirty pans and dishes were all that was left.

Church and Nevver had played a couple of games of pool afterwards. Daniel watched. At the end of the first game he had tried to shoot a few balls, but stretching his left shoulder out was too painful, and he couldn't make any shots. He had an ice pack on it now, and had for the last hour. Once the ice melted and the hand towel was saturated and wet, Daniel would switch it out for more ice and a clean towel. The ice seemed to be helping as Daniel noticed that there was some swelling to his upper arm and shoulder. To him it still felt out of place, though he had nearly full range of movement, even if it did hurt like hell as he rotated it. The pain was the combination of a dull, nagging ache punctuated by sharp, random stabs of agony.

After Nevver won the two games of pool they decided to watch a movie. Nevver had tapped into the Maker's Mark as *Pulp Fiction* started, Church had helped himself to one glass on the rocks, then switched back to the beer. Daniel wasn't much of a hard liquor person, so he strictly stuck to the beer.

He washed down two aspirin and two more ibuprofen a half hour earlier in an attempt to cut the pain in his shoulder down to a more manageable level. He was mad at himself for getting too careless and for not listening to the better thought of just holding on and letting the roll cage do what it was designed for.

You should listen to me more, his mind told him. You'd be way better off, in a lot of ways.

Daniel ignored the thoughts in his head, but he was regretting not taking the advice or the path that that inner voice had suggested on many occasions. Daniel lamented the fact that he could not go back and do things differently. No one could. A jolt of pain in his arm and shoulder ripped those thoughts from his mind.

He thought about going to the hospital, but he had been drinking and he really did not want to go there at all. He was hoping that time, along with the ice and the mild pain medication would fix the problem. He was hoping that his shoulder was just deeply bruised or dislocated slightly. He'd broken his thumb when he was in high school during a wrestling match, other than that he had no frame of reference to what a broken bone felt like. He just knew that it hurt.

Daniel was in pain and feeling tired, but he didn't want to disappoint his friends. As they watched there was some playful banter and commentary on the movie, which was their ritual. He pushed himself to stay alert as they then watched *Sin City*, again commenting on the action and various scenes. As soon as that movie ended Daniel announced, "Guys, it's been fun, but I gotta take my drunk, injured ass to bed." His friends laughed and bid him a good night. "Feel free to play pool, watch another movie, play video games, whatever you guys want. My house is your house," he told them.

He went into the master bedroom and closed the door. He struggled to take his clothes off, stripping down to his underwear. With much pain he put on a fresh T-shirt and crawled into bed. He lay down and the stab of pain in his left shoulder almost made him cry out. He awkwardly pulled the second pillow on the bed close to him and laid his arm on it. Next, he placed the ice wrapped in the hand towel onto it at the upper arm and shoulder. He gently let his arm's weight sink into the pillow, testing the support and how it made his arm feel. *Tolerable*, the thought.

I think you messed something up. It's more than a dislocated shoulder. It's probably broken, his mind told him.

He didn't want to acknowledge it, but the pain now radiating throughout his body and throbbing in his shoulder proved to be more forceful than his wishful thinking. *I need some sleep now*, he thought. *I'll go do the hospital in the morning.*

He then slowly drifted off into a drunken sleep.

The sleep Daniel desperately sought did not come easy. He had hoped that if he could fall asleep he would not feel the pain in his shoulder and time would pass quickly. Which did happen, but only for a couple of short hours. Being primarily a side sleeper, Daniel found himself rolling over onto his left side, only to wake up abruptly with a sharp, piercing pain shooting through his arm and shoulder.

The ice in the hand towel had melted, leaving just a wet cloth laying on his arm. Daniel grabbed it and tossed it towards the bathroom. It sailed through the doorway and hit the porcelain tile with a wet slap. Trying to keep his arm pressed to his body and as immobile as possible, Daniel struggled to turn himself and grabbed his cell phone from the nightstand. He pressed one of the side buttons to illuminate the small display. The time read 3:14AM. Too soon to get up.

It seemed like his entire body was throbbing from the pain. Grudgingly, Daniel struggled out from under the fleece blanket and out of bed and made his way to the adjoining bathroom. He turned on the faucet, cold water only. He then got out the bottle of Aleve. The directions said only take one per every 12 hours. Daniel ignored that warning and shook out three of the tablets. He tossed them into his mouth then bent down, ignoring the jolt of pain in his shoulder, and put his mouth into the stream of running water. He sucked the water into his mouth, swallowing the pills. He kept drinking in that manner pulling in much-needed water to his alcohol dehydrated body. He righted himself and shut off the tap.

He looked into the mirror, and though the room was dark and his reflection dim, he could see that his face was drawn, his hair disheveled. His eyes seemed sunken. He leaned forward, focusing on the reflection of his eyes. It was said that the eyes were the reflection of the soul. Daniel tried to see if he could glimpse his own in the mirror. He did not like what he saw, wasn't sure who this man was that looked back at him.

He was on the verge of contemplation, of trying to sort out the things in his mind and in his life. He was on the edge of realization, perhaps even revelation. But the pain in his head and in his arm pushed any clarity from his mind with a thick fog of misery wrapped around not just the physical pain, but also the mental anguish of the events of the previous months.

Too much to think about, he thought as he scuffled back to the bedroom. He crawled under the covers, careful not to move his arm too much. He once again propped the pillow under his left arm and shoulder in an effort to support and stabilize it. He took deep breaths and soon his weariness overtook him and he fell back to sleep.

CHAPTER TWENTY-THREE

It was just after 7AM, and the throbbing pain in his arm and shoulder was now a constant ache. Almost as if some creature was attached to it, digging its claws into his flesh and muscle, down into the bone, piercing the marrow. The weight of the creature pulling and tugging on his arm was making him struggle to even hold it in place. As Daniel's mind cleared the fog of sleep, he thought he could almost hear an evil laughter. As he pushed himself out of bed, the pain in his arm shot up into his brain and his whole body seemed to throb with every heartbeat, Daniel knew that laughter was from his conscience.

Keeping his arm close to his body, Daniel struggled to pull clothes from his dresser drawers one-handed. Underwear, socks, blue jeans, and a gray sweatshirt. With the clothes in a small pile he carried them into the adjoining bathroom and shut the door. The bathroom had a large garden tub and a separate standup shower with an etched glass door. He pulled at the door and broke the magnetic seal, reached in and turned on the water instinctively knowing how much to turn the cold and the hot knob to get his preferred temperature. He closed the door and took a deep breath before attempting to take his T-shirt off.

He braced himself for the shot of pain he knew was coming. He figured it was like ripping off a Band-Aid: do it quickly and the pain will be over in less time. With that strategy Daniel reach back with his right arm and grabbed the collar of his T-shirt. He took one more deep breath, then pulled the shirt over his head and stretched his right arm out as far as it would go. At the same time he carefully pulled his left arm through the armhole and out of the fabric. He then shook his right arm until the T-shirt fell to the floor.

Still in his underwear, with the hot water beginning to steam in the shower, Daniel looked at himself in the mirror that hung above the sink. He turned so that his left side was facing the mirror. He was almost horrified at what he saw. His shoulder and upper arm nearly down to his elbow was a deep black and purple, and seemed fatter than normal, a bit unusually shaped. This he knew was from the swelling.

Shit, that does not look good at all, he thought. But he knew there was nothing he could do to prevent it now. "Looks like were going to the hospital," he said aloud to himself. He was still holding out hope that it would not be as bad as it felt. But he knew he was kidding himself, as it actually felt worse than it had the day before.

After pulling down his underwear and stepping out of them, Daniel quickly opened the door to the shower and stepped in and closed the door behind him in a smooth, practiced motion. The hot, steaming water startled him as it hit his skin and poured down his body. He turned to face the showerhead and ducked his head under the water, letting the rain-like spray soak his hair as the hot water cascaded down his back and face. He stood there for a few long minutes, letting the force of the water massage his head, and turning away from it allowed it to beat on the muscles of his back. He then grabbed the shampoo and squeezed some directly from the bottle onto his head. Instantly the fresh, clean smell of the soap hit his nostrils and lifted his spirits a bit. Using just his right hand and arm he massaged the glob of gel into a lather, spreading and rubbing the soap over his shoulders, under his arms, down his torso and the rest of his body. He then grabbed the shower scrubber and worked the soap across all parts of his body spending a little extra time carefully on his feet. Daniel usually used shower gel and not just the shampoo, but given his injuries he decided it was quicker and easier to minimize his movements.

After scrubbing, Daniel again just stood under the water, letting it rinse him clean. He turned from the spray, purposefully letting the water directly hit onto his left shoulder and arm. He had hoped that the massaging action of the hot spray would help soothe the pain. But he quickly found that was not the case. The force of the water beating on to his bruised and battered arm seemed to intensify the soreness. He quickly shut the water off, standing drenched and naked as he took in deep breaths. Instantly gooseflesh appeared across his body as the colder air wafted in from above the door opening, pulling the steam and heat from the shower. Daniel opened the shower door and awkwardly reached out with his right arm and grabbed a towel that was hanging on the metal loop that was attached to the wall. It was an easy grab with his left arm, not so much with his right. He pulled the towel into the shower and closed the door, trying to ward off the cold air as he began to shiver while awkwardly attempting to dry himself off with only one arm.

After drying himself the best that he could, Daniel stepped from the shower and closed the glass door behind him. He stood on the small rectangle of rubber-backed carpeting as he clumsily used a towel to dry his feet and in between his toes. It took him longer than usual to get dressed mostly one-handed. Though, he did use his left hand and arm sparingly, with much pain, to pull on his jeans, button them and to pull his sweatshirt on and get his socks up. It was then that Daniel realized how much he took for granted the use of a fully functioning body. He had sympathy before for those who lost a limb or the use of one of them. But now he had some empathy, even if it was just a small glimpse of what it would be like.

After dressing, Daniel applied deodorant and cologne and even managed to gel and style his hair before exiting the bathroom and walking in the living room. Beer bottles and bowls of snacks littered the coffee table. Seeing immediately neither of his friends had opted to crash on the couch, Daniel quietly made his way down the short hall to the spare bedroom that shared a wall with the third bedroom that served as his office. Because of Faith's children for that bedroom he had purchased a steel bunk bed that had a double size mattress on the lower level, and a twin on the upper. The door was partially open, so Daniel walked up to it and pushed it slightly so he could see in. He smiled to himself as he saw both of his friends effectively passed out, Nevver sprawled out on the bottom bunk, and Church barely visible wrapped in covers on the top. He turned and walked slowly back towards the kitchen.

Daniel grabbed a piece of paper from the small desk in the corner and quickly scribbled a note letting his friends know that he had gone to the hospital and would be back afterwards. He looked at the clock on the stove and it read 7:35 AM. He figured most likely he would be back before they even got up. It was early Sunday morning and he assumed that the hospital would not be busy, though it seemed, busy or not, it was always nearly a two to four hour stop going to the emergency room.

As he drove towards the hospital down the all-too-familiar streets, passing the same businesses, the same houses he noticed that everything was quiet and calm. The sun was just starting to come up, promising a brighter day. The early morning light painted the world in sepia. Everything seemed to have a tinge of brown and gray. The world seemed cold, being on the verge of winter and not wanting to go forward into that season. But like many things there was no choice, no other option. Time moved on.

A dark blue Chevy Malibu passed him. The driver was a woman wearing a stocking hat, brown and white striped. In the vehicle it looked like she had three or four children, one in the passenger seat and two or three in the back. She was not smiling. She did not look happy. A few minutes later a red Dodge Ram pickup with a 6 inch lift and large, all-terrain tires that made an audible *whirring* as they sped across the pavement, drove up quickly on his rear and got so close that all Daniel could see in his rearview mirror was the front bumper. Daniel checked his speed and saw that he was going 3 miles over the limit. *This asshole is in a hurry*, he thought. Daniel knew that there was only one, maybe two places to pass on that stretch of road that led out of Alanson through Conway and Oden before entering the northern part of Petoskey and the highway that connected it to Harbor Springs. They were coming up on the first such stretch, so Daniel slowed down just as the big truck veered into the oncoming lane and roared past him. Daniel sped back up to the speed limit as he watched the big truck roar into the distance. He calculated that he was probably going 70 miles an hour or more. He just shook his head.

A few minutes later Daniel arrived at the hospital and parked as close as he could to the emergency entrance. He walked into the reception area went through the motions of presenting his ID and insurance card, filling out the prerequisite paperwork and then taking a seat and waiting to be called.

Twenty-seven minutes later a nurse came and called his name. Daniel followed her back and endured the weigh in and blood pressure check before he was put in an examination room and told to disrobe down to his underwear put the waiting hospital gown on. Daniel did as he was asked then sat on the paper-covered exam bed for another 13 minutes before a doctor entered the room.

"Mr. Gibson," the doctor said as he entered the room. "It seems you had a little accident this morning. Can you tell me about it?" The man was tall, very tall, Daniel guessed probably 6'5". He had a gray beard that was curly and trimmed neatly, his hair was salt-and-pepper, mostly salt, that was wavy and though it seemed messy it was neat and professional. He wore a tan shirt under a white lab coat minus the stethoscope around his neck. His slacks and shoes were brown. The man did not show his teeth when he talked, and he did not smile. There was a hard edge to his voice, Daniel noticed.

"Yes. I got up this morning--later today I'm having friends over--so I decided to take the go-cart out for a spin to make sure it was in good running order. I guess I was going a little too fast for the rough conditions and the cart began to tip. Instead of rolling with it, I stuck my left arm out in an effort to brace or push me back over, but the cart tipped and fell onto my shoulder. I think I dislocated it.," Daniel explained quickly.

"You were out on your go-cart at 7 o'clock this morning?" The doctor asked suspiciously.

"Yes. For work I get up at about 4 o'clock, so being up and going out and doing something at that time is not unusual for me," Daniel explained. The doctor just eyed him and nodded his head, as he turned and walked out into the hall.

Daniel had thought he might get some resistance having an accident so early in the morning on a Sunday. He had heard that in Michigan you could get a DUI ticket for impaired driving on any sort of vehicle, even a riding lawnmower or a go-cart in your own yard. *In your own yard!* He thought incredulously. For that reason--aside from his futile wish that it was dislocated or deeply bruised--just to be safe, Daniel did not come to the hospital the night before, and had waited until nearly 8 AM the next day to come in. He knew that any alcohol in his system would've been out by then and any blood test or breathalyzer would show no alcohol in his system, and thus he would be cleared from any ridiculous impaired driving prosecution.

As he suspected, Daniel looked out into the hall and saw the doctor conferring with a State Police Trooper. Daniel braced himself as the trooper walked in the room and approached him. The trooper asked the same question as the doctor had. Daniel gave him the exact same answer, looking the trooper in the eye. The officer accepted his answer and walked from the room.

Seven minutes after that the doctor returned and told Daniel they were going to take some x-rays. A nurse showed up and Daniel followed her to the x-ray room. Once there, he was seated on a little stool at a table that had an x-ray camera mounted to it. The nurse pulled and twisted his arm into an awkward position and told him to hold it there. She then positioned the camera over it and pressed a remote button that took the picture. She repeated the process, contorting and pushing his arm into painful positions as she took x-rays from multiple angles. She then led him back to the examination room where he waited for the doctor to return with the results. "Would you like something for the pain?" She asked pleasantly. Daniel replied in the affirmative. The nurse left and returned within two minutes with a small cup of water and a large Vicodin tablet. Daniel knew that Vicodin was basically Tylenol and some hydrocodone which was a mild opioid. He swallowed the tablet and thanked the nurse. She then told him that he could get dressed.

After painfully and carefully putting his sweatshirt back on he easily pulled his pants on and slipped his shoes over his socks. He then waited another 17 minutes before the doctor returned with the results.

The doctor walked in with a scowl on his face, looked at Daniel and said, "Well, you broke it." He almost shouted at him, like he was the doctor's own child who had disobeyed the master and had gotten hurt doing something that he was warned not to do. *One hell of a bedside manner you got there, doctor,* Daniel thought to himself. Daniel assumed that part of the doctor's animosity toward him came from the fact that he probably felt Daniel was full of shit with his early-morning go-cart accident story. But, Daniel didn't care. It was mostly the truth, he just left out the part that would've got him into even more trouble.

The physician walked over to a panel on the wall and stuck two x-ray films into clips at the top that held them vertically in place. He then switched on the fluorescent lights that illuminated the panel allowing the x-rays to be seen more clearly.

"You broke your Humerous just below the Humeral Head, or the shoulder ball, in two places. Luckily for you, there was no damage to the shoulder socket, and the two breaks appear to be pretty clean and should heal fairly well," the doctor explained, though still surly in his tone. The doctor walked over to the countertop and unwrapped a white and baby blue sling. "We'll have to refer you to an orthopedist so they can determine how best to set and immobilize the arm. But, seeing how it's Sunday and they're not open, you're just going to have to wait until tomorrow, maybe even Tuesday," the doctor said with no hint of sympathy in his voice. "Until then, keep your arm in this sling and try not to move it. You can use over-the-counter pain medicine. An ice pack will help with the swelling and the pain as well."

The doctor helped Daniel get his arm into the sling and position it correctly. His arm was throbbing and aching from the exertion and the awkward positions he was forced to put it in during the x-ray procedure. He was not looking forward to having to go back to another doctor to have something else done to his injured arm.

Daniel remembered when he had broken his thumb during a wrestling tournament it was on a Saturday. He had been a freshman in high school and during this particular tournament he had won his first match, lost the second, and on his way to winning his third and thus gaining a third-place medal for the tournament when he tipped his opponent on his shoulder and the weight snapped his left thumb. He remembered looking down at his hand, had his thumb pointing off in the distance somewhere in an awkward angle. He held it up for the referee to see who then immediately halted the match and told Daniel to go see the trainer, which he did.

The trainer thought it had just been dislocated as they righted the thumb and Daniel was able to move it. He went back in to finish the match but within a few seconds the thumb was again at an awkward angle pointing off somewhere in the bleachers. The referee stopped the match then. Daniel had lost by default.

The trainer had put his thumb in a splint and they called his mother to come pick him up, though the tournament was being held at a school over an hour and a half north of Bay City. They had gone directly to the hospital where the emergency room could do little for him except give him a better splint and arranged an appointment for the orthopedist the following Monday. Since the bone in his thumb had been healing itself for the previous two days, the doctor had to re-break the bone in order to set it so it could heal correctly. During the re-breaking process Daniel did not cry out or even make a sound, though he had gritted his teeth and tightened up seemingly all of his muscles to brace himself for the pain. "Your son is pretty tough," the doctor had told his mother. Daniel remembered smiling at the comment.

Thinking back to that now, he was hoping and praying that his shoulder would not have to be re-broken when he saw the orthopedist, hopefully the following day. He was remembering and thinking these things as he made his way to the checkout counter. He paid his co-pay and got the information for the orthopedist. He was told that he should get a confirmation call from them, but if he hadn't heard by 10 or 11 o'clock the next morning that he should call and verify his scheduled appointment. Daniel thanked her then walked to his car, thinking about all the things that had happened in the last few days, and what lay ahead in the next few.

The outside air blasted him with a cold breeze as he exited the hospital. The wind was coming across Little Traverse Bay and brought with it the smell and feel of the oncoming winter. Just the day before it had been near 70°, but today the high was now only forecasted to reach 53°. To Daniel it seemed much colder even through his sweatshirt and the spring fleece jacket he wore half on and half off trying to shield the sling holding his broken arm from the cold. *So much for three days a warm weather*, he thought.

He got into his Toyota and cranked the heat to full, though keeping the fan on low until the engine had heated up. *I guess it's a good thing it's my left arm*, he thought. Being right-handed, Daniel obviously relied on his right arm for most of his daily duties and tasks: writing, eating, answering the telephone, using the adding machine, putting toppings on pizzas...*even wiping my ass*, he thought. His mind was a swirl of what if's and if only's...*Welcome to the show. What's next?* He thought bitterly.

    *   *   *

When he arrived back home his friends were up and nursing hangovers. Nevver was in the kitchen preparing breakfast: crispy bacon, a seasoned potato hash with green pepper and onions, scrambled eggs with cheddar cheese, and wheat toast. Church was seated at the dining table drinking a steaming mug of coffee. Nevver was in mid preparation when Daniel walked through the door.

"Hey Dan-O! What did the doctor say?" He asked as he looked over his shoulder at him though still stirring the potato hash as it sizzled in the frying pan.

Daniel removed his jacket to reveal his arm in the sling. "It's broken," he told them. "In two places, just below the shoulder."

"Geeze, buddy, that really sucks," Church said as he stood up from the table. "Sit down. Do you want a coffee?" Church asked.

"Yes, please. One Splenda and about a second's worth of the chocolate creamer," Daniel said.

As Church prepared the ordered beverage in Daniel's favorite 20 ounce Superman mug he asked, "Did you damaged the rotator cuff at all?"

"No, thank God. Two clean breaks of the humerus, just below the shoulder ball. I have to go to the specialist, hopefully tomorrow after work and see if I need a cast or whatever. The sling is just temporary."

"Did they give you any good pain meds?" Nevver asked.

Daniel snorted a laugh, "Nope. They give me one Vicodin and didn't even offer a prescription for anything else. The doctor was kind of an asshole. He just told me to take over-the-counter medications as directed. I don't think he believed my go-cart accident story," Daniel told them.

"You didn't tell them you were drinking, did you?" Nevver asked.

"Absolutely not. There was a state cop there who asked me what happened, and I told him the same story that I told the doctor. I got up early this morning and was out screwing around in my go-cart, and the rest is what actually happened," Daniel said.

"They didn't say your bruising looked a little advanced to have happened just this morning?" Church inquired as he handed Daniel his mug of coffee.

Daniel took a sip and smiled at the deliciousness of it. "No, they didn't mention it. But that's probably part of the reason why they didn't believe me. What could they do?"

"Not give you any fucking pain meds, that's what they did," Nevver said.

"That's true," Daniel said as he took another sip of coffee.

Four pieces of toast popped up in the toaster. Church got up and walked over to it and began spreading vegetable spread that looked and tasted like butter onto each piece. Nevver reached down and opened the oven door, revealing a broiler pan full of crisped slices of bacon. He was an advocate of baking the breakfast meat instead of frying in a pan, as the pieces stayed flat while cooking and they tended to cook more evenly, and it was less dangerous as the bacon grease flowed into the bottom of the broiler pan through the large slits on the top section. He carefully scooped the pieces of bacon off with a large pancake flipper and placed them on a waiting plate. He continued stirring and folding the scrambled eggs in a large frying pan for just a few more seconds before turning off the flame beneath them and announcing, "Breakfast is ready guys."

The three of them were more hungry than what they knew, devouring everything. Daniel told them to leave the dirty pans and dishes, along with those from the night before, that he would clean up. But Church and Nevver would not hear of it, especially since Daniel was injured. The two quickly and expertly cleaned all of the pans and utensils, but did shortcut the plates by just rinsing them and putting them in the dishwasher along with the silverware.

Afterwards, they sat down in the living room, still drinking their coffee, each one on their third or fourth mug, the coffee pot having been drained and filled twice already. Nevver took control of the satellite and turned on a football pre-game commentary show. It was Sunday after all.

Shortly before noon Church announced, "All right Nevver, we gotta get going. At least I do, so if you want a ride, let's hit it."

"Awww, duuuude! That sucks! Who's gonna take care of Dan-O, and wipe his ass when he needs it?" Nevver said with playful sarcasm.

"Don't worry, my friend. I wipe and jerk with my right hand," Daniel said with a smile. They all laughed.

Daniel stood by as his friends gathered their overnight bags, then followed them out to Church's vehicle. Daniel hugged them with one arm and shook their hands firmly. All three vowed to keep in touch more often and make the time to get together. He stood on the dirt and rocks of his driveway in the October chill as the wind kicked up the dust, blowing it in his face as he watched with sadness his friends drive away.

He quickly walked into the warmth of the house, shutting and locking the door behind him. The television was still on and he made his way into the other room, but first he exchanged his coffee for beer. To his dismay he saw that there were only six Michelob Ultra and one Labatt Blue remaining. *That's enough for today*, he thought to himself. He saw the half empty bottle of Maker's Mark silently cursed himself as he was going to give that to Nevver because he knew he wasn't going to drink it. *Well, it will be here for him next time*, he thought.

As he sat on his leather couch the throbbing in his broken arm pulled his focus back to his injury. He thought about getting an ice pack for it, but was too lazy and tired to bother with it just then. Aside from the announcers' bantering about the upcoming games, the house was quiet. Just then, his cat jumped up onto the couch from out of nowhere. He had hidden most of the previous day and night because there were people over. But now he knew it was just him and his master. The black feline cuddled up next to him as Daniel pet the soft hair with his right hand, holding his bottle of beer in his lap with his exposed left.

Not being much of a football fan, Daniel grabbed the remote and started cycling through the channels, looking for something more entertaining to watch. He found the movie *Back to the Future* was playing on a pay channel with no commercials. It had just started within five minutes. *Perfect*, he thought. *If only time machines were real.*

CHAPTER TWENTY-FOUR

Daniel stood in front of the mirror in his bathroom, wearing only what the doctor had called an "immobilizer" wrapped around his healing arm and torso. It was a harness of sorts, made from cotton and elastic and Velcro closures. The main band wrapped around his torso with a strap that crossed his chest and went up and over his clavicle resting on his trapezius muscle settling halfway between his neck and right shoulder. It reminded Daniel of his paperboy days and carrying the large canvas bag in much the same way. There were two bands that essentially held his broken arm at a 90° angle and fixed it to his body. One wrapped around his upper arm, the other around his forearm, his arm being bent at the elbow and essentially attached at his stomach. "Don't get it wet," the doctor told him. So began the frustrating daily ritual of sponge bathing himself before work.

He ran hot water into the sink and wet a blue washcloth, adding a small amount of body soap to it. After very carefully removing his arm from the immobilizer sling and setting it aside, Daniel carefully and methodically began washing himself. He moved his left arm away from his body a few inches, still keeping it at the recommended 90° angle. Moving his shoulder sent shocks of pain through his arm as he held it in that precarious, awkward position while his right hand rubbed the wet soap up under his arm down the side of his torso. He was careful to get under his arm and wash both sides of the broken and still healing appendage with great care. It was still sore and badly bruised, even three weeks later. Though the deep black and purple bruising had faded somewhat, even turning greenish in some areas. A sign the bleeding under the skin was healing as the bones knitted back together. The swelling had gone and the pain was subsiding, though there was still a constant ache.

He set the blue washcloth down on the edge of the sink and grabbed a green washcloth that was folded on the counter. He quickly turned on the hot water and ran the green washcloth under the stream until it was soaked. He turned off the tap and squeezed the cloth in his right hand to shed the excess water from the fabric. He then gently rubbed the cloth over the parts of his body that he had just applied soap to. Satisfied that he had effectively rinsed those areas he hugged his left arm to his body once again.

Daniel shivered as he stood naked, using the blue washcloth, soaping and cleaning the rest of his body. He had turned the propane-fired forced air furnace up 3° before entering the bathroom, which helped take the chill from the November air that hovered inside the bathroom. Even so, his body shivered from being wet. After effectively soaping his body, Daniel repeated the rinsing process with the green washcloth.

Daniel then carefully dried himself with a fresh towel, taking great care once again to get under his broken arm and ensure that his torso and left arm was completely dry. He then slipped the mobilizing sling over his shoulder and carefully attached his arm to it. Daniel took deep breaths as he absorbed the pain from the minimal exertion that moving and washing his arm caused.

He had to wear his arm under his shirt, something that looked awkward and strange he was sure. He would pull the left sleeve inside-out and would leave it that way, in an effort to minimize the odd look. He didn't like the way an empty sleeve looked just hanging off the shirt. But before getting dressed, Daniel washed his hair in the sink and then shaved his face, being as careful as he could to not get the fabric of the immobilizer went in the process. Luckily he was right-handed which made this tedious routine easier, if it could be called easy.

Having to wash and dress in this way added another layer of stress to Daniel's life. Though he washed, the scent of his sweat and body odor from his daily exertion clung to the cotton fabric of the immobilizer. Even the smell of the damn washcloths seemed nauseating. Just the odor of himself now clogged his nose and his mind, making him feel *less than*. He wanted to take a shower badly, but he wasn't even supposed to take his arm out of the immobilizer at all. But he could not live like that, his sense of hygiene would not allow it. He just hoped that by him doing so it wasn't prolonging the healing process, or worse yet damaging his arm irreparably.

Work was still stressful, though in his impaired state he had less to do, because he physically couldn't do more. He had delegated the food ordering and putting the truck away to his assistants. He even had one of them, Girl, doing the scheduling, though he had to go over it to modify and change it most of the time. But at least the beginning parts of that headache were already done. Thanksgiving was only a week away. They were at the end of their slow period between Labor Day and Black Friday when the Christmas shopping rush began. The Wednesday before Thanksgiving was traditionally one of the biggest pizza nights of the year, even eclipsing Super Bowl Sunday. They would be busiest on weekends, as usual. Though they would start to sell gift cards and be busy with shoppers wanting quick food as they made their way home with the items they had bought to give to others.

At work Daniel focused on the work. He tried to have as much fun as he could with the people who were there, though the job itself was stressful and he felt little joy in the near mundane but necessary tasks. When he went home to his empty house it was just him and his cat. He was thankful for his cat, for the unconditional love and companionship that the small animal gave him. The quietness and emptiness of his house led Daniel to drink even more than he previously had in an effort to not only cope with his limited ability to do normal things as he once had, but also the crushing feelings of loneliness he was battling. Because of his broken arm he was eating more fast and junk food and he drank himself to sleep every night.

His thoughts frequently went to Faith and the times that they shared. They drifted to her during the day while he worked as he remembered fondly the days when they worked together and he relied upon her. Though it was at night when thoughts and memories of her assaulted his mind and emotions. But it compartmentalized nearly everything, blocking out and shutting away the horrible times and the bad things that she had done, that he had been through because of his relationship with her. He focused only on the fun and laughter, the companionship, and the sex.

He missed how in those good times she often pampered him. He thought fondly on the times when she would rub lotion on his calloused and sore feet just before he went to bed. How she massaged the lotion in and then put fresh socks on him. Oftentimes she would rub his back with lotion, even though he complained that the lotion was cold and it shocked him as she applied it. Several times she would try breathing on the lotion in an effort to warm it before, but Daniel knew she got a perverse thrill from seeing him squirm and holler as the cold, thick liquid hit his back unexpectedly. She would even trim his toenails and file his fingernails for him. He assumed it was the mother in her wanting to take care of another person. But he also believed she did it to show him that she truly loved him and wanted to repay him for his love and kindness. Daniel was thankful for that, he did enjoy the pampering even if it wasn't offered all the time. He missed it.

He missed her smell. He missed the warmth of her body on the other side of the bed. He missed her laughter, her smile, and her touch. He missed her being there when he got home from work. He missed cooking for someone other than himself.

Quit feeling sorry for yourself, his mind told him. *You're better off. We'll get through this.*

"I don't like where I'm at," he said aloud to himself as he stared at his naked reflection in the mirror. He absently pulled on his underwear, then the rest of his clothing as competing thoughts bombarded his mind.

She's broken and needs my help, he thought. *What if that's what I'm supposed to do? What if that is my purpose, to help her and her kids have a better life?*

Remember what she did to you, his mind prompted. She had no remorse, no guilt over anything. She was using you. What she gave was way less than what she took. You need to *know* that and move on.

Once dressed, Daniel looked at himself in the mirror, his focus going to the arm-shaped bulge beneath his shirt. He didn't like how it looked. He didn't like how he felt. Though he had gotten up less than an hour before, he was tired and felt drained. Even so he took a deep breath and attempted to push all of the thoughts of Faith and self-pity aside.

"Time to go to work, mother-fucker," he said to himself in an attempt to rally his strength for the work that lay ahead.

*   *   *

Daniel struggled and pushed himself through the next two weeks. He had worked a grueling Thanksgiving Eve, breaking store sales records. Everything had gone smoothly, for the most part. He counted only three small catastrophes that happened that evening. All in all it was a good day, especially since it was over.

He had spent Thanksgiving at his mom and stepfather's house in Midland. He drove down early that morning and returned to his house in Alanson late in the evening. The weather had cooperated. It was cold, but it did not snow and the highways were clear pavement. Daniel was thankful for the time with his family and enjoyed it. It was like a mini Christmas, without presents being exchanged. His grandparents on his mother's side were there, his sister Aubrey was in attendance, though her husband did not make the trip. Daniel wished that he did not have to work the following day, Black Friday, but it was the nature of the business that he was in. Customers and sales dictated his life, and though he was growing weary of the stress and chaos, he knew he was good at his job, and he wasn't sure what else he was supposed to do. So he pushed on.

It was the first week in December. The angry monster known as Winter descended upon Northern Michigan with an Arctic fury. Winter temperatures in the region normally hung around the mid-20s, though for the past week and for a few weeks forecasted the temperatures were to be in the single digits, not including the wind chill factor. The only positive about that was snowfall was not expected when it was so cold, except for lake effect snow which seemed nearly constant though without much accumulating in the area.

Daniel cringed as the propane-fired furnace kicked on for the third time that hour. He had checked the gauge on the large, green propane cylinder that sat just 10 feet off the side of his house a few days earlier. The needle read below 40%, which meant Daniel would have to get it filled again probably in January, maybe sooner if it stayed so cold. *I get an extra check that month, so I should be all right*, he thought. To help conserve, Daniel closed the vents to the back bedrooms and guest bathroom. The large wall of windows in the kitchen, which was pleasant and inviting three seasons of the year, were now a burden to the house maintaining a warm temperature. Even though they were double-paned, Daniel could still feel the cold leeching through the glass, though they were sealed well and no drafts could be felt.

He shivered as he carefully pulled on a hooded sweatshirt over the gray sweatshirt he was already wearing, his arm in the immobilizer tucked up underneath it. He had on long thermal underwear underneath sweatpants and his feet were clothed in thick socks. It was 11 AM on a Wednesday, three weeks before Christmas.

As Daniel walked to the refrigerator he looked out the wall of windows in the kitchen and gazed at the winter landscape. Snow devils blew off the low mounds of snow that lined the driveway. The black Toyota looked gray as it was covered with a dusting of snow. The first large snowfall had happened a week earlier netting over eight inches. In Daniel's condition he could not shovel snow, and he had only a small, single-stage snow thrower that was only suitable for less than 3 inches, and even then with Daniel's long and wide, gravel driveway it was more of a hindrance than a help. He paid his neighbor to plow his driveway out and it cost him twenty dollars. He wasn't sure what he was going to do if they got more snow. He supposed he could continue to get his neighbor do it for him, but if they got any amount of snow regularly, that would be too expensive. Wouldn't be able to afford it. Luckily with the forecast being so cold he wouldn't have to worry about that until maybe Christmas. And he figured with the Christmas money he usually got from his father and others he could get it plowed out a few times and still pay the bills. The thought of his bills and mounting credit card debt made his mind go back to the propane. *Son-of-a-bitch*, he thought. *My life is good, yet so shitty at the same time.*

Suddenly he felt tired, standing there in the kitchen at the counter in front of the coffee pot. He stared at the coffee pot, then turned and looked out the window again. The sight of the blowing snow did not help the feeling of desperation that was closing in on him.

He decided he should go take a shower, get cleaned up and let the hot water warm him up. Then he laughed, *Stupid idiot*, he scolded himself. *You can't take a shower with your broken arm.* The realization of him not even able to undertake that simple pleasure with his current injury broke through the thin barrier that was holding depression at bay.

As he turned from looking out the window back towards the coffee pot, he reached for it and was about to fill it with water and make a pot as he caught a whiff of his own body odor. The smell made his stomach turn. It was as a sweet-sour smell, a mixture of failing, day-old deodorant, grease from the restaurant from the previous day's work, and the sweat that soaked into the immobilizer, staining it with the new, unpleasant smell. His brain knew this scent now, having categorized it over the preceding days and weeks. It was the nauseating smell of sickness, of incapacitation. *The smell of my failure*, he thought bitterly.

To his stressed and worn out mind the smell reminded him that he was in some ways handicapped. Even his laundry had been suffering, since he could not fold the clothes he just left them in the basket to get wrinkled. His work clothes he would throw back in the dryer in an effort to get the wrinkles out before he wore them. He could not do everything that he once had. Even though he realized it was just temporary, that he should be healed in another month, his situation pulled his drive and desire from him.

Disgusted by how he smelled and felt, Daniel left the cold kitchen made his way back to the master bathroom. Even though he was not looking forward to the daily ordeal of washing himself from the sink, shivering naked before it, washing and rinsing as fast as he could, though still trying to be thorough, he wanted to be clean. He needed to feel better. He mentally prepared himself for the uncomfortable and humiliating ordeal that he willingly undertook. With a deep breath he closed the bathroom door, turned on the hot water and undressed as quickly as he could.

    *   *   *

He was dressed in comfortable clothes, sitting on his couch, under a blanket, his cat resting on his lap. He was flipping through the satellite stations trying to find something worthwhile to watch. He didn't feel like watching a movie, or was too lazy to get up and search through the cabinet to find one. He hadn't decided which. He was on his second beer. It was one in the afternoon.

His cell phone rang, piercing through the quietness of the cold house. Daniel jumped in his seat, his cat leapt up off of him and took off running. His heart was pounding from the unexpected and loud noise. Part of the reason his heart thundered was also the ring itself. It was *hers*. He quickly grabbed his phone and looked at the small display for confirmation. His hand trembled, more from his anxiety than from the vibration setting on the phone. *Should I answer?* He asked himself. He wanted to. But he knew he probably shouldn't. *Let her go to voicemail*, he thought. *We'll see what kind of message she leaves, if she leaves one.* He stared at the lit up dial and listened to the harmony blast through the tiny speaker. In five seconds the phone went dim and silent.

Daniel's mind began to twist with the thought of what type of message she could be leaving, if she was leaving one at all. He continued to look at the phone in perverse anticipation. Waiting. A long minute later the small rectangle display lit up and the symbol for voice message appeared.

Without hesitation Daniel flipped open the phone and held down the one button, speed dialing his voicemail. The computerized voice asked him to enter his security code. Daniel quickly punched in the four digits with his thumb and then the #.

"You have one unheard message," the voice told him. Then the message began to play. It was definitely Faith's voice. Her telltale crackle and smokiness was evident, and Daniel could hear anxiety and sadness coating her words. *Some things will never change*, he thought absently as he tried to listen to what she was saying.

Hey, babe. I know it's been a while, but I wanted to tell you that I'm sorry for everything. I was just lonely and just wanted some friends. Those guys are such assholes, I didn't even know! But I swear I never had sex with any of them. I would never do anything to hurt you, she said, and as she did so her voice broke and Daniel could tell she was crying. *Um, Scott is doing some nasty shit, so I can't stay there anymore. Going to go stay with with my mom--my fucking mom!--Because I don't have anywhere else to go. I was just going to let you know where I'd be, in case...Well in case you wanted to talk. I'm sorry, Daniel. I do love you. I just want you to know that...Okay...Bye.*

Daniel pressed nine to save the message. He listened to it three more times, absorbing every word, discerning every nuance and break in her voice. He thought that he should probably call her, talk to her, now that she had sincerely apologized. He could only imagine what "nasty shit" she was talking about, but he knew it had to be pretty bad for her to leave her kids and go stay with her mom of all people.

She blamed her mother for what happened to her and her siblings when they were young, and even not so young. According to Faith, her mother turned a blind eye and a deaf ear to their cries and their pain when Faith had gone to her for help and protection. Daniel didn't blame her. If he would of had of a mother and so-called father like that, who knows how he would've turned out. His heart broke for her as he listened to the pain in her voice. Adrenaline was making his heart pump faster. A thick mixture of anxiety and excitement filled him, though it was tempered with apprehension.

You know you shouldn't do this, his mind warned him. You may be sad and lonely, but that will pass. You have taken a step forward, don't take three steps back.

Daniel ignored the thoughts in his head as he flipped open his phone and speed dialed Faith. His heartbeat pounded in his ears as he listened to it ring, two, three times.

"Hello?" She said, her voice still thick with tears. Daniel knew that she had to know it was him calling, but still that was all she said in way of greeting. It made him pause and question his decision one more time. "Hello?" She said again, pulling him from his wavering thoughts.

"Hey, Faith. You okay?" He asked her. He knew from her message that she wasn't okay, but he thought it was a way for him to convey, first thing, that he still cared for her.

"Scott's been a fucking asshole, as usual. He locked me out of the house a couple days ago and wouldn't let me back in until I told him I would sleep in his bed. I didn't want to do that! That's not why was there, I was there for the kids! I was freezing in the garage and I didn't have a vehicle, my phone and everything was in the house--even my boots! My fucking boots were inside the house! So, I told him I would, but I kept all my clothes on and I tried to figure out what to do. I called my brother and he was no help. The sick fucking bastard would not keep his hands off me, I couldn't get any sleep! I just wanted to sleep! I was sleeping in Tara's room this whole time, now he says I can't sleep in there anymore if I want to stay! And I didn't want to stay, didn't want to be there at all! So I had to call my mom! My stupid, fucking mom! She should be the one who's dead, not my dad! But she did come and get me, but I had to leave while the kids were at school, and the asshole took Tara to day care, so they don't even know I am gone. I didn't get to say goodbye to my kids!" She shouted in a long, rambling, hard to follow explanation. She was fighting tears, though her sobs pushed her words.

Daniel was feeling sorry for himself, and now he was feeling sorry for Faith. There was a heaviness, a weight that was pushing down on his chest. His head was throbbing, and his heart felt heavy. He wanted somebody, needed somebody, to help him through the daily struggle that had become his life. She was available, and she had been there for him in the past, even if he had not been her true focus. But right then, Daniel figured a little help and affection was better than emptiness and being alone. *Besides,* he thought *she needs me now probably more than I need her.* The combination of all the emotions, now coupled with hearing her latest predicament broke him down even lower. He felt the sadness welling up within him, bring him close to tears as he clearly heard hers pouring from her as she spoke.

"Did he hurt you?" Daniel asked her.

"No... Not really. He sure as hell didn't get any sex, I can tell you that!" She stated defiantly, and he detected a hint of triumph in her voice. "I fought him off all night, finally got up and just started making the kids breakfast at 5 AM, just to get away from him. I called my brother, you know him, all he did was holler and swear, calling Scott an asshole. But, he didn't do anything to help me. Not that I want to stay with him, but where else was I to go?" She said, rambling again.

"Did you get all your things?" Daniel asked.

She laughed at the question. Actually laughed. It served to shut her tears off for the moment. "That's funny, right there. All I have is what I took that night you made me leave. A suitcase and duffel bag full of not fucking much," she told him, anger now coating her words, though he did hear sarcasm in her words as well. He didn't think the anger was launched at him specifically, he could tell she was just angry at the whole situation even as she tried to make light of it.

What she said wasn't lost on Daniel. He corrected her by saying, "Hey, I didn't make you leave. You packed those bags and left on your own. Without saying a word, I might add."

"I know, babe. I was just giving you shit," she said, again with a small laugh. Her mood seemed to be lightened now as she got a chance to vent to someone who actually cared. "It's good to hear your voice," she told him after a short pause. "I'm very sorry for what happened. Sorry that those assholes stole from you, but I did try to my best to get stuff back for you. And, honestly, I never had sex with them, never! I know you probably hate me and don't believe me, but I want you know that I do love you, and I'm sorry," she told him, tears flooding back into her speech.

It was good to hear her laugh. He missed that. He missed talking to her, even though it seemed there was always some major drama going on in her life at any given time.

"I know you don't want to hear it, but Faith if you hang around better people you won't have these problems. You hang around users, you're going to get used," he told her.

Good advice, his mind told him. He pushed the chiding thought aside.

"I know, I know. It's just that I don't have very many friends...I don't have any real friends except you.," She told him and was quiet for a few long seconds. He could hear her breathing, it was coming in a ragged gasp's. He could almost see her chest shuddering under waves of sadness. "I don't even have you anymore," she said as tears flooded her voice once again.

He was on the verge of saying it, then he bit his tongue. Part of him wanted to so very much, but another part resisted. *She doesn't have anyone else*, he thought. Before his mind could react he suddenly said, "Do you want me to come get you?"

It was out there now. He couldn't take it back. Part of him felt a sense of relief, while another part of him was filled with a foreboding anxiety, all of which was awash in a wave of adrenaline that mixed the emotions and made them all feel akin to excitement.

"Yes," she began. "I'd really like that. I miss you. And I am really sorry," she said again.

"Okay...But no more bullshit, Faith. We got to find you better friends."

She breathed laughter at his words. He could see her smile in his mind and it made him smile. "I know," she admitted. "When you gonna be here?" She asked, lightness returning to her voice now at the ray of hope he just provided her.

As Daniel had already washed, shaved, and dressed he could leave within five minutes. He calculated the time it would take him to get to East Jordan. "I'll be there in half an hour," he told her. It would really take him closer to 45 minutes, but she was never ready on time, and he figured if he told her he'd be there earlier, she should be ready by the time he got there. She said she would be. He didn't tell her about his broken arm, he figured it would give them conversation for the drive back. She told him she loved him before hanging up. Daniel did not return the words.

As Daniel stepped outside, a blast of frozen air slammed into him at 35 miles an hour. The gust slammed the storm door closed as he stepped off the porch, ducking his head trying to shield it from the onslaught as he made his way to the icy Toyota.

The car door creaked and crackled as he opened it. He quickly got in and slammed the door shut, jamming the key in the ignition and turning it. The starter struggled to turn the engine over. Daniel swore as he could immediately tell the battery was stressed from the low temperatures. Finally, the engine caught and slowly came to life. He breathed a sigh of relief and he automatically flipped the small switch to turn on the rear defroster.

Even through the thick winter coat, Daniel was shivering as he sat on the cold cloth seats waiting for the engine to warm up. Because of the wind and the light snowfall he did not have to brush or scrape the windows, though they were icy but on the inside of the vehicle due to the snow and moisture that were on his floor mats. All he could do was wait for the engine to warm up and the defroster to start to work.

As his teeth chattered and his body shivered, his muscles tightening from the cold and a jolt of pain at the breaks in his left arm, he could not help but think that this was just one more thing he was willing to endure to help Faith, to be with *her*. His left arm was aching now, Daniel thought he could feel where the mending bones were straining against the cold, as his arm muscles tightened and increased the pressure in that still sore spot.

He sat in the car for only a minute before deciding to go back in the house and wait for the car to warm up. He cranked the fan dial to maximum before getting out of the car and hurrying back inside as the icy wind again assaulted him with every step.

Daniel entered the house and quickly shut the door behind him. Almost immediately the warmth and shelter eased his shivering body. He walked over to the coffee pot which was still on and poured himself another cup. The sweet, hot liquid warmed him as he felt it run down his throat into his chest and stomach. He sat down at the dining table and looked out at the Toyota, watching as the heated air from the engine slowly removed the thin layer of ice and frost, gradually clearing the windshield. He smiled to himself as he thought that within a couple hours his house would be a home again.

CHAPTER TWENTY-FIVE

He helped her by carrying the suitcase to the car, while she carried the duffle bag. She also had two plastic bags from the grocery store filled with only she knew what. They loaded everything into the hatch and he slammed the door. The car was still running, the heater still on full as they stood outside in the wind. Snow flurries whipped about them, dancing an erratic patterns. A gust of wind blew snow off of the roof of the house, coating them with a cold, wet mist.

"You have everything?" Daniel asked her, eager to leave. Even though it had taken him over an hour to get to her mom's from when he had disconnected the phone call, Faith was still not quite ready, though she did have her bags packed, but she was searching for a last few items, arguing with her mother nearly the entire time. Daniel felt an uneasiness being in the house. He thought he could feel a heaviness and it raised his anxiety level. He cold only stay inside for a few minutes before retreating back outside where he waited by the idling car. He did not want to come back, do not want to give her an excuse to have to come back a couple days later.

"Yeah, I think so," she told him as she got in the car and shut the door. He went around to the driver side and got in, shutting his door, sealing out the cold.

"You sure you got everything, I don't want to have to come back. Sure you don't want to go back in to check?" He asked her, silently praying that she didn't go back in and thus prolong the already taxing journey.

She shook her head, "No, I got everything."

With that said, Daniel put the car in gear, backed out of the driveway and headed for home.

"So, you gonna tell me what happened to your arm now?" She asked.

Daniel told her the entire story. It took him over half the way home to recount all the events as he remembered them, including the police officer and the surly doctor.

"It's a good thing you didn't go in that night," she told him. "You would've got a DUI for sure. It's wrong, but I know this guy who was an alcoholic that lost his license, and he was driving back from the party store on his riding lawnmower with a six pack, and the asshole sheriff busted him for driving on a suspended license. Driving a lawnmower, to a store that was only a quarter-mile from his house! The dumbass should've walked there, it being that close. But still!" She said in a rambling story.

Daniel smiled at her as he looked at her. Her face seemed sunken and drawn, her hair unclean. She looked tired, and she smelled of dog.

"You look tired. Do you want to take a shower and then lay down when we get back?" He asked her.

"That would be great. I haven't slept in like two days, and I didn't shower either. I haven't shaved my legs for over two weeks. I feel gross and disgusting," she admitted.

Daniel cringed at the mental picture that her words conjured in his mind. He thought of black stubbly legs and armpits, and overgrown pubic hair. His dick was ready and willing, but Daniel had to subdue the thoughts and urges. *Yuck, no sex until she's cleaned up and ready*, he thought. Being on the subject of hygiene, Daniel told her of his difficulties and what he had to do to wash himself daily.

"Well, it's probably better now if you wash when you get home from work, instead of in the morning. It will keep the sheets cleaner. I can help wash you, babe," she told him.

Daniel had always been a pre-work shower person. He'd never thought of his dirty work body soiling the sheets and blankets as he slept. But she was right. He should be taking showers after work, or both.

"I'd really like that," he told her. He wanted desperately reach over and put his hand on her thigh, as he always did when he drove. But seeing how he only had his right arm to drive with he could not very well take it off the steering wheel to do that. So, he just looked at her and tried to convey his love and affection with his eyes and his smile. She smiled back and leaned her body sideways over the console and put her head on his shoulder and her hand in his lap.

"I'm sorry, babe. Thank you for rescuing me. Again," she said.

"You're welcome," he said as he kissed her on top of the head as it lay on his shoulder. He could tell it was unwashed. Playfully he said to her, "Yuck, babe! We need to get you in the shower, quick!" They both laughed.

"I know. I'm sorry," she said.

As they neared the house and were only a couple minutes from the Mickey's party store and gas station, Faith asked, "Daniel, I hate to ask, but can we stop at Mickey's and will you buy me some cigarettes and some orange soda?"

Some things will never change, he thought.

He slowed down as they neared the station, pulled in the driveway having to avoid an exiting car. He made his way to the side of the building and parked. The car still idling, he turned and looked at her. She looked back at him and they both just sat there.

"Well?" He said to her.

"Babe, I can't go in looking like this! You're all showered and clean, plus I got no money, you know that," she reminded him. "Please?" She said, looking into his eyes and putting a pouty frown on for more effect.

"Fine," he said as he opened the door started to get out. "But you owe me."

She smiled back and said, "After a shower and sleep, I'll make it worth your while."

Daniel smiled back at her as he shut the door and made his way into the store.

*   *   *

Daniel had timed it nearly perfectly. While Faith was taking a long, much-needed shower and attending to her personal hygiene needs, he made brunch. It was nearly 3 o'clock, but for some reason bacon, eggs, and toast sounded good to both of them. As they ate at the dining room table, Daniel could smell her shampoo and her cologne. It was a good smell, one that he had missed. Even though she was clean, she did not put on makeup and that seemed to add to her look of tiredness. Daniel was tired as well. Being out in the cold, thinking of everything--still trying to sort out and make sense of the past and present, looking towards the uncertain future--was making him feel weary.

After putting the dishes in the dishwasher, Daniel followed Faith to the bedroom. She was wearing her pink and baby blue striped pajama bottoms and a white T-shirt. She climbed in her side of the bed and closed her eyes with a smile on her face. Daniel undressed down to his underwear and T-shirt and climbed in beside her. Almost as if it was a natural response, their bodies gravitated towards one another. They both lay on their right side, assuming the intimate spoon position. The warmth of their bodies under the covers was welcomed from the colder air of the house. Feeling her body, the heat of it, made his heart speed up. As her left ankle snaked around his he smiled. It was awkward with his left arm in the immobilizer to lay on his side pressed up against her. He desperately wanted to wrap that arm around her and hold her tight against him. He kissed the back of her neck and she told him she loved him. Within minutes they were both fast asleep.

*   *   *

He woke from a deep sleep. His mind was a fog, not knowing what time it was or the day. Waning light shone through the blinds of the bedroom. The sun was in its setting arc, pushing the day to its end and pulling evening behind it. A gust of wind whipped at the window, rattling the glass. He took a deep breath in an effort to help him become fully awake. With that breath Daniel tasted cologne. He was lying on his back. He turned his head to the right toward what had been for weeks the empty side of the bed.

There was a shapely form there now, wrapped in white and pastel striped cotton. The covers had been pulled down to her mid thigh. Pajama bottoms had been pulled down slightly past the curve of her hips, the white T-shirt pulled up several inches exposing the bare skin of her back and the bottom portion of her dragonfly tattoo. At the top of the pajama bottoms Daniel could see the top of the divide of her round as cheeks. It was something he had not seen in what seemed a very long time. The sight of her curves, the smell of her clean and perfumed body, the undetectable magnetic pull of her feminine allure aroused Daniel, making his heart quicken as his desire intensified.

He reached with his right hand and touched her softly on her exposed lower back. He gently began to caress the curve of her hips and her buttocks. She stirred at his touch, rolling from lying on her right side onto her back, effectively breaking free from his touch.

"What are you doing?" She asked, her voice pleasant.

"I'm enjoying having you here," he began. "I was enjoying touching your body, seeing and feeling your curves." He smiled at her and she returned it with a giggle and a smile of her own.

She rolled onto her left side and lay her head on his right shoulder. She began caressing his stomach, sliding her hand under his T-shirt, swirling her fingertips in the patch of hair, lightly scratching with her long fingernails. Daniel's arousal became more intensified as he thought with hopeful anticipation of what might happen next. He started to hard as your action became more prominent beneath his cotton boxer-briefs.

"What's this about?" She asked, noticing his growing erection. She reached down for it, using her palm and her fingertips to massage him through the fabric. His right arm was underneath and around her as her head still lying on his chest and shoulder. With his right hand he slipped it into her pajama bottoms and began caressing and rubbing her ass.

She rolled into him and pushed herself up, being mindful of the healing arm bent across his chest. She leaned in and gave him a kiss, which he returned. He pulled her closer to him as he tried to kiss her passionately, pushing his tongue gently in her mouth. She returned the kiss briefly before breaking the connection and smiling at him. Without saying a word she got to her knees and positioned herself on the side of him, leaning over at his groin. She grabbed his underwear with both hands and slid them down, exposing him.

She took him into her hand, pulling and massaging briefly before opening her mouth and taking him there. Daniel breathed out a moan of pleasure as he felt her touch once again. It seemed like it had been such a long time. As she continued her sensual work, Daniel looked down at her half exposed buttocks, the cotton fabric having been pulled down as she got to her knees. He reached towards it and began gently caressing her cheeks, then sliding his fingers in between her legs and feeling the warm folds of skin that beckoned him.

At his touch she began sucking and pulling faster and more excitedly. Daniel probed and found the entry, wet and sticky. He slid his finger in and began caressing her insides, trying to match her rhythm. She began to moan now as he did. He looked down and witnessed her head slowly bobbing, feeling her with every second. His eyes drank in her short black hair, the side of her face, her lips. The motion of her slender fingers wrapped around him, how her long fingernails looked, with their chipped white paint. The sound she was making as he continued to pleasure her with his hand. He could feel himself growing larger and coming closer to the point of climax.

"Babe, you should stop," he warned her before it was too late. "I wanna get behind you."

She stopped and looked at him, still holding him in her right hand. She smiled and let go.

Daniel rolled off the bed and stood on the floor facing it. Faith rolled onto her back and pulled her pajama bottoms completely off, then she backed up towards him, on her knees, her feet hanging off the edge of the mattress. He inserted himself into her, slowly. She let out a yell as he pushed himself all the way into her. He started out in a slow rhythm, she was matching it as she bounced slightly back into him.

This must be a weird site, he thought as he looked down at his left arm in the immobilizer as his right-hand caressed her back as their bodies created a symphony of sex and pleasure. His nostrils were now filled with the scent of their lovemaking. It was sharp and sweet, mingling with the aroma of sweat, cologne, and shampoo. The bouquet was welcomed and familiar. He had not realized until then that he had missed *their* smell, that it held such a powerful adhesion and attraction for him.

He intensified his rhythm now, pulling her back with his right hand as she continued to bounce, matching his thrusts.

"Oh, God! Right there, right there!" She yelled as she thrust herself back at him harder. "Don't go any faster, don't go any slower," she instructed him.

Daniel complied, concentrating on the rhythm and the amount of force that he was currently applying. In a little over a minute, she was moaning louder as she pulled the blankets toward her and shoved her face down into the folds, yelling as she climaxed.

Daniel could feel himself swelling as he now thrust harder into her. Less than half a minute later he felt himself release inside of her. As his legs began to shake he pulled her to him holding himself inside of her as the wave of euphoria and pleasure flooded his body. All of his stress and anxiety, all of his energy was then drained from his body. Still standing on the floor he slumped awkwardly over her and she collapsed onto the bed. They lay like that for long moments, both breathing hard. Daniel could still smell their aroma in the air and he smiled.

It's good to have her back, he thought, as the winter wind once again rattled the window of the bedroom.

CHAPTER TWENTY-SIX

The landscape along Interstate 75 was usually a welcomed sight. The green rolling hills, patches of land thick with trees, farmland, sporadic houses in the distance. Of course there always were many billboards and signs announcing the exits, though those too became welcomed in the sense of familiarity and helped to mark distance and progress. But during the winter months the freeway was a reminder of how insignificant humans were compared to mother nature.

Thick blankets of white snow covered the rolling hills and farmland. The once lush trees were barren of their leaves, standing like spindly remnants of a proud Army that was laid waste from the onslaught of Winter, destined to stand in their death poses until the magic of Spring broke through and revived them once again.

It was Christmas day throughout the world. Daniel drove down the stretch of highway toward Saginaw where his family on his father's side would be gathering for their holiday festivities. This year, Faith was going with him. It was the first time his family would meet her en masse. Understandably she was nervous. Daniel was nervous as well. He knew she would get questions and he was unsure of what the answers might be. Aside from that, Daniel knew that when she was on her medications at their full dose she became confused and often times would be out of it.

"Faith, please don't take all of your meds today, okay?" He had pleaded with her as they were getting ready for the day. "I want you to be alert and have fun. I want them to see the real you," he told her with a smile.

"Okay, babe," she said with a smile of her own.

She had been sick for the past few weeks, ever since she came back from staying with her children. She had flu symptoms and lay in bed most of the day. Daniel bought over-the-counter cold meds for her and tried to pamper her back to health, but it was a stubborn illness. They did not have sex for nearly two weeks after she moved back in because of how she felt. But about a week before Christmas she seemed to get over her cold and back to her old self. Her smile had returned and the sex had resumed. Daniel was happy for both.

The holiday traffic became thicker as they neared the larger cities. North and southbound traffic were utilizing all three lanes, everyone seemingly pushing their vehicles' capabilities to their limits as they maneuvered on the slippery, snow-covered highway. From I-75 Daniel took the I-675 bypass that hooked around and brought vehicles into the city of Saginaw. The place of his birth.

Daniel took the exit for Tittabawassee Rd, which led them past several big-box stores, chain restaurants, and the Fashion Square Mall. He continued on that road past the movie theater, the hospital, and other big-box stores, until there was just open farmland and scatterings of houses. It had been years since Daniel had been down that road. Things had changed, businesses had changed, some closed down, others came in. One of the stretches of farmland now held a new subdivision, with two-story stately houses built on fenced-in, postage stamp lots.

He remembered fondly of the times in his late teens when he and his cousin and their friends would drive the summer streets, day and night, going to the record store to buy heavy metal T-shirts or the latest cassette tape. He laughed at how sometimes they would score a 12 pack of beer, drinking it warm as no one thought to bring a cooler or ice. He remembered the times late at night they would sneak onto the golf courses and creep into their ponds collecting the wayward golf balls and selling them for two dollars a dozen. They did it more for the entertainment and excitement--as the night grounds keeper in his old, blue pickup truck was never far off--than for the small amount of money they gleaned. One night there were four of them evading the truck and its driver. They hid in a port-a-potty, all four crammed into the confined space, the smell of the urine and feces almost gagging in the summer night's heat, praying the groundskeeper wasn't heading in their direction to use that very same toilet. He laughed at himself and at the folly of his youth.

He tried to remember what dreams he had had for his life back then. Whatever they had been, he was certain that his current life did not reflect those hopes and dreams even in the smallest sense. He subdued the nagging feelings of regret, of chances and opportunities squandered or not taken, and smiled at the wonderful joy of the holiday and the celebration that was just ahead.

The Toyota sped over a set of railroad tracks, the sudden jolting and loud *thump-thimp-thump-thimp* as the car hit the steel tracks pulled him from his memories and alerted him that his turn was coming up quickly. A few minutes and a few turns later they had arrived in a small subdivision at his grandmother's house.

As Daniel found a parking spot in the street behind a Ford Explorer, he noticed the other vehicles parked in the driveway and out on the street. A few of them he knew who the owners were, others he had to guess at. He shut the engine off and turned to Faith who returned a smile.

"Can I have a cigarette before we go in?" She asked.

There was nervousness in her voice and Daniel saw it in her eyes. He imagined she felt like she was going to court to stand in front of an accusing judge and jury. *In a way, she kinda is*, he thought. *She'll be fine.*

"Sure, it'll take a few minutes for me to get the presents ready," he told her as he got out and went to the vehicle's hatch, opened it up, and began inspecting the colorfully wrapped packages for any damage.

He brought a black, plastic clothes basket into which he had carefully put the gifts. Faith sat in the passenger seat with the door open while she smoked her cigarette, blowing the acrid smoke into the winter air. In the cold stillness of the day, Daniel could smell the pungent odor of the burning tobacco, it flared his nostrils and made him wish she could quit that habit.

He lingered as long as he could with the wrapped gifts, giving her time to smoke and hopefully calm her nerves. But, the winter chill was starting to eat through his clothes and chill him more than he was comfortable with. He wanted to get inside where it was warm, eat some food and have some beer, all the while reminiscing and catching up with his family.

He grabbed the basket and awkwardly balanced it on the edge of the rear bumper, with his left knee, as he reached up with his right arm and slammed the hatch shut. It was times like this that Daniel really missed having the use of both arms. He would be forced to use the immobilizer for at least two more weeks, the doctor had told him.

Daniel was thankful for all the help that Faith had provided him. As promised, she helped him wash daily, and was back to doing the household chores, including shoveling the driveway by hand as he could not. She would even get up early with him and while he was in the shower she would make coffee and go out and start his vehicle so it was warmed up for him before he had to leave. She even made dinner for him now and then. She seemed happy and less depressed now that she was back. Daniel prayed that it was a turn for the better and a sign of things to come. As far as his arm, Daniel could feel that it was healing and the daily pain had lessened considerably. Though as he looked at it in the mirror he noticed that the muscles had atrophied substantially. It shocked him that his left arm seemed so much smaller than his right. He wondered how long it would take for his arm to be back to normal. His father told him that the muscle would return quickly and without much effort other than using it daily. Daniel hoped that he was correct.

"Faith, can you grab the clothes basket for me?" He asked from the rear of the vehicle. With that she took one last drag and flipped the smoking partial cigarette into the snow where it reluctantly died with a hiss.

"Ready?" He asked her with a smile. He could tell that she was nervous as she returned a weak smile. He leaned in and gave her a long kiss on the lips after which he reassured her, "It's fine. It's just my family, we'll have fun! There's food, snacks and cookies, beer and booze. Just be yourself. We won't stay too long."

"Okay," she told him as she grabbed the basket with both hands and followed him up the snowy sidewalk to the front door.

*   *   *

Daniel and Faith were sitting next to each other on the couch, she took the seat on the end and was leaning on the arm listening to conversation. Next to Daniels sat his uncle and one of his cousins. The loveseat, two rocker recliners, and some kitchen chairs that been brought into the living room bordering on the dining area were all full. The kitchen table was full, mostly of Aunts, his two sisters, and a female cousin. All were engaged in lively small talk, questions and answers about each other's lives, monologues and stories about recent trips, even mundane musings about the weather, and of course talk about football.

They had eaten and were now grazing on the sweet treats of Christmas time: chocolate and colored marshmallow church windows, rich buckeyes, sticky and sweet cornflake wreaths with the cinnamon Red-Hot candies, frosted cookies, assorted nuts both in and out of the shell, plus an assorted list of must-have goodies all displayed on the large dining table begging for over-consumption. Cans of Miller Lite and Labatt Blue were out in the small entry, being kept cold by the frigid atmosphere. When one person went out to get a can for themselves, they always brought back two or three more and passed them out as needed.

As the multiple conversations crisscrossed, Daniel tried to focus on the more interesting ones, and interjected a thought or two as he mostly listened. He looked to Faith and noticed she was starting to nod off, her jaw resting on her fist as her elbow was perched on the arm of the sofa. He nudged her with his elbow, harder than he anticipated. She jolted from her half sleep but managed to stifle a shout.

"What?" Was all she said, irritation in her voice as she looked at him with sleepy eyes.

Daniel leaned in and whispered into her ear, "You are falling asleep," *and you're embarrassing me*, he thought. It was the first time that she had met most of his family. The first time she'd actually interacted and talked with them. For the most part, Daniel was pleased with how she conducted herself, though she did tend to swear too much, using the limited vocabulary that she used with her friends, her family, and her kids.

Daniel had to admit that he swore a lot, though he was able to curtail it depending on who's company he was in. His family swore very little, so he made a point to not to, or at least keep it at a bare minimum when one or two slipped out. If he was alone with his cousins, that was a different story altogether. But he still held the older generation of his family in high regard and treated them with respect.

Daniel caught a glance from his grandmother who was sitting in her rocking chair looking directly at them. She smiled a warm smile. "Honey, are you tired?" she asked sweetly. Daniel could feel his cheeks flush and his face redden, his temperature rose and he began to sweat. Embarrassment flooded through his body and he hoped it wasn't evident to those who were sitting around.

Daniel wanted to answer for her, but before he could say anything Faith said, "I'm sorry. I didn't get much sleep last night."

"Do you want to go lie down in the bedroom?" His grandmother offered.

"Yea, that would be nice," Faith replied.

Daniel stood from the couch and motioned for Faith to follow, which she did. He smiled and thanked his grandmother as they walked out of the living room to his grandmother's bedroom. Daniel closed the door slightly as Faith walked directly to the bed and plopped down upon the thick, maroon comforter and began snuggling against the pillow. She was already nearly asleep.

Daniel wanted to yell at her, to scold her for her behavior. But, he knew at this point that wouldn't do much good. He bit his tongue and stifled his anger and embarrassment. He thought about just taking her and leaving right then, but he didn't want to. He was having fun and enjoying his family, something he didn't get to do very often. So, he decided he was going to enjoy the day himself, let Faith sleep for an hour or two, and when she woke or when he decided it was time to go they would leave.

He looked at her as she slept. His anger and frustration was then tempered by pity. He felt bad for her and all that her mind struggled with, but he was angry with her for obviously taking all of her meds even after he practically begged her not to. He wanted to avoid just this sort of situation. He wanted his family to like her, and she like them. It was too late to change the first impressions now, so Daniel would go back and make excuses for her behavior and deflect any unwanted questions as best he could.

I need another drink, he thought. He knew that he had to drive nearly three hours home, so he had to be careful about how much he drank. But one more would be okay. Maybe two.

*   *   *

As they drove out of the subdivision the late afternoon light was quickly receding. There was no sun visible that day, as a thick cloud cover obscured it which served to make it feel colder as the warming rays from the sun were blocked as well. The icy landscape served to chill Daniel's mood even further.

"I asked you to not take all your meds today," he said to her. He couldn't hold his anger any longer. "But you did any way, didn't you?"

"I had to," she said. She was looking out the window, avoiding his looks. She was still groggy from the medication-induced nap she took. It was only a few minutes after she had awoken that Daniel was ready to leave and put the events of the day behind him.

"What's wrong with her?" His sister, Aubrey, had asked him. He didn't have a good explanation, so he told her the truth as he knew it.

"She's on pain and anxiety meds. They knock her out when she takes them at the same time. I asked her not to, but she did anyway," he had told her and anyone else who had inquired about why his girlfriend was falling asleep and needed a nap less than two hours after arriving.

"No, you *didn't* have to," Daniel snarled. "For some reason you wanted to because you were stressed about going. I get that, I do, *but* I needed you to be normal today."

"Well, I guess I'm *not normal!*" She said, spitting his words back at him.

"You know what I mean," he said. "It was embarrassing for me and for you! If you didn't want to go so bad you should have said so. It would've been better if I had left you at home alone," he told her. He shook his head and didn't say another word. Neither did she. Faith, without asking, then lit a cigarette and rolled the window down partially to help expel the smoke. The selfish act angered Daniel, but he kept silent, enduring the unwelcome smell and the blast of frigid air. He felt that it was her way of covertly telling him to *fuck off.*

They drove in a thick silence for nearly an hour, listening to the radio. Daniel was starting to calm down and he hoped Faith was as well. He reached over quickly, steadying the steering wheel with his knees, and gently squeezed her thigh in a gesture of peace and love. He quickly grabbed the steering wheel with his only free hand again as he said, "I have to stop and get gas. Do you want anything? A soda, or candy bar?"

She looked at him and sheepishly answered, "An orange soda and Almond Joy...and can you please get me some smokes?"

The request grated on his nerves. He was getting tired of supporting her habit. He didn't smoke, but was buying nearly ten packs of cigarettes a month all in an effort to keep her happy. He pushed down the urge to quip about her smoking and just smiled as he got out of the car. After filling the gas tank he walked into the store. He returned a few minutes later with the items she asked for and a Coke and Take 5 candy bar for himself. He made a point to tip the worker five dollars for having to work on Christmas day, something he always did when traveling on Christmas.

"Thank you," she said as she accepted the treats. Faith tore into the candy even before Daniel had the car started. He tuned the radio to a station playing all Holiday music in an effort to lighten their moods. He hoped the sugar and caffeine would help as well, though he knew that he had eaten enough sugar for months, but it was a long drive.

*   *   *

They arrived back home in the dark. The headlights of the Toyota lit the driveway and the side of the house as its tires crunched on the frozen gravel beneath it. Daniel pulled the car closer to the house and he usually did. Faith had fallen asleep shortly after eating her candy and drinking her soda, although she did have another cigarette thereafter. His anger and frustration had subsided, but was still bubbling beneath the surface. He was thankful that she had slept for the final hour of the journey, for it saved him having to pretend that everything was okay, pretend to be interested in whatever story or topic she talked about. On the downside of that was he was then stuck in his own mind, replaying everything that had happened to him because of her. He tried to focus on the good memories, but the traumatic episodes kept pushing their way to the forefront of his consciousness, commanding a prominent position in his mind.

He shook her leg and pushed on her shoulder, trying to wake her. She blinked her eyes open and looked around, almost confused.

"We're home." He told her as he opened the door, allowing the frigid wind to blow through the car.

The unexpected harshness of it jolted Faith fully awake and she unbuckled her seatbelt and got out of the car just as Daniel was shutting his door. He walked quickly to the house, not waiting for her. The motion sensor light kicked on as he stepped up onto the porch, opened the storm door and unlocked the steel door. He pushed it open and hurried into the house letting the storm door close behind him, not holding it or waiting for Faith. He clicked on the kitchen light before removing his coat. As he sat down and removed his boots, Faith made her way into the house and closed the door behind her.

"Fuck, it's cold," she shouted as she shivered and stomped her feet. She then began the process of taking her boots off, though she still kept her winter jacket on.

The smell of pine and cinnamon from the scented oil air freshener brought to the forefront of his mind that it was Christmas. It was usually a happy and joyous day for him, and though he did enjoy visiting with his family, Faith had soured the day for him. It was just a handful of minutes past 8 PM and Daniel felt overly tired. All of the food, alcohol, and sugar he had consumed over the course of a few hours was now clenching and churning in his stomach. Thankfully, he knew that he did not have to work the following day, as he purposefully did not schedule himself for the day after Christmas. It was one of the small perks of being the GM and doing the schedule. He usually gave himself the day after Christmas off, the day after Thanksgiving if he could, and Easter Sunday off as well. Every other day he was pretty much open to work. So, though he did not have to, right then all he wanted to do was go to sleep.

Usually, if he had the night off and didn't have to work the next day, he would buy some wine for Faith and beer for himself and they would play pool, listen to music, and have sex. It was usually something he really look forward to and enjoyed doing. But her actions of the day had disappointed him to the point where none of those things held any attraction for him. As he looked at her as she took off her boots and her jacket, he wished that she would see how her actions hurt him. He wasn't sure if she ever would.

"I'm cold and tired," he told her. "I want to go lay down in bed, maybe watch some TV before I fall asleep."

She looked at him with a frozen stare. He could see the tiredness in her eyes and in her slack features. Her mouth was drawn, her cheeks slightly sunken. She looked older and more frail. The anger he was holding slowly melted away, replaced with empathy and pity. She looked like she had a question, so he just waited for her to ask. He looked back at her with kindness and his eyes.

"Can I watch with you?" She asked, the question coming out like a child asking a parent if they can stay up late on a school night. The tone suggested to him that she was afraid that he was going to say "no."

He gave her a half smile and said, "You can do whatever you want." He then turned and walked from the room. Half of him wanted a beer, but the other half just wanted to shut his mind off and sleep. The second half won.

After putting on sweat pants and climbing into bed, Daniel decided not to turn on the television. In a few minutes, however, Faith entered the room and turned it on before she changed clothes and climbed under the covers with him. Daniel grabbed his earplugs from the nightstand and inserted them, cutting the noise from the TV way down.

He rolled onto his side away from Faith, careful not to put too much weight on his still healing arm. He felt her hand on his hip, gently rubbing him as she flicked through the channels. He touched her hand with his and squeezed it gently, silently letting her know his disappointment and anger were waning, before settling in and trying to shut his mind off.

You love her too much, his mind said.

But love conquers all, he thought back.

"I'm sorry," he thought he heard her say an instant before his mental fatigue caught up with him and he fell asleep.

CHAPTER TWENTY-SEVEN

*Y*ou *need to get control of yourself, girl,* she thought. But that was easier said than done.

As Faith sat up in bed switching channels, the volume low so as not to disturb Daniel too much, she thought of the day and how she had let Daniel down. It wasn't what she intended. It seemed every Christmas lately was not a good day for her. She wanted to meet his family and was honestly eager for them to like her. But she was so nervous about the meeting that she couldn't not take her medication as he had asked her to. She feared she would have been much worse if she hadn't. She had told him she was sorry, and she was, but for more reasons than he knew.

Faith had a secret that she was keeping from Daniel. *What he doesn't know won't hurt him*, she kept telling herself. She didn't tell him, *couldn't* tell him...

She was grateful to be back with Daniel, living with him again. He had saved her again from elements of her life she couldn't seem to pull herself away from. She told Daniel what Scott was doing to make her life hell again. Most of it. What she didn't tell him was that her new doctor had put her on morphine pills, 30mg, twice a day. She was also still prescribed Xanax for anxiety. But the prescribed dosages would barely take the edge off of her pain and panic attacks. She had been self-medicating for months, using additional and higher doses of mostly opioids for recreation in that time as well. As a result her body had built up a high tolerance to where she needed, or thought she needed, higher dosages taken more frequently to get the same affects.

To help her out, and to hopefully drag her back into his life permanently, Scott had been supplying her with the additional meds, all the while keeping mental track of what she owed him. This stopped, however, when she refused to sleep with him and eventually decided to move out to avoid the harassment. She tried to hide it from

Daniel, her withdrawal symptoms. Faith tried weaning herself off of the drugs, but her prescribed supply was so depleted by the time she left Scott's she only had enough for less than one week at the lowest dose she dared. Within a few days of being back at Daniel's she was completely out of her meds and she was not scheduled for a refill on her prescriptions until December 28th, nearly two weeks away. And with the Holidays that could be delayed.

A narcotic prescription had to be hand written and brought in to the pharmacy. Because of DEA regulations doctors could no longer just call in narcotic medications, and the pharmacy was bound by law not to fill any prescription early. Every thirty days meant every thirty days at minimum. So, not only did she have to wait until three days after Christmas she would have to get in to see her doctor on that day and then to the pharmacy as well.

You can do it, girl! Fight it! She told herself as panic filled her thoughts and her body rebelled against itself. Her muscles would contract in hard spasms, agonizing to endure. She tried to push back against the unexpected tightening of her muscles, but the effort only served to increase the pain. Her breathing came heavy and quickly as the spasms overtook her. It was even difficult to draw a breath. Her mind screamed and sometimes so did her mouth as she clutched at the sheets, making fists in the fabric, biting into the pillow as waves of agony slammed through her.

Please, God! Her mind begged, *Just make the pain stop!*

Her bowels would let loose unexpectedly and she would hurry to make it to the bathroom. Several times she didn't, the spasms coming on too quickly, their affect unavoidable. She cried as she defecated in her pajamas and struggled on wobbly, pain wracked legs to shower and cleanse herself. She was doing small loads of laundry several times a day as Daniel was at work, hiding the effects. She vomited uncontrollably at times to where only bile would dribble from her mouth as her stomach muscles contracted and tightened seemingly beyond belief. Her stomach burned from the exertion, her throat raw and sore. She lost her appetite and even cigarettes held little comfort for her.

Faith was overcome by the alternating hot and cold sweats as her body tried to cope with being without the opioids it had known for so long. She would go from burning up hot, kicking the covers off and lifting up her top to expose her bare skin to the cool air, to freezing cold where no amount of blankets or layers of clothing could keep her from shivering. Her clothing and the sheets were soaked with perspiration as her mind screamed in torment, *You can do this, you're strong.*

Daniel thought she was sick. She was, he just didn't know how bad. *He couldn't and wouldn't do anything for you even if he knew*, she told herself. She knew in her heart that he would do almost anything for her, and he had done a lot. But, she knew he wouldn't get her the meds she needed, not illegally anyway. He'd want her to go to the hospital, or worse into rehab. *He just doesn't understand my situation, and probably never will*, she thought as tears of pain ran from her eyes and soaked the pillowcase.

Faith pushed herself into a ball of anguish and tried to sleep away the withdrawals. She thought it had been a week that she had fought the good fight. Her cries unto God had gone unanswered. The pain did not lessen. Her cravings for the opioids and the affect they had on her mental wellbeing and calming of her body was all she desired. She thought of suicide more than once, but she fought those feelings off successfully so far. Faith wasn't sure when her will finally broke and she reluctantly decided a different kind of help was needed.

She had lost count of the times she had vomited that day and had pushed herself to do two small loads of soiled laundry. She was tired of crying, tired of the pain in her muscles. Tired of the constant war within her mind that screamed at her to do what she must to save herself. With an unsteady hand, lying on her side curled into a fetal position on the bathroom floor, she opened her cell phone and called her brother.

"Zacharia?" Faith said as he answered. She almost always used his given name, a name which he despised, having been branded with a Biblical name for life. He preferred to be called "Z" or Zak. He hated his full name and gave hell to anyone who used it, except for his sister. She got a pass.

"What up?" Z said in greeting.

"I need some meds," she told him, a wavering in her voice.

"Can't help you. I'm not holding. You shoulda got a hold of me yesterday," he said casually.

"Zak, I'm not fucking with you!" She shouted. "I have been off my meds for a week and my body can't take it anymore!" Faith yelled as she started to cry. "If I can't stop the pain I think I'll just fuckin' kill myself," she threatened.

"Whoa, slow down, BS," he said, using the nickname he gave her which were the initials for Big Sister, but also carried the connotation of bull-shit. He thought it was funny. "You got kids--little kids--who need their mom. Plus, who would give our so-called mother shit if you were gone?" He joked.

His comments managed to solicit a laugh from Faith. "Don't make me laugh, it hurts, and not in a good way," she said.

"Geese, don't get all sexual on me, I told you I don't want to hear about your fucklife!" Zak told her with lightheartedness.

Faith again giggled at the comment. "Zacharia, please! You're not helping!" She scolded.

He let out a deep breath. "I really don't have anything, but I can probably get you...something. I can get the pain to stop...but you may not like it," he told her.

"If you can get the pain to stop I don't care what it is! Just please help me, I don't know what else to do," she told him, tears streaming down her face and coating her words. Faith sobbed into the phone as she pushed herself up from the bathroom floor. The tile was wet from perspiration and she almost slipped and fell as a lightning bolt of pain shot through her back as she struggled to her feet and wobbled to the bed, falling onto it.

"Z? You still there?" She asked.

"Yea, I was just thinking...Where you at?" He asked.

"At home, in Alanson," she told him.

"What time does your old man get home?"

"Don't call him that!" she scolded. "He closes, so about eleven-thirty."

"Alright, calm down. Geese!" Zak said. He paused for a moment, thinking. "It's five now. I'll make a few calls and get back to you soon. If I can get--and I said *if*--I'll head up there and get you squared away. I'll let you know. When I call you fuckin' answer," he said.

"I will," she assured him, a hopefulness in her voice. "Thanks, Zacharia," she said before the connection was broken.

*   *   *

Zacharia Collins pulled down the gravel driveway at 8:12 PM, the square headlights cutting the cold darkness with yellow light. He was not alone. He got out of a dented and fading maroon Olds Cutlass Supreme, circa early 80s. By the look of the classic vehicle it had barely made it the distance. Z stood five foot five inches tall, just a few over his sister. Like Faith he had black hair cut short. He kept it short almost in a military buzz cut, though longer on the top. He was small in size but made up for it with his quick mouth and quicker temper. He had fierce, green eyes and naturally straight teeth. He was clean shaven and had a strong jaw, thin lips, set under an Indian's nose. He carried a small toiletries bag as he approached the house.

With him was another man. He was taller, just over six foot. His hair was long and unkempt. He sported a full beard and mustache that made him look ten years older. He had a lanky frame clothed in soiled jeans and a button-up mechanic's shirt with an oval patch that read: KURT.

Z knocked hard on the door. "Open up! It's the police!" He shouted and both men laughed. He continued knocking obnoxiously until Faith appeared and opened it.

"What the fuck are you doing?" She scolded. "You're *not* funny, and you're making a lot of noise!" She said as she backed from the door and let them in.

Zacharia could tell his big sister was in pain. She looked like she hadn't showered in days, which was very unlike her. Her eyes were glossy and bloodshot, her facial features drawn and sagging. Her lips were dry and cracked. He noticed she was having trouble standing as she was wobbling, almost teetering as she took a few steps back giving them room to enter.

"BS, this is Dennis," Z said as he introduced the man with him.

Faith looked puzzled as she read the name on his shirt which did not match the introduction. "Then why does your shirt say 'Kurt'?" she asked.

"Cuz Kurt didn't need it no more," the man said, his voice low and raspy.

"I don't have time to socialize," she told the men. "Daniel will be home in awhile, so give me what you got and be on your way," she said.

"Well, like I told you, I can make the pain go away, but you may not like it," Z reiterated.

Faith looked puzzled again, looking from one man to the other, not getting any clues to the meaning. She knew she could trust her brother, well mostly. He was a thief and would sell out anyone to save his own ass, she knew, but their blood bond was always thicker than water. And he knew she had endured horrible, unspeakable things trying to protect him.

"What do you mean?" She said, apprehensive now. But as she said the words her body went through another spell of spasms. They were so fierce they doubled her over and she fell to her knees, then onto her side on the kitchen floor as she let out screams of agony and frustration.

Almost instinctively Z and Dennis got on either side of her and tried to calm her as her body twitched and kicked uncontrollably. She continued to let out cries of pain and anger as she tried to withstand the onslaught of her body rebelling against itself.

After a minute, Zak stood and unzipped the toiletries bag and removed a bullion spoon bent in an arc where the handle met the bowl. It was discolored and looked burned. Next, he removed a thin, clear syringe that had a three-inch needle attached. These he set down on the countertop of the island. Dennis was kneeling on the far side of Faith, holding her left arm and pushing up the sleeve of her pajama top, exposing the cleft of her elbow.

Zak turned on the sink faucet and put a small amount of water into the spoon. From a small, inch and a half square plastic reclosable bag, Zak then dumped a grayish-white powder into the spoon's bowl and the water. He looked over to see that Faith was starting to calm down from the spasms. He pulled a pack of cigarettes from his jacket pocket and removed a menthol from it. He placed it on the side of the stainless steel sink and with a flick of his wrist he opened a pocket knife and cut off a half inch of the cigarette's filter. He expertly peeled the paper from it and set the round piece of cotton-looking filter down.

He picked up the syringe and with the needle end he swirled and mixed the powder into the water. Zak then turned around and twisted the knob on the gas stove igniting a front burner. He held the bent spoon with the mixture over the blue flame until it began to boil. He stirred with the needle a little more then turned the burner off. Turning back to the sink he carefully sat the spoon down and placed the filter piece into the mixture. Then he pierced the filter with the needle and pulled back on the plunger of the syringe. He watched as the solution was pulled through the filter and needle into the syringe. Once all of the liquid was drawn from the spoon, Zak depressed the plunger on the syringe pushing out any air slowly until a couple of drops trickled out from the end of the needle.

Taking the syringe and grabbing a shoelace from the bag he walked calmly back to where Faith was still lying on her side with Dennis beside her. The whole thing had taken less than three minutes.

"What--what are you doing?" Faith asked, her eyes wide when she saw her brother approach with the needle attached to the syringe.

"I'm gonna make things all better for you," he told her as he knelt down beside her.

Faith's mind filled with memories of seeing her mother lying helpless on the couch as her step father did unspeakable things to her. The visions flashed to her seeing her brother slumped in a chair, needle hanging from his vein, sores on his face and arms.

"No, no!" she cried and tried to sit up, but Dennis held her down, pushing on her shoulder as he held her exposed arm tightly. "I don't want to do that!" She told them. "I promised myself I would *never* do that shit!" Faith was crying now. The man was too strong for her to pull away from him. She smelled dirt and automotive grease and stale cigarettes as she struggled against him.

"Calm down, Faith," her brother said as he touched her gently on the face. "I am trying to help you, okay? Your body *needs* this, okay? This will take the pain away in a fuckin' *second*, believe me. You can continue to go through withdrawals without help and without meds, but Dan is going to find out and you may die from it. Do you understand that?" He told her. He wasn't completely sure you could die from opioid withdrawals, but you for sure felt like you were and you wanted to just to end the agony.

He slowly and calmly handed Dennis the shoelace as he looked his sister in the eyes and smiled.

She was scared. She knew needle users and didn't want to be one, had *refused* to be one. Her mind was raging with conflicting thoughts. She desperately wanted the pain to end, but she just wanted her body to heal naturally, just much quicker than it was. Faith could feel the shoelace being tied and tightened around her upper arm. She struggled to get free. Zak pushed her onto her back and straddled her chest, pinning her right arm to her side with his leg. In seconds the veins in her left arm were starting to bulge from the pressure.

"No, no! Please Zacharia, don't do it, don't do it, don't do it," she begged through free-flowing tears. She couldn't watch, but she felt a sharp prick of the needle as it entered into her arm. "NO!" She screamed as Zak pulled back on the plunger, bringing Faith's blood into the syringe, mixing with the drug solution. He watched as the liquid turned red in a swirl. He then pushed the plunger in slowly, releasing the fluid into her vein and bloodstream.

In less than five seconds Faith was quiet. Her screams and pleas had been silenced just as the pain in her aching muscles and bones had been. Her mind felt light and airy. Her cares had been instantly carried away. Her breathing became normal. She had a hard time thinking or remembering where she was or what was happening. She knew something bad was going on, but she couldn't remember what. She couldn't focus, and that seemed to be okay. It fact, to her then it seemed to be much more than okay. When she opened her eyes to look at her brother sitting beside her she saw him smiling.

"Wow," was all she managed to say.

Zak and Dennis had carried Faith to the bedroom and had lay her down. Zak covered her up with a blanket. He had explained to her what they had done and told her he was leaving the "kit" for her. Inside was one more dose, he told her. After that she was on her own, but he could get more stuff for her, but no freebies. Faith told him to put the kit in her large black purse that hung in the back of the walk-in closet, which he did.

"Call me if you need anything," he said to her. Then they left, locking the door as they did. Zak had thought about going through the house and taking some things to pawn, but fought against the urge just then. He knew there would be another time, a better time to do so.

Faith was still in bed a few hours later when Daniel came home from work. She was feeling better than she had in a long time. Her body, though still aching and sore, was not wracked with spasms, her mind was calm, and she was in a safe place. She smiled as Daniel kissed her on the forehead.

We'll get through this, she told herself. *We'll make it right.*

She couldn't think past the moment, even though she tried. Deep down Faith was horrified about what had happened, what her brother had done to her, but at the same time she felt relieved. The pain was gone except some residual effects from the near constant battle her body had with itself over the last several days. She was exhausted but she found that she could sleep.

When she woke up she would cope with her new situation.

When she woke up she would deal with being a heroin user.

CHAPTER TWENTY-EIGHT

The sun was shining, not a cloud in the sky. It was a pale blue, a harbinger of Spring and warmer weather, or so Daniel hoped. It was the middle of February and the snow banks were still two feet high. Even with the sun the temperature was only forecasted to reach the high 30s, though because of the sun it felt ten degrees warmer.

It was Daniel's day off and he was headed into Petoskey to meet a good friend of his for lunch. Church was in Gaylord on business and they decided to split the difference in miles and meet in Petoskey, though it was much closer for Daniel. He had offered to meet Church in Gaylord, but his friend insisted on driving most of the way, making it easier on him. They were meeting at the Mitchell Street Pub for some beers and a good burger.

They had only spoken once since Church and Nevver had been to the house in October, the day of Daniel's accident. He was very much looking forward to seeing his friend again, even if it would only be for an hour or so. Neither one had seen or heard from Nevver, though both had left voice messages for him, but they had not received any reply. They left the invitation open to him, letting him know when and where they would be meeting, just in case.

Daniel's mind absently noted the make and models of the vehicles he passed: a Chrysler Town and Country minivan filled with a family, a Ford F-150, new, with a single woman driving, a Mercedes of some sort, a lawyer-looking man driving, and old Econoline conversion Van, rusted and looking out of place. *Strange*, he thought, *those things were common and looked upon as a status symbol fifteen years ago.* Times and what was considered "in" seemed to change almost as frequently as the weather.

Daniel arrived ten minutes early for their one o'clock luncheon, which was on-time for him. If he arrived anywhere less than ten minutes early he felt like he was late. He found a spot in a free parking lot on the back side of the restaurant which was situated downtown in a row of other businesses. He knew that parking on the main street was a hit-or-miss proposition most days, so he decided to park in the back where he knew there would be several open spots and only a short walk.

He walked quickly through the winter wind, squinting from the harsh sunlight, across the alley and entered through the back door, passing the kitchen and storage via a narrow hallway. The smell of charred meat and frying grease hit his senses and made his stomach growl. the hall opened up into the pub/restaurant. There was a long bar with a dozen or so stools, on the other side of the main aisle were six booths and a couple of tables. Another room to the right held ten or so more booths. The décor was dark stained wood and green upholstery, quaint Irish Pub signs adorned the walls adding to the ambiance.

As he made his way to the front and the hostess stand he heard his name being called, "Hey, Dan-O!"

He looked and saw Church waving his arms from a booth in the adjacent room. He smiled and waved back as he headed in that direction. The room was only half filled with patrons, the bright sunlight streamed in through the large windows that faced the street, dust particles were illuminated as they danced in the beams. As Daniel got to the table, Church stood up and the two hugged briefly.

"Good to see you, man," Daniel said as he removed his coat and placed it in the booth before sitting down across from Church. "You look good."

"Thanks, good to see you, too. But, you're looking tired," Church said.

Daniel snorted a laugh and smiled. "Yea, life's been interesting lately to say the least," he said.

"You hear from Nevver?" Church asked as he sat across from Daniel, taking a sip from a glass of water.

"No," Daniel replied as he picked up the drink menu. "I was hoping to, but no word. I left another message yesterday. Maybe he'll show up unannounced."

The server came over and introduced herself. She was in her mid-thirties, Daniel guessed, thin and pretty. Her dark hair was in a long braid that ran to the middle of her back. She wore tight black slacks and a loose green polo with the Pub's name embroidered on the left side. Daniel asked what was on tap and she dutifully rattled off the half dozen offerings. He picked an amber ale brewed locally. Church ordered an oatmeal stout. Daniel stared at the woman as she walked away, admiring her figure.

Church laughed, "Why don't you take a picture?" He joked.

Daniel laughed, "They don't like that, not one bit," he said with a smile. "How's work going--what is it that you are doing now?" Daniel asked.

"I am a consultant and a counselor of sorts," Church said. "I work for businesses, sometimes just owners of the businesses. I help them find new marketing opportunities, search out new clientele, help them build a workforce culture. I also do some interpersonal communication training which sometimes leads to relationship counseling."

"Wow, sounds like a lot," Daniel remarked.

"It can be. Just depends upon the situation. They're all different, which is why I like it. Plus, I get satisfaction from helping people in a variety of ways," Church said.

The server arrived and sat down their drinks, asking if they were ready to order.

"Sorry, I haven't looked at the menu yet, could you give us a few minutes?" Daniel asked. She told them she would be back as Daniel and Church both picked up a menu and began reading the options.

Daniel's eyes followed her again as she walked away, "Yea, I'd definitely eat pretzels out of her butt crack," he said, soliciting a laugh from his friend.

"So, how goes the search for a new woman?" Church asked. "Why don't you ask her out?"

Daniel's face instantly flushed as blood rushed in. He had not had a real conversation with his friend since his accident and the last Church knew he was single. After a silence he answered. "Ah, I don't think servers like being hit on while they work, probably happens a lot. And...Faith is back," he finally said. "She moved in after Thanksgiving."

Church set his menu down and looked at his friend, reading his face and looking into his eyes. Daniel averted his friend's gaze.

When Church remained silent, Daniel felt a nervous compulsion to keep talking. "She was having issues living with her ex and her kids, he was trying to get her to sleep with him and be a family, I guess. I was needing help with my arm still healing as well. But things have been good since she's been back," Daniel told him.

Just then the waitress returned. They both ordered burgers from the specialty menu, a side of fries for both. Daniel asked for a water as well. The server smiled a warm and pleasant smile and thanked them before walking away, Daniel's gaze following once again.

"Let me ask you something," Church said. Daniel's heart picked up its pace at the thought of what was coming next. He was practiced at avoiding questions and not answering them about his personal life, but with Church he knew that he could not sidestep him, at least not for long. "Why do you feel responsible for her?"

Daniel sat for a moment and took a drink of his beer in an effort to give him more time to respond. "I don't know...I think that maybe I'm supposed to help her, like God has me with her for some reason?" Even though it was supposed to be a statement, Daniel posed it like a question as he was not totally sure why he kept doing what he did for her.

"Possibly. You *did* almost die at birth, which suggests that God does indeed have a plan for you," Church responded. "Though I'm not so sure Faith is your purpose.

But, it's obvious she has 'daddy issues' and you seem to be filling the role of that--protector, provider, strength," he added, letting his words hang in the air, letting Daniel absorb them.

Daniel didn't want to admit it, and hadn't seen it before, but having heard the observation from Church he grudgingly agreed. "I guess you're right, but it's more than that," Daniel told him. "I am *drawn* to her for some strange reason. She has her flaws and drama, but for some reason I have a hard time *not* wanting to be with her."

"Is it really *her* you have a hard time not being with, or is it just not being with *someone?*" Church asked.

Daniel took another long drink of the beer. The tangy brew tasted good, more flavorful and potent than his usual Michelob Ultra. He thought about what Church was saying, what he was getting at. Daniel didn't like looking too deeply into himself as he didn't want to admit certain things that might push him out of a crumbling comfort zone.

When he did not answer, Church continued, "You didn't have many relationships when we were in high school, or after--none successfully lasting more than a month or two. Not until you met Stacy. Then, if I may be so bold, you held on to that for longer than you probably should have. Am I right?"

Daniel's face flushed again at the accusatory statement. Not because of anger or defensiveness toward Church for saying it, but for the truth that it held. *The truth hurts sometimes*, he thought.

"Yes," he admitted. "But, I felt, at the time, I was following God's rule about only being with one person," Daniel said in his defense.

"Commendable following our faith and belief. But, have you considered that you weren't supposed to be with Stacy for that long, that you weren't supposed to be married to her?" Church asked.

The thought was a little too much for Daniel to process. "I agree I probably should have walked away when she left. But I wanted her, just like I want Faith now."

"You, my good friend, have a control issue," Church said.

Daniel was slightly offended at the statement, "I do *not*," he said.

"Well, okay, it's more of a possessive issue. You look at 'your woman' as that, *yours*, no one else's," Church said. It was a statement, not a question. "When they leave or behave in a way you don't agree with, you get angry and your ego goes into possession mode and you do whatever it is you think you have to do to get them back...Back with you...Away from anyone else," he concluded.

Daniel was saved by the server returning with their meals. The smell of the hamburgers and fries was nearly heavenly. She asked if they wanted another drink. Daniel did, Church asked for more water.

They were silent as they prepared their burgers, placing the lettuce and tomato on. Church reached across and grabbed the slices of onion from Daniel's plate and placed it onto his burger along with his, then applying ketchup and mustard before placing the homemade bun on top. Daniel used only mayo as a condiment, and he did not like onion and Church knew that he was welcome to it any and every time. After they had each taken a second bite and tasted their fries, the server came back with Daniel's second beer and asked how things tasted. They both said it was great and she left again. Daniel did not watch her leave this time.

"So, back to the issue," Church said. Daniel had hoped that he had forgotten what they were discussing and was going to let the conversation take a new course. That didn't happen.

"You're right again," Daniel admitted. He couldn't deny his behavior especially not to Church who had witnessed every relationship he had. "I never really saw it before, but I guess I do get possessive. I don't like losing what I have. Having something is better than having nothing," he told his friend, feeling pretty good about his answer.

"True, that's human nature. But, to use some cliché sayings, *nothing lasts forever,* and *all good things come to an end.* The key to happiness lies in one's ability to realize and accept when things change, when they have ended--which could be in a lot of ways--and *moving on,*" Church said.

"When did you get so wise?" Daniel chided, though he was serious.

Church laughed. "I told you I am a counselor now, on a lot of different issues and subjects," he said with a smile.

Daniel thought about what his friend was saying and it made sense. "But, I am conflicted between what I think I should do and what I think I'm supposed to do," he said.

Church nodded his head as he chewed. "Ah, the moral dilemma. You have to search your own heart for that one. The only advice I have for that is this: if you feel anxiety over a decision it's probably not the right one. If you have peace and feel good about it, then it probably is the right one."

Daniel thought as he chewed. The burger was delicious and the amber beer made it more so. He drained half of his glass of beer as he considered what his friend was telling him.

"Okay, let me ask you this now," Church continued. "What about Faith makes you want to be with her so badly?"

Daniel didn't mind the question, he thought it was an easy one to answer, one that he didn't have to delve into his deep self to get. "The way she looks: her eyes, her smile, her ass. I like her cockiness and her strength. I like her short, punky hair. And, she has a sex appeal that I find alluring--and so do most men I've noticed. I think that leads to my possessiveness, to be honest. I know others want her and I have her, so that makes me feel good about myself--that I have something others want," he said. Daniel was almost surprised at how quickly and honestly the answer had come.

Church didn't comment on the answer yet, but chose to pose an additional question, "In the first place, what made you want to be with her, knowing that she had baggage and drama?"

Daniel thought as he chewed is burger. "Part of it was the secrecy, and aside from the looks and the way she carried herself, there was something about her that was..." He didn't know really what it was, didn't know what word to use to describe it.

"Dark? Seductive? Dangerous?" Church offered.

Daniel nodded his head and looked at his friend with a puzzled look, he thought that Church was reading his mind or looking into his soul. "Yes. How did you know that? You haven't met her, I don't even think I've shown you a picture of her," Daniel asked.

Church smiled a knowing smile and laughed, "I read you like the cover of a magazine, Gibson," he said.

Daniel laughed as he finished his meal and pushed the plate to the edge of the table along with his now empty glass of beer. "Seriously, why did you say that?

"I've been studying different areas for my work and I came across some interesting reading on the human psyche with regards to relationships. It's a newer theory that says there are three main categories of personas that people tend to gravitate toward. Meaning, that usually depending upon which stage someone is in in their personal life they will desire and seek out, on a subconscious level mostly, a certain type of person to fulfill those needs and desires at that time," Church told him.

Daniel sat quietly, trying to understand what he was being told. Just then the server came and grabbed Daniel's empty plate and glass, asking if either of them would like another drink and if Church was finished with his meal. They answered in the affirmative on all questions.

"I guess that's too highbrow for me. I don't understand," Daniel admitted.

"Okay. In the reading I did the person explaining the theory referred to the different categories as *hands*," Church said.

"Hands?" Daniel asked, lost again.

Church let out a laugh. "Yes, as in *hands*," he said holding both of his hands up, palms facing Daniel. "They were talking about relationships and seeking out a mate, right? So, the categories were referred to as hands, as in *holding hands*, get it?"

Daniel nodded his understanding. The server brought their drinks and set them on fresh beverage napkins. She asked if they were wanting dessert and they both declined. Church told her to bring the check whenever, but he wanted to pay for both.

"You don't have to do that, Church," Daniel said.

"I know," his friend said with a smile. "I want to."

"So, we're holding hands," Daniel said, getting back to the subject. He was actually a little intrigued by it and was curious to hear more.

"Yep, three hands, or three main categories is what they came up with. The first is called the Black Hand. Now, these are just color representations, they have *nothing at all* to do with a person's race, okay? They're just colors on a wheel, though each does represent a specific subconscious mindset when searching, again based upon one's own stage in their personal life," Church clarified.

Daniel nodded that he was following so far. He took a drink of his beer as he listened.

"So, it says that usually during one's adolescent years they seek out the Black Hand, though not exclusively. Some people subconsciously seek out this category of persona later in life, again it all depends upon where the person is in their personal life's journey, what they are wanting and seeking for their fulfillment at that particular time," Church explained.

"Got it. Just try not to go too far over my head with the explanation," Daniel said.

Church laughed and nodded, "Okay. I'll try and keep it simple. So, the Black Hand is basically the persona of the *bad boy*, or *bad girl*, right? It seems every woman wants, desires, craves the bad boy at least one time in their life, some all their life. This is why most 'good guys' don't get the girls they want, because the women are not seeking or desiring a good guy, at least not when they are subconsciously seeking the Black Hand to hold. Make sense so far?" Church asked before continuing.

"Yes, that makes a lot of sense," Daniel admitted. It helped him realize why it was he had failed so many times with girls in his past. He was always the nice guy, the good friend, the shy one. He wondered if there were a "hand" category that he belonged in. He was eager to find out.

"That's where Faith comes into your life," Church told him. "She has a dark past, mysterious, sexy, alluring, has tattoos, has been in trouble with the law. Has a strong, sometimes aggravating personality, stubborn and not willing to change easily. Most likely has a temper and is a little dangerous. Typically these personalities usually prove themselves to be selfish and untrustworthy, their mates complain about being used by them in a variety of ways as a consequence. These are traits all Black Hand personalities seem to share. So, in the recent part of your life you were seeking--consciously or subconsciously--the Black Hand and you gravitated toward Faith, as she seemed to fill your desires and wants to where you quit looking for another woman, correct?" He asked.

Daniel nodded his head. "That's crazy, man," Daniel said, smiling. He couldn't help it. He was a little amazed by the accuracy of the theory so far, and more than a little embarrassed by it.

"Moving on," Church said as he continued. "So I'll use you as an example. We've established you were seeking and found your bad girl, satisfying your subconscious need and desire for the Black Hand to hold."

Daniel nodded and took a drink from his beer as Church paused for a drink as well before continuing.

"The next category is referred to as the Red Hand," Church began. "This one is similar in some ways to the Black Hand, but these personas tend to be more mature and grounded, tend to be more appreciative and giving, less selfish. They have less dark and dangerous traits, but usually have the same strong sexual and charismatic personality traits. People subconsciously seeking the Red Hand persona crave and desire almost just that--desire. They seek someone who elicits within them the fire of lust, for starters. The explosion of emotion, mostly sexual, that ignites when they are near that person. Though they also tend to gain an enhanced sense of self-worth being with them as well, as Red Hand people will build up their partner with praise and compliments, unlike the Black Hand who have a propensity to tear the other person down with insults and belittling. In this heightened emotional state partners of the Red Hand think about them all the time and can't wait to be with them, especially alone with them. These feelings lead people to believe in *love at first sight*, and usually become emotionally attached quickly. So, Red Hand--hot, passion, lust, a near insatiable desire to be with someone, almost a purely physical and emotionally-based relationship.

"Though, they said this type of relationship rarely keeps the red-hot passion for very long, because the mystery and excitement starts to leak out of the relationship at some point. The subconscious seeking of this type of *hand* often leads to people cheating in their relationship or dating multiple people at the same time, which in and of itself has an element of excitement and passion. It is said that these types of personas are frequent drug and alcohol users because those outside stimuli helps to create the Red Factor, as it were. The Red Hand relationship tends to fizzle out quickly or maybe the relationship lasts, but the initial desire and passion doesn't. Which can lead to more and more seeking of the same, and sexual promiscuity," Church explained.

It was a lot to take in and consider, but Daniel understood it and it seemed plausible to him. A question hit him then, "Church, what about those of us, maybe all of us, who are seeking the *one*, you know, the one we were *meant to be with*?" Daniel asked. "Is there such a thing?"

"Good question. Actually the answer to that, at least in part, is the third category. Now, I can't say whether there is the 'perfect person' for everyone and you just have to let God bring you together. Some people believe that, others can't wait on a deity and actively seek on their own," Church said.

"Most people don't wait," Daniel offered.

Church nodded, "I agree. To your question of their being a *one*, the researchers say the third category or White Hand is the one *most* people truly desire and want, though they tend to settle for one of the other two categories or a mixture, staying with what they have for a multitude of reasons--as you said, having something is better than having nothing. Given that, they say the White Hand is the very best one desires. This persona will genuinely be uplifting, encouraging, inspiring, you will have an enhanced sense of euphoria being with them, the feeling that you were meant to be together. The couple will share the same interests, likes, desires, have similar or complimentary goals, even have similar dislikes. There will be a sustained level of passion and excitement. But more than that, they will truly enjoy being around each other nearly all the time, and when they are apart they will honestly miss the other, like a part of them is missing. This would be your 'match made in heaven,' the best either could possibly do, and so thankful that they found each other," Church said.

"That would be awesome. Yes, please," Daniel said with a laugh.

Church laughed as well. "I hope I didn't bore you with that. Hopefully it helped you see which relationship you're in and what you truly want. Just be aware and be careful to which hand it is you choose to hold," Church advised. "The hand you hold can bring you up to a new level in your life, or it can pull you down to a depth you never wanted to experience...In either case you must learn when to hold on tight or when to let go."

"It's very interesting, I'll admit that," Daniel said.

The server walked up to the table asking if they wanted another drink. They both declined. She presented the check and Church handed her his debit card.

"Well, buddy, it was great to see you. I unfortunately have to hit the road. I have a meeting in Ann Arbor tomorrow morning and I have some prep to do before then," Church said.

Daniel stood from the booth and hugged his fiend. "Thanks for making time to get together. I appreciate it," Daniel told him.

"We'll have to keep trying to get in touch with Nevver and get together this summer for sure," Church said.

"Absolutely," Daniel agreed.

"Keep in touch. And keep searching for the White Hand to hold, my friend," Church said. "If anyone deserves to find the *one*, you do."

Daniel walked his friend to his car and watched with sadness in his heart as he drove away. An icy wind blew off the bay, chilling Daniel and making him shiver. He walked back through the pub, stopping at the restroom to relieve himself, then hurried out the rear entrance to his car.

On the drive back home Daniel could not help but think on his life as it was, which choices he had made to get him to where he was. He then started thinking about his future and if he was making the right choices.

God, help me find the way, he prayed.

CHAPTER TWENTY-NINE

He was working the day shift. It was a rare occasion that there were enough managers and employees on that he could leave before the dinner rush, while it was still light outside. He had full use of both arms again. His father had been right, the muscles in his left arm came back quickly and full range of motion and use followed. One of the best things was taking long, hot showers again. Just the feel of the warm, rain-like water pouring over him was something that he took for granted most days. But having to wipe himself down with a soapy washcloth for over two months made him appreciate what a luxury showering was.

Gone was the immobilizer strapped to his chest, and with it the coldness of winter. It was early Spring in northern Michigan, and it had come unseasonable early to nearly everyone's surprise and delight. Rarely did warm weather blanket the north and stay in the month of March. Warm was a relative term, as the daily temperatures were steady in the low 50s, some 15 degrees higher than normal, but compared to temperatures in the mid-30s it seemed much warmer. No one was complaining, except the farmers.

Daniel had a few things to finish up and he was hurrying to do so. He had allowed Faith to drop him off that morning so she could go to her doctor's appointment and she had arrived to pick him up ten minutes previously. She was early which surprised him, though she had been trying more in regard to their relationship in the past few months.

Instead of sitting in the car and waiting she came into the restaurant. Since she still knew many of the workers she was welcomed and it was a good reunion of sorts for her. As Daniel finished his manager work for the day he noticed Faith smiling and laughing with the people she knew and had worked with. She was getting hugs and having short conversations with nearly all of them.

It did him good to see her in a pleasant mood. Watching her walk about the back-of-the-house of the restaurant reminded him of the times when they had to conceal their relationship. He fondly remembered and felt the rush of the excitement of hiding their passion, how they would brush against one another in seemingly innocent ways, conveying with just a touch their intent and desire. He smiled to himself at the memories of her winking at him, touching him. The smile of hers beckoning him. Her eyes broadcasting her want.

Just as he was grabbing his coat and preparing to tell Faith he was ready to leave, a strange and familiar figure suddenly appeared at the counter of the pickup window. Daniel stopped and stared for a few long seconds as his mind tried to comprehend what he was seeing. As soon as the man smiled and gave him the double-middle-finger salute it pulled Daniel from his confusion and he smiled, returning the gesture. Nevver was there.

Daniel walked quickly up to him and they shook hands. "What are you doing here?" Daniel asked. "It's good to see you. Church and I tried to get a hold of you last month. He was up for the day and we had lunch. Wish you could've made it." The tone and volume of his voice projected his joy at seeing his friend so unexpectedly. What added to that fact was that he was just getting done with work and Faith was there, so two of the most important people in his life could finally meet.

"Ah, I couldn't make it, but I've been around, my brother, I've been around," he said still grinning from ear to ear. "I just stopped in to say hi, not looking for anything, don't need a place to stay," Nevver assured him.

"You want something to eat, man?" Daniel asked. It was the least he could do for his friend, and he, and probably Faith, had not eaten all day either. Nevver just shrugged and nodded his head.

"Hey, my girl's here! Why don't you go have a seat in the side room over there and I will be there in just a minute," Daniel said as he handed Nevver one of the large menus. Nevver thanked him and turned and walked into the dining room.

Daniel, still smiling, scanned the kitchen area for Faith. He found her talking to one of the long-term servers, the only one besides Faith who stayed with them during the transition. Daniel walked up behind her and put his hand on her lower back, brushing the top of her butt with his fingers. She turned and smiled at him.

"Hey, Nevver is here," Daniel said with obvious delight in his voice and eyes. "Do you want something to eat? We'll sit down and I'll buy us all early dinner," he said.

The women finished their short conversation and Faith then followed Daniel through the server area, out the double doors into the dining room, snaking their way around some tables and chairs into the side room that served as overflow for the main dining area. At this time of day no one was seated there besides Nevver.

He was seated facing them, the sun beaming through the windows casting a warm glow about the room. Upon seeing Daniel and Faith enter, Nevver stood, his smile beaming, yet mischievous as always. As Faith saw him she stumbled a bit and seemed to freeze. Daniel had to catch her to keep her from falling down.

"I sometimes a trip over my own feet," she said with a laugh. Daniel did not notice, but as his two friends locked eyes on one another a flash of recognition passed between them. As Daniel was looking toward Nevver he did not see how Faith's eyes went wide and the color momentarily drained from her face. She recovered quickly, however, and the look of shock was replaced with a smirk and a flash of white teeth.

Still smiling his mischievous, devilish grin, without missing a beat, Nevver stuck out his hand. "This must be Faith," he said. "I've heard a lot about you. Pleased to meet you finally," he added.

She reluctantly took his hand and shook it quickly, "Nice to finally meet you, Nevver," she said before sitting down across from him. Daniel took the seat by the wall next to her.

"So, what's good here?" Nevver asked as he pretended to scan the menu while gazing at Faith, trying to catch her glance. She kept her face down, staring intently at the menu which she already knew from memory.

"Babe, I need a drink," Faith blurted out.

"Good idea," Nevver added. "You get the food, Dan-O and I'll buy the drinks," he offered.

"Deal," Daniel said.

Faith then shoved her chair back and began to get up. "I have to use the restroom. I'll get Carol to come wait on us," she said as she winked at Daniel before turning and walking out of the room.

Daniel noticed how Nevver watched her leave. "So, what do you think?" Daniel asked.

"Duuuuuude!" his friend began. "She's a wild one...I can tell by the way she walks."

"Oh, whatever!" Daniel said with a laugh in disbelief.

"I'm serious! I can tell you for a *fact* that she's not wearing underwear, not even a thong. Am I right?" Nevver asked. Daniel did not answer. "I'll take that as a *yes*," he said. "I'm telling you, she's got that primal, sexual vibe and she *knows* it! She's working you, just like she works *every* man she comes in contact with," Nevver told him.

"How would you know that? You *just* met her a minute ago!" Daniel protested. He knew his friend thought of himself as the quintessential male player, that he knew all the angles and all the games that people played. And maybe he did. *But, how the hell would he know that about Faith at first glance?* Daniel thought.

"I know her *type*," Nevver explained. "The way she moves, the way she looks at you, and at *me*...probably almost every guy she looks at...yeah, I know her type, all too well. She is *exactly* the type of girl I zero in on when I go to the clubs and bars.

Even the grocery store. She gives off a vibe that says she wants it, but she also projects that that shit aint free!"

"Fuck you, asshole," Daniel said playfully.

"I'm serious, my friend. Okay, I'll prove it to you," Nevver told him. "Do you get jealous at how she looks at other guys, at how she approaches them, how she touches them on the arm, how she smiles at them, how her eyes fixate on them?" Nevver asked as he mimicked the gestures in theatrical fashion as he said them. "Do you even *notice* that shit?"

Daniel paused and took in what his friend was saying. And it was true, Daniel *did* have flashes of anger and jealousy when they were out at how casually and easily she approached other men, telling them--in his opinion--way too much of her personal information. How she would ask them for things, even if it was just a cigarette or lighter. Or how she would want to play them at pool while he sat and watched. That was the main reason Daniel had bought the pool table for his house, so they could play whenever, but also so he didn't have to worry about other men moving in on her, or her being too friendly with them. It did seem to him that she was being more than friendly, that she was flirting. But it felt even more than that, like she was actively seeking something. Something he couldn't, or wouldn't, give her.

He pushed the feelings off as just his jealousy, that he was overreacting to his perceptions. He knew she was a social butterfly and flirtatious. Those were some of the qualities that had attracted him to her in the first place. But, watching how she interacted with other men bothered him. It aggravated his insecurities and it had started several heated arguments between them. It seemed like she gave more attention to strangers at times than she was to him. *Maybe she was trying to make me jealous those times*, he thought. He wasn't sure, but what Nevver was saying did not ease his mind nor his suspicions about what she was doing behind his back.

"I do notice. And I don't like it," Daniel finally replied.

Before either man could say more, Faith and Carol walked into the room. Faith sat down and Carol stood at the end of the table, waiting to take their order.

"Go ahead, guys, order your drinks," Nevver prompted. "I'll have a bottle of Labatt Blue, and some cheese bread sticks for an appetizer. But I'll need a few minutes to look over the menu," he said to Carol. As he pulled his gaze from the server he looked at Faith whose eyes were locked on him in recognition. He stared into those blue-green eyes and smiled a mischievous smile, giving her a wink. "Damn, everything looks good enough to eat!" Nevver said, holding her gaze and licking his lips before looking down at his menu.

266   M E Karbowski

CHAPTER THIRTY

A warm, humid breeze blew through the few open windows of the house, bringing with it the smell of summer. The night sounds of crickets and other nocturnal creatures were drowned out by the stereo as Bob Seger's *Roll Me Away* played through the speakers. The *crack* of the cue ball slamming into the triangle formation of striped and colored balls was satisfying to Daniel as he watched with anticipation the balls split apart and two of them headed for corner pockets. One of them, a stripe, fell. He was on his fourth beer and Faith on her third glass of Merlot as they played their fourth game of pool. She was up two games to one.

She was wearing a pair of her short, tight denim shorts with a frilly black tank top over a black bra. White and black striped ankle socks covered her feet. Daniel was wearing black basketball style shorts and a black T-shirt with the Batman symbol screen printed on the front.

It was a Wednesday night and he did not have to work the following day. It was 9:30 PM, Daniel had gotten off of work two hours previously and had raced home to spend time with Faith. He had stopped at Wal-mart to get a large bottle of wine for her and a case of Michelob Ultra for himself, as well as some snacks.

The work week had been stressful so far, as Memorial Day had come and gone and so the Peak Summer Season had begun. The Fudgies and Snow Birds were in full invasion mode returning to the Petoskey and Harbor Springs area for the warm months, opening up their summer homes and cabins, or filling the hotels and motels on the weekends in their pursuit of the "good life."

A week earlier Faith's doctor had dropped her as a patient, stating that he could no longer treat her condition as it was chronic and required a pain management specialist. He had referred her to three others in the area and she was impatiently waiting for a response from them as to whether or not she would be accepted as a new patient. Luckily for Faith, her doctor filled two thirty-day prescriptions of morphine, one for 30mg tablets and one for 60mg along with 180 Xanax, so she would have enough until she secured another physician.

Her kids were back to the every-other-weekend routine of staying with them, which gave Daniel a taste of parenthood. It seemed stressful for Faith as they tended to give her a hard time, pushing their limits and her stress buttons, as she tried to be a good mother to them. As an outsider, Daniel could do little in way of helping her discipline or control them when they acted out, though he did set "house rules" and he could enforce them with Faith's help. All in all it was a stressful situation for everyone, especially the children.

Daniel pushed all of those worries aside that night as he focused on the recreation of playing pool with Faith, looking forward in anticipation to some great sex later on.

Daniel missed his next shot and watched as Faith stepped up to the table, bending over slightly and she lined up her shot. Daniel stared at the tight denim that hugged her ass and her bare legs as she leaned forward. On instinct, he took a few steps towards her and just as she made her shot he slapped her on the ass.

"Hey!" She shouted as she rubbed her cheek with her left hand. "Not so hard."

"Sorry," he told her as he looked at the dark lipstick enhancing her mouth, which had been transferring to the wine glass and some how still managing a full coat on her lips.

She made her shot and continued around the table eyeing up her next. Daniel drained the bottle of beer and went to the kitchen to grab another.

"Will you bring me some more wine?" Faith asked him. "Can we switch the music?"

"Yes, I'll bring more wine. I don't care what you switch the music to," he told her. Which wasn't exactly true, as he did care what they listened to, but she knew what his musical tastes were, and he assumed that she would not put on the Dixie Chicks or Wilson Phillips, not while they were playing pool anyway.

"Did you miss?" He asked her as he filled her glass with the dark red wine. He looked over at her lustfully as she was bent over at the waist searching for a CD that apparently matched her mood. Within a few seconds Pat Benatar's *We Belong* filled the room.

"Yea, it's your shot," she said as she walked back to the table. She sipped her wine as he eyed up a shot. He sunk one in the side pocket and smiled up at her. "Um, I'm going to go have a cigarette, okay?" She framed it as a question, but it was really a statement. He just nodded his head as he lined up another shot.

He watched her walk through the kitchen and out the side door which she left ajar. He missed the second shot, so he grabbed his bottle of beer and stood with pool cue resting on the floor in his left hand, listening to the music and studying the balls on the table.

He sang along to the song and drank his beer as he tried to wait patiently for Faith's return. A second, then a third song played from the stereo and Daniel became impatient and agitated. "How rude, she knows we are playing a game. It shouldn't take that long to smoke a damn cigarette," he said aloud to himself.

He finished his beer and set his pool cue leaning on the table as he walked into the kitchen to grab another. He looked at the small desk in the corner of the kitchen where two cell phone chargers were plugged into the socket. His black cell phone was there. Her purple one was gone.

Daniel's heart rate immediately spiked as he realized she was out talking on the phone. Which, in and of itself was not something to be concerned about, but it added to the rudeness of the act as it kept him waiting for what he thought was no good reason.

He walked as silently as he could toward the side door, pulling it further open. He peered out and saw that she was not on the porch as she usually was when smoking. His heartbeat was thundering in his ears as his breathing became more rapid. He held his breath in an effort to calm his nerves and lower his heart rate. He strained to hear over the pounding in his ears and the sound of the summer breeze.

I should go outside and see if I can hear who she's talking to, he thought. He still had his jealous suspicions, and though he said he forgave her and had put the past troubles behind him, Daniel still had the nagging, sickening feeling that she was still up to her normal tricks and hiding things from him. Faith had proven herself to be a very good liar, keeping to the same story months and even years later, never wavering in the telling, never slipping on the details.

I don't want to risk her hearing the door opening, he thought. *I want to catch her in the act, hear what she's saying, know who she's talking to.*

He then had a better idea, knowing that she was in the front of the house, probably sitting on that porch. The vinyl blinds to all the kitchen windows were down and the windows were closed. The windows next the pool table were open, however letting the summer breeze in.

Daniel quickly made his way back to the pool table and got down on his hands and knees. He crawled as quietly as he could, positioning himself under the open windows. The blinds were pulled half way up, so he could not overtly listen at the window, otherwise she would see his shadow not to mention his form in the window if she looked that way. He strained to listen, but the stereo was too loud, obscuring any of her words. He could not even tell that she was actually talking, though he could smell the burning menthol-laced tobacco from her cigarette, so he knew she was still out there.

He backed up and made his way to the kitchen and crouched down beside the desk at the first window closest to the front door where Faith was. He slowly raised the blinds a few inches, just enough to expose the bottom of the window sash. He then lifted the window with as little force as possible. The seal broke with an audible *thuuuuttt*, Daniel froze at the minor sound, his head still thundering with his beating heart.

He waited and did not detect that she had heard. He did hear her talking now in a low voice, but above a whisper. Daniel strained to make out actual words and not just her voice. Between his heart beating, the anxiety-inducing thoughts racing through his mind, and the stereo, Daniel could not make out a single word. He couldn't tell what she was saying and thus could not ascertain who she was talking to. *Damn it!*

He wanted to storm out there and stand right next to her to see if she would continue her conversation. Part of him wanted to do that, but then he had another, almost silly idea. He grabbed his cell phone and his beer and walked back to the pool table. He flipped open the phone and speed dialed Faith's number. He managed to smile at himself as his heart was still thundering within his chest. He pressed the phone to his ear as it rang on his end two, then three times.

Then he heard her voice. "Hello?" She said, her voice was light, she was laughing. "What are you doing?" She asked, laughter bubbling as she spoke.

"It's your turn," he said, trying to keep his voice light. "It has been for about 15 minutes, what are you doing? Who are you talking to?" He asked.

"Talking to my aunt," she giggled. "I'll be there in a minute," she assured him. Daniel didn't reply, he just stayed silently on the line. "Okay?" She asked politely, waiting for a response.

"Okay," he said, putting anger in his voice as he snapped his phone shut.

He walked over to the CD player and stopped the Pat Benatar. He was in the mood for something more aggressive. He selected Candlebox and started the song *Changes*.

As promised, Faith came in and walked into the living room, still smiling and laughing. "You're such a goof," she said to him, remarking on his phone call. She held out her empty wine glass towards him, thick with red lipstick marks. "Will you pour me more wine while I go potty?" She asked him, smiling.

Daniel took the glass from her and managed a weak smile back. His anger and frustration was building at her lack of consideration for him. "Do you even still want to play pool?" He asked her angrily.

She stopped and turned toward him, "Yes, I do. We have all night, babe. You don't have to work tomorrow," she reminded him, she turned and continued walking towards the bathroom. But not the one adjoining the master bedroom, the guest bathroom.

The truth of her statement did nothing to calm him. In the back of his mind he was still thinking about who she was talking to. He did not believe that it was her aunt. Not for one minute. He watched her walk down the short hall and saw the light of the bathroom turn on, then become blocked as she shut the door.

He thought it was odd how she kept all of her stuff in the guest bathroom almost ever since she was back. Before they had shared the master, but now she exclusively used the guest bath. She also seemed to take much more time to relieve herself and always closed the door, something she rarely did before. Faith claimed that morphine made her constipated and he believed that, but still he found her behavior odd. And at times frustrating.

Daniel poured her more wine and sat the glass on the windowsill to the open windows next to the pool table. He took a deep breath of the summer air that gently spilled into the room, trying to calm himself. He plopped down in the thick leather chair that was positioned in the corner by the front door at the end of the pool table. Two songs played and ended and the next one began before Faith emerged from the bathroom. She grabbed her custom pool cue and asked him, "I forgot, am I solid or stripes?"

The question nearly enraged him. "Well, you'd fucking know if you weren't outside for the last half-hour, talking to who knows what!" He said nearly shouting, scolding her.

She ignored the anger and let out a giggle as she responded, "Talking to 'who knows what?'" She repeated his words, laughing at the error.

"You know what I fucking meant!" He yelled. His anger pushed through now, past the barrier of calm that he tried to keep in place.

"Whoa, calm down!" She yelled back sternly. "I didn't do anything wrong, I was having a fucking cigarette and my aunt called *me*! Excuse the Hell outta me for fucking talking to my relatives," she said angrily as she took a drink of her wine, giving him a hard stare over the glass.

"Yeah, I'm sure that's who you were really talking to," he spat.

She shook her head and her face scrunched into an incredulous, questioning look. "I know you don't believe anything I say anymore," she began. "But that's who I was fuckin' talking to!"

"And I should believe you...because I only know what you tell me, right? Every time you're on the phone you go outside so you can have these...secret conversations! If they're so innocent why don't you talk inside in front of me?" Daniel demanded. He was tired of tired of her so-called friends, tired of her lies.

Faith rolled her eyes and shook her head as she took another drink of her wine.

"Well?" Daniel yelled, again demanding an answer to his question.

Anger flashed crossed her face then, her eyes becoming cold and hard, "I don't talk in front of you because, number one, I'm having a fuckin' smoke and I can't in *your* house," she told him. "Second, who I'm talking to and what I'm saying is really *none of your fuckin' business*!" She yelled.

"It *is* my fucking business, because you got shitty fucking friends that can't be trusted! And you always come running to me to bail you out of some fucked-up situation that your bad decisions and asshole friends put you in!" He yelled at her as he stood up from the chair.

His anger was building and he needed something to expend energy on. Their pool playing was over as far as he was concerned now. So, he walked over and slammed his cue in the rack, then started angrily pushing the balls into the pockets where they were stored. He did this as Faith continued the argument he had started.

"Oh, I forgot all my friends are fuckin' lowlife dirtbags, huh?"

"Yes, they are! They stole from me, treat you like shit, never there when you need them," Daniel reminded her. "I told you, if you got better friends you wouldn't have so many fucking problems!"

"Oh, your friends are so great?" She asked with attitude and defiance in her voice and her body language.

"My two best friends, yes they are," he told her.

She snorted a devilish laugh as she said, "Then you don't know your friends as well as you think you do."

Daniel just finished putting the vinyl cover over the pool table as he looked at her. She was glaring at him in defiance, her stance was cocky as she clicked her fingernails on the wine glass. The look on her face made him want to slap her, it was smug and superior, he could tell she was holding something back. It grated on him. Her comment intensified his anger. *How dare she speak badly about* my *friends!* he thought.

"What do you mean by that?" He asked, giving her a hard stare.

"Nothing...Just that Nevver isn't as much of a friend as you think he is," she said accusingly. She walked to the loveseat and sat down, effectively turning her back on him.

Daniel walked over to her and sat down heavily next to her. "Why do you say that? How the fuck would you know? You just met him one time!"

"Hmmmm....did I?" She said, raising her eyebrow and giving him a smirk.

Daniel knew for sure now that she knew something, or at least she thought she knew something, and he wanted to know what it was. The tone of her voice and the look on her face was making it hard for him to control his anger.

You need to calm down! his mind warned him. She's not being combative tonight, you are, and this will not lead to anything good.

Daniel pushed the warning out of his mind. His stress, frustration, and anger, coupled with the alcohol, was fueling his animosity towards Faith and what she had done to him in the past. What he allowed her to do to him. But right then, he was singularly focused on knowing what it was she thought she knew. He wanted to put her in her place and let her know that she was wrong about so many things.

"Well, you tell me. You seem to think that you know Nevver pretty well for some reason," Daniel said accusingly.

"No...I don't think I should. Because you won't believe me anyway," she said matter-of-factly.

Daniel was not going to let her off the hook that easily. "I knew it...you're just full of fucking shit, as usual, trying to get me angry," he said to her, trying to push her buttons for once, trying to get her to answer questions with what he hoped would be the truth and not more lies.

Faith took another drink of her wine, finishing the glass, obviously stewing in her own anger now at his accusations. But her pride and defiance, and her knowledge, would not let her stay silent.

"I'm not full of shit. I happen to know that Nevver thinks he can get any woman he wants to, that he thinks he's so cool and sexy...Please," she said. "You honestly didn't notice how he was acting towards me when we all had lunch a few weeks ago?"

Daniel laughed. "*That's* all you know?" He laughed again. "I know that. He's a man-whore, he hits on almost every woman. That's not a secret."

"That's *not* all I know," she spat. His laughter set her off then. Even if it hurt him she was going to tell him what he was so desperate to hear. "Do you remember the night you called me, practically *begging* me to come over?"

"When was this, supposedly?" Daniel asked. He didn't remember what night she was referring to.

She rolled her eyes again. "It was like, before Christmas, when I was back at Scott's," she began. "You called me and I told you I didn't have a ride and I was out with friends," she said.

Daniel did remember then. It was a night of weakness when he was drunk and lonely, missing her. He remembered thinking she was at a bar because of the noise in the background. He remembered his angry thoughts of her being with another guy, even though they were broken up. "I remember," he admitted.

"I didn't know who he was, didn't know he was your friend--not until that day we ate at Pizza Hut--but he was at the Keyhole that night. And he tried everything he could to fuck me!" She said with that tone of superiority.

Daniel was taken aback at the revelation. He wasn't sure he understood. "Did you?" he finally asked, it was the only question that he could think to ask, his mind was flooded with doubt and confusion.

"What, fuck him?" she asked, surprised at the question. "Hell no! But, I did let him buy me drinks and I won twenty bucks from him playing pool," she admitted.

"You didn't do anything else?" Daniel asked, not wanting to hear the answer. His head was spinning now from his speeding heart and the alcohol, and from adrenaline-fueled anger.

"Well, he followed me and my friends to the dance floor," she began. "He was grinding on me for a while, I'll admit it was kinda fun...he was kissing my neck and grabbing my ass, but that was...about it," she said coyly, the look in her eyes conveying there was more, but she wasn't about to tell him.

About it? his mind raged.

"So...when I was here, actually *needing* you, you were out dirty dancing and grinding

on--and God only knows doing what else--with some stranger who turns out to be my best friend?" He yelled the question at her.

"Apparently...some friend you got," she replied smugly.

Something then snapped inside of Daniel.

In that instant, the slow burning fuse of his subdued rage that had been lengthened by his calmness, patience, and acceptance had reached its end. For months and months he had pushed down and compacted all of his life's stressors-- those brought on by work, brought on by his relationship with Faith, brought on by his debt, brought on by unanswered prayers, brought on by his self-doubt and insecurities, brought on by his failures and struggles.

These things he kept a tight lid on, continually pressing them down and subduing them, forbidding the release of the stress, for fear that he could not control the full release in whatever form it manifested. When it came to his relationship with Faith, however, he could only keep things in check for so long, then specific stresses would be let out in measured doses--like small earthquakes releasing the earth's energy--usually manifesting in heated, verbal arguments. It had never reached the physical level, aside from the occasionally thrown item smashing against a wall. After such an outburst, which usually lasted less than an hour, Daniel would again push down and set aside the pain and fury caused by his stress, until another major episode would occur and the anger and frustration would fight its way out in the form of another argument.

This time the shock of what she had done with Nevver coupled with her arrogance and smugness sent him over the edge. His mind could no longer contain all of the anger and frustration that he had intentionally imprisoned deep within him. Rage consumed his mind and overtook his body. Like an exploding volcano of emotion, Daniel lost control.

CHAPTER THIRTY-ONE

"*I want you out!*" He screamed, louder and with more force than he ever had before. "You fucking sleazy bitch, get out of my house!"

He stood up quickly and towered above her as she sat still on the leather loveseat. She was looking up at him with confusion and fear in her eyes. His mind was racing, not thinking clearly. The rage flowed from him in barely thought out sentences as it fueled his muscles like nitric oxide. He was running on instinct as a jumble of thoughts ran through his mind. The barrier that had kept his frustration and fury in check had been washed away by the jealous and hurtful revelations of Faith being so unconcerned with his feelings and how her actions affected him, like a tsunami washing away buildings of concrete and steel as if they were merely cardboard caught in the deluge of unstoppable seawater.

Pick her the fuck up, and throw her out the door!

Blindly obeying, Daniel reached down and grabbed her by both shoulders. Faith let out a scream, dropping her now empty wine glass, as she instinctively grabbed at the arm of the loveseat with both hands holding herself to the furniture. "Daniel, please!" She begged. "I'm sorry you're mad, but I didn't do anything wrong!"

Bullshit! That's what you always say!

Her words stoked the flames of his anger and resentment.

He pulled, trying to throw her off of the shortened couch, but her grip was too strong. He absently thought she might rip the cheap leather with her fingernails, so he stopped.

Grab her by the ankle and drag her ass out of the house! He thought then.

Daniel grabbed her right ankle with both hands and began pulling on her leg. Faith screamed again, still clutching onto the side of the furniture with both hands, still pleading with him, "Stop it, please!" She yelled, thoughts of her being six years old again, hanging on to the furniture in fear of her safety filled her mind with dread and panic.

You need to stop this, his mind told him. Get control of yourself, before it's too late.

Fuck that! I'm tired of doing what I should, tired of doing what is right! Tired of all of her lies and betrayal! Tired of this life! The thoughts raged in his mind as his body seemed to be controlled by his primal instincts. He could feel the anger welling up inside of him, filling his body with a dark energy almost like that of helium into a balloon. His head felt light, yet heavy as the blood and adrenaline rushed through his body.

You're losing control of yourself! His mind screamed at him, trying to reason and calm him.

Yaaaaaaaahhhhhh! Daniel let out a guttural shriek.

Daniel knew he was going bezerk, but he didn't care. The tremors of his stress and anger were finally being let out and it felt good.

He let go of her ankle, letting her foot fall the floor. "*I want you to leave!*" He screamed.

"I don't want to go," she cried, her voice still beseeching the good man she knew him to be. She was honestly frightened of him then. She had never seen him like that before and it scared her. "Please, Daniel calm down. Don't make me leave. I have nowhere else to go!"

"*I don't care! Get out, get out, get out!*" He screamed as he paced back and forth, not sure what to do. He had never been in a physical and emotional state such as that before and he was having a hard time processing what he was doing, what he should do.

You need to go outside and calm down, his mind told him. You need to stop this before it cannot be stopped.

It was Faith, then, who decided that she needed to get outside, needed to get away from him. She swiftly got up from the loveseat and walked quickly towards the kitchen.

Maybe she's going for a knife, he thought. *Better go after her.*

Daniel hastily followed her into the kitchen. "What the fuck are you doing?" He yelled.

"Trying to get away from you, so you can calm down!" She screamed, tears streaming down from her eyes.

As Daniel took another step towards her, she grabbed the dishtowel that was hanging on the handle of the range. She slapped at him repeatedly with the cloth, in an effort to get him to back off and give her some space. Even though it was a weak gesture and hardly a threat, it only served to enrage him further.

Daniel let out another guttural yell as he reached out and grabbed the collar of her frilly tank top and yanked down hard, tearing it from her neck down to her stomach, exposing the black bra beneath. Faith screamed and her body shook from fear.

"Get away from me! Leave me alone!" She screamed at him through tears as she backed away from him, instinctively trying to cover her exposed body.

Now's our chance, she's almost to the door, he thought, his mind still wild.

Daniel kept moving towards her as she continued to back her way through the kitchen. She turned quickly and stepped through the storm door outside onto the porch and kept walking in her bare feet on the dirt and gravel of the driveway.

Shut and lock the door! He did.

Still in a rage, still having too much energy to stand still or even think clearly, Daniel paced back and forth in the kitchen. He opened the refrigerator and grabbed another Michelob Ultra, twisting the bottle cap off in a quick motion, then drinking half of it in a series of swallows.

As he drank he walked to the window and opened the blinds, looking outside. The outside light illuminated the side porch and driveway, where he saw Faith with her cell phone pressed to her ear. Daniel quickly unlocked the window and heaved it up. The summer breeze brought with it the words she was speaking clearly.

Fuck! Fuck! Fuck! She called the cops on me!

Well, what did you think was going to happen? His mind asked him. You can still stop this. It's not too late.

Daniel again ignored the urgings of his mind. He tried to quiet the thundering of his heart so he could hear what she was saying.

"...He pushed me out of the house and locked the door," she was saying, her words coming out as whimpers and cries. Normally, Daniel's heart would break and he would have sympathy and compassion for her as he saw her crying and in distress, but not this time. His rage had taken control of him.

Get all of her stuff and throw it out with her! Yes! He thought. *Get her and all of her things--all of her bullshit and lies--out, once and for all!*

Daniel grabbed a large, black trash bag from the pantry and quickly went into the bedroom. In a mad frenzy he opened the drawers of the dresser that held her clothes. As fast as he could he pulled the clothing from the drawers and stuffed them into the plastic bag. He ignored the clothes hanging in the closet, but went to the guest bathroom and threw all of her toiletries, makeup, lotions, even her toothbrush and shampoo into the bag as well. He didn't care if the containers opened and ruined her clothes, didn't mind that most of those things he had purchased for her were probably getting ruined.

He carried the stuffed bag to the door and threw it onto the side porch, some of the contents spilling out. Daniel glared at her as she continued to speak into the cell phone. He closed and relocked the door. He stood by the opened window and stared at her through the glass, listening.

"...He just threw a garbage bag full of my stuff outside," she sobbed into the phone. "I just want to go back inside...I don't even have my shoes...he ripped my shirt, it's getting colder and I don't have a jacket," she was telling the 911 operator.

Oh, shit! She just told the cops I ripped her fucking shirt!

Daniel focused through his rage and clearly saw her shirt was hanging from her. Panic now mixed with his anger, fueling him to merely act instead of thinking.

Grab her jacket, then go out there and rip the rest of her fucking shirt off, there won't be any evidence then, he thought.

In a frenzy, Daniel grabbed her purple spring jacket from where it hung on one of the dining chairs. He went to the side door and unlocked it, quickly darted out. She was still talking into the phone while she smoked a cigarette. She didn't see him coming.

"I just want you to make him let me come back inside...I don't want to leave," she was saying.

She was still talking with the 911 operator as Daniel grabbed at her, and with two violent tugs he was able to tear the rest of her shirt from her. Faith screamed again and again with each violent motion, her raspy voice shrill and broken as her shouts filled the night. He then threw her jacket over her left shoulder and walked quickly back to the house, locking the door once again.

"*Oh, my God!*" Faith screamed into the phone, sobs coming out with each breath. "He just came outside and tore my fucking shirt off of me!" She yelled into the phone. She was in a panic now, not knowing who this person was that Daniel had suddenly become. Her protector, her lover, her only true friend was in a rage and had just assaulted her. Her world once again was turning up-side-down.

It's your word against hers, he thought. *There is no evidence of a torn shirt, only that she's outside in her bra, but she does have a jacket. That should work*, his frenzied mind thought.

You're losing control of yourself! Calm down and go talk to her, apologize before it's too late! This isn't you, you don't really want this! His mind pleaded with him.

Daniel went to the trash can and shoved the torn, black tank top deep under the garbage. He guessed that the cops would be on their way by now. They would want Faith to stay on the phone until they arrived.

Shit, they're coming...what do I do? He thought, trying to plan a way out of the situation he created. *They can't break in*, he thought. *I need to shut off all the lights and lock all the windows, then hide.*

Back in motion, Daniel slammed the two open kitchen windows shut, locking them. He knew all the others were already closed and locked, shutting out the summer humidity. He then did the same for the few remaining open windows in the house. Then he began turning off all the lights, including the motion light over the side porch. The house, inside and out, was plunged into darkness. He could faintly hear Faith relaying into the phone what was happening. As Daniel stood in the living room, contemplating his next move, something shining caught his attention.

He looked down at his shirt and to his dismay he noticed the Batman symbol was glowing in the dark! *Shit! I didn't know it did that!* He thought. Quickly, he pulled it off of him and threw it into the bedroom. Then he saw the red and blue flashing lights of a police car pulling into the driveway.

His heart was still thundering, but his rage had subsided, now replaced by fear. *Lock yourself in the guest bathroom, there are no windows in there*, he thought.

The guest bathroom had no windows, only a row of glass block along the top of the tub/shower that allowed light in. He locked the door and lay down on the floor. His heart beat was thundering in his head as his mind continued to try and formulate a plan of action, tired to anticipate what was going to happen next.

I'm fucked...I'm so fucked, he thought. *Why did I let it get so out of control?* He asked himself. He wasn't sure if it was the alcohol or the stress, or both, but whatever allowed him to lose control was not going to help him regain it.

She only wanted you to calm down and let her back into the house, his mind reminded him. You fucked that up when you wouldn't listen and let your ego and anger take over. I can't even help you now. What's done is done. You can't unshoot a bullet.

Daniel had never been in this type of situation before. He didn't know what was going to happen next. Not exactly. As he lay on the cool linoleum floor of the bathroom, his heart thundering in his chest, fear and anxiety filling is body--replacing the rage and anger that had consumed him just minutes before--in his mind he saw the look on Faith's face. How the tears were streaming down from her eyes, the fear in those eyes. The fear caused by him.

Son-of-a-bitch! He thought. *Now what?*

Daniel lay on the floor for what seemed like half an hour, but was only a few minutes, before his curiosity urged him into action. He slowly got up from the bathroom floor, unlocked the door and slowly walked out into the hallway. The flashing lights could be seen through the window blinds, an eerie colorful swirl in the summer night, piercing through the opaque blinds, casting erratic shadows across the walls and the floor. Shirtless, he tiptoed to the master bedroom and slipped under the covers.

I'll pretend like I'm passed out, that I didn't hear them knocking. Which they were now.

Forceful pounding thundered through the house, on the side and the front door now, a Sheriff deputy and a State Police trooper announcing themselves, asking him to come outside so they could talk.

Fat fucking chance of that, Daniel thought. The single window in the bedroom had protruding from it a small air-conditioning unit.

I should turn that on. It will help the story that I couldn't hear them, he thought. But it was off, and he thought it was too late to turn it on. He then had a horrifying realization, that with the air conditioner in the window it was not secure. The window was essentially open.

I should go quickly and pull it out of the window and shut and lock it, he thought. But with his heart thundering and his mind still racing he didn't know if he would have time to do that. *Probably not,* he thought. So, Daniel just lay under the thin summer blanket, sweating and thinking, his mind not finding any easy way out.

In less than five minutes the police were at that window, their flashlight beams searching through the blinds then. As he had feared, the window was slowly pushed up and the air conditioning unit was removed, pulled out into the summer night. Then two flashlight beams cut the darkness and played across his form under the covers as he lay still, his heart thundering, his body sweating.

"Mr. Gibson," an officer called. "Wake up!" he shouted.

He heard one of them giggle, then a shoe hit him. *What the fuck?* He thought angrily. His shoes were on the floor under the window and apparently the cops were using them as a means to wake him. *This is borderline unlawful entry,* he thought as another shoe hit the headboard and dropped onto him.

Daniel bolted upright in bed, acting like he had just been awakened. "What the hell?" he said loudly.

The flashlight beams were now shining directly into his face. He squinted to see past the harsh light, but could only hear the voices.

"Mr. Gibson, we need you to come outside and talk with us," one said.

"About what?" Daniel asked.

"About what went on tonight. We just want to hear your side of the story."

"We were having an argument and I wanted her to leave," he told them.

"Okay...can you come to the door, sir. We'd like to talk to you further."

Daniel reluctantly got out of the bed. He could feel the night air had become colder as it wafted in from the open window, chilling his bare skin. As he made his way to the side door, he grabbed his blue fleece jacket and put it on, leaving it unzipped. Daniel flipped the switch to the outside light, flooding the driveway and porch in a harsh glow. He slowly unlocked the side door and pulled it open. As he looked through the glass of the storm door he saw Faith standing with a Sheriff deputy, talking with him as he wrote in a notepad, the red and blue lights of the Sheriff's vehicle and the big, red gumball light of the State Police vehicle, along with the flashing headlights and turn signals were lighting the dark night like a strobe show from Hell, announcing to all the neighbors that something bad had happened.

The State trooper stood off the side of the porch and stared at him as a second Sheriff deputy walked up on the porch and opened the storm door. He was tall and thin, maybe an inch or two taller than Daniel was. He had brown hair that was trimmed short, no facial hair.

"Mr. Gibson, may I come in?" He asked pleasantly.

Daniel's heart was still beating fast, his mind still spinning and trying to think one step ahead. He nodded and moved back into the kitchen, allowing the officer to enter.

"Okay, you and Miss Collins are a couple, and she lives here, is that correct?" The Deputy asked.

Daniel processed the question before answering, "We are a couple, but officially, no, she does not live here. She stays here, but her address is in East Jordan," he said.

"So, she does not reside here?"

"No. She did and I had to file a notice to quit and evict her last year. She moved back in with her ex and her kids. She just recently has been staying here again," Daniel explained as the sheriff wrote notes on a pad of paper. They could check those facts, Daniel knew. That and the address on her ID.

"She says the two of you were drinking and playing pool tonight, is that correct?"

"Yes, we were," Daniel admitted.

"Then an argument broke out?" He asked.

"Yes," he said reluctantly.

"Tell me what happened."

Daniel took a deep breath trying to collect his thoughts before responding. "We were arguing, which is not unusual, and she told me about a time recently when she was out dirty dancing at a bar and it upset me. I yelled at her and told her I wanted her to leave and she wouldn't."

"She says that you grabbed her, then tore her shirt and pushed her out of the house," the deputy said, looking him directly in the eyes, probing for signs of deceit.

"I did not rip her shirt and I did not push her out of the house. She was hitting me with a towel in the kitchen and she ran out of the house, that's when I locked the door," Daniel told him. He could feel his face reddening as he spoke the partial truths, hoping that he looked and sounded convincing.

"Did you tear her shirt off of her? Did you touch her at any time?" The deputy asked him.

Daniel thought for a moment, then responded, "I did not tear her shirt off of her--she wasn't wearing one. But, as she was sitting on the couch I did grab her ankle and I started to pull, but thought 'No, I'm not going to do that,' and I let her go."

"So, she's sitting on the couch and you grabbed her ankle and pulled on her leg?" The deputy asked.

"Yes, but only for a second then I let her go," Daniel replied.

The officer looked at him for a long second, Daniel just stood there staring back at him, waiting for the next question. The deputy put his notepad into his shirt pocket then took a step toward Daniel.

"Mr. Gibson, since you've admitted to grabbing her, I'm taking you into custody for domestic violence," the deputy he said as he opened a pouch on his belt and pulled out a set of handcuffs.

You gotta be fucking kidding me! Daniel raged.

I told you you should have controlled yourself. You did this to yourself, his mind told him.

Standing in his kitchen in shorts and the blue fleece jacket, Daniel felt his world tilt. He felt sick in the pit of his stomach as the fog of adrenaline and alcohol quickly dissipated and left him feeling empty and exposed.

He thought about running. He thought about hitting the cop. He imagined grabbing his gun and going out in a blaze of cowboy glory. Daniel acted on none of those thoughts. He just stared blankly, his mind frozen in a dark moment of time.

"If you promise to stay calm and cooperate, I will cuff your hands in front of you," the deputy offered.

Daniel was still in dismay, only able to nod his head. As an after thought, Daniel asked, "Can I get my phone, keys and wallet?"

The deputy allowed him to get his items and slip on a pair of shoes before placing the handcuffs around his writs. Daniel winced as the metal was forced tightly down upon his skin, the sound of the handcuff teeth clicking rapidly as they locked around his writs, pinching muscle, skin and bone. He could almost feel his circulation being cut off they were applied so tightly.

The sheriff then led Daniel out of his house to the waiting brown Ford Crown Victoria, placing him in the back seat. The other Sheriff deputy was in the front seat passenger side, apparently he was a rookie learning the ropes. There was a computer screen that Daniel could see attached to the dashboard. He tried to nonchalantly read the green text that was displayed. What he could make out was a history of Faith's calls to 911 and some of her previous encounters with the police. *Interesting*, he thought. Most of what he could make out Daniel knew about, but there were a couple that he didn't and it was those that he tried harder to read, but because of the angle and the second deputy sitting in the front passenger side it made it difficult.

The Sheriff deputy and the State Police trooper were still talking to Faith outside of the house. Daniel wasn't sure what was going to happen to him, but he was thankful that he did not have to work the next day. At least that was one thing he wouldn't have to worry about. One more embarrassment he would not have to endure. The deputy then walked back to the car and got in the front seat. He spoke into the radio's microphone some codes and said they were in route to the jail for booking.

"So much for getting a warning the first time, huh? Damn!" Daniel said, both of the deputies tried not to laugh, but they did. "So, what happens when I get home and all my shit's gone because she stole it?" Daniel asked. "Call you guys again?"

The rookie deputy turned in his seat and looked through the partition at him and said, "If that does happen, yes. Call 911."

"Not very reassuring," Daniel said. His wrists were in pain from the tightness of the handcuffs, but he was powerless to do anything about it. He sat back in the seat as the deputy closed his door and put the car in gear, backing out of the driveway.

Daniel watched his house through the window as the car pulled away. He was starting to crash from his alcohol and adrenaline high. His emotions had been spent, his anger was all but gone. Except that he was angry at himself for his inability to stay calm. Especially since Faith was being mostly reasonable and non-combative, which usually wasn't the case when they argued. She was usually the one that wanted to keep going and keep arguing, and he just wanted to be done with it and go to sleep and move on.

But not tonight, he thought. *Your dumb ass couldn't let it go tonight.*

You realize that if you would have kept calm you would be having sex right now instead of going to jail, his mind told him.

Fuck me, Daniel thought as he closed his eyes and laid his head back, praying that it was all just a bad dream.

But Daniel knew that it was not dream. It was a living nightmare from which he could not escape. Anger and regret burned in his mind as he silently prayed for a way out. But, like so many of his prayers of late, he knew that one, too would go unanswered.

Once a choice has been made, his mind told him, once something has been done, it cannot simply be undone.

End of Book One

Choices...Decisions...Right versus Wrong...Good versus Evil.

Everyone deals with daily struggles in their own way. Some breeze through life seemingly making the right decisions....others ostensibly always choosing wrongly, and suffering the consequences. Every action has an equal and opposite reaction...every decision delivers an outcome, whether it is good or bad, whether that outcome is immediate or manifests itself at some future date. One mistake can lead to others, forging a chain of misfortune and misery that can bind even the best of us. Everyone needs a helping hand at one time or another, though the conclusion will greatly depend upon the choice of the hand you hold.

For Daniel Gibson his life needs to make sense. The choices he makes are all geared toward one ultimate goal: to achieve the American Dream--nice house, good job that he enjoys...and mostly someone special to share life with. Someone to love, and to have that love returned in kind.

But things aren't always what they seem...and sometimes believing a lie can be better than the truth...until everything you think you know comes crashing down around you. Can one good man overcome obstacles and his own inner demons to defy the odds and prove that nice guys don't always finish last?